TIDAL WAVE 23

- A NEW WORLD ORDER THRILLER -

Thomas J. Ryan

www.TidalWave23.com
www.ConspiracyFactPress.com

TIDAL WAVE 23 – A New World Order Thriller

Copyright © 2012 by Thomas J. Ryan

www.TidalWave23.com
www.ConspiracyFactPress.com

Edited by Booker T. Boffin

Cover Art and Design by:
www.studiogearbox.com

The Library of Congress has catalogued this first edition:
TIDAL WAVE 23 – A New World Order Thriller / Thomas J. Ryan

Library of Congress Control Number – 2012911400

ISBN-10: 0-9856263-0-5 (Paperback)
ISBN-13: 978-0-9856263-0-3 (Paperback)
ISBN-10: 0-9856263-1-3 (eBook)
ISBN-13: 978-0-9856263-1-0 (eBook)

PRINTED IN THE UNITED STATES OF AMERICA

This book is dedicated to Alex Jones who woke me up to the New World Order and helped me unplug from the propaganda matrix. Keep up the good fight and long live the Infowars!

2012 USA Best Book, Finalist
2012 New England Book, HM
2013 Novel Rocket, Thriller Winner
2013 National Excellence, Finalist
2013 International Book, Finalist
2013 IBPA Ben Franklin Silver, Cover/Art

"Countless people will hate the New World Order and will die protesting against it."

- H.G. Wells

CHAPTER 1

Special Agent Tristan Wood observed the hustle and bustle of Massachusetts Avenue buzzing with late morning activity, the sweet spring air merging with exhaust from the taxicabs idling in front of Union Station. Through the foliage of Chestnut Oaks, Tristan took in the view of the United States Capitol while his FBI partner scanned stations on the radio of the unmarked car.

Though not a residential part of town, this was one of the most densely populated areas of the country during the week. Within one-half square mile sat the White House, Library of Congress, Metro Center, the Smithsonian museum complex, the State Department, Navy Yard, Washington Monument, and the J. Edgar Hoover FBI building to name a few. This part of Washington, DC, was America's ground zero.

The red digits of the car's clock read; *11:11 a.m.*

"Unbelievable," Tristan said, as the familiar acid-rush of adrenalin burned his gut. He blinked to make sure he was reading the time right.

"What?" Agent Jason Graves mumbled as he continued searching the radio.

"Can I ask you a question?"

He received a familiar look that clearly meant; *NO.*

A handheld police scanner sat upright on the dashboard and hissed with occasional chatter over the frequency dedicated to the perpetually short-staffed Secret Service. Another threat on the president's life had prompted FBI to grant them four agents as additional security. Tristan and Jason kept watch over the front entrance while a second team covered the lot on the north side of the building. FBI special agents considered this kind of work both demoralizing and boring. Today they were glorified security guards.

"Do you ever have a sense that something is wrong, drastically wrong, in the world? Something you can't quite put your finger on?"

"This again?"

"You don't feel it? Like the wool is being pulled over your eyes?"

"There we go." Jason sank back into the worn cloth seat as clear voices of several ESPN announcers discussed sports highlights.

Tristan continued, "Think about it. Everything we learned today, all the news, was what the media decided we should know."

"You lose your tin foil hat? If so, I can probably make you a new one."

"I can't be the only one." A gust of wind entered the window blowing Tristan's tie up over his shoulder like a noose.

"You want my advice?" Jason gibed.

"Not really."

"Do your job, go home and enjoy a ballgame with a cold beer. Cash your paycheck, take vacations with the wife, and one day you can retire on a beach somewhere." Jason checked his appearance in the side mirror. "You think too much."

Tristan's attention turned to the front entrance of the building. "People seem to be in a hurry all of a sudden."

The President of the United States was at Union Station for a ceremonial ribbon-cutting of the debut trip of the new Amtrak Next Generation high-speed commuter rail system. The first of its kind in the country, Next-Gen used magnetic levitation to connect DC to Philadelphia to New York City and ending in Boston. The MAGLEV technology allowed the train to float above the tracks at over 220 mph providing a smooth ride. An expensive project, watchdog groups criticized its bloated cost during an anemic economy that seemed to have no end in sight.

"Seriously, what's up with you lately?" Jason kept on him, unaware of the activity a short distance away.

"I've had this feeling . . ."

"What feeling?"

Tristan hesitated before finishing his thought. "Like I'm at a mad tea party—"

The scanner abruptly came alive with voices.

"Phoenix is leaving the building!" *Static.*

"Bring in the Stagecoach!" *Static.*

"What is condition of Phoenix?" *Static.*

"Phoenix is on the move!" *Static.*

"Where?" *Static.*

"Heading to the Castle!" *Static . . .*

The two young FBI agents were out of the car and running across the street toward the Main Hall. They pushed through the heavy revolving doors and headed for the Next-Gen terminal, careful not to slip on the highly polished floors.

"Bravo Team, are you on your way?" Tristan spoke into the scanner.

"Already here," came the reply.

With only two teams from FBI they kept the codes simple. Tristan and Jason were designated *Alpha* and the others, *Bravo.* They weaved in and out of casual shoppers and weary travelers on the middle of three levels that comprised Union Station. Both men raced past Amtrak Police, arriving at the location of the ceremony. Tristan was now limping.

"You okay?"

"I'm fine."

He attempted to conceal the pain, the hard concrete surface causing unwelcomed stress on his bad leg. Tristan reached into a pocket for the meds he carried but resisted the urge to take a pill.

They approached two Secret Service agents, easy to spot since they dressed in similar dark suits with the addition of the trademark earpieces.

"What happened?" Tristan asked, holding up his badge.

"Somebody tried to set off a bomb in a piece of luggage."

"The president?"

"He's safe. We got him out of here right quick."

Tristan recalled the codes they had used. If *Phoenix* was in the *Stagecoach* going to the *Castle*, the president was in his limo going to the White House. A common misconception, the unambiguous and easily pronounced words were chosen simply for identification purposes and were not secret. The White House Communications Agency, created under FDR, chose code names to identify the commander-in-chief, his family, and prominent persons and locations.

"Where's the bomber?" Jason asked, scanning the area.

Union Station was quickly emptying of people, now aware something was amiss.

"We don't know."

"You don't know?"

"He walked off, into the crowd. We're reviewing the security tape to try and ID him."

"No time for that," Tristan stated the obvious.

"The guy over there?" the S.S. agent pointed to an older gentleman surrounded by Metro Transit Police. "So far he's the only real witness."

"Who are we looking for?"

The other Secret Service agent paced with adrenalin. "A male, jeans and a short sleeve, striped golf shirt is what he remembers. Thinks the color was blue. Exits are covered and my guys are on the upper and lower levels."

"What about the parking lot?"

"I sent a deuce, but there's serious ground to cover. It just happened, he can't be far."

"We'll help search the outside perimeter," Tristan said.

The pair rushed over to Bravo Team, a young man and younger woman speaking with a civilian.

"Anything?"

"Nothing." Jennifer was a newer FBI agent, her long red hair tucked loosely under a baseball cap.

"Head out back and comb the lot. Jeans and striped blue shirt, right?"

"10-4." Both special agents hurried off.

"Seems they have all the bases covered. I don't remember seeing anyone fitting that description as we came in, do you?" Jason asked.

"No. Doesn't mean we didn't miss him though." Tristan was drawn to the sound of the departure board, a massive split-flap display hanging from the ceiling. The new boarding status updated to: ON HOLD.

"The trains."

"Let's go." Jason led the way.

At the platform, two Amtrak commuters sat idly on opposite tracks. Each man entered a different car. Tristan advanced up the aisle, making sure to get a clear visual of every person as he progressed. He swept through the first four cars with diligence, ending up in the fifth and last.

The restroom was occupied.

A conductor clipped tickets for anxious passengers. No one matched the description of the suspect, so he backtracked.

"I need your help." Tristan flashed his badge. "Can you unlock the restroom for me?"

"Sure thing."

They headed for the forward end. The conductor located the right key on his chain. Tristan motioned to stand-by, then knocked on the flimsy door.

No answer came.

"Anyone in there?"

Again, no reply.

He nodded to the conductor who inserted and turned the key. Tristan drew his Glock and racked the slide. He quickly swung open the door while pointing the gun inside. A young Middle Eastern man in jeans and a blue striped golf shirt leaned against the back wall, hands by his side and a dazed expression on his face. With little resistance, Tristan pinned him face-down on the aisle floor.

"Do you have any weapons on you?"

The question was repeated, still with no response. Tristan FlexCuff'd his hands and searched the pockets finding only a used Amtrak ticket stub. He Mirandized the young man and escorted him off the train, in the direction of the terminal. Jason caught up, grabbing the suspect's other arm.

"I knew you'd get him, I have no luck."

A Metro Transit cop ran up to assist. They locked the suspect in a small holding cell in the Amtrak Police Station. The high-tech control center reminded Tristan of an air traffic tower in its sophistication.

He spoke into the handheld, recalling Bravo Team from outside.

"Anything on him?" Jason asked.

"Just this." He handed over the stub. "If there was a wallet, he ditched it."

"One-way from Philly. Interesting."

"Is that the bomb?" Tristan referred to the carry-on sitting nearby.

One of the cops opened the bag, revealing multiple blocks of C4 bricks linked in series by wires. "Check out his little toy."

"Wow. How much explosive power is this?" Jason called upon Tristan's military experience.

"This would have taken out everyone in at least a hundred yard radius including the president. In fact, I'd say it would have leveled this entire section of Union Station."

"Damn."

Tristan picked up one of the blasting caps, shook and then smelled it. A black substance on the end rubbed off on his thumb. "This is a fuse cap."

"So?"

Before he could answer, Bravo Team arrived. Jennifer, the female agent, assessed the young man in the cell.

"That him?" She studied the suspect. "What's wrong with him?"

"What do you mean?" Tristan asked.

"He looks doped up."

"Yeah, I noticed that. We'll run a tox-screen on him."

The other FBI agent leaned in, "See his hands?"

With head down and eyes wide open, the suspect continued to impassively stare at the floor. Hands folded, the scars were clearly visible.

"Been practicing the art of bomb-making, buddy?" Jennifer knocked on the glass window but elicited no reaction.

Jason pointed to the computer screen. "Here's our guy!"

The video showed an Amtrak train lumbering to a stop. Passengers began to exit, including the bomber suspect with his luggage.

"So we know he was on the train. Let's go to the ceremony," Tristan instructed.

The Metro cop switched to another shot of Union Station where spectators jammed in for a better view of the president. After searching different angles they located the culprit, standing at the rear of the crowd. He unzipped the top of the bag, took a lighter from his pocket and lit two fuses before walking away. The sparkling light began to capture the attention of those nearby. Both wicks rapidly burned down and extinguished with a *poof.* Twin plumes of smoke rose upward, intertwining in a dance.

"Rewind that?" Tristan asked. "Check this guy out."

He pointed to a man in a red sweatshirt, facing away from the group and fixated on the suspect. Obscured by other onlookers, the face was indistinguishable. After the fuses burned-out he calmly pulled the hood over his head and walked off.

"Strange," Jason said.

"This guy's familiar. Can you go back to the video of the platform?"

The Metro Transit cop replayed the previous frames.

"Freeze it."

Jason pointed at the screen. "Well, what have we got here?"

The same man in the red sweatshirt, with no luggage, exited the train behind the Middle Eastern man and casually followed.

"Can we get a copy of this video?"

"I'll have to put in a request. We're under the jurisdiction of Department of Homeland Security, it's their call."

Tristan offered his FBI business card. "Do you still have the witness?"

"They took him down to the eatery to get food, he's a diabetic."

Tristan said to Jason, "Let's find out what he remembers."

The FBI agents left the police station and walked downstairs. The witness sat with two Metro Transit cops silently eating a burger and fries, his face pale.

Jason flashed his badge as they settled down at the table. "Can you take us through what happened?"

"I was standing right next to him," he said, clearly shaken. "This person opened his luggage, which seemed strange to me. But then the crowd reacted to something the president was doing so I turned away. Next, I heard a fizzing sound and saw light out of the corner of my eye. I remember thinking a fuse must lead to a bomb, the president is here, this is a terrorist, and I'm going to die."

"We got him. He's in custody right now, thanks to your description," Tristan attempted to relieve some stress.

"Oh, thank God."

"Do you remember anyone else acting suspicious, or was the bomber with anybody?" he continued, hoping to jar the man's memory without leading him into an answer.

Considering the question for a moment, he answered, "No, that's all I remember."

Jason asked, "Does anything out of the ordinary come to mind?"

He thought again before saying, "I don't, I'm sorry. I gave the police my contact information. Can I go?"

Frustrated, they let the only credible witness return to his life.

"Well, let's see if we can get something out of the bomber?" Jason suggested.

"Worth a try," Tristan replied.

They were headed back upstairs when Bravo Team approached. Jennifer attempted to communicate between breaths. "They came and got him, and took him away. We told them he was under our jurisdiction but they had paramedics and rushed him out on a stretcher."

"Who? Who took him?" Tristan asked her.

"Homeland Security."

CHAPTER 2

Allyson sat by herself in the cafeteria of Walter Reed National Military Medical Center. The meatloaf with macaroni and cheese reminded her, food was consistently unappetizing no matter what the hospital. She dropped the fork and concentrated on a television mounted to the wall. A local station had interrupted the regularly scheduled sitcom for a breaking news report from Union Station. She was about to turn up the volume when a nurse stopped to look at her.

Not again, she thought.

"Are you Allyson Wood?"

"Yes, I am."

"Do you work here now?"

"I'm a chief resident, second year." In conspicuous discomfort, the woman was so pregnant Allyson thought she might pop at any minute. "Please, sit."

"Thank you. Carrying a bit of a load here."

"You must be close?"

"Another month if you can believe it?" She beamed with happiness and reached out to shake hands. "I'm Joann."

"Nice to meet you."

"How is your husband?"

"Tristan's doing well, thanks."

The couple had become minor celebrities this year. The mainstream media did not seem particularly excited in them at first, not unusual, as little news came out of the wars in the Middle East these days. Then USAA contacted them for an interview and, to their surprise, ended up on the cover of their magazine. Others began to catch on, and before long it had snowballed into a national drama.

Allyson knew what was coming next.

"I loved the article."

The title of the piece was, "Life in the Valley of Death." She found it peculiar that, although familiar with the story, folks still wanted to hear it from her. The downside was the hype it had generated. Allyson was accustomed to receiving attention, but felt uncomfortable with the advances by strange men.

"May I ask about the trauma care?" Joann asked. "We train in 'Core 5' and 'Trauma Twelve' here. The article didn't get into the specifics of his injuries and how you kept him alive until the rescue team came?"

An unexpected question. Usually the women wanted the romantic angle, or as Allyson called it; the soap plot. "Sure, I'd be happy to. Let me try and remember."

Angst compelled her to glance back at the TV. Though she could not hear what was being said, the reporter motioned with dynamic hand gestures. The news ticker at the bottom of the screen read;

President evacuated from Union Station . . .

Allyson forced herself to concentrate. "Well, Tristan was hit three times in his left leg. I didn't know what he would die from first; blood loss or exposure. We were under fire at dusk making it difficult for me to tell how much blood he was losing. After I secured the area he lost consciousness so I administered plasma and tried to keep him warm."

"And no one else survived?"

The question was undoubtedly rhetorical.

"Everyone in his platoon was killed, and the article described what happened to the helicopters and my team. If the MEDEVAC that rescued us had arrived a few minutes later I don't think Tristan would have made it. It was only a matter of time until he bled to death and I didn't even know it."

"So a bone fragment punctured the femoral artery?"

About to answer, Allyson felt a hand on her shoulder.

"Doctor Wood?" asked Lawrence Woo, one of the resident physicians on her team.

"Yes?"

"Doctor Michaels needs to meet with everyone; right now."

"Okay."

After a long day—and up since dawn—it appeared she would not be leaving anytime soon.

"Have you seen Doctor Corrigan? I need to find him as well."

"He was just here, eating lunch." Allyson picked up on his urgency. "Why don't you page him over the intercom?"

"Doctor Michaels wants to keep this on the down-low," he said, clearly not comfortable using the slang.

"This sounds important?"

"Not sure, but we'll know soon." Woo scurried away.

Allyson wondered if it was related to the event at Union Station, just as the report went to commercial.

"Pleasure speaking with you Joann, congrats on becoming a mom," Allyson hurried off before the nurse could respond.

She moved through the corridors with haste. The National Institute of Health, NIH for short, was a huge complex in Bethesda, Maryland. The personal doctors for the president and VP resided in the Naval Hospital, the familiar high-rise building often shown in the news.

A wall of glass in an observation lounge presented a wonderful view of trees thick with fresh green leaves from the spring rains.

Entering the Trauma Center, Allyson rounded a corner and almost bowled-over the group of resident doctors, including Lawrence Woo who had apparently found the rest of the team.

"Doctor Wood, how good of you to join us," her boss said as he escorted them into his office, closing the door.

Dr. Michaels, the current NIH Director, oversaw the largest biomedical research team in the world. A member of Mensa, the gifted surgeon often wandered around the hospital bumping into people and getting lost. He was constantly deep in thought, socially introverted, and the best mentor Allyson could ever hope to have.

"There was a bomb attempt at Union Station a short while ago where the president was campaigning."

"What happened?" Allyson asked.

"All I'm told is the suspect suffered burns. They are bringing him to us."

"They need a team of doctors for one patient?" Dr. Woo wondered.

"I want you close by, to document everything. Eyes open."

Allyson pulled her lab coat tight, attempting to warm up in the frigid office. "Anything you're worried about?"

"We are being instructed to keep it quiet, which makes me nervous—" A knock on the door interrupted. "Yes?"

A portly nurse named Julie stepped in. "I think they're here, doctor."

The residents poured into the hall where the activity level was mounting. Employees and patients gathered around televisions to find out what all the excitement downtown was about. A nearby TV tuned to a cable news channel rolled an updated ticker.

Presidential assassination attempt at Union Station . . .

Two unmarked cars with tinted windows pulled into the sheltered driveway of the Emergency Room. Multiple federal officers exited the vehicles. The ambulance drove in next, lights on and brakes squeaking as it came to a stop. Two men in dark sunglasses entered through the automatic doors carrying walkie-talkies. Each navy blue Polo shirt was embroidered with the circular *Department of Homeland Security* logo.

"I believe you're looking for me."

"Are you Doctor Michaels? We were told to see Doctor Michaels," one man asked.

"Yes, yes, that's me. You can bring him into ER-5."

He pointed to a security door, next to the receptionist behind bulletproof glass. A tone sounded, opening it automatically. They removed the bomber suspect from the back of the ambulance, strapped down and secured to a gurney. A blanket partially concealed the restraints.

They rushed him into ER-5 at the direction of Nurse Julie.

"No one goes in but him," the Homeland Security agent said, pointing his walkie-talkie at Doctor Michaels who followed them into the examination room.

"What are we supposed to do now?" Dr. Woo asked.

The residents indecisively shuffled around.

Allyson turned to notice her reflection in a glass partition. Placing a hand on her flat stomach, she imagined being pregnant with a round belly underneath maternity clothes. The sadness in her emerald eyes reminded of the question that had haunted her all these years.

Is God punishing me for what I did?

Allyson quelled the guilt, as she had so many times in the past.

"I'm going to check on my patients," she announced with no protest.

Tristan was on an assignment at Union Station, she needed to find a television with volume.

She ducked into a private recovery room. Their newest patient arrived early this morning from Iraq; and was rushed into surgery. His injured left arm became infected during the lengthy overseas trip. Doctor Michaels had hoped to save it but was forced to amputate. Apart from the slow beep of the vital signs monitor, silence consumed the small space. The morphine drip in his remaining arm kept him comfortable and asleep; he would live.

Nineteen years old.

Careful not to wake him, she turned on the television with the volume low. A generic media report detailed a failed bombing attempt at the Next-Gen terminal by a white right wing extremist—odd since the man they brought in was clearly Middle Eastern. Several patriot groups were mentioned followed by an interview montage of angry and terrified people on the streets; the emotions angle.

Allyson checked the fresh bandages and switched out a new bag of Lactated Ringer's solution. Lifting the sheets revealed both stumps that used to be his legs, taken from him by an IED just days prior. She recalled hearing nothing in the news about that particular attack. Three other marines had been killed.

Iraq had been all but forgotten, unless a story had political value for one of the two parties. Even roadside bombs and suicide attacks, which still occurred regularly, rarely got so much as a mention anymore.

Injured soldiers continued to enter the hospital on a daily basis from the Mid-East and often confessed they had no mission. Most of their time was spent guarding roads, bridges, or worse; opium fields. Patrols sought to make friends with tribal leaders who despised them, ending up in cash bribes for intel, and still the locals did not cooperate. The problem, as with Vietnam, was the near impossibility of spotting the enemy until they started shooting. Platoons were ordered to fight an aggressor they could not classify and who did not dress in uniforms.

She would know. Allyson was stationed in the Korengal Valley, in Afghanistan, for over a year.

"Hey doc," her patient awoke, his speech slow from the medication. "I'm in a lot of pain."

She turned off the TV and reviewed his chart.

"You're not due for pills for another hour. You're maxed out on morphine too."

"The morphine only dulls the pain; the pills get rid of it. What are they called, oxy-something?"

"Oxycodone; terribly addictive."

"Doc, I'm never gonna walk again. I have one arm left, are you really worried about me getting addicted to medication?"

"Actually, yes I am." She wrapped new medical tape around his hand, securing the IV needle. "Before you're discharged we will set you up with an After-Deployment physician who can help with pain management . . . counseling, or anything you need." She hated assuming these combat vets would require psychiatric care, but many would. *Counseling* was the word they were instructed to use as it sounded relatively benign. Allyson replaced the chart at the end of the bed and headed out.

"Let me see what I can do."

"Thanks," he said weakly.

At the front desk, she leaned in toward Nurse Julie. "My patient in room 24?"

Julie grunted in sympathy.

"Let's move his meds up one hour."

"You got it."

She joined her peers who remained waiting outside ER-5.

"Anything going on?"

"This is strange," Lawrence Woo spoke up when no one else seemed willing. "A judge showed up. He's still in there."

"A judge?"

"Yes," he continued. "He arrived right after you left."

The door opened and Doctor Michaels walked out murmuring and cursing under his breath. "Wasting my time, wasting my time! I've got soldiers suffering and dying, and you're wasting my time with this?"

The residents followed, as he stormed off.

"What happened?" she asked.

"The man has no injuries. They won't allow a blood or urine panel, and he's obviously narcotized," Dr. Michaels fumed. He slammed the office door, shaking the walls. "Wasting my time!" his voice carried through.

Confusion lingered among the residents.

Finally giving in, Allyson took out her cell phone and hit the speed dial labeled; TRISTAN.

CHAPTER 3

The two young FBI agents thought hard as police cars and other official vehicles, including news trucks, jammed in the front of Union Station. The sun had burned off the morning dew and a cool breeze kept them comfortable in their dark suits. Tristan Wood and Jason Graves were in the FBI's counterterrorism division, a part of the Bureau officially formed after the 9/11 attacks.

"What now?" Jason asked.

"I don't know, but it's going to be a zoo in there."

"I can't believe this, we're gonna get chewed out for sure."

Leaning against the car to take stress off his leg, Tristan finally gave in and swallowed a pain pill.

"Let's go to Philly."

"I'll drive," Jason insisted.

Tristan tossed him the keys, per their *understanding*.

In no time at all, the unmarked was cruising north on I-95. The flashing red dash-light allowed them to exceed the speed limit unhindered. The inaccuracies on the local news station were astonishing, the line between fact and speculation quickly blurring. Some said the bomber was a Timothy McVeigh type, others a Tea Party member and everyone seemed to have figured out his political motives.

A detailed call from Allyson reinforced his bad feeling.

After a three hour trip, they double-parked in front of the Pennsylvania 30th Street Station. Tristan attempted to shake off the hazy effects of the medication as the special agents entered through the brass-framed doors of the main concourse.

They passed the *Angel of the Resurrection,* a thirty-nine foot bronze statue of the archangel Michael created by the American sculptor Walker Hancock, one of the Monument Men who recovered art looted by the Nazis. Tristan knew this because their father, Steven Wood, never missed an opportunity to take his sons to an American landmark and teach them its significance and historic background.

The FBI agents made their way across the Greek-influenced complex, the pillars reaching a full hundred feet to the ceiling. *Amtrak Police Center.*

They flashed their badges to the lone cop, an older gentleman who reclined in his chair and casually sipped a drink. Tristan handed him the ticket stub now protected in a plastic bag.

"We need to see the security video from the time this train left the station to about a half-hour prior," Tristan gave the order politely.

"Any particular location?" the cop asked.

"Start with the counter," Jason said.

"What are we looking for?"

"We'll let you know."

After some work he located the video, scrolling frame-by-frame as passengers moved through the ticket lines.

"Stop there. Okay, play it in real-time now."

At normal speed, the same Middle Eastern man in jeans and blue striped shirt bought a ticket with bills. He ambled away with the black carry-on in tow. Tristan pointed to someone in the background; a young white male in a red-hooded sweatshirt.

"Gotcha," Jason grinned.

"You're looking for the Train Bomber!" the cop said, repeating the media's new catchphrase.

Tristan directed him back to the screen. "Do you have a view of the platform?"

Locating the feed from the train's departure gate, they crawled through video stills until the bomber suspect came into sight. He glanced around nervously and sat down, clutching the carry-on as if his life depended on it. Close behind, the man in the red sweatshirt relaxed on the opposite end of the same bench and rolled up his sleeves.

Immediately, both FBI agents spotted something.

"What's on his forearm?"

"Are you able to zoom in?" Tristan asked the security cop.

"Sorry, that's as good as it gets," he responded.

Jason strained to focus. "A tattoo, but I can't read what it says. The letters are gothic. Looks like a capital I, a lowercase n, and an f, or is it an s?"

"Oh, no."

"What?"

Tristan covered for himself. "Nothing, I think you're right. Appears to be an I and n, for sure."

After a few clicks of the mouse, the Amtrak cop checked the computer records. Both tickets were paid in cash, the signatures illegible.

"We need video of this," Tristan said.

"I'm not able to—"

"Yeah, yeah, yeah," he interrupted, "you have to get permission from Homeland Security." Tristan took out another business card, trying to conceal his frustration.

Upon arriving back at the J. Edgar Hoover FBI building, Tristan and Jason went straight from the underground parking garage to their boss's office. Special Agent in Charge Murphy expected them.

"What happened?" he demanded.

"I'm sorry, sir. Homeland Security swooped in," Tristan admitted, reluctantly.

SAC Murphy leaned back and glared at both men now seated in front of him. The desk chair creaked loudly, his massive physique threatening to crumble its aluminum construction. His chronically taught shirts invariably missed at least one button, as did this one.

"How does DHS come in and take our man? You mind telling me how the hell that happens?"

"Tristan, I mean, Agent Wood, arrested him on one of the trains, hiding in the bathroom. We had him in custody, in a cell at Amtrak Police. We went to talk to a witness and when we got back—"

"Two of you to interview one witness?" Murphy's abrasive personality did not go over well with many who worked under him. Thick skin was requisite. Tristan believed he'd be a spectacular drill instructor in the marines.

"It was strange, sir. They hurried him off in an ambulance, but he wasn't injured. My wife was at Walter Reed when they brought him in. Homeland Security wouldn't let anyone examine the guy. Then a judge showed up to arraign him right in the hospital."

"A judge?"

"Yeah," Tristan continued. "Have you ever heard of that?"

Murphy wiped the perpetual sweat from his forehead and ignored the question. "I'll call DHS. Maybe we can team up on this and get some cooperation."

"They took the suitcase bomb too, probably held about twenty bricks of C4; super powerful. But the blasting caps were useless"

"What do you mean?"

"They're fuse-caps. You don't want to use these with C4, they are totally unreliable. I worked with this stuff overseas."

"Explain."

Tristan picked up a pencil to utilize as a visual. "The lit fuse ignites a pyrotechnic mixture in the metal cylinder that blows it out the back and sets off the primary charge; in this case C4. C4 is a plastic explosive so it needs extreme heat and a shock wave to cause an explosion, otherwise it just combusts. We used C4 on cold nights in Afghanistan as kindling. Light it with a match and it slow burns for hours, great for boiling water too. Of course, you have to be careful not to breathe it in, the fumes are poisonous."

"You said it's unreliable." The SAC was growing impatient.

Tristan continued, "You want to use a solid pack electric blasting cap, those are tried-and-true. Any number of things can go wrong with a fuse. Plus, why would you draw attention with all the light and sound of a big long fuse? It goes off like a sparkler. From the video we saw, the people around him detected it right away. Fuses are okay for mining or construction sites, in a tight space where you need time to get out. But if you're going to blow up C4 as a weapon, you don't want to wait around for a wick to burn down."

"Maybe the guy wasn't so bright?"

"You can research blasting caps in five minutes on the internet and figure this out; not exactly top secret information. If he's smart enough to find C4 and put a bomb together, does it make sense he'd use the wrong type of fuse?" Tristan shifted in the chair, his leg starting to bother him again. "But here is the kicker. There was no pyrotechnic mixture. I took it apart, the wick just burned-out inside the cap. The bomb wouldn't have detonated."

"Are you sure?" the SAC asked.

"Oh yeah, I'd be able to smell it."

"Could it have leaked out?"

"Even if it had, the odor is strong." He set the pencil on the desk. "No, it was clean."

"You know what else is fishy?" Jason said. "We discovered a guy within feet of the suspect at both Union Station and the 30th Street Station, like he was overseeing the operation."

Murphy looked to Tristan who backed up his partner. "He wore a red sweatshirt and was never more than arms-length away. Real suspicious."

"You get a make on him?"

"We either got bad camera angles, or his hood was up."

"If he rode on the train he bought a ticket." Murphy declared.

"Paid for in cash, along with a bunch of other passengers."

Jason added, "He had a tattoo though, on his right forearm. We could only make out a partial; I, n, and f, or s."

"I think I know what it is." Still reluctant to speak, Tristan gave in. "A couple outfits in the Korengal Valley inked 'Infidel' on themselves."

"Why would they do that?"

"Because the enemy considered us infidels. By the time I deployed, the guys were calling each other that, just joking around. Later I learned a whole outfit got the tattoos."

"How do you know from three letters?" Jason asked.

"You said it looked gothic? Well, you're right. They all got the same font. I've seen the tattoo several times." Tristan was unable to hide his guilt for holding out, catching the evil-eye from Jason.

Murphy leaned forward in his chair. "You think you can identify him? How many guys have that tattoo?"

"Hard to say. I'd guess twenty at least, and no telling who's still alive, home, injured, or dead. Won't be easy since we never got a good look at his face. They're sending over the surveillance video, from both Amtrak stations. Hopefully we can clean up the image and get something useful."

"Neither of you have had an informant in a while, you need to step up, and I mean fast."

The Bureau strongly urged each agent to recruit, develop, and operate at least one Confidential Informant at all times. Considered an essential tool for combating crime and collecting intelligence, a special agent was deemed "fully successful" when working an informant. But the world wasn't perfect, it did not always happen.

Confidential Informants could be hard to develop, tough to monitor, and even more difficult to control. It was not uncommon for a C.I. to fabricate evidence and make false statements especially when promised money or leniency in jail time. On the flip side, most senior law enforcement personnel would agree a good C.I. could be a real asset to an investigation if properly managed. But FBI's principle guideline was to maintain control over an informant—at all times.

"This is our C.I., the guy in the red sweatshirt. Whoever he is, we'll find him before Homeland Security does."

"I want a full report on my desk by the end of the week. DHS has the suspect, but try and get a make on this guy. Do what you need to do, I've got your backs."

Tristan and Jason stood up and left the office, the glass door rattling behind them.

"Why didn't you tell me about the 'Infidel' tattoo?"

"I guess I didn't want to give him up so easily, the guy is my brother. It's a marine thing." This had sounded better in Tristan's head.

"So am I. I'm the one risking my life for you on a daily basis." He turned and walked away.

"I'm sorry, okay?" the plea ineffective. "You're still coming over tonight, yeah? We'll get a pizza and watch the game?"

"Got a date. It's a single guy thing." And he was gone.

Tristan let out a sigh and headed for the elevator. He pushed *LL* to return to his Jeep in the parking garage. Jason was meeting up with a Russian girl Tristan had never met. This was odd, as he usually flaunted his girlfriends like trophies.

For some reason he was keeping this one under the radar.

Tristan guessed the night would be a long one as the elevator began its ascent with a *woosh*.

CHAPTER 4

Tristan Wood sat alone in his Wrangler on a dark Georgetown street watching *The Tombs Saloon and Restaurant* through a pair of binoculars. The cobblestone streets reflected the glow from nineteenth century gas lamps long since converted to electric. Along with the original row houses, it was not difficult to envision times past.

The door to the pub opened. Tristan directed the binoculars toward a couple leaving the establishment, but it was not who he expected. So far the stakeout was a bust.

The Tombs was a landmark rathskeller situated near the entrance of Georgetown University campus. High-backed booths, vintage crew and sporting prints, and colorful leaded glass made the bar a popular hangout for Hoya fans. Tristan had attended the rival Catholic University of America, all the way across town, but had a soft spot for Georgetown; his wife's Alma Mater.

Though only two months apart in age, Allyson had graduated one year later than Tristan for reasons she had never revealed. The question naturally came up. However, based on her dodgy response he decided not to ask again. Truly remarkable, was that it took a war in the Middle East to bring them together.

The front door opened once more, interrupting his thoughts. Finally; Jason and his girlfriend. On impulse, he glanced at the digital clock on the stereo.

11:11 p.m.

"Again?" he said to himself.

Tristan studied the girl; blonde hair with dark roots, extremely short skirt, high heels, and a tight top. She looked like a prostitute.

For all he knew that's exactly what she was. A flashy guy, this was Jason's ideal type. He loved dating head-turners, brains or not.

Moving in for a kiss, she tactfully rejected his advance, and they vacillated down the street. It perplexed him the way Jason drank multiple times a week and still showed up for work.

Of course, I'm one to talk, Tristan thought to himself. *I do it on heavy pain medication.*

He exited the Jeep and followed, keeping in the shadows, feeling deceitful. They had a tacit agreement—Tristan looked the other way with the drinking and Jason, the same with the medication. But tonight was different. Something was not right and it wasn't his comrade's taste in women.

The couple headed east on M Street through downtown Georgetown and turned south toward the C&O Canal. Tristan kept his distance. Arriving at a small stone bridge, they walked down the staircase to a dirt path where a large tree hung over the water as if reaching for a drink.

The path reminded him of another in his past, triggering an unsettling memory.

Moments later, a thin man with a pony tail approached Jason and his girlfriend. The three appeared to have a conversation that quickly became animated and resulted in shoving. Then a gun came out.

Ping.

Ping.

Before Tristan could react, he recognized the sound as bullets exiting a silencer. Jason's body buckled.

"No!"

He drew his firearm and rushed down the stairs to where Jason lay, conscious but not coherent, the girlfriend and assailant gone. Even in the low light, the gravity of the situation was obvious. Blood spread through the fabric of the white shirt from two entry wounds in the gut.

He dialed 911 on his cell phone.

"This is FBI Agent Tristan Wood, badge number . . . my partner is down and I need an ambulance at 33rd and M Street north-west."

After confirmation, he lifted Jason and carried him back down the path and up the stairs to the bridge. By the time they arrived at M Street his leg was in terrible pain.

They both collapsed on the sidewalk as pedestrians stopped to watch. Without warning, a DC Metro Police car screeched to a halt and two cops jumped out, guns drawn.

Tristan held up his FBI badge as a rescue siren grew louder.

The paramedics rushed Special Agent Jason Graves into the Georgetown University Hospital ER. Tristan fell into a waiting room chair and took a pain pill, chewing the bitter tablet to hasten the effects.

He dialed a number on his cell phone.

"Hey baby, it's me," he spoke to the answering machine. "I'm at Georgetown Hospital, Jason was shot and he's going into surgery so I'll be awhile. I'm okay, I'll call you later."

He leaned back with closed eyes waiting for the opiate to take effect. After a year, the pain continued despite the physical rehabilitation. Although they retrieved all the bone fragments in surgery, the bullet that shattered his femur had done permanent damage to the sciatic nerve.

The medication hit and he slipped into a delirious slumber.

Stark and dour images flashed through his mind. Fellow marines in desert camo moved in slow motion, dodging gunfire. Torrid air choked Tristan's throat from the inside out and he clawed at the sand of the trail beneath him. The palsy that engulfed his body forced him to spectate, his brothers falling one by one. Above him a helicopter spun out of control with aureate flames projecting like fire from a dragon's mouth, the nose dipping—

"I'm Doctor Croft, are you the one who brought the shot man in?" a surgeon in scrubs asked.

Tristan attempted to wake up, dazed and lacking an awareness of time. After a few moments he regained his composure.

"Yes, I'm Special Agent Wood, his FBI partner. How is he?"

"Both bullets passed through the gut. Neither hit the spine, which is good news, but one penetrated the liver and made a bit of a mess. He needed a partial hepatectomy."

"What is that?" Tristan asked.

"We had to remove about forty percent of the liver. There was an excessive amount of alcohol in his system and possibly some drugs. He's stable but in critical condition."

"I need to call his father in Detroit. The number is probably programmed into his cell phone."

"I'll have someone bring it out. No reason hanging around, he can't have visitors until morning. You look like you could use some rest yourself."

The surgeon turned and headed back for the ER.

"Thanks doc," he said, rubbing the sleep from his eyes.

Minutes later, a nurse approached with Jason's smart phone. Tristan left the hospital and set off for his Jeep parked just blocks away, unsure whether to be worried or relieved. He powered up the cell and scrolled through saved numbers to the one labeled; DAD. Their very first conversation and it was to give him devastating news about his son.

". . . I'll leave the keys to the apartment and the phone in the mailbox," Tristan offered before saying goodbye to Sebastian Graves.

R Street was quiet and misty, thick with humidity. He spotted the lawn jockey that graced Jason's yard, a creepy statue of a gargoyle holding a skull in its hand instead of a lantern. It sat in a crouch with wings extended, resembling a tiny fallen angel. This was the perfect representation of his friend's other personality, the dark side. Passing the ghastly ornament, he arrived at the ground-level apartment.

The lid of the corroded wall-mount mailbox creaked. About to deposit the house keys, a noise made Tristan pause. The door was ajar. He reached for his holster and eased inside, searching for a light switch.

The gun was knocked loose followed by a blow to the face, dropping him to the floor.

Although disoriented, Tristan attempted to locate his firearm in the black, until two of three kicks connected with his bad leg. Stars filled his vision and a bolt of lightning rose from the left thigh up to the base of his neck. This must be where the term *blinding pain* came from.

Rapid footsteps indicated the attacker darted outside and down the walkway. By the time Tristan regained his composure and got to his feet it was too late. He limped out to the front yard anyway. The street remained still without so much as a breeze. Nothing stirred. He bent over to catch his breath as sweat dripped from his forehead.

Staggering back inside, Tristan collapsed in the chair. The laptop computer glowed. His head began to pound on top of the leg pain so he reluctantly downed another pill.

Overall, the apartment seemed intact except for the work station, with open drawers clearly searched. A yellow legal pad with groceries and other scratched notes of no apparent importance remained untouched.

He placed Jason's wallet and keys on the desk, then scrolled through unfamiliar outgoing and incoming calls on the smart phone. Tristan checked the word-processor function which contained no data. Next, he reviewed the list of GPS coordinates, all associated with businesses such as restaurants.

All but one.

The most recent position was saved as a latitude-longitude. He wrote it down.

38°54'16" N ~ 77°02'9" W

Then Tristan saw something attached to the key ring; a flash drive. He moved his finger across the computer's mouse pad to get rid of the screensaver. The C-drive window was open. Someone had been searching for something on the computer. He plugged the flash drive into a USB port and discovered only one thing on it; a video file with a Russian title.

— Приливная волна 23 —

Tristan opened the file. A bleak map of Russia and the states of the former Soviet Union popped up. A military green hue filled the screen, gray outlines differentiating the countries. A cursor appeared in the lower left corner, a thick vertical bar that pulsed slowly. On the right, a time code idled.

00:00:00

A jolt shot through his body as animated missiles launched from different parts of Russia, Ukraine, and Kazakhstan. The time code ticked-off a standard numeric code. The map turned into a 3D image. It rotated, tracking the missiles as they circumnavigated the North Pole and Canada, striking targets in the continental United States, Alaska, and Hawaii. Additional locations were hit by rockets launched from the Atlantic and Pacific Oceans, as well as the Bering Sea. Tristan guessed they must have come from subs.

Accompanying the nuclear blasts, tiny mushroom clouds popped up and faded away. The cursor tabulated names in Russian.

Шайеннский Аэродром Горы,

Дуайт Д. Эизенхауэр,

Химический Центр Войны, Юта . . .

Mesmerized, Tristan played the strange video over and over. Finally, having enough, he ejected the flash drive and attached it to his own keychain. Overcome by fatigue, he stretched out on the couch. With the familiar euphoria of the medication, the pain ceased.

In seconds, FBI Agent Tristan Wood fell into a deep sleep.

CHAPTER 5

Robert Wood turned over again, not awake but not really asleep. The seat in the *Gulfstream V* reclined into a single, and extremely comfortable, bed. If not for the occasional bout of turbulence, he never would have known he had spent the night on a plane.

"Wake up, son."

Robert forced open his eyes, his boss standing over him. A lever on the side of the chair returned the seat to its upright position.

"What time is it?" he asked, a cup of coffee placed in his hand.

"Washington or Moscow?" the deep voice revealed a hint of southern drawl.

"On second thought, neither," Robert grumbled.

Senator Matthews, one of the longest serving United States congressmen, was a career politician in his sixth term. A large man in both height and weight, he towered over most people at 6'5" with the build of a linebacker, which he had been five decades earlier at Yale. Although the senator had lost his hair long ago, his distinguished presence commanded authority. Robert had never seen him without a suit, perfectly straight necktie, and spit-shined shoes.

"I will confirm our E.T.A., and then we will begin." The senator lumbered off toward the cabin.

The chartered flight had left Andrews AFB on schedule at approximately 5 p.m. the day before. It was due to land at

Domodedovo International Airport in the early Moscow morning, ten hours later.

Turbulence struck as Robert sipped the bitter brew, almost spilling it. He liked his coffee loaded with cream and sugar but it didn't matter. The senator found some humor in bringing it to him the complete opposite way. At least it always arrived in an extra-large cup.

Waiting for the caffeine to kick in, he took a moment to admire the jet plane. The Gulfstream V was pure luxury. The interior consisted of leather and wood, with multiple televisions and computers complete with working internet. The senator had taken full advantage of the stocked bar the night before.

In addition to the two pilots, a flight attendant had served them a five course meal for dinner. From the smell making his stomach growl, she was also preparing breakfast. Robert reached in his back pocket and took out a photo, inducing a smile.

Senator Matthews returned and settled into the opposite seat.

"What is that?"

"A picture of our kids. Sarah slipped it into my luggage when I wasn't looking, she's got a thing."

He offered the photo, unsolicited. It showed his two year old daughter Maggie grinning cheek to cheek, sitting next to a bassinette that held their newborn son, Rory. Robert's children were the joy of his life and often hinted that he wanted eight of them. The joke did not go over well with Sarah. The senator expressed some forced interest and handed it back without comment.

"We'll be on the ground in an hour. Can you hand me my file?"

He removed a briefcase from under the seat, each brass latch opening with a *snap*. He took out a thick folder packed with photos and official documents. The senator put on his reading glasses and began to sift through the papers.

"I'm sorry, I didn't have much time to study the START treaty."

After dinner Robert had sat down with the file, but the combination of a big meal and champagne had knocked him out. Worse, his daughter Maggie had come down with a stomach virus and kept both parents up most of the night before. It had taken all his energy just to get to work, only to discover they were leaving for Moscow later in the day.

"I can trust you, can I not Mr. Wood?"

"Sir?" The question caught Robert off-guard.

"I need to trust you," the senator held up the file, "to keep this new knowledge in confidence and not leak information to the press, or anyone else. Can I trust you, Mr. Wood?"

"Of course," he replied.

"Working for me, you're going to learn things. Some will seem counter-intuitive."

"I feel like I already have."

"No, you haven't. You hear what I let you hear and you read what I let you read. Always remember, those in power control information. So far, you have only seen the reflection on an immensely deep lake. Now that you are accompanying me to Moscow, the equation changes. I cannot keep the truth from you forever, nor do I want to. It's time to look beneath the surface and study the depths."

"Yes, Senator."

"We're not going to Moscow to discuss the START, or any other arms treaties."

"Sir?"

"Ambassador Bullitt is missing."

"Missing?"

Robert took the black and white glossy showing a group of men standing side by side in front of the Moscow Kremlin.

"You'll recognize President Putin and acting Prime Minister Medvedev on the left. In the middle, you have Finance Minister Ivan Nikitin, to his left is Andrei Tarasov, Putin's Chief of Presidential Staff and on the right is Yuri Ushakov, the Russian ambassador to the United States. Next to him is the US ambassador to Russia; Walter Bullitt."

Senator Matthews had been the real force behind the president's choice, and the senate's confirmation, of Walter J. Bullitt as the newest US ambassador to the Russian Federation. Robert remembered the senator did not have to work exceptionally hard to get him approved. Bullitt was born in Boise, Idaho, to an American father and a Russian mother. He grew up speaking both languages and attended Leningrad State University.

The only issue that emerged at his senate hearing was the revelation that his mother's family still lived in Russia, and therefore questions as to where his loyalties may lie. However, in the overall frenzy of a new president entering office, this was a minor issue and Bullitt was easily confirmed.

"We lost contact with him two weeks ago. Prior to that he was recalled to Washington, several times, but refused. Then we discovered he moved his family to Moscow. Walter and I are dear friends and he hasn't return my calls either."

Robert handed back the photo. "So we were sent to find him?"

"No," the senator snapped. "We are on a diplomatic trip to discuss arms inspections per the START treaty. Are we clear?"

"Of course."

"We didn't want any leaks to the press, no one outside my committee knows. As far as nuclear arms talks go, it is a useless endeavor anyway. The Soviet Union has yet to abide by even one of its treaties with the United States."

"You mean Russian Federation, right? Not the Soviet Union."

"I meant 'Soviet Union.' They may not be unified at the moment, but they will be again."

"I thought the USSR fell, it doesn't exist anymore?" Robert chugged the rest of his coffee.

The senator laughed. "That is the modern view, yes. Don't believe everything the media tells you, son."

Needing clarification, he asked, "I'm sorry, I don't understand?"

"Are you ready to look below the surface of the lake?"

The way it was presented, he wasn't so sure. Robert had been working as an aide for less than a year, and had done his best considering the steep learning curve. Up until now, however, it was mostly administrative work. The senator received habitual classified reports called "eyes-only," which he delivered but never saw. This information required a higher level of security he did not have.

"I'm ready to move beyond taking phone calls and making coffee," he said, exaggerating somewhat.

The flight attendant served them trays of food and juice. The senator waited until she walked away before speaking.

"The Soviet Union did not collapse, it was a grand deception. We've been so distracted with Islamic terror and the Middle East wars that we have taken our eye off the real threat. Call it Russia, the Russian Federation, or the Soviet Union, it doesn't matter. Ever since the Bolsheviks took over in 1917 the goal has been the destruction of Capitalism and the building of a world empire under Communism. They have never taken their eye off the ball. Unfortunately, we have."

"But the Berlin Wall came down, the Soviet Union went bankrupt!"

"Yes, the Berlin Wall did come down in 1989, and the Soviet armies did leave Europe in 1990, but the overthrow of Communist regimes by the so-called reformers was allowed to happen, under supervision. And when the new leadership took over, they were able to act the part of reformers and hide their allegiance with the Communist Secret Police. Those Communist leaders are still in charge today. It was a ruse."

"I thought Russia was our friend, the media is always telling us the Cold War is long over," Robert said, as he scarfed his food.

"Since 1990, Russia has been feigning weakness as the Kremlin plans a resurgence. With Vladimir Putin as president again, they are full-steam ahead. The Russian Federation is the largest conventional arms dealer on Earth, quietly selling to smaller nations and converting them to Communism, one by one. The START treaties are a tool in a greater plan to weaken, and eventually disarm, the United States. No, Russia is not our friend, Mr. Wood."

"I've always thought of Russia as wanting Capitalism; to be like us?"

"Because the media repeats it over and over."

This simple statement, that the Soviet Union's collapse was a ruse, was tough to swallow. The source certainly was credible, yet a part of him did not want to believe it. Robert glanced out the window as the plane entered clouds so thick the tip of the wing disappeared.

"And the economic collapse?"

"Some of it was real. The civilian economy was in shambles and allowed to buckle, but most programs moved underground. While being told Russia was becoming democratic, essential elements such as private property rights and transportation were never freed from Soviet-style control. And when Russia complained about their economic woes and threat of famine after this so-called collapse, President Clinton and European leaders gave them billions in foreign aid, both in money and food. But there was no famine, Russian farmers had plenty of crops. They were just displaced by US food-aid, sold back to the people by Russian leaders for a hefty profit."

"What about the military?" Robert asked.

"Only the manpower side of the Russian military was allowed to collapse. They purposely failed to pay troops or maintain normal living standards, leading to discontent in their armed forces. However, production and development of high tech conventional military equipment never slowed. Huge stockpiles of tanks and mobile artillery were simply taken out of current inventory and hidden away. They remain dispersed in depots in and around deep underground military bases as part of the *Conventional Forces Treaty* signed with the United States and NATO. This treaty allowed Russia to match US reduction in forces without actually destroying equipment, requiring them only to put their tanks 'out of reach.' In fact, the Russian Ministry of Defense brought back some of that inventory during the various Chechen and Georgian conflicts starting in 2004, and the US let them get away with it without a peep of protest. Many of the low-level troops left the army in the 1990s, but Russia kept their huge corps of officers and NCOs. This strategy will allow it to refill the low ranks of enlisted soldiers in a matter of months when war breaks out.

"*When* war breaks out?"

"Are you familiar with *The Art of War?*"

"I know of it, but never read it."

"They are implementing Sun Tzu's classic war doctrine; feigning weakness prior to a strike."

"A strike?"

"We're still in a Cold War, Mr. Wood. These days, we fight it through third world countries. Every time we bomb or invade a new country such as Libya, Syria, Egypt, Tunisia, Yemen, or Iran, it further erodes our global image, stretching our military and economy thinner. Unfortunately, cold wars lead to hot wars—"

The pilot interrupted with the approach and landing announcement as the flight attendant took away their food trays.

"It's not easy being on the inside, seeing what is genuinely going on in the world, even when it runs contrary to what's reported in the news," the senator said as he stood up. "We'll have much more to talk about, this is only the beginning."

He gave his young aide a pat on the shoulder and then buckled himself into a seat on the other side of the aisle.

Robert turned on his smart phone and downloaded his emails and texts, plus the latest news headlines. Most were analogous reports pertaining to yesterday's historic event at Union Station such as, "Presidential Assassination Attempt at Next-Gen!"

But the one that grabbed him was further down.

"US ambassador Missing in Russia."

The story hadn't stayed under wraps for even the length of their flight.

"Unbelievable," he said to himself.

Robert Wood tightened his seat belt as they approached the runway at Domodedovo International Airport in Moscow, Russia.

CHAPTER 6

The Wrangler circled through the underground garage of the J. Edgar Hoover building on Pennsylvania Avenue, the headquarters of the Federal Bureau of Investigations. On sunny days Tristan liked to roll back the soft-top and enjoy the weather. He had dreamt of owning a Jeep Wrangler since he was a child, and upon completing rehabilitation for his combat injuries had treated himself to his first new car.

The extra wide tires howled in every turn as Tristan maneuvered around the garage looking for a space.

FBI Headquarters, nicknamed the *Seat of Government* by Hoover, was originally headquartered in the Department of Justice until 1974 when they began the transition into the existing multi-level fortress constructed specifically for the Bureau. President Gerald Ford dedicated the building in 1975, and by '77 the move was complete.

Tristan parked in the first available spot, turned off the engine, and examined himself in the rear view mirror. He had quite a shiner. The blow, as he entered Jason's apartment, caught him square in the face. In his younger years he would have worn a black eye as a badge of honor. Now it embarrassed him.

He arrived at the elevator and waited with an unfamiliar woman about his age.

"Dangerous job, huh?"

"Excuse me?" Tristan asked.

She pointed at her own eye.

"Oh, yeah. Could be worse, believe me."

After some small talk he realized she was flirting. Marriage had dulled his radar. At just over six feet tall, he had thick dark hair, straight white teeth, and mahogany eyes, as Allyson described them. Although he no longer had the brawn from his days as a marine, his health was excellent—except for the bad leg. But he was tough. Afghanistan had made him that way.

The elevator stopped and the doors opened.

"Bye." She turned with a smile and was gone.

Tristan exited on the fifth floor and walked to an office where a secretary sat at her desk typing on a computer keyboard.

"I've got an appointment with SAC Murphy."

She glanced over at the half-open door. "I believe it's okay to go in."

He knocked and stuck his head inside.

"Agent Wood, come in," his boss grunted.

Tristan nodded hello to ASAC Andrew Tufts, his assistant special agent in charge, who sat in a nearby chair. An unfamiliar man stood reading over Murphy's shoulder.

"This is SAC Seth Pascal, he's the chief of Foreign Counterintelligence Investigations for the east coast."

"Are you Tristan Wood? The war hero?" The new guy adjusted his wire-rimmed glasses and reached out to shake hands.

Great, Tristan thought, *another desk-jockey bureaucrat.*

"Actually, my wife is the hero."

"Yes, of course."

No matter how many times this happened it didn't get less uncomfortable.

"Any update on Agent Graves?" Murphy asked in his usual grumpy way.

Tristan had called their boss after waking up on Jason's couch early this morning to give him the news.

"Nothing new. He's still stable but critical."

"What is his prognosis?"

"Lost a lot of blood; one bullet went through the liver and did some damage. The doctor seemed optimistic. His father caught the first flight out of Detroit. He's retired FBI actually, his name is—"

"Sebastian Graves," Pascal cut him off.

"You know him, sir?" Tristan was surprised.

"Not personally, but I've been with the Bureau a long time. I'm familiar with the career guys. He's been on some of the more famous cases. A bit of a hot-head from what I've heard, good agent though."

"I've never met him." Tristan suppressed his irritation at the back-handed compliment by the stocky and unassuming man.

"Sit, Agent Wood." Murphy broke out of his trance, closing the folder in front of him. "Just what in the hell were you doing last night?"

"Jason's been acting strange lately. We had plans to watch the game, but he went to meet this girl instead."

"Why did you follow him?"

"Suspicious of his new girlfriend, I guess. I'd ask about her but he never offered to introduce us. The Tombs is his regular hangout, so I took a chance they'd be there. I wanted to see what was going on with him, I didn't expect anything like this to happen."

"Is that all?" Murphy asked.

"All what?"

"Is that all you know? That he's been acting strange lately?"

Tristan felt a nervous rush, thoughts passing through his mind at the speed of light—*drinking . . . pills . . . Tidal Wave 23?*

"I don't understand your question."

"We've had Agent Graves under surveillance for six months," Pascal interjected. "He's been selling classified intel to the Russians."

"Spying?"

"Specifically for the SVR, the—"

"The Russian Foreign Intelligence Service?" Tristan interrupted. "No, that can't be."

"I'm not asking you, I'm telling you."

After the break-up of the Soviet states, the KGB went through changes under President Boris Yeltsin. The Russian Foreign Intelligence Service was the counterpart to the CIA. Headquartered in Moscow, the SVR engaged in electronic surveillance, intel gathering, and general espionage activities outside the Russian Federation. It had become the primary spy agency of Russia since the end of the Cold War.

"There must be some kind of mistake." He asked Murphy, "Did you know about this?"

"He wouldn't. These investigations are covert." Pascal moved to the window and gazed outside, the white dress shirt underneath his suit jacket struggled to keep his gut contained.

Murphy slid the file, full of photos, printed emails, and wiretap transcriptions, across the desk to Tristan.

Pascal continued, "My men were just days away from arresting him. We had a little more evidence to gather first."

"This is unbelievable," Tristan flipped through the pages. "Does his father know?"

"Not yet, but he will," Murphy said.

Pascal walked over and took the file away. "The investigation is being turned over to Internal Affairs. This conversation stays in this room, understand?"

"So, how was he doing it? Passing secrets, I mean."

"Dead drops. He used a pen-type device to photograph documents here in the Bureau. The others he downloaded off our computers, directly to flash drives, and smuggled them out of the building."

A *dead drop* was an old Cold War method of espionage using a pre-planned location so the parties were not obligated to meet face to face. The spy hid the information at one locale and picked up their payment at another, sometimes requiring hours of driving or moving around to shake off any tails.

"I never would have imagined—"

"SAC Murphy says you called him from Agent Grave's apartment?" Pascal asked.

"Yes, sir."

"Did you find anything that could assist in our investigation?"

Tristan clutched the flash drive in his pocket and considered this new guy he did not know. "I didn't think to snoop around. I was there to leave the keys for his father."

"Agents just finished searching his apartment. Your prints were on his laptop," Pascal said, studying him.

"It was powered on. I shut it down, that's all." Tristan had not thought to check the hard drive for *Tidal Wave 23* before leaving in the morning. "Did you find anything useful on it?" He knocked the ball back into Pascal's court.

The SAC did not answer. Tristan could tell by his reaction they did not.

"What did you do to your eye?" Murphy finally brought it up.

Thinking fast he said, "Jason's elbow must have got me while I carried him to the ambulance." A terrible liar, Tristan hoped they could not see through him. He changed the subject. "Was the canal his regular dead drop?"

"They used a different location every time."

"Who is the girl?"

"Her current alias is Lara Fedorov, and she's got quite a résumé." Pascal opened the file and pulled out a photo, handing it to Tristan. "These Intelligence Officers are always looking to recruit both Russians and Americans, but with different tactics. With Russians, they actually go to the person's home and knock on the door. If they're unable to reach an understanding the spy will threaten the would-be recruit's family in Russia, with both legal prosecution and physical harm."

"And for Americans?" Tristan asked.

"For Americans, they learned long ago that the best way to recruit is with money and sex. And it doesn't matter if they're single or married, the Russians have found their methods work equally well with both. The Intelligence Officer will follow the person to restaurants and bars and meet them under a pretense of chance. We believe Ms. Fedorov approached Agent Graves in this manner. Apparently, she met him in a bar and seduced him. She was exceedingly good at what she did."

Tristan pondered this new information. "How did I not see this? I thought something was wrong, but I'd never guess spying?"

"How would you? He didn't live extravagantly. In fact, it appears he did not spend any of the money." Murphy scanned the figures. "We checked his credit card bills and bank statements. He lived completely within his means and all his payouts went into one offshore account—"

"It doesn't matter," Pascal cut in. "The reason is always greed. The M.O. is what changes with each individual but it's almost never about helping the Russians or the Chinese. We've had spies who bought half a million dollar homes all cash, spent twenty thousand a month on credit cards, and purchased brand new cars they could obviously not afford on their salary. But Agent Graves was smart, and low-key. He had almost three hundred thousand dollars in the account."

"How did you find out?"

"I can't disclose that."

"If he wasn't spending the money, what was the point?"

"I believe saving up until he had accumulated a specific amount, then he'd flee the country."

"How can you be sure? Did he have a passport or a plane ticket? I don't remember him travelling outside America, wouldn't he scout places to live, and have a plan?" Tristan asked.

Pascal paused before answering, "Those details are restricted."

Tristan began to fidget in his chair. He rubbed his thigh and stood up.

"Leg bothering you?"

He ignored Murphy's question. "Put me on this case."

"No, this is what counter-intel does," Pascal said.

"So transfer me over. I know Jason better than anyone."

"Even if we were to consider it, you have zero experience in espionage. The answer is no."

Though his impulse was to argue, the man was right. In the months spent recovering in the hospital, Tristan had read numerous books on the FBI. The Bureau had quite a record of blown cases as a result of inexperienced agents.

One particularly dark period was 1985; "the year of the spy." Of the several major examples, the case of Navy Officer John A. Walker, Jr. was one of the most damaging in US history. Walker almost got away when FBI sent a special agent with no experience in foreign counterintelligence to interview his ex-wife.

The agent failed to recognize, through the rambling stories and vodka drinking, that the details she cited were genuine signs of a Soviet spy operation.

FBI eventually arrested Walker during a dead drop as he attempted to pass on documents his son had stolen from the USS Nimitz, the ship he was stationed on. By that time, however, eighteen years of spying had provided the Soviets with an abundance of classified information including Navy vessel and submarine locations, weapons data, covert military operations, and emergency plans in the event of a nuclear war.

"I need you to concentrate on the Train Bomber case." Murphy now used the media's label.

"Did you get a copy of the security video from Amtrak yet?"

"Still waiting, I'll inform you when I do. You're dismissed."

Tristan stood up. It occurred to him that he should give them all the tools they needed to investigate Jason's case, and reached into his pocket for the flash drive.

"I'm going to be assigning you a new partner." Murphy said, not looking up.

A rush of anger became difficult to suppress. "Jason is my partner." He gave his boss an opportunity to renege, which he did not. "I'll wait for him to come back to work, but thanks."

Special Agent Tristan Wood slammed the door behind him.

They would not get the flash drive yet.

CHAPTER 7

Through the rain and mist, the Spaso House appeared out of nowhere as the limousine turned down Spasopeskovskaya Square, the street it was named for. Originally built in 1913 by the textile industrialist Nikolay Vtorov, the mansion had served as the residence of the US ambassador since 1933 after a long period of not recognizing the USSR.

The official title changed in 1991 from "Ambassador to the USSR" to "Ambassador to the Russian Federation." An important distinction, it meant the world media would refer to the US conduit without the term *Soviet* anywhere to be found.

Robert stopped his research and turned off the smart phone.

The pictures of the Spaso House did not do it justice. The structure was considered *Neoclassical Revival* and resembled a small version of the White House imbued with Russian flair. Painted a rich gold color, the alabaster pillars and trim gave it a grand appearance. The grounds were meticulous even in the doldrums of April in Moscow, the cold and damp weather normal for this time of year.

If it's this inspiring from the outside, he thought, *I can't wait to see the interior.*

The senator had seemed distant ever since they left the airport, so he decided to stay quiet until spoken to. The limo came to a stop in a short circular driveway and the trunk popped open. The chauffeur opened the door for the senator who stepped out onto the walkway underneath an awning that provided some protection from the drizzle, a major improvement from the downpour that hammered the car for most of the ride.

The driver then went to retrieve the luggage.

"Let me help you," Robert offered.

He was waved away, apparently in lieu of speaking English.

"Wood! That is not your job, now come along." Grabbing his aide's arm, the senator said under his breath, "By the way, the entire house is bugged." He winked, then led them inside.

"Welcome, welcome, welcome!" A young man in a dark suit, and brandishing a Russian accent, walked up to them. "My name is Lev. I am new caretaker of the residence." He helped the senator with his overcoat.

"I wish to speak with Ambassador Bullitt right away, please have him meet us in the library," he said, getting to the point.

Lev hung their coats in the entry-way closet.

"The ambassador is not here at the moment, Senator Matthews," Lev replied, his heavy accent straight out of the movies.

"Does he know I flew all the way from Washington, DC, to meet with him?"

"If he is watching the American news then I'm sure he does. A shame you do not have control over your media like Russia does, yes?"

"We have much more than you realize."

Robert didn't understand the senator's response, but was not about to ask.

Lev led them into the Chandelier Room where he witnessed the true grandeur of the Spaso House. The colonnade extended from the wood floors to the first tier ceiling and engulfed a rotunda that soared over two stories. A balcony overlooked the space.

The chandelier was one of the biggest he had ever seen. A dome of hundreds of crystals comprising the bottom half and gold laced electric candles on top, it drew the focus to the center of the room.

"Amazing!"

The senator was about to respond when a man dressed as a butler joined them. Lev spoke to him in Russian.

The limo driver caught up, struggling with the luggage. Robert insisted on carrying his own bag, this time without protest.

"We will show you to your rooms and lunch will be served in an hour," Lev announced.

The butler led them to the most famous part of the house, at least for Russians. The main stairway had inspired a scene in a 1937 novel called *Master and Margarita* by author Mikhail Bulgakov.

The steps were lined with red carpet and the wall adorned over twenty past US ambassadors. Several of the more recent photos were different than the others, each man posing with his right hand partially inside his jacket as if exhibiting some kind of veiled message. Though it reminded Robert of portraits he had seen of Napoleon Bonapart and George Washington, it was familiar from somewhere else he could not recall. The picture at the bottom of the staircase was instantly recognizable.

Robert stopped to read the name on the plaque.

Walter J. Bullitt.

Arriving upstairs, the butler unlocked the doors for them. The limo driver followed Senator Matthews into the first room wheeling the oversized suitcase inside. Robert entered the second bedroom with his own bag and closed the door, thankful for some privacy.

The modest space was furnished with a bed, small desk, and sitting chair with an end table by a large window overlooking the garden. Four framed photographs hung on the wall, each showing a different scene from the annual Fourth of July celebration.

Two showed scenes from the parade. The one of the proudly marching marines, with spectators cheering, reminded him of his older brother Tristan. Unlike now, July in Moscow was warm and sunny. The other pair of photos were taken inside Spaso House during the after-party with guests dressed to the nines.

Robert checked his smart phone again. One text was from his brother.

"Any idea what *Tidal Wave 23* means? Can you ask the senator? Seems to be a Russian phrase. Hope you had a good trip. Don't get recruited by the KGB!"

Leave it to Tristan to make him laugh.

He opened his suitcase and pulled out some clean clothes. After a long hot shower he relaxed on the bed and closed his eyes, but his mind raced. The stress of working in politics had started to take its toll on his health, as well as his marriage. Sarah pointed out he was often distant, tired, and in a cranky mood. If it solely affected him, he would cope. Lately, however, the tension was impinging upon the little quality time he had with his children. And despite all the food available as a senator's aide, he had lost weight.

Robert began to dream.

He was at home with his youngsters. Maggie played with toys on the floor and little Rory lay on his belly, pacifier in his mouth and rattle in hand. Their innocence made him want to weep with joy. He searched for Sarah but she was not here. The increasing volume of the rustling leaves outside drew his attention.

A light flashed on the horizon followed by a mushroom cloud rising up to the sky. In the distance, a wave of smoke and debris headed toward them. He wanted to pick up his children and head for the basement, but his feet would not move. He tried to scream over the progressive bedlam. The house began to shake and oscillate, the noise resembling a freight train. A pounding indicated to Robert that a structure failure was imminent.

He snapped back into reality as his conscious mind realized it was coming from outside the room.

"Chow time, son," the senator banged on the door. "Wood, you awake?"

The temperamental weather rattled the glass window while Robert tried to regain his senses.

"I'll be right out!" he yelled.

The boss led the way downstairs to a banquet room with a long table and two formal place settings on opposite ends. The aroma of cooking filled the air and Robert realized he was famished.

"It appears we will be dining alone," Senator Matthews mumbled, referring to the absence of the ambassador. "Have you ever had real Russian food?"

"Can't say I have, Senator."

A servant entered, placing two large bowls of cold soup in front of them and left without saying a word. Robert tried to guess the ingredients as he ate. Although unappetizing to look at—like a dark green wet salad—it was divine.

"I taste carrots and cucumbers, and fish?" he guessed.

"This is called Okroshka. Russians love their stews and soups. There are several ways to make it, this is perch or cod, I can never tell which. Yes, carrots, cucumbers, and a green onion base gives it its color."

"Delicious," Robert realized he was almost done with the entire bowl.

"Russian food has evolved over the centuries. It started with the peasants and was refined by the aristocracy, influenced in their travels to countries such as Britain, France, and Austria," the senator seemed to be lightening up.

Next, they were presented with a plate of pies called pirogi; small stuffed lightly-fried pastries. The filling was mainly rice, hard-boiled eggs, and some kind of meat. To wash it down, each had their own pitcher of a refreshing fruit beverage. Robert hummed in approval as he drank.

"Kvass," the senator said. "A fermented bread based drink, with fruit added. This is raspberry. It is considered non-alcoholic but go easy, it's not an exact science and might sneak up on you."

Dessert was a scoop of chocolate ice cream followed by coffee.

"I believe Russian coffee is the reason the Communists are so aggressive. Drink enough and you'll want to take over the world."

"Wow!" Robert took a sip and smiled. "That is the complete opposite of smooth."

"Just wait until the caffeine kicks in."

His energy returned, mainly from the food and drink, but also because they had gone the entire meal without speaking business or politics. Then he recalled his brother's text message.

"Sir, does the phrase *Tidal Wave 23* mean anything to you?"

The senator almost choked on his coffee, "What?"

"My brother Tristan wondered if it's a Russian expression. He thought you might know the meaning?"

Blood left the old man's face.

"Have him search 'Tidal Wave 21'," was the reluctant reply.

"Okay." He returned the text.

The servant walked in to take their empty desert bowls away and top off their brew.

"Please let Mr. Lev know that we will be in the library and would very much like to meet with him."

The woman silently walked back into the kitchen.

"Does she speak English?" Robert asked.

"She understands everything."

The senator grunted as he arose from his chair, leading the way through the Chandelier room and into the library. They both sat down and continued drinking their coffee.

"What do you think is going on? Why won't the ambassador return your calls?"

"Do you remember what I told you when we arrived this morning?" the senator winked, referring to the bugs.

As they waited for Lev to join them, Robert had a look around. The Spaso House library was a warm room with comfortable chairs and an abundance of lamps to read by. He wondered what the book collection was comprised of, guessing there would be no shortage of pro-Communist publications, Soviet Union history, plus novels by famous Russian authors such as Trotsky and Testikov.

Lev finally entered the room.

"Have you been able to contact Ambassador Bullitt?"

"I'm sorry, we still cannot locate him," Lev said.

The senator thought for a moment. "Well, then we have no choice. How would you like to take in the Russian countryside young man?"

"Um, sure," Robert went along.

"As Mr. Lev knows, Ambassador Bullitt's mother is Russian and has a family home in Bologoye, isn't that right Mr. Lev?"

Lev appeared to become agitated.

The senator continued, "Bologoye is a quaint town in Tver Oblast, about halfway between St. Petersburg and Moscow. Shouldn't take us more than a couple hours to drive."

"I do not think that is good idea Senator, once you leave the premises, we cannot guarantee your safety," Lev struggled with his broken English.

"Don't be foolish, I have been a guest at the ambassador's dacha many times, I know the way by heart." He turned to Robert, "Wait until you see the Volga."

"The what?"

Lev walked out of the library in a huff.

"The Spaso House has quite a car collection. We'll take the 1956 Volga, from the glory days of the Soviet Union. But we'll need to be cautious, like the old USSR their cars tend to be big, bloated, and can turn you into a Communist when you're not paying attention," the senator bellowed. "Let's get our coats, we will need to dress warmly."

They walked back through the Chandelier Room to the coat closet and bundled up, adding scarves and gloves.

"Watch how an old man can drive, son."

Turning for the door, the sound of automatic weapons loading echoed in the hallway. Before them stood two Russian military police, AK-47s held high. Lev approached from behind holding a walkie-talkie.

"I'm afraid I can't let you leave the residence Senator Matthews."

CHAPTER 8

Tristan sat waiting for the computer to boot as white noise from the shower filled the room.; he was anxious for an update on Robert and Senator Matthews. A full moon shone like a spotlight through the upstairs bedroom window of their small red-brick colonial, the style of home Allyson had dreamed of owning her entire adult life.

By the time they decided to buy, however, the second housing market crash of the twenty-first century had set in as media personalities sat around scratching their heads. Unlike the sub-prime lending crisis back in 2008, the Federal Reserve could no longer artificially suppress the zero-percent bank rates, making this downturn much worse. With interest rates rising and personal debt at historic levels, fewer people qualified for a mortgage despite the continuing decline in home prices.

With the combined salary of a new FBI agent and a doctor in her residency, plus student loans, even the Department of Veteran Affairs had been unable to approve them for a VA loan, once easy money for vets. Demoralizing as it was, the couple was forced to rent.

Tristan sat at a desk in boxers and a T-shirt searching for news reports, most of which were about the attempted assassination of the president. Scrolling down the page he found what he was looking for.

US ambassador missing in Russia.

Below that was another.

Senator held hostage in Moscow!

Tristan perused both extremely speculative stories, searching for anything about his brother. The shower turned off and moments later Allyson entered, holding something in her hand.

"What are these!?"

She inspected the label of a prescription bottle.

"You're a doctor, you know what they are."

"I don't appreciate sarcasm, Tristan. Oxycodone? This is heavy stuff!"

"Doctor Stanley prescribed them. It's the lowest dose they have and I only take one when I need it."

"That's how it begins. Do you realize how addictive these are? Law enforcement is shutting down *pill mills* on a regular basis now, there's a reason for that."

As a returning service member, Tristan was under the care of a pain management consultant since being honorably discharged for his war injuries. Though no longer a marine, he was eligible for treatment at the VA Medical Center where they attended to current and former troops with everything from chronic pain and PTSD, to anger and sleep disorders.

"I have a prescription from Doctor Stanley, it's legit."

"Is that why it was hidden under the sink?"

He pulled her to him.

"I didn't want you to worry, that's all. I'll be careful, I promise."

Allyson gave him an unconvincing look.

"My wife is a medical doctor, I believe I'm in good hands," Tristan said with a hint of flippancy.

"I'm serious. Don't keep things like this from me."

"You're right, I'm sorry."

She held his head back and examined his black eye. "You'll have this for a while." After composing herself she noticed the news article open in the browser. "Worried about Robert?"

"He's not returning my texts anymore."

"Are they reporting anything new?"

"Not really. The rumors are, Senator Matthews and an aide are being held against their will at the Spaso House. The mainstream media says they don't want to speculate, while speculating they're hostages," Tristan complained. "No mention of Robert by name."

"They love coming up with buzzwords like 'hostage'." Allyson began to dry her long dark hair.

"I hate not knowing what's going on."

"Speaking of not knowing what's going on, I've been thinking," she seemed reluctant to bring it up, "we should get a fertility test."

"You mean me."

"No, both of us."

Tristan wondered when this would come up. Now married nine months, at Allyson's insistence they had started *trying* before their honeymoon was even over. This precipitous urgency had blindsided him. Most couples spent the first few years enjoying marriage, getting settled in their new lives, organizing finances and planning for the future.

Tristan had thought long and hard about past conversations regarding family and children. He could not remember discussing it while they were dating, other than in vague generalities. In fact, Allyson tended to avoid the subject altogether. Since their marriage, however, she had become obsessed about having children and it vexed him.

"So how many kids should we have?" he asked apprehensively.

"Four, maybe five?"

"Seriously?"

"Sure, why not?"

"I'd say we better start making more money. Or win the lottery."

The look on her face gave him a pang of guilt, but so far, getting pregnant was far more difficult than they had anticipated. Some couples succeeded the first night and others took a year, or more. It did not mean something was wrong with either of them, just that it was not yet meant to be. This was where their personalities differed. Tristan was patient and allowed things to resolve in time. Allyson over-analyzed, intervened, and forced outcomes.

"Hey, I almost forgot to show you this!" Desperate to change the subject, he plugged Jason's flash drive into a USB port and saved it to the hard drive as a backup.

Tristan opened the file, the time code set to zero, the drab white cursor blinking hypnotically. He played the now familiar video. The map moved, following the nuclear missiles as they cruised over the polar cap. The time code counted. After clearing the northern border the nukes reached their targets.

"This is what you found on Jason?" Allyson asked in disbelief.

"It's wild, right?"

"What are those? Little mushroom clouds as the missiles hit?"

The cursor began tabulating.

Пентагон,

Аэродром Морской пехоты . . .

"What do these mean?" Allyson continued.

"They're military targets."

"How do you know?"

"At first I noticed that not every word translated exactly." Tristan reversed the video and paused. "Look at this one," he pointed to Arizona.

Дэвис-Monthan AFB.

"AFB is air force base, and Monthan is part of Davis-Monthan Air Force Base. It's in Tucson. When I got to the office today I spent some time in the computer room and confirmed it with an English-Russian translation website. From what I can figure, the first wave is military. The second is civilian."

"Civilian?"

"Hospitals, monuments, power plants, ports . . ."

"What was Jason doing with it?"

"I don't know that yet."

"The title is in Russian, what does it mean?" Allyson asked.

"It translates to *Tidal Wave 23*."

"What's that?"

"I found nothing about it on the internet, absolutely nothing, so I texted Robert to ask the senator. Before I lost contact with him, he hit me back and said to search *Tidal Wave 21.*"

"*Tidal Wave 21?* I don't get it."

"It's in a speech."

He clicked on a saved bookmark. The webpage that loaded showed a photo of a woman behind a podium, and under it a transcript of her address titled; "Financial Crisis Will Sweep Away Governments."

"Only a couple websites post the actual speech." Tristan scrolled down the page as he explained, "So on June 29, 2001, the Russian Duma held an official hearing called, 'On the Measures to Provide the Development of Russian Economy in the Environment of Destabilization of the World Financial System.' It featured a Kremlin advisor," he pointed to the name under the photo of a middle-aged woman, her hair cropped short and parted on one side, "Tatyana Koryagina. The theme of the hearings was the rapidly approaching economic crash of the United States and focused on preparations for President Putin as to what Russia should do to soften the consequences of the coming catastrophe, which she called *Tidal Wave XXI.*"

"It's a short speech." Allyson began to read, "I shall try to sketch the development of the research done by our group, which is a group of independent experts studying the world financial crisis, but in a more global context than merely financial . . . I shall not go into details, but the fact that ultimately Putin came to power, I consider to be positive." She chuckled, "Great, a Putin supporter. She must be happy he's president again."

"No kidding," Tristan agreed.

Allyson continued where she left off, "Many colleagues here know me, and that I have studied the shadow economy of the Soviet Union and then Russia, in parallel with studying the ordinary, normal economy. So, when I was dragged by the ears into politics, as well, while studying our domestic shadow economy and expanding that to the study of the transitional shadow economy, I unavoidably landed in the realm of analysis that is sometimes called conspiracy theory . . . My forecast is that major events will unfold, once again, in August. In a strange way, it seems to me that the date may even be known. It will be August 19."

"That's August 19, 2001. Remember that date as you're reading," Tristan said.

She went on, "I have provisionally called this scenario, *Tidal Wave XXI*, where XXI denotes the new century, in Roman numerals . . . The main blow will be inflicted on the United States of America." She asked, "Main blow?"

"Keep reading."

"My colleague, Andrei Kobyakov said here, that his analysis shows that the eye of the cyclone will be in America. I would only add, that it will emerge there, but this will be done on purpose . . . Thus I make this determination. It will be the United States this time, and it will be a crisis developing at a different rate than the one in 1997-98. At that time, the action was drawn out. Here, it will be more of a precision strike. It will be like the explosion of the universe. And it will spread throughout all continents. Many governments will be swept away. The monetary and financial systems of the world will change. In Russia, beyond a doubt, the free exchange of currency will be shut down . . . Those who have a lot of money will use their greenbacks to wallpaper the bathroom, where they'll be able to admire the portrait of a past President of the United States. Insofar as I nevertheless fear to say too much, and I could say very much, thank you. God grant that my forecast turn out to be wrong. May God grant that!" Allyson finished reading the speech. "I don't get it, what was she predicting would happen on August 19, 2001?"

"It wasn't what happened on that date, but about three weeks later."

"9/11? It doesn't sound like a terrorist attack, it sounds like a financial downturn."

"Or something causing a financial downturn. I found an article that might explain it. Thirteen days after these Duma hearings, Pravda did a page one report on *Tidal Wave XXI* called,

'Will the Dollar and America Fall Down on August 19? That's the Opinion of Dr. Tatyana Koryagina, Who Very Accurately Predicted the August Default in 1998'."

Pravda was the newspaper considered the establishment voice of Russia's old guard Communists who controlled the military and intelligence agencies.

"In this article," Tristan continued, "they interviewed Dr. Koryagina to clarify what she meant in her speech. She talks about international *super-state* and *super-government* groups in control of the shadow economy that can be collapsed at any time, on purpose."

"Why America?"

"She claims that the US has been chosen as the object of the economic collapse because the financial center of the planet is located here."

"It does sound like she was predicting a 9/11 size event, but she got the date wrong," Allyson said.

"She says in the interview that August 19 could fluctuate. But here's the problem with that date; August 19, 2001, was a Sunday. The financial markets weren't open. I found a NewsMax article from September 17, 2001, verifying that Russian citizens were warned to get out of the US dollar pending an economic collapse following some kind of attack."

"How would Russia know what was being planned in the Middle East, or what bin Laden was going to do?"

"Sponsors of state terrorism including Iran, Iraq, Libya, Cuba, North Korea, Sudan, and Syria have a history of close ties with Russia and her military and intelligence agencies. They documented many trips to Russia by Anwar Awlaki in the 1990s."

"The Al Qaeda mastermind who helped the *Underwear Bomber*?" Allyson recalled.

"And the Fort Hood shooter, the Times Square bombing attempt, and possibly the 9/11 terrorists." Tristan continued, "Remember when Fox News discovered that Awlaki had dined at the Pentagon about a month after 9/11, for a Muslim outreach program, even though he had preached to at least three of the hijackers at a Mosque in Falls Church, Virginia?"

Tristan did not like conspiracy theories, he didn't want to believe in them, but a gut feeling had been getting stronger since he started work at FBI a year ago. Something in the world was not right. His intellect told him to keep an open mind and not dismiss facts simply because they did not fit into the mainstream narrative. And he was particularly wary of anything the media said.

"So let's say *Tidal Wave 21* was 9/11, and assume that a future nuclear war is *Tidal Wave 23?* What's in between? What is 22?" Allyson wondered.

"Not sure."

"What did your SAC say when he saw it?"

"I didn't exactly show it to him."

"Tristan!"

"I was going to, but he started talking about giving me a new partner and—"

"What were you thinking? That may be an important part of the investigation? You could get in a lot of trouble for withholding evidence."

"You're right," he admitted.

"Turn it in tomorrow, tell them you forgot you had it and apologize."

The ring of his smart phone saved Tristan from getting chewed-out further.

"Hello? Hi Sebastian, how are you?" He slumped into a chair, the proverbial wind knocked out of him. "Oh no, I'm so sorry . . . Okay, I'll see you tomorrow." He hung up.

"What's happened?"

"Jason passed away."

CHAPTER 9

Tristan eased into a conference room in the J. Edgar Hoover FBI building. He hated being late for anything, but was exhausted. The news of Jason's death had brought back memories of friends killed in Afghanistan causing him to toss and turn in a sleepless fit most of the night.

Afraid of nodding off, Tristan decided to lean against the wall.

He was surprised at the presence of FBI Director Richard Dufour, who paced around as he addressed FBI's counterterrorism division. Tall and lanky—with slicked-back gray hair—he barely filled out the Armani suits he wore exclusively. A dapper man, Dufour spoke with eloquence and seemed to choose every word carefully.

The director appeared to shoot a scathing glance at Tristan.

"As I was saying, nothing is going to change; you will continue to report to your SAC as usual. The Train Bomber case is not our only priority. There are daily security threats to investigate and we are short staffed. If anyone has questions or concerns," he paused for effect, "the assistant director's door is always open." A roar of laughter spread through the crowd.

The FBI Director, appointed by the President of the United States, was a position not without its controversies. There had been good and bad ones, but no matter what their background or who gave them the job, if they didn't go to Quantico and carry a gun there was an automatic credibility gap. Director Dufour had never been a cop, served in the military, or even worked as a security guard.

As far as the field agents were concerned, he was another Ivy League lawyer who created an us-versus-them perception within FBI. Intimidating and unapproachable, Dufour was looked at with suspicion by his subordinates. Politicians believed experience was never necessary as long as one had a degree from Harvard or Yale. Though he may occasionally crack a joke, the consensus among the FBI special agents was one of distrust.

The director continued, "For those of you who haven't met him, I'd like to introduce SAC Seth Pascal who is the chief of Foreign Counterintelligence Investigations for the east coast. We've had some problems in the Bureau recently, I'll leave it at that. He is here to try and keep us honest."

Tristan scanned the suits looking for familiar faces. He didn't see his SAC, whom he was going to give the flash drive to, along with his confession and apology. He hoped Murphy would understand. ASAC Tufts sat in the front row, legs crossed and acting interested. In fact, he looked uncharacteristically happy.

Director Dufour shook Pascal's hand then left the room.

"I'm thrilled to be back at the Seat of Government, I've floated between field offices for years, mainly New York and DC. I returned because of a growing problem in this office, so it looks like I may be here for a while. There are two topics I want to address, the first being the news media. We have a special relationship with the media, we want to cooperate with them and help them get the information they need to report. Lately, however, they've been receiving unauthorized details about ongoing investigations. Any agent caught leaking to the press will be let go."

Tristan did another visual sweep of the room for SAC Murphy.

Strange he would not be here.

Pascal drank some water from a glass and continued, "The second thing I want to talk about is spying. My specialty is espionage, mainly with the Russians. I've been doing this for a long time and seen it all. FBI has a colorful history of spies and zero tolerance for it. I'll be reviewing individual cases, just as another set of eyes and only to monitor your progress. At the same time we'll be conducting random lie-detector tests . . ." Pascal was forced to pause as a rumble of dissent distracted him from his speech. "If anyone's spying for the Russians, or other foreign governments, we'll find you." He found it difficult to speak above the drone of the crowd.

Tristan knew J. Edgar Hoover's reputation for purposely creating fear and paranoia within FBI to accomplish his personal agenda, even if it hurt morale. During the Vietnam War, Director Hoover discovered that one of his field supervisors, and a well-respected one, had a son who was a Catholic priest and was arrested at an antiwar demonstration. To send a message, Hoover transferred the field supervisor which meant his family had to pull up stakes and move.

As expected, the news spread quickly through the halls and offices by hushed voices. This action accomplished exactly what it was supposed to. FBI special agents became apprehensive and afraid to make mistakes, thus not taking chances or exercising initiative. Understandably, they wanted to hang on to their jobs.

And now the tactic was being used again.

"Anyone caught deceiving on a polygraph will be fired and prosecuted to the fullest extent of the law. I've thrown spies in jail for life. That's all, have a good day and go get 'em." Pascal tried ending on a positive note, but it did not work.

At least he didn't mention Jason or use him as an example, Tristan thought.

Word spread fast within these walls. It would not be long until everyone in the Bureau knew, if they didn't already. It saddened him to realize his friendship with Jason was based on keeping each other's secrets. They hung out to watch sports, but when it came down to it, they weren't really pals.

Tristan headed for the door, a long day lay ahead.

"Agent Wood!" Pascal raised his voice over the clamor of the exiting group.

"Sir?" Tristan approached his superiors.

"We're sorry to hear about Agent Graves," Pascal commented, with Tufts in agreement.

The contrived sympathy gave Tristan another gut feeling. Now both men stared at his black eye that seemed to get darker by the day.

"Do you have any information on the funeral?"

"Not yet, I'm meeting his father later on this afternoon."

"Well, let me know when you find out," Tufts continued.

Tristan found it interesting he used *me* instead of *us*.

"There's no easy way to say this, so I'll just say it. SAC Murphy is no longer with us," Pascal said.

"What?"

"He was leaking information to the press. Due to his years of service we gave him the option to retire early, and he took it."

"Doesn't sound like Murphy, the guy is a clam. He's been my SAC since I was a rookie. There must be some kind of mistake?"

"I'm afraid not." Pascal exhibited a complete lack of emotion. "ASAC Tufts has been promoted to special agent in charge, effective today, you will report to him."

"Yes, sir." Tristan's gut had been right again. "Were you able to get the surveillance video from Amtrak? It will be a big help locating the guy in the red sweatshirt."

"No, and it's not promising. Homeland Security is acting territorial. Like a rabid junkyard dog, territorial. From the looks of this case, he's probably long gone or dead anyhow."

"What makes you say that?" Tristan asked.

Pascal hesitated. "Decades of experience, Agent Wood." Changing the subject, "I realize it's a sensitive issue, but we do need to get you a partner. I'll take any suggestions into consideration before making a decision."

Pascal spoke with the pretense of lead SAC, instead of Tufts.

"I can't discuss this now. I'm going to find my suspect." Tristan walked away, knowing full well he was being disrespectful, again.

Speeding along in the unmarked car, Tristan found it burdensome to concentrate. A new FBI partner was inevitable, whether he liked it or not, but Jason was still lying in the morgue at Georgetown Hospital. Several hours remained until he was due to meet Sebastian, and decided the best way to keep his mind off it was to investigate the leads he'd pulled off FBI's Investigative Data Warehouse.

Tristan had found a total of six marines with "Infidel" tattoos who had returned from the Middle East. One was in Ohio and another in New Mexico, both currently being investigated by special agents from their local field offices, per his request. The other four stretched from Baltimore almost down to Richmond.

The digital clock on the car radio read; *11:11 a.m.*

The experience continued.

He entered the addresses into the GPS program of his smart phone. One of the four was listed as deceased, but he still had to check them all out. He decided to start with the location furthest north and work his way south.

The first stop was at the home of a twenty year old marine living with his parents just outside Baltimore City. After an hours' drive, Tristan was standing on the front stoop of a modest row house. The sun warmed him, its rays perforating the branches of the pine tree overhead. Less than fifteen minutes later he was back in his car driving south on I-95. This private had lost a leg below the knee from an IED attack in the Korengal Valley and was learning to walk with a prosthetic. Tristan wanted to stay and talk but was interrupting his PT. He understood the importance of physical therapy.

The second was a small brick rambler in Silver Spring, Maryland, and the home of a marine stationed at Firebase Phoenix who had been killed when a sniper bullet caught him in the head as he walked to the latrine. Tall unkempt grass sprouted up and around a *For Sale* sign in the front yard. The late marine's father had been laid-off and his mother had various health problems. Without their son to help make ends meet, they had been foreclosed on. After hearing the story and seeing photos of the funeral it was on to the next.

Number three was in a planned development in Herndon, Virginia, ostensibly built during the first phony housing boom of the new century. Either that or it was the result of the more recent, and equally bogus "recovery" preceding the second collapse. Hindsight certainly was 20/20. Cement bricks outlined house foundations on broken ground long since abandoned, orange banners on wooden stakes still thrashing in the light breeze. The modern brick homes, appearing new at first glance, were dilapidated and neglected. Privacy fences added to the perception that communities were a thing of the past. These days folks kept to themselves, staying indoors to watch television rather than socializing with neighbors.

This marine's mother did not hide the fact she was not a raving fan of the military and would not let Tristan inside. But he caught a glimpse of her son in the living room, in a wheel chair, both legs gone, and that was sufficient.

The fourth and last stop was further south in Virginia, and the most depressing of all. A doublewide trailer rested on a cement block foundation with grass and vines creeping up the sides. A small front porch had been added on to give it more of a house-feel, but the weeds had even found their way up between the wooden planks. Moments after knocking, the door opened.

"Jill Johnson?" Tristan asked a woman in cut-off jeans and a tight T-shirt that revealed too much.

"Yes?"

"Special Agent Wood, FBI." He flashed his badge. "Is your brother James Johnson, the marine who was stationed in Afghanistan?"

"Yeah."

"Is he in, I'd like to speak with him?"

"I haven't talked to James in months, since he . . ." she paused.

"Since he was let go from Special Forces?"

"That's right."

"Your home is listed as his last address."

She pulled on the curls of her long blonde hair, a nervous twitch, or a tell.

"I don't know why, he never lived here."

"Did you see him after he returned from Afghanistan?"

"No. He uh . . . no," she said, growing impatient.

"Ma'am, I'm an ex-marine. I was in the Korengal Valley. No 'Infidel' tattoo though."

He studied her reaction.

A gust of wind bristled through the tall grass surrounding the trailer. Clouds moved in random directions in the sky above, unsure whether to unite in a meteoric front.

"Did you know James?"

"According to his service record, he deployed after I left."

"Why are you looking for him?" she asked.

It struck Tristan how tired she looked, not from a day of work but rather a lifetime of hard knocks. "I'm just following up on some leads regarding the assassination attempt on the president."

"The Train Bomber? You think my brother's involved?" Her piercing blue eyes finally came to life.

"Do you know where he is? Address, phone number, or email?"

"Like I told you, I haven't talked to him in a long time." Her mood changed on a dime. "I know my rights, I don't have to talk to you. Get off my property." The door slammed, shaking the entire trailer.

Tristan returned to his car and drove away. His gut was talking to him again. This James Johnson was out there somewhere or she was hiding her brother inside the house right now. He could have a warrant emailed to his phone in less than an hour, but it would be prudent to establish a relationship and try to get voluntary cooperation.

Anyway, it was time to meet retired Special Agent Sebastian Graves, one of the best known career agents in the Bureau. He had been involved in some of the biggest FBI cases, starting out first in the organized crime division before transferring to counterintelligence after 9/11.

Tristan was aware of their rocky relationship, but always believed Jason chose his vocation because of his father. Sadly, he never admitted he was proud of his dad.

As a spontaneous shower began to drench the car, it dawned on him that this case was falling apart. Homeland Security would probably not cooperate and his only potential lead might never be found. He needed a new FBI partner; someone with experience.

Well, Tristan thought to himself, *it wouldn't hurt to ask*.

CHAPTER 10

Tristan entered Jason's Georgetown flat, this time in the daylight. Sunshine pierced both ends allowing him to see straight through to the patio. FBI had ransacked every inch of the place in their search for evidence, with the furry of a tornado. The sofa was overturned and the kitchen a disaster. A chair propped the refrigerator door open causing the smell of rotten food to fill the air. Framed pictures lay on the floor, one with cracked glass. He recalled how much Jason liked living here.

"Hello?" Tristan called out.

"If you've come to do more damage to this apartment you can leave, it's already trashed!" a voice came from the back.

In the bedroom, a man struggled to fit the box spring onto the metal bedframe.

"Mr. Graves? I'm Tristan Wood."

"Tristan, nice to meet you," Sebastian shook his hand. "I've heard a lot of good things."

Shocking was the similarity between father and son; the same gray eyes, same broad-shoulders, and the same crushing handshake. Apart from Sebastian's razor-shaved head, they were carbon copies of each other, give or take a quarter century.

"They did quite a job on the place, didn't they?" Tristan bemoaned.

"They were still searching when I arrived."

The two men adjusted the box spring and replaced the mattress on top.

"I'm sorry about Jason. I did my best to save him."

"I know you did."

"The surgeon said he was stable. He sounded optimistic."

They began picking up clothes strewn across the floor.

"The bullet that went through his liver did more damage than they thought. The internal bleeding started again and his body just crashed, there was nothing they could do. I'm glad I was with him when he passed, so he wasn't alone."

"I don't know what to say."

Sebastian replaced drawers and straightened the dresser. "SAC Tufts called me. Seems like a strange guy."

"I won't disagree with you there."

"He told me you and Jason were on the Train Bomber case?"

"It's not much of a case."

"What do you mean?"

Tristan sat to take the weight off his leg. "Ever get the impression, that some cases aren't meant to be investigated?"

"How so?"

Reluctant to bring it up, he said, "Nevermind, I'm probably just being paranoid."

"Look, I was in FBI for thirty years. No matter how paranoid you are, you're not paranoid enough."

Feeling uncomfortable, Tristan brushed it off and changed the subject. "So, what are your plans?"

Sebastian appeared to want to continue on the topic, then let it go. "I'll have the funeral service here in the area and bury him locally. I'm his only family, except for some cousins out west but we're not close with that side."

Tristan watched him choke back his emotions.

"I have to ask you a question, if I'm out of line . . ."

"Okay."

"How about rejoining FBI?"

"What? No way, sorry."

Tristan had not expected such a prompt response, nor had he considered how to persuade him otherwise.

Jason built walls and hid behind a mask of false self-confidence, but after a few drinks he became confessional. His father lived alone and had lost much of his retirement in the stock market several years back, as many Americans had. After retiring from FBI in January 2010, Sebastian had stayed in Detroit, the city of his last assigned field office.

The reason for their falling-out remained a mystery unable to be pried open by alcohol. Tristan suspected it had something to do with Sebastian's temper, which Jason had recounted with indignation many times. However, they had recently started talking again after an extended silence. It was obvious both harbored regrets, and now it was too late.

"Eventually, they are going to assign me another FBI partner. I need help, our case is falling apart, I'm at a loss."

Sebastian took a photograph from his wallet.

"What's this?" Tristan asked.

"My new home. I'm leaving the country."

The photo was of a small rust colored cottage surrounded by tropical trees and plants. Snow covered mountains ascended in the background above the ceramic barrel-tile roof.

"Where are you going?"

"I bought a house in the Pacific. Macquarie Island, about halfway between New Zealand and Antarctica."

"Why so far?"

Sebastian seemed reluctant to elaborate. "Do you know 90 percent of the world's population lives in the northern hemisphere, and that's where 95 percent of the pollution is? If you wanted to get away from populations, pollution, crime, and military targets where would you go?"

"The North Pole?" Tristan guessed.

"Actually, you want to be in the Southern Hemisphere. Pollution doesn't cross the equator."

"That's why you're moving to the other side of the planet? To avoid the pollution?"

"Nuclear fallout doesn't cross over either."

"Nuclear fallout?"

"I don't want to be here when everything goes to hell. The republic is over Tristan, it's only a matter of time."

"The United States of America?"

"The big one is coming. I'm not sure of the timeline, but it will be soon. I intend to be far away when it does."

"The big one? What is that?"

"It's nothing, I'm just venting." Sebastian seemed to back off from the statement and resumed picking up clothes.

"I have to show you something." Tristan took out the flash drive attached to his keychain, then remembered FBI confiscated Jason's laptop. "I need a computer."

Sebastian reached into a suitcase. The white airline baggage tag on the handle read; *DTW* for Detroit Metropolitan Wayne County Airport. He took out an iPad and powered it up.

Tristan inserted the thumb drive into a USB port and played the video; missiles launched, the time code counted, nukes detonated, the cursor indexed targets—

Учебный центр Горы,

Интегрированная Поддержка Кливленд . . .

"What is this?"

"It's called *Tidal Wave 23*. I found it on Jason the night he was shot. Then I was attacked by someone, in here, looking for something."

"Is that how you got the black eye?"

No answer was necessary.

"I realize it's not a subject we want to talk about, but if Jason was spying for the Russians and they were looking for this video file, there must be something to it."

"Do you think this is what he was killed over?"

"I don't know."

Sebastian played the video one more time.

"Why don't you download it to your iPad," Tristan suggested. "You may want to watch it again."

"Was this saved on Jason's computer?"

"No, I don't think so. He left a pretty cold trail."

Sebastian ejected the drive after backing it up.

"What did your SAC say, when you showed him?"

"I haven't exactly given it to him yet."

"Good man."

Tristan was surprised by his response, the opposite of Allyson's.

"I searched Jason's cell phone for anything out of the ordinary before I left it in the mailbox for you. The only thing I found odd was a GPS location, a stop he made before I tracked him down at the Tombs."

"Well, they took the phone."

"I already checked into it. There's no 411 information associated with the address but a satellite map shows it to be a residential building. Thought I'd take a drive-by and check it out."

Tristan held up his keys, leaving an opening.

"Well, I wouldn't mind getting out of here for a while," Sebastian said. "But I'm not rejoining FBI."

The open windows cooled the interior of the unmarked car as Tristan drove east through Georgetown, the GPS on his phone guiding them.

He explained in detail what he and Allyson had discovered, thanks to Senator Matthews, about *Tidal Wave 21* including the prediction of the financial collapse of the United States, or an event triggering it. Sebastian listened intently but offered no commentary.

"What trouble are you having with your case?"

"Well, let me think," Tristan could not resist the sarcasm. "We captured the Train Bomber suspect but Homeland Security took him from us and a judge arraigned him in the hospital. They fired our SAC—Murphy. The one you talked to, Andrew Tufts, is my new boss and that doesn't exactly thrill me. Then there's the guy from counterintelligence who was investigating Jason. He wants to give the entire department polygraphs in case we're spying for the Russians. And the one lead we have is illusive. He's on the surveillance video following the Train Bomber, watching over him."

"Really?"

"I've never seen anything like it but I can't seem to get the video from Amtrak, and so far FBI is not much help. A cloud of gloom is hanging over the Bureau right now, it's depressing."

"If Homeland Security thinks it's their case, and they have the only suspect, you're not going to get a lot of enthusiasm from FBI. The Bureau doesn't like to put its resources or reputation behind a case if it doesn't completely own it."

"I'm noticing that."

"Hold on to the *Tidal Wave 23* video for now. It never hurts to have an ace in the hole."

The female voice of the GPS directed them south on 16th Street, past the Masonic Temple, with the White House in view. Their destination was on a block mixed with aged row houses and modern apartment buildings.

They parked in an empty space under a cherry blossom, giving the car shade. Birds began to sing, with the engine off.

"It's the old Soviet Embassy, check it out," Sebastian observed.

Tristan grabbed a pair of binoculars from behind his seat and inspected the residence, surrounded by a black iron fence. The Russian flag with its red, white, and blue stripes, swayed gently in the breeze from a prominent position on the building.

"This structure has been recorded by the Historic American Building Survey of the US Department of the Interior for its archives at the Library of Congress," Tristan read the brass plaque next to the front door.

"That's what it is. In 1994 this property became the embassy of the Russian Federation and the home for the ambassador to the United States."

The quiet of the street was interrupted by a nondescript van that pulled into the service road on the south side of the residence.

"So Jason was here before he went to the Tombs?"

"Right before, according to his GPS." Tristan passed over the binoculars.

"Did you ever meet his girlfriend?"

"He never introduced us. I didn't even know her name until Murphy and Pascal told me."

"Pascal?"

"Lead agent, investigating Jason."

"Sounds familiar."

"He's heard of you."

While Sebastian racked his brain, Tristan grabbed a Manila envelope from the back seat. "Borrowed from FBI; don't tell anyone." Inside was a large glossy surveillance photo of his son and the girl.

"What's her name?"

"Lara Fedorov."

Sebastian studied the face in the picture then got out of the car and headed across the street. Tristan followed him down the service road where the van had entered moments before. Two men unloaded crates of what looked like food and cooking supplies.

The side gate was propped open for the delivery and they took advantage by slipping inside. With full hands, one of the deliverymen tried to protest, but they were already around the front of the building. Sebastian rang the doorbell, then impatiently knocked on the heavy door.

A voice in Russian came over the intercom.

"English!" Sebastian demanded.

"Can I help you?" a thick accent asked.

"We're here to speak with the ambassador."

"I'm sorry, do you have an appointment?"

"I want to talk to the ambassador."

"If you do not leave immediately I will call the police." The voice was calm and cool.

"We are the police!" Sebastian peered back at Tristan who, against his better judgment, displayed his FBI badge for the camera pointed down at them.

A buzzer sounded, unlocking the latch and admitting them into the breezeway, followed by another that opened the main door.

They entered the foyer of the grand home where a large man, clearly security, stood before them. He moved his jacket to one side revealing a semi-auto.

"Please tell the ambassador an American citizen needs to speak with him."

The security guard did not respond. Good chance this man only spoke Russian. As they waited in uncomfortable silence Tristan glanced at the staircase, coiling its way up three stories like a snake. The architecture was old-world, typical for the time period in this part of the District. Red carpet ran up the stairs, enclosed by an ornamental black steel banister adorned with gold. In fact, gold detailing was everywhere: the molding on the walls, the furniture trim, and the Oriental rug.

"Hello gentlemen." A man in a navy one-button Armani suit sauntered into the foyer and shook their hands, flashing a fake smile. "I am Serge, assistant to the Russian ambassador to the United States. What can we do for you?" His accent was so heavy, it was difficult to understand.

"I'd like to speak with Lara Fedorov."

"Who?"

"I'm Sebastian Graves. My son was an FBI agent. He had a Russian girlfriend named Lara Fedorov. He picked her up here a few hours before he was shot. I'd like to speak with her."

"Would you care to sit, please?" Serge asked.

"Thank you, but no. I just want to talk to the girl."

The cadence in Serge's voice changed. "We have many important Russian families who stay as our guests, however, I do not know anyone by that name."

Sebastian held up the photo, keeping it out of arm's reach. Serge momentarily glanced at it, uninterested and indifferent.

"I do not recognize her."

Tristan was unable to discern if the Russian was telling the truth or lying.

"Where is the ambassador?" Sebastian pressed him.

"In Russia at the moment, on personal business."

He referred to a portrait on the wall, an abstract oil painting of Ambassador Ushakov's family. Two daughters posed in front of their parents, everyone with an austere expression. His wife, endowed with the features of a model, was some thirty years younger.

"We respect the privacy of our guests and you must understand, we are under no obligation to give you any information."

"We will sit across the street day and night and wait for her to leave. You can sneak her in and out the back door for the next year if you want, or you can make it easy and let me talk to her."

"What would your FBI Director say if I called him?"

The comment made Tristan break out in a nervous sweat. Sebastian had put him in a position to get in serious trouble.

"So, you won't help us?"

"Well, it is time I became, how do you say—blunt? Even if this girl you seek, if she herself murdered your son, we have diplomatic immunity. Therefore, I must ask you to leave."

Sebastian stared down Serge then headed for the door before turning back. "Oh, by the way. Do you know what *Tidal Wave 23* is?"

"I'm afraid I don't," Serge answered.

The guy would make a hell of a poker player.

"We do." Sebastian stormed out.

Both men dodged a fast moving roadster as they crossed the street.

"What was that?" Tristan demanded.

They got back in the car. The armed security guard gave them one more dirty look before closing the front door. After a prolonged silence, Sebastian finally spoke.

"Take me to where Jason was shot."

CHAPTER 11

Tristan led Sebastian down the path extending along the C&O Canal in Georgetown. The afternoon sun revealed what the night had concealed. Old brick buildings lined this part of the waterway, reminders of early nineteenth century Washington, DC.

"He walked this way with the girl." Tristan retraced his steps.

The sandy path, imprinted with fresh tracks, was a popular route for joggers. They reached the familiar old-growth tree hanging over the water. By now there was little indication a man had recently been in this spot fighting for his life. He crouched down, careful of his bad leg, and raked his fingers through the sand. A small clump crumbled in his palm staining the skin dark red.

Sebastian looked away at the site of his son's blood.

"The girl, and the man with the pony tail, took off from here." Tristan pointed east. "Jason wasn't moving so I called 911 and carried him up to M Street. All I thought about was getting him to the hospital as fast as possible."

Tristan stood up with a *grunt* and leaned against the red-brick retaining wall.

Sebastian asked, "Earlier, when you said you were paranoid, that you felt your case wasn't meant to be investigated. What did you mean?"

"Not just on this case." Tristan sighed, knowing he was getting into this bizarre subject again. "It's everything—the whole system."

"So when you look at the 'system,' what do you see?"

"I'm not sure I understand what you're asking?"

"When you read the news or listen to the talking heads in the media, what do you think?"

"Well, for the first time in my life, I question everything. I used to just accept what I heard, without thinking twice about it. Then I started noticing something."

"What?" Sebastian encouraged him.

"It seems whenever a big news report comes out, the media immediately creates the simplest and most accidental explanation. They advance the version they want and ignore anything that appears to contradict it. Do you know what I mean?"

"Like there's a story behind the story that no one wants to talk about?"

"So I'm not the only one?"

"Not by a long shot," Sebastian said.

"There's something else." Tristan now felt emboldened. "I keep seeing '11:11' on clocks. It's a hard experience to explain. It's an awareness, a sort of pre-déjà vu. I'm compelled to look, and when I do, the clock reads; 11:11. Have you ever heard of that?"

"It's been happening to me for years. Let me guess, something is troubling you, you don't know what it is but it's there."

"It's worse. I've got a sense that something really bad is coming. A world changing event." He massaged the thigh of his bad leg. "It's not just a feeling, it's an actual physical experience that makes me sick to my stomach."

"You are ready to wake up, Tristan."

"What does that mean?"

"Wake up from the *propaganda matrix*. Do you know what I'm talking about?"

"I think so, but I'm not sure?"

Sebastian continued, "For years it seemed there was knowledge, an alternative history in the world I either didn't know or wasn't being told. It was like searching for a hidden picture within a landscape painting, intentionally created to hide the truth. I'd watch television and listen to talk radio, I read newspapers and magazines, I thought I was well informed. Every election cycle it was Democrat versus Republican and left versus right. But when I looked closer, there didn't seem to be a difference between the two parties. Presidential nominees were so much alike it didn't matter who was elected. It was frustrating but I knew someone out there could explain it, to put it into context for me. Then a friend told me about Alex Jones."

"Who is that?"

"He's a radio host, activist, and documentary filmmaker. The first day I listened to his show at www.infowars.com, I woke up. It was amazing. Things immediately started to make sense. He broke down the phony left-right paradigm used to keep us blind and fighting amongst ourselves. When I watched his documentary *End Game*, that was it. Alex Jones was the one I was looking for." Sebastian asked, "Do you know about the New World Order?"

"I've heard the phrase, but I'm not sure where?"

"I'll tell you what it is and what I've learned, and you can decide what to do with the information. I can't push this on you, you have to want to know. It's what you don't hear anyone talking about."

"Okay," Tristan said, unsure how to respond. "What is the New World Order?"

"In a nutshell, it's a movement to create a one-world government supported by a global tax in which sovereign countries no longer exist."

A jogger ran in between them.

"The New World Order is a global system of control by the very few super-rich elites who influence and manipulate politicians, governments, people, and economies using the vast wealth of the international banks. The end game is to bring us back to the pre-industrial age with the United Nations as the world government and all of us as 'world citizens.' The plan has been to implement a one world government by first creating up to five super-states including the North American, Asian, African, Pacific, and European Unions, which would eventually be merged. You've seen this symbolized in the Olympic rings."

"In this new order there will be two classes of people; the elites and the serfs. The elites live how they want, in luxury, and the rules they create will not apply to them. NATO is the framework for the global military to enforce a worldwide police state, additionally supported by citizen spies. A global tribunal with a world constitution will override our US Constitution and limit, among other things, the right to bear arms. The serfs will live in city-prisons connected by super highways and rail systems, with the rest of the country re-wilded through the UN Agenda 21 project and off-limits to anyone without permission to enter. Everyone will be micro-chipped, the RFID technology analyzed by super computers to track our movements."

Sebastian waited for a couple to pass by before speaking again.

"Working for the mega-corporations that control all commerce and production under protection of the state, zombie worker-citizens will be socially engineered with propaganda to feel content by dumbing them down through state-controlled education, diet, medications, injections, and injunctions. Environmentalism will be the world religion. Individualism will be sacrificed for the 'greater good' as the obedient slaves are rewarded with food and water rations, vacation allowances, and other movement restrictions, all the while living in environment-friendly utopias under constant fear of being cast into the slum-cities or FEMA camps with their fellow dissidents who dare question the state. They will control information by deeming anything they don't like as hate speech or politically incorrect. And for troublemakers who cannot be reeducated, they will face extermination."

"World population is to be kept around 500 million through a one child policy with forced abortions and sterilizations. This will rid the gene-pool of undesirables as determined by the 'science' of eugenics, giving the elites moral justification to treat their fellow humans like animals and kill us off. National healthcare, through death-panels, will decide who dies and who gets treatment and the occasional lab-generated pandemic, such as a bird or swine flu, will be used for quick results. And these world policies will be dictated to us by the elites through exclusive secret societies without any input from citizens."

"How can they get away with this?"

"By dumbing down the population and keeping us distracted. They've been slow-killing us for decades, Tristan, using silent weapons to fight a quiet war. They poison our water with fluoride, chlorine, and heavy metals, they taint our food with GMO and Aspartame, they saturate our bodies with aluminum and pharmaceuticals like Prozac and Ritalin, and inject us with vaccines containing mercury and adjuvants such as squalene. They keep us preoccupied with sports and entertainment, pornography, video games, and recreational drugs. And to be sure citizens don't wake up and get thoughts of ending this tyranny, we are kept in constant fear and emotionally off-balanced with false flag terror attacks and manufactured threats while the media creates phony debates pitting left against right, man against woman, and white against black. Because of this we allow the state to do whatever it wants whenever it wants under the guise of keeping us safe. Welcome to the New World Order."

"That's a lot to swallow . . ." Tristan experienced his mind wandering off to other thoughts, his beliefs conflicting.

"I've been studying this for years. It sounds crazy at first, then things start to click, your eyes open, and one day it all makes sense."

Tristan moved around to loosen his leg muscles.

"This is only scratching the surface," Sebastian said. "Most of what I've told you is going on right now. It's all out in the open. The elites discuss it publicly and write about it in their books, but the corporate-controlled media won't even mention it. If it somehow gets reported, it's not questioned or challenged. And the mainstream media is where almost everyone gets their news. This is why you probably feel like you're living in an information vacuum."

Tristan asked, "Do you know something about *Tidal Wave 23* you're not telling me?"

"Not specifically. But after seeing the video, something occurred to me."

"What?"

"The globalists have always used incrementalism to move us toward tyranny; small steps under the radar. A little here, a little there, while we're not looking. So far it's worked well for them. But from what I see, they are becoming impatient. Too many of us are resisting, especially with the push to take our guns. They've been working their entire lives for this, and many of them are getting old. Where generations before them were content to pass the baton to their children and grandchildren, this gaggle doesn't seem to want to do that, which is why they're so brazen and out in the open about it. They may want to bring in the New World Order now, to finally witness what they've worked so hard to create. I believe they're going to make their move as we approach the worst economic collapse in world history."

"I've had the feeling a collapse is coming. But the politicians are still making speeches about ways to fix the economy, which the media says is just fine, and then do nothing," Tristan said.

"That's because there *is* no way to fix it. Those are political talking points meant to keep us passive until it happens."

"There must be a way? Cut spending, balance the budget, increase manufacturing . . ."

"It will only delay the inevitable. There's upwards of $700 trillion in derivatives in the world economy thanks to Goldman Sachs, JP Morgan, the US Treasury, Federal Reserve, and the international bankers. It can never be repaid."

"Okay, so what is the solution?"

"Let's say you lived in a decrepit run-down home and you kept taking out loans, but every time you made repairs something else would break down. No matter how much money you spent the house never improved and no one would buy it, and all you did was create more debt for yourself. How would you fix it?"

"I guess you couldn't," Tristan gave in.

"Actually, you can. You burn it down and start over. Before the economy comes down on its own, which is very difficult to control, you engineer the crash and bring the entire system down."

"How would you do that, a nuclear war?"

"It must be a colossal event. Whatever is used to bring in the New World Order, it will have to eclipse all previous man-made world crises. I used to think it would be a pandemic like a swine flu, but those are unreliable and can be easily contained. It can't be conventional wars which are isolated and drag on for years. Another stock or banking crash would be unpredictable and the inevitable riots could backfire on them. But a nuclear war would be perfect."

"Why would the super-rich want to destroy the system? Wouldn't that wipe out their wealth too?"

"Not in a cashless society, which is the goal. They will always be in control of the monetary system. When the New World Order emerges from the ashes they will have their birth-right aristocracy again. There will be a few hundred million slaves to keep the world going, grow food, produce goods, and provide basic services. We'll be told the elites are the only ones with the ability to manage things. They will emerge from the ruins and say, 'We're sorry, we didn't see this catastrophe coming but please put us in charge because we've learned from it and we will protect and take care of you.' What we will have returned to in the blink of an eye is a modern-day feudal society, a class system with a few kings to rule over the commoners. Their motto is *order out of chaos*."

"Why would they want to wipe out the entire planet with a nuclear war?" Tristan tried to wrap his head around it.

"Actually, the nuclear winter scenario is a misconception. The initial blasts will destroy their targets and the radiation will kill millions within days, but the radioactive fallout will only last a few weeks. In the aftermath when things have calmed down, except for the major cities, most of the country will be physically undamaged. The worst consequence will be commerce and other services shutting down. People will soon grow hungry and thirsty, followed by civil unrest and widespread riots. The American citizens who don't perish in the war will be dependent on FEMA shelters, as they were after hurricane Katrina, but on a massive scale."

"I've heard the average person has food and water for four days or less in their homes," Tristan added.

"The elites have bomb shelters with years' worth of supplies, plus homes outside the country, in the southern hemisphere, and private jets to take them there. Defectors from the Soviet Union, or the Russian Federation as they call themselves now, have been trying to warn us that Moscow has been planning an offensive nuclear war with the United States for decades."

Tristan felt like he was going to get sick.

"There are vast underground bunkers in the US and Russia, cities below cities, connected by a network of MAGLEV train tunnels. When the time comes, the select few will be given shelter. The elites are prepared."

Sebastian picked up a rock and tossed it into the canal, the ripples resembling waves moving away from a blast site.

"But if Russia were to try to nuke us, as soon as we saw their birds in the air we'd fire back. How do you win a nuclear war?" Tristan asked.

"Do you know what a Presidential Directive is?"

"Is that an executive order?"

"Yes, they were called Presidential Directives under Clinton. One in particular was PDD-60, which did a number of things intended to purposely weaken the defenses of our country."

"What did it do?"

"I won't get into Clinton's personal politics or his history of visiting prominent families in the Soviet Union beginning in his early twenties, but let's just say Moscow was thrilled when the Bilderberg Group picked Bill Clinton to become president. He issued PDD-60 at the end of his presidency. Eclipsed by scandals, it was never mentioned in the news, but the purpose of PDD-60 was to show good faith toward his friends in the former Soviet Union."

"Good faith for what?"

"To send a signal, that we were not a threat. PDD-60, which works in tandem with the START treaties, took Reagan's philosophy of *Peace through Strength* and the policy of *Response on Warning*, and threw them out the window with no congressional debate or approval. This happened with one executive order. Instead of launching our missiles as soon as we detect theirs, PDD-60 declared we would have to absorb a nuclear strike, and then threaten a response based on how much damage was done."

"You're kidding?"

"PDD-60 is online, hidden in plain sight. Executive orders must be nullified by successive presidents, and from my research it has yet to be reversed. George Bush issued NSPD-14 in 2002 which was supposed to reflect his own policies, but all it did was allow Russia to stockpile more weapons and did nothing to change the underlying premise of Clinton's order. There has been no other related Presidential Directive since. I believe the policy is currently in effect, both officially and in ideology. It's up to the White House to give out the launch codes. All the power to defend ourselves lies, not in the hands of the armed forces, but in one man who is under the control of the New World Order."

"You can't just start a nuclear war, how would Russia justify launching first?"

"They'll need a catalyst to trigger it."

"Like what, a presidential assassination?" Tristan swallowed a pain pill, relieved Sebastian did not ask why.

"Not on its own. But the Train Bomber could be the start of something bigger, something we can't see."

"This handler is the only lead I've got. If I don't collar this guy, I'm afraid this case will be swept under the rug."

Sebastian turned his back to Tristan and dropped his head.

"Do you think you can help me get back into FBI?"

"Really? What about your new house?"

"I guess it can wait."

CHAPTER 12

Robert Wood had never been held hostage, with the exception of playing cops and robbers with Tristan as children. The brothers were sixteen months difference in age, and though interested in most of the same things, were far enough apart that Tristan had a clear physical advantage.

Robert never liked being the robber, but with older brothers there was rarely a choice. In cowboys and Indians he got Indians, in Sherlock Holmes he got Watson, in Batman and Robin he got Robin. The younger sibling always got the short end of the stick.

I'll bet Tristan has never been a hostage in the capital of a Super Power, Robert thought to himself.

Senator Matthews seemed to be taking it all in stride. The term *hostage* was somewhat melodramatic anyway, as there were worse places than the Spaso House to be held captive. Aside from the cell phone withdrawal, courtesy of the Russian military police, it wasn't all that bad.

They had another amazing meal the night before, and at the senator's insistence had indulged in too much wine. After dinner, Robert found an English translation of short stories by Fyodor Dostoevsky in the library and retired to his room, but the alcohol knocked him out after several pages. The bed was quite comfortable and he slept soundly.

This morning he was rested and refreshed . . . and still a hostage.

The senator rapped on the door announcing breakfast, but didn't wait. After getting dressed, Robert headed downstairs. In the dining room, his boss sipped coffee while reading an English version of the *Moscow Times*. Robert took a plate full of eggs and some strange looking sausages from a silver serving tray and sat down to eat.

"I am trying to get in touch with President Putin. I've sent a message to him through the embassy," the senator broke the silence from behind his newspaper.

"You mean through Lev?"

"Unfortunately, yes."

For anyone familiar with Russian politics, the reelection of Vladimir Putin was hardly a surprise. Elected for two consecutive four-year terms, from 2000 to 2008, he could not run a third time. But after one term served by Dmitry Medvedev, Putin became eligible to stump for a potential two additional terms. In true Communist style, the Medvedev-Putin party had been able to change the rules by increasing the presidential limit, per the 1977 Soviet Constitution of the USSR, from four to six years.

During the Medvedev presidency, Putin had kept himself in a high-level position as Prime Minister. To remain in the limelight, he staged regular photo-ops participating in activities such as karate, rock climbing, and scuba diving.

Eventually, Putin won reelection with overwhelming support of the Russian people, securing more votes than the nominees in the two opposing parties combined; or so it was claimed. In Russia, the Kremlin had full control of the voting results.

Most analysts were aware that during the Medvedev regime, Vladimir Putin was de facto president. When both men walked into a room together in a public setting, Putin entered first. This was not coincidence, but rather a sign of authority. When conversing, Putin addressed Medvedev with the informal "you" in the Russian language, while Medvedev acknowledged Putin with the formal tense.

What shocked Robert was the senator's explanation, in detail, that the current Communist-corporate economic system in Russia was essentially identical to the crony-Capitalist economy of the United States. Both countries were controlled by elite families through the international banks and operated under a similar political-economic structure. He had a name for it.

A corporatocracy.

Disturbing as the information was, it was exciting to be confided in with a crash course in the insider's history of the Soviet Union.

"Does anyone on the outside know we're being held against our will?" Robert asked with a mouthful of eggs. "My wife is going to start wondering why I haven't called or texted her."

"Hard to say. It depends on whether the KGB decides that releasing the story is useful. If it turns into an international incident, it's because they want it to."

"Do you think Putin will let us go?"

"That's not the question to ask," the senator mumbled. "Russian political corruption is different than in the United States. In our country, corruption is when a representative is elected and becomes corrupt. With Russia, prior to gaining a position, they must understand and agree to become part of the corruption. The Russian government *is* the Mafia. When accepting a governmental office, if a politician does not go along with the malfeasance, or tries to do the honest thing, they are considered corrupt."

Robert motioned to the ceiling, referring to the bugs most likely planted in every room.

"This is nothing our Russian friends don't already know, you can speak freely."

"Do the Russian people like Putin?"

"There was resistance at first, but with a steady flood of propaganda the opinions softened. Now they believe he instills a sense of patriotism lacking since 1989 when their leaders embarrassed the country by admitting defeat to the United States. The average Russian did not understand this was necessary for their long-held plan. Unlike Americans, the Russians are remarkably patient. A corrupt American politician will do or say anything, then repeat the same pattern for their reelection. They do it strictly for themselves and their short-term interests. Russian politicians will sacrifice their own short term political goals for their country."

"So the question is, will the KGB let us go?"

"That remains to be seen."

"Well, I'm sure they won't start a nuclear war over us," Robert joked.

"Wars have been started over much less, young man," the senator said as he put the newspaper down. "Come, I want to show you something."

He led the way into the kitchen and through the door to the wine cellar. The feeble wooden stairs creaked with every step until they arrived at an uneven concrete-slab floor. Hundreds of bottles lined the walls, the vintages dating back over a century.

At the rear of the subterrane it appeared they hit a dead-end.

"Did you wonder how the Russian military police arrived with such haste, before we were able to leave the residence?"

Before Robert could formulate a guess, the senator opened a hidden door and they stepped onto an aged train platform.

"What is this?"

"A tunnel for a high speed rail system."

The platform was composed of antique ceramic and glass tiles of various colors, but the tracks below appeared new. Each pitch-black end of the passage reminded Robert of the New York subway, which he had been in once. The damp smell was intrusive and stung his eyes.

"This is amazing. Is it a working subway?"

"The tunnel was excavated shortly after building the Spaso House in case the original owner and his family needed to escape. Over the years it has been upgraded to its current form; a magnetic levitation subway. There are underground tunnels under just about every major industrialized city on the planet now, all with a network of MAGLEV trains."

"I had no idea."

They returned to the kitchen where Lev stood talking to one of the caretakers.

"Ah, Mr. Lev, were you able to contact the ambassador? Holding us captive will eventually leak to the press, even the Soviet controlled press."

"I have done better than that, Senator, please follow me."

Lev escorted them to the library where Ambassador Bullitt waited. The two shook hands and sat down, a strange handshake Robert had never seen before.

"I apologize my old friend, I did not know you would be prevented from leaving the House."

"Walter, where have you been? I came all this way because we recalled you to Washington weeks ago."

The ambassador spoke apprehensively. "I'm not going back. My family and I will be staying in Russia. You may inform the committee, I appreciate their support during my tenure." He reached into his jacket and pulled out an envelope. "My resignation letter."

"I'm sorry to hear that," the senator said.

Robert got the impression this was not a surprise. Their conversation felt contrived—for the benefit of whoever could be listening.

"The plan is now in motion—"

Senator Matthews held up his hand to cut the ambassador off. They began speaking Russian in hushed voices, then slipped back into English.

"You should not return. I can find you a lovely dacha in Bologoye."

"Mileva is gone," the senator lamented.

"Yes, I am sorry. However," Bullitt commanded his full attention, "the storm is coming."

After contemplating the offer again, he labored to stand and hugged his colleague. "Goodbye, Walter."

Following Senator Matthews out of the Spaso House library Robert thought to himself;

A storm is coming?

CHAPTER 13

The heat from the tarmac created blurry waves on the horizon, giving the illusion that the runway at Andrews AFB had no end. The air traffic control tower rose above the 89th Aerial Port Squadron passenger terminal, the home of *Air Force One* and the fleet of private jets that chauffeured the political elites around the world.

Tristan hit the END button on his cell phone and wiped the sweat from his brow. Looking down, little Maggie clung to one leg. Sarah held Rory in her arms, bouncing him up and down. Both wore hats to shield them from the intense midday sun. Tristan loved his niece and nephew so much he could not imagine how he would one day feel for his own children.

They relaxed as the private jet safely touched down, an effortless landing.

"I think I'm going to melt," Sarah said.

"Allyson says hello. It's a comfortable 72 degrees in her hospital. She's drinking a cup of coffee to warm up."

She glared at Tristan.

"I know, too hot to joke."

The jet taxied in between two rows of cones, marshaled by a ramper waving orange wands. After powering down the engines, a pilot exited the plane and was handed luggage by a female flight attendant. The senator stepped out, struggled to keep his balance, and climbed down the stairs. Robert came out next. Maggie began to wave and yell, then ran off toward her father.

"Maggie!" Sarah called out to the toddler.

Robert intercepted his daughter, picking her up and swinging her around in his arms. He hugged Tristan and gave his wife a kiss.

"Senator Matthews, you remember Sarah. And this is my brother Tristan."

They shook hands and the senator said, "Nice to meet you, son, I've heard a lot about you."

"Likewise, sir. Just so you know, there are reporters waiting for you inside."

"Yes, yes, I wish they would not be granted access. I will go in first and talk to them. You and your family can pass by, they won't recognize you, and you can be on your way."

"Are you sure?" Robert asked. "I'm pretty good at the 'no comment' thing now."

"No, let me take care of it."

The senator entered the terminal, immediately bombarded with questions and camera flashes. Tristan waited until the diversion was complete, then ushered everyone past the crowd.

"Can you tell us why you were held hostage in Moscow, Senator?" one reporter yelled above the others.

"It was all a misunderstanding, a bit of a language gap. They thought we were going to drive outside the city of Moscow, but wanted us to stay in the embassy for our own safety. Russia is experiencing unprecedented social unrest and high crime rates."

"Did you locate the ambassador?"

"No, I was not able to make contact with him."

Tristan stopped to listen to the questions as Robert took the car keys and swiftly escorted his family out of the terminal.

"How did the arms talks go?" another reporter called out.

"The Soviet Union continues to ignore their side of the START treaty, any disarmament is from the United States only."

"Don't you mean Russia?"

"Pardon?" the senator asked.

The other reporters quieted down, waiting for an answer.

"You said the Soviet Union, you meant the Russian Federation, didn't you?"

"Of course. Now please, it's been a long flight and I'm an old man. I need to get home." The senator attempted to push through while struggling with his luggage.

One more question caused Tristan to pause at the door. "Do you have any statement to make about your ordeal?"

The senator turned back to them, saying, "The KGB is alive and well in Moscow. Good day."

Tristan escorted the politician outside to a stretch limo where the driver loaded his suitcase into the trunk.

"Thank you, Agent Wood."

"You're welcome."

Tristan opened the car door and to the senator's surprise, followed him inside.

"Sir, I need a moment of your time please. I'm lead agent on the Train Bomber case. The other day, my partner was shot and killed."

"I'm sorry to hear that."

"He's been accused of spying for the Russians." Tristan worked up the courage, then asked. "Senator, I have to ask for a favor . . ."

Sebastian Graves sat parked in his son's Jeep Cherokee, across the street from the Russian ambassador's residence. He stared at the photo of Lara Fedorov memorizing her face. The lump in his throat was physically painful. Sebastian had succeeded at keeping it together this morning, going over arrangements with the funeral director.

He lowered the visor to give his eyes relief from the sun and a photograph fell into his lap. A faded color picture of the family at Disney World brought back a flood of memories. Sebastian and his wife Miriam hugged and smiled, their young son Jason looking up and laughing.

The good ole' days.

This was many years after the incident in the Georgetown bar that changed his life, and career. A time he wished he could forget . . .

Studying the photograph caused the hurt in his throat to move down into his chest, like a kick from a horse.

Then he broke down.

Sebastian realized how alone he was, with both wife and son gone. There were no brothers, sisters, or other relatives to speak of. In fact, there was no one. A part of him wanted to leave for his new home right now, and never look back. However, he had a nagging urge to return to FBI and finish Jason's case—that is, if they were to reinstate him. He could not imagine they would.

Retiring before the completion of his own last investigation— the *Underwear Bomber*—had tormented him. Since unplugging from the propaganda matrix, Sebastian had felt a deep void inside. Learning about the New World Order was a double-edged sword. On the one hand he was happy to have the knowledge, but on the other, ignorance was bliss.

The clash of beliefs he had struggled with, the tussle between the illusion of the propaganda matrix and reality reminded him of what he called "The Santa Conspiracy."

Children believed Santa Claus flew around the world in his sleigh delivering presents to good boys and girls every Christmas. They accepted this because their parents insisted he existed. There was no reason to think otherwise. When a child began school, the belief in Santa was strengthened by others in the class who had been given the same information by their own parents. Thus, acceptance of Santa Claus was reinforced by society. And since the goal of public schools was to socialize students, rather than educate them, conforming to group beliefs was a top priority.

Those who did not conform, and believe in Santa Claus, were ostracized as outsiders.

Ultimately children would begin to ask questions. Could reindeer fly? Did elves exist, even though one had never actually been seen? Was it possible to carry millions of toys in a sleigh or to climb up and down a chimney?

In due time, all parents were forced to admit to the hoax, yet the tug of war between fantasy and reality would continue. If Santa did not exist, then neither did the Easter Bunny or the

Tooth Fairy. But the power of the human mind to want to believe was incredibly strong. As long as society reinforced these axioms, they were extremely difficult to sway.

Eventually, in a domino-effect of awareness, a majority of the class would repudiate the existence of Santa. Each child needed to come to grips with the truth in his or her own way, and in their own time. This would be strengthened by others in the class who had been given the same information by their own parents. Thus the disbelief in Santa was reinforced by society.

Those who did not conform, and reject Santa Claus, were ostracized as outsiders.

There was nothing worse in the public school system than independent thinking, and was the reason the state worked so hard to outlaw homeschooling. If a child showed independence and did not rely on the group to form their opinions they were considered antisocial. An antisocial child was a danger to the collective and labeled as shy.

Shyness was now a diagnosed mental disorder in the Diagnostic and Statistical Manual of Mental Disorders. The DSM was the politically influenced and heavily lobbied psychology Bible, which strongly recommended shy children be put on Ritalin. Unfortunately, too many were.

This same belief pattern followed people into adulthood due to their public school "training." The desire to conform to groupthink was a powerful force and well understood by the social engineers. The best way to create a belief was by attaching it to an emotion, and an emotional experience almost always won out over a rational thought. This is why terrorist attacks were so effective as they required virtually no critical thinking to work.

A child believed in Santa because the parents, or authority, said so and it was reinforced by society.

An adult believed bin Laden was responsible for 9/11 because the government, or authority, said so and it was reinforced by society.

A voter believed a new president elected from one of the two parties every election cycle would bring about real change because the media, or authority, said so and it was reinforced by society.

The social engineers knew "believe" was the most hypnotic word in the English language and was the reason every political candidate fought to use it exclusively in their campaign slogans. Evidence was not a prerequisite to *believe* in something, only a strong emotion reinforced by the general populace.

Anyone who thought differently was a danger to the group, ostracized, and called a conspiracy theorist, kook, nut, or other derogatory name. The reality was, a majority of adults could be convinced to believe in anything, and hold on to it, regardless of any facts to the contrary. The American people were literally hypnotized by social engineers working for the globalists, and they had absolutely no clue.

The cell phone roused him from the daydream.

"Hello?" he answered.

"May I speak with Sebastian Graves please?" a woman's voice said.

"Yes, that's me."

"This is FBI Director Dufour's secretary. The director would like to meet with you."

"Of course, just let me know when."

"Can you be here in half an hour?"

"Yes, I'll be there." The urgency caught him by surprise.

"I'll tell him to expect you. Park in the underground garage, your name will be on the guest list at the gate. I believe you remember where we're located." She hung up.

He left his space in front of the Russian residence and headed west on Pennsylvania Avenue in midafternoon traffic. In a matter of minutes he pulled the SUV into the security entrance of the J. Edgar Hoover FBI building and waited for the guard's acknowledgment. Sebastian gave his name and showed his driver's license.

"Hold on," the burly man in a military green uniform said from behind two-inch bulletproof glass. He wrote on a clipboard and handed over an envelope. "Guest parking is on lower level one. Put the pass on the dashboard and the sticker on your shirt."

Sebastian parked the car and sat thinking. He could drive away right now, head for the airport and leave the country today. Meeting with the FBI Director would commit him to something his conscience wouldn't let him abandon.

This was it, he thought, *the moment of truth.*

Sebastian Graves took a deep breath, got out of the Cherokee, and headed for the elevator.

CHAPTER 14

Tristan Wood sat in an unmarked car surfing the web on his smart phone as the pouring rain battered the steel roof above him. Combined with the roar of the air conditioning he could barely hear *Proud Mary* by Creedance Clearwater Revival playing on the classic rock station. Tristan often listened to talk radio, though lately he had a strong aversion to it. Not because of what the hosts talked about, but rather what they didn't.

Typing "11:11" into the search window produced vague results, so he tried "I see 11:11." This brought up some interesting websites suggesting the experience was anything but rare. One page professed it to be "a beneficial act of Divine intervention telling you it is time to take a good look around you and see what is really happening. It's time to pierce the veils of illusion keeping us bound to an unreal world."

After some additional research, he concluded it was a sign he was unplugging from the propaganda matrix, as Sebastian would put it, and reinforced his commitment to keep an open mind about what he was learning.

There was nothing wrong with asking questions.

Tristan broke out in a cold sweat and noticed a tightening in his chest. He had resisted taking pain medication this morning, purposely trying to back off. The anxiety was too much, however, and a strange new urge, like a voice he could not hear, compelled him to pop a pill.

As small hailstones began bouncing off the hood, the passenger door opened and Sebastian jumped in, soaking wet.

"I thought FBI had a special going on; a free Bureau-approved umbrella for all new agents?" Tristan joked.

"No, but they gave me a gun and badge instead."

"Congratulations Special Agent Graves. I hope Director Dufour was civil?" Tristan pulled the car into light traffic.

"I would describe him as politely annoyed." Sebastian wiped the water off his shaved head. "He emphasized the point that I'm back to base pay-grade. Of course, I'm not doing this for the money."

"I bet this is the first time he's ever had a retired agent actually request to come back to work?"

"And probably the first time a sitting United States senator called to demand it. I'm not sure whether to hug you or kill you."

They headed south through the green expanse of the National Mall.

"Did you meet Tufts?"

"Yes, and SAC Pascal. I can't put my finger on it, but I swear I've heard his name before."

"He told me you never met," Tristan said.

"We didn't meet, I'm sure of that." Sebastian pulled back on the slide of his new FBI issued 9mm Glock to check the chamber, then engaged the safety. "The guy gave me a bad vibe."

"I'm right there with ya."

In no time at all they had crossed the George Mason Bridge into Virginia.

"Tell me about this lead?"

Tristan spoke as he concentrated on the slick highway. "Well, so far I haven't had much luck tracking down this suspect. Without the surveillance video, the only clue is 'Infidel' on his arm. Most marines with that tattoo are still overseas. I had a couple agents from the Cleveland field office investigate a lead in Akron, but he's been recovering from injuries there for months. Another in Albuquerque checked out too. I got four local names—the one in Baltimore lost a leg below the knee, one is dead, the guy in Herndon, Virginia, is in a wheelchair, and we're going to visit the sister of the fourth."

"What's her deal?"

Tristan reached behind his seat and pulled out a folder. "I get the impression she's holding out. It seemed like she wanted to talk to me, I think with a little persistence she'll open up."

"When is the last time she saw him?" Sebastian asked as he scanned the file.

"Well, the guy came back from Afghanistan to train in Special Forces down at Camp Lejeune and flunked out. This is his last verified address but the sister claims she hasn't talked to him and doesn't know where he is."

"What's his name?"

"James Johnson."

The highway expanded into additional lanes as the rain slowed to a drizzle, allowing Tristan to step on the gas.

"How do you want to handle this?"

"Let's put some pressure on her, ask more questions and try to get her to cooperate on her own."

"And where are we going?"

"A quaint little town called Thornburg," he said facetiously, "about halfway to Richmond. Since we have time, why don't you tell me how you woke up to the New World Order? How you unplugged?"

"Are you sure? I realize I hit you with a lot the other day. Just remember, you can't unlearn it."

Thinking for a moment, Tristan gave his answer; "I'm ready."

"Fluoride."

"What?"

"If I told you the government was knowingly adding poison to our drinking water, what would you say?" Sebastian began.

"I'd say that sounds like a conspiracy theory."

"Do you know fluoride is a poison?"

"Poison?"

"When you get home tonight, check out the back of your tube of toothpaste. The warning states, 'If more than the recommended brushing amount of toothpaste is accidentally swallowed contact a Poison Control Center immediately.' And what is the recommended brushing amount? The size of a pea for children and the length of the brush for adults."

"You're kidding?"

"It's hidden in plain sight, a fact that can be checked by anyone right in their own medicine cabinet. So the next obvious question is; why do we have public water fluoridation?"

"Well, to keep our teeth healthy. Fluoride prevents cavities."

"Then what is toothpaste for? You can buy it anywhere. You can brush your teeth whenever you want, so why add it to drinking water?"

"Huh." Tristan realized he had never thought of it that way before.

"The controversy surrounding sodium fluoride in municipal drinking water has been growing over the decades, and many cities are no longer adding it. The average person just assumes it prevents cavities, and that those putting it into the water must know what they're doing. Fluoride occurs in nature in varying amounts, but what is added to our drinking water is a waste product of aluminum manufacture and phosphate fertilizer production. It's been used as rat poison, later to be replaced with substances found less toxic to the environment. Fluoride has also been linked to bone cancer with many scientists stating it's responsible for more human cancer death, and causes it faster, than any other chemical. Every major city fluoridating their drinking water shows higher cancer rates. Many European countries such as Germany, Italy, Norway, Sweden, Denmark, Belgium, Austria, France, and the Netherlands, have stopped adding it."

"Did you say rat poison?" Tristan asked incredulous.

"It's still used in roach poisons and other insecticides, even Sarin nerve gas. It is so toxic the shipping containers have a skull and crossbones warning. Almost no one knows the history of fluoride, and where water fluoridation comes from. In 1954, a prominent US industrial chemist named Charles Eliot Perkins wrote a letter to the Lee Foundation for Nutritional Research stating he had learned the Nazi regime had used sodium fluoride as a means of mass control of the German people to reduce their resistance to dominance, authority, and loss of liberty. Doctor Perkins had been sent by the American government to help reconstruct the I.G. Farben chemical plants in Germany at the end of World War II. In his letter he wrote that he was positive, the reason behind water fluoridation was not to benefit children's teeth but rather to reduce the individual's power to resist domination by slowly poisoning and narcotizing the area of brain tissue making the person submissive to the will of 'those who wish to govern him.' He went on to say, with all the earnestness and sincerity of a scientist who had spent over twenty years' research into the chemistry, biochemistry, physiology, and pathology of fluorine, that anyone drinking fluoridated water for a period of one year or more will never again be the same person, mentally or physically."

Sebastian stopped to watch Tristan's reaction.

"Normally, this is the point in the conversation where you should be experiencing cognitive dissonance."

"Cognitive what?"

"Cognitive dissonance. The dictionary defines it as a condition of conflict resulting from inconsistency between belief and action, such as opposing killing animals and eating meat. When a person has a strong ideological belief and is presented with indisputable facts contradicting that belief, the denial urge is so strong their thought process appears to completely shut down. It's quite amazing. You can hand someone their tube of toothpaste so they can read the poison warning, and yet they will still laugh it off, change the subject, call you a conspiracy nut, or even forget the conversation ever happened. Pavlov was the first to observe this. He trained his dog to drool for food with the ringing of a bell. Next, he trained it for the same response with a buzzer. Then when he played the bell and buzzer simultaneously, the dog experienced cognitive dissonance and refused to eat. It would curl up in a corner, confused and depressed. Humans experience the same thing. I've told numerous people about the poison warning on their toothpaste tube and they will outright refuse to walk into their bathroom and verify for themselves." Sebastian tossed the file onto the back seat. "You still with me?"

"I'm with you."

"Now I'll really blow your mind. Guess what common pharmaceutical drug is made of fluoride?"

"I'm not sure I want to know."

"Prozac; the most popular in a family of Serotonin Reuptake Inhibitors, or SSRIs. These drugs contain over 90 percent fluoride. The American population is being medicated on a daily basis in their own drinking water, it's out there in the open but they don't want to know it."

"What about the American Dental Association? They still say it's good for our teeth, although, it didn't help me much. I'm full of cavities," Tristan realized.

"Even if science could demonstrate that the topical application of sodium fluoride reduced caries, which they've only been able to do in children under the age of twelve, one could still logically ask why it would be added to drinking water for everyone in the population, when the ADA admits there is zero benefit from ingesting? If a pea-sized amount of toothpaste is toxic, then how can the government possibly regulate how much water a person consumes? The more water you drink, the more fluoride you intake, right?"

"Of course."

"Now, guess where we buy the sodium fluoride being added to our water?"

"No, don't tell me."

"The People's Republic of China. The same country shipping children's toys with lead, pet food with rat poison, and toxic drywall for home construction. Who do you think was behind the first push to fluorinate drinking water in America? After all, it must have been lobbied to politicians in our government to create the policy? The answer? Where almost every eugenics program of the twentieth century has come from; the Rockefeller-Soviet axis. Water fluoridation is being done on purpose, it's just one part of the slow-kill plan by the New World Order."

"I swallow some toothpaste every time I brush, how can you not? And I've been doing it almost my entire life!"

"That's nothing. Wait until I tell you about the history of the Rockefeller-funded public school system and what the true goals are, and how SSRIs like Ritalin were advanced to purposely poison children. It's mind blowing."

They arrived at their exit and Tristan drove the car off I-95, heading west.

"I've got some homework for you. The first chance you get, watch *End Game*, the documentary by Alex Jones. It's free on YouTube."

"*End Game?*"

"He's produced lots of amazing documentaries, but that's the one you want to start with. It's the most important film ever made about the New World Order."

"*End Game*. Got it."

The town of Thornburg consisted of a few mom-and-pop businesses and historic properties with large expanses of land. Following the GPS voice prompts, Tristan pulled the car into the familiar driveway. After such a long drive he hoped she was home, but dropping in was a better way to prevent the person from avoiding a visit. Although they had left the rain behind, the air was thick with humidity and puddles checkered the landscape.

"What is the sister's name?"

"Jill."

"Jill Johnson and James Johnson? Parents weren't too creative," Sebastian said as he stepped out of the car and into a pool of water that was deeper than it looked.

The gravel driveway crunched under their shoes as they walked. Tristan led the way to the covered porch and knocked on the screen door of the trailer. He listened closely, hearing a television inside.

"FBI Ms. Johnson. We spoke the other day?"

The door cracked open and a face appeared behind the chain of the security latch.

"You again?"

"Can we talk please ma'am?" Tristan made a conscious effort to be polite and respectful.

She slammed the door. The security chain came off and Jill Johnson walked out onto the porch, her flip-flops clapping with every step.

"I thought we talked about this, James could be dead for all I know."

"I have a source at Camp Lejeune who believes your brother flunked out of Special Forces on purpose."

"I don't know anything about that," she said, irritated. "What do you want from me?"

"I don't think you're telling me everything."

"I'd appreciate it if you didn't bother me anymore." She tried closing the door, but Tristan wedged in a foot.

"Look, I'm a marine," he spoke to her intimately. "I was in Afghanistan. James and I never met but we're still brothers. If he's involved in the attempted assassination of the president, believe me, you want me to find him first. If another agency gets to him, or the people he's in with decide he's no longer useful, I hate to think what will happen." By the expression on her face, Tristan surmised he was getting through. "Any idea where he might be?"

She shuffled her feet and shunned eye contact.

"He never told me he was back from Afghanistan, or even in Special Forces, he just showed up on my doorstep one day. I was so happy to see him I didn't ask any questions. I could tell he was depressed. He wouldn't talk about it, but I knew he was unhappy with the wars and his experience at Camp Lejeune. Then one morning I woke up and he was gone."

"When was that?"

"Two months ago, give or take."

"Did he say anything while he was here? Anything to indicate where he is or what he might be doing?"

"The night before he left, we had plans to go out to dinner, but he got into another mood so we ate in. The thing I remember him saying was, he had finally found a cause he believed in, people he fit in with. He was making comments about hating the government, but that wasn't him. I know him, he didn't like big tyrannical government but he was not an anarchist. I didn't believe what he was saying, and he knew it. He got so angry I shut up."

"Is that all?" he asked in a dubious tone.

She pulled on the curls of her blonde hair—her tell.

"We're the good guys ma'am, we just want the truth. I'll do my best to help him if he's in trouble." Tristan handed her a business card. "If you want to talk, here's my cell number. Call me any time."

He felt her gaze as they got in the car and drove off. They stopped to eat at a diner and were back on the road in an hour, heading north on the interstate. Tristan's cell phone rang, the caller ID displaying a Virginia number.

"This is Special Agent Wood."

"Agent Wood, this is Jill Johnson."

"Yes, is everything all right?"

"I'm worried about my brother," she said hesitantly.

"I'm listening."

"I have an address. I don't know if he still lives there."

"Okay, I'm driving so let me hand the phone to my partner who can write it down."

"Agent Wood?"

"Yes."

"He's your brother, right?"

"We're marines, ma'am."

"James is the only family I've got. Promise me . . ."

"I promise."

CHAPTER 15

Robert Wood attempted to balance his coffee as he walked the halls of the Russell Senate Office Building in downtown Washington, DC. Filled to the brim, it was too hot to sip and required his complete concentration to keep from spilling. He breathed easier as he arrived at the door of Senator Matthew's office.

"Welcome home Robert," a fellow aide said, with a slap on the back. A wave of coffee left the cup and splashed on the floor in the doorway.

So close.

Stepping over the puddle, Robert decided he was lucky he didn't hit the wall-to-wall rug. It was beautiful, with red and gold fringe, and had come from the Orient on one of the senator's yearly jaunts. It was also sickening to look at.

Congressmen did this on almost every trip, buying personal items paid for with money from various slush funds slipped into legislation just for this purpose. There was upwards of twenty thousand dollars in decorating within this small room, all thanks to the American taxpayer.

"Hi Robert, how are you?" asked another aide who looked familiar. "I heard you had quite an adventure?" The young girl hurried down the hall as she called back, "We should have drinks sometime and you can tell me about it. See you later."

He mopped the floor with paper towels as the desk phone rang, again. So many calls for interviews had come in, he was burned out from saying "no comment." The senator did not want to tell the press anything. After the beep, a female voice left a message begging to ask some questions about the Russia trip, but that was not going to happen.

A man pushing a cart rolled by and handed over a stack of mail without stepping inside. Robert went to drop it into a basket on the senator's desk when he noticed a large white envelope labeled; *eyes-only*. It was open but poorly hidden below some letters. Curiosity got the better of him. He sat down at his makeshift work station, a small desk and chair in the corner.

Above him loomed a framed picture, a skull and crossbones with the number "322" underneath. With a little research, he had discovered its origin. Yale was the senator's alma mater, and this was the logo for *Skull & Bones*, an elite secret society he had belonged to. Robert once asked what 322 meant, but received no answer.

Two infamous modern-day members were George Bush and John Kerry. When confronted about Skull & Bones in interviews before the 2004 general election, both men refused to discuss it.

Aside from the pentagrams contained in some of the art, what particularly bothered him was the portrait. It jarred his memory from Spaso House. Senator Matthews was posing with the same hidden-hand gesture as the ambassadors in their photos, right hand partially inside the suit jacket and resembling a claw.

It gave him the creeps.

A rush of adrenalin reminded him that although he had an automatic low-level security clearance as an employee of the senator, he was not officially authorized to view eyes-only documents. The envelope contained satellite photos and an official CIA report. The first page read;

Progress Underground Base Construction in Yamantau and Ural Mountains: Mining project in the Russian Yamantau range area and Ural mountain range, known as Beloretsk 15 and 16, appear to be completed. Included satellite photos show; Ural mountain complex, intelligence indicates a series of underground nuclear bunkers and weapons production facilities including nuclear, biological, chemical. Ural mountain complex exceeding depths of 1000 feet, bunkers reinforced with concrete, steel, and other unknown materials. Complex clearly designed to function and withstand multiple blasts during nuclear exchange.

Note especially, estimated size of Yamantau Mountain mining complex, comparable to District of Columbia, believed to be largest nuclear-secure project in the world with train tracks entering mountain at numerous locations; five track widths. Estimates suggest Yamantau underground base reinforced to withstand minimum six direct warhead strikes in simultaneous location before compromising structure. Each base believed to require approx. 30,000 workers and 10+ years to construct.

Current inspection status: Closed to Russian public, closed to foreigners, closed to US military and Pentagon officials.

Robert almost choked on his coffee. This was something you would read in a science fiction novel or on a conspiracy theory website, but it was a CIA intelligence report. He flipped through photos of the bases, marked in red pen to show the points of interest.

A recurring highlight included the multiple tracks entering the mountain complexes. One blurry image showed a train heading toward the Ural Mountain base. He was no expert, nevertheless, this was obviously not an industrial-type vehicle used for mining. It appeared to be a commuter.

In fact, it closely resembled the Washington, DC, Metrorail.

The report mentioned upcoming Russian war games, but no dates. Then he read something strange. Comparisons were made between the underground bases in Russia and two in the United States, including one under the Pentagon and another beneath the Denver International Airport, each with its own state-of-the-art central command center. Robert would never have guessed they existed.

It went on to cite concerns CIA had with President Putin's speeches where he was calling for a strong and patriotic Russia, as well as a new unified Soviet Union. He was also talking openly about Communism again, even quoting Lenin and Stalin.

There was one phrase in particular that Putin used often.

Ola Gigante.

He would need to research it, but for now he closed the folder and rubbed his tired eyes.

"Good afternoon Mr. Wood," the senator said, entering the office with rare vigor.

Startled, Robert awkwardly returned the greeting and stood up, the classified intelligence in front of him. There would be no wiggling out of this.

"So? What do you think?"

"Um, well . . ."

"Relax, son. I was going to discuss this with you today."

"I'm sorry sir, I know it's eyes-only, but it was open and—"

"I said it is all right, you're on the inside now."

Breathing a sigh of relief, Robert sat down and took in the view of Constitution Avenue through the window. The Russell Senate Office Building opened in 1909 to relieve overcrowding in the US Capitol. It was renamed in 1972 for Senator Richard B. Russell, Jr. of Georgia perhaps most famous for being a white supremacist with decades-long opposition to the civil rights movement. This was one of the best known secrets in Washington.

"Remember when we talked about the staged collapse of the Soviet Union?" The senator plopped down into his chair.

"How can I forget, my mind is still reeling."

"What would you estimate two underground nuclear-proof bases cost to build, with one approximately the size of Washington, DC?"

"I can't even guess."

"Russia claimed they could not afford $200 million for the service module on the International Space Station, which they were obligated to pay for. They do not have the capital to support the infantry and provide them housing, or help their poor and hungry citizens. Yet, the money pit for weapons projects has no bottom. Even with the billions in foreign aid sent over annually, we are not permitted to inspect, what are undoubtedly, secret underground bases."

"We've never been inside them?"

"Not for lack of trying. A US military attaché stationed in Moscow was turned back when he attempted to visit the region a few years ago. We can't even get a response to questions about them anymore."

"I don't understand, why would they build these? What are they for?"

"All along the claim was, they were enormous mining projects. But we knew better. Multiple defectors have confirmed our suspicions."

"Which are?"

"In addition to the military, these bases will shelter the most important civilians, business people, and politicians during a world war."

"Why isn't this all over the news? It seems pretty big to me?"

"Actually, in 1996, the *New York Times* printed photos of the Yamantau complex on the front page of an issue, and the CIA was given a chance to respond. Keeping pace with the long-standing secret government policy to protect Americans from any information that would point to a Russian threat, a spokesman for The Agency stated they weren't worried, claiming the massive Russian facility was purely 'defensive.' And since no US official has ever been allowed to visit the site, it's been dismissed as a conspiracy theory."

"Because Russia is not supposed to be a threat?" Robert asked.

"Back in 2009, in public testimony before a House Armed Services Subcommittee, KGB defector Colonel Oleg Gordievsky claimed they had maintained a separate top-secret organization, known as Directorate 15, to build and maintain a network of underground command bunkers for the Soviet leadership. This included the vast sites beneath the Yamantau and Ural Mountains, including their weapons repositories."

"Are they storing nukes there?"

"Building and stocking a brand new ICBM." Senator Matthews leafed through the photos and handed one to Robert. "This is a TOPOL-M class thermonuclear ICBM, a seventy-five foot long, three-stage solid propellant rocket with a 7000 mile range. These can be fired from silos or mobile launchers. They have been deployed since the 90s."

He passed over another photograph.

"Here is the RS-24 Yars, in service since 2010. The previous model held up to four MIRV warheads."

"What kind of warheads?" Robert asked.

"MIRV; multiple independently targetable re-entry vehicle. It's a system that deploys warheads one after the other, either striking several targets or the same target multiple times. Each warhead carries the explosive power of up to twenty Hiroshima-sized weapons. The TOPOL-M and RS-24 Yars comprise about 80% of Russia's nuclear arsenal."

The senator held up another photo, not letting Robert hold it.

"This is the Yars-M, the first modernized intercontinental ballistic missile. We believe this is the top secret ongoing project in the Yamantau Mountain underground base. The Yars-M can carry up to ten warheads, and is still light enough for a mobile launcher. What makes it so deadly, is that it is immune to any current and planned US antiballistic missile defense systems. It is so fast we're unable to calculate its trajectory."

"We can't shoot them down?"

"That is correct." The senator placed the envelope, with photos, in a desk drawer. "Yet another Russian weapons project funded by the American taxpayer. The Russians have been using our financial aid to upgrade and improve their nuclear arsenal, and to build missiles we cannot protect ourselves from."

The office phone rang.

"Calls from reporters have been coming in all day," Robert said. "I've been letting them go to voicemail."

"Please do."

The phone's answering machine picked up.

"Hello, this is Lieutenant Sam Hornell. I'm calling for Senator Matthews. I'm a navy pilot stationed on the USS Carl Vinson . . . I'd rather not leave a message, it's important I speak with you directly. I don't want to give out my number so I'll try calling back another—"

"Hello? Hello, lieutenant?" Robert pressed a button, engaging the speakerphone.

"Yes, Lieutenant Hornell speaking. Is this Senator Matthews?"

"No, this is his assistant." His boss nodded. "The senator is here."

"Hello lieutenant, this is Senator Matthews."

"Is this the congressman who was held hostage in Moscow?"

Robert got up to close the door to the office.

"How may I help you?"

"I understand you've traveled to Russia many times and have experience dealing with the Russians?"

"That is correct," Senator Matthews opened a desk drawer and rummaged through papers, taking out a map.

"I heard your press conference. You used the term 'Soviet Union,' and said the KGB is alive and well, if I remember the phrase correctly?"

"That was a slip of the tongue, I misspoke."

"Yes, sir."

"Lieutenant, you're stationed on the Vinson?" the senator asked.

Another pause. "Sir."

"So I can verify you are who you say you are, can you disclose your current position?"

"We're in the Bering Sea at the moment."

"And where is your home port?"

"San Diego, sir."

The senator pointed to a red dot in the Bering Sea, labeled; *CVN70*. The map's key listed CVN70 as the *USS Carl Vinson*, and San Diego, CA, as the home port. Robert knew this map; it indicated the current deployments of the United States Atlantic Carriers, Pacific Carriers, and Big-Deck Amphibious Warfare ships.

"How is the weather up there?"

"I don't mind it right now, sir, as long as we get out before the fall."

"It gets cold at the top of the world—" a coughing fit overtook him.

Robert asked, "Lieutenant, you had something important to talk to the senator about?"

"I've recently become concerned with the war games we are conducting. Over the past year we've shifted into a defensive response to a Russian nuclear first strike."

"Russia often runs war games with a nuclear scenario," the senator affirmed.

"Yes, sir. But what's new is we're not practicing to fight, or retaliate. We are assuming Russia has taken out major cities and military targets with nukes. Trouble areas in America are hit with chemical and biological weapons . . ." Static began to cut in and mask his voice. ". . . we're following the guidelines of the MIAC rep . . ."

"I'm sorry son, you're breaking up. What are you trying to tell me?"

"The exercises are no longer to fight Russia. We're training to police the American people after we lose a war to them. I thought you might have some insight into this? I've been a pilot for almost twenty years and this is new to me. No one seems to know why."

Robert sat watching the senator's reaction, which was strangely innocuous. He seemed about to respond when more interference muddled the connection.

"Something's not right," Lt. Hornell said. "I have to go."

A *click* indicated the line went dead.

CHAPTER 16

Tristan and Sebastian sat in the parking lot of a non-descript housing complex, one of hundreds strewn across the Washington, DC, area; not old, not new, just built, just there. A five level apartment building rose up over the horizon, rust stains crawling down the white siding like wet mascara. Realtor *For Sale* signs peppered the area. The grounds were not manicured enough to disguise the fact that this was representative of the new American slum.

The middle class had been eroding for decades, but since the second housing bust of the century it was well on its way to being wiped out completely. Tristan imagined families sitting in their homes feeling the depression no one would talk about while the Ministry of Plenty told them things were good and getting better. Somehow, most people convinced themselves it was true.

"Got it."

Tristan handed his smart phone to Sebastian who read the electronic search warrant they had been issued, sent by email.

"So what's the plan?" Sebastian asked.

"I was thinking, you should head around the back in case someone tries to escape that way. I'll knock on the front door and see who answers. This is the last lead we've got and I don't want to take a chance losing this guy," Tristan said.

"I agree, let's do it."

Sebastian walked off, disappearing behind the end of the row of townhomes, the alternating red brick and white vinyl fronts creating an illusion of choice.

While waiting for his new partner to get into position, he had time to reflect on their conversation during the ride. According to Sebastian, the way to help others unplug from the *propaganda matrix* was to start them out with a few smaller truths to create doubt about the status quo, and eventually arrive at the big picture; the New World Order. He had stressed the word; *help*. Some were more willing to unplug than others. Tristan knew he was the exception, since he had willingly sought answers.

The average person was perfectly content to accept what they were told by the media, without question. But how could one assume the veracity of the information when over 90 percent of the news was controlled by six multinational corporations?

GE-NBC, News Corp-Fox, Disney-ABC, Viacom, CBS, and Time Warner-CNN.

News was regurgitated from one source; the Associated Press. The major TV networks would shift the words around and add their bias, with little or no fact-checking for accuracy. Reporters were reprimanded and threatened to stick to an angle while cramming as much information as possible into simplified sound bites for mass consumption. Those who did not comply, like CNN journalist Amber Lyon, were fired.

Sebastian believed the only truth came from the alternative media. After listening to a replay of the Alex Jones show the night before, Tristan was hooked.

Realizing he had been daydreaming too long, he left the car and walked to the sidewalk where cracks in the cement meandered like distended veins. These townhomes did not have yards so much as small patches of feral grass. The entire area was depressing.

At the front door, he reached inside his suit jacket and released the holster lock on his sidearm. He rang the doorbell and waited. With no response he knocked again, but nothing. He spotted a well-window below. The grime on the glass made it even darker inside, except for a beam of . . . *wait—*

Something moved through the light.

The storm door grated on corroded hinges. The knob was locked. He glanced up and down the deserted street, then stepped over the railing and onto the grass below. The dirty well-window allowed a partial view of a vacant basement room.

The window gave way with a loud *squeak*.

This was his last chance. If they blew it and the suspect got away, the case would be handed over to Homeland Security. Or shut down.

He dropped to the floor, landing on his bad leg with too much force.

Agh!

Tristan clenched his teeth to try and stay quiet. He drew his Glock and limped to the door, avoiding the direct sunlight entering the room. Ahead of him, in the main part of the basement, sliding glass doors led out to a patio surrounded by a rickety wooden privacy fence. He knew Sebastian would not have a view into this level from his position on the other side.

Tristan cautiously headed for the sliders, unlocking them.

An arm wrapped around his throat cutting off his oxygen. In order to pry loose using both hands, he had to drop his gun. Whoever held him from behind was strong—very strong.

Tristan tried unsuccessfully to get free.

He pulled away for a moment, enough to catch a glimpse of a tattoo on the forearm.

The clutch strengthened; a classic military death-grip.

A rush of adrenalin overcame him and his vision clouded, resembling the snow of an old analog television with fuzzy reception. He began to lose consciousness.

"James Johnson, James Johnson, I just want to talk."

Tristan's legs started to buckle.

"Damn the valley."

As if outside his body, he heard himself say it one more time as everything went black;

"Damn the valley . . ."

CHAPTER 17

James Johnson wiped the sweat from his forehead and tried to catch his breath as he walked the final few yards to his outfit resting in front of their barracks. At the end of the early morning 6k run, he had not only finished last in the platoon, but in the entire company. Disapproving looks pierced him like invisible knives. Embarrassment was an emotion he was not getting used to.

It had been just three weeks, and in that time James had gone from first to last in everything. The men he was training with, those depending on him with their lives were once again forced to wait. And James knew they would all pay for it.

"First Platoon, fall in!" came the always-commanding voice of their drill instructor, Sergeant Black. "I said, fall in!"

The group filed into place and stood at attention. James tried brushing off the sand that clung to his shoes and socks, picked up from the beach part of the course. It was a nice run, except for the fact that he was at the end of the pack the entire way.

Little did his fellow marines know it was on purpose.

"First Platoon!" Sergeant Black yelled as he began pacing around the men. "We seem to have a weak link, do you agree?"

"Yes, sir!" they answered back.

The early morning sun was starting to burn off the humidity on the base of Camp Lejeune and it looked like another beautiful day on the North Carolina coast. James, or J.J. as his friends called him, was quickly flunking out and everyone knew it. Of course, no one here was his friend so he was officially "James" or "Johnson" or any number of rude nicknames.

TIDAL WAVE 23

The newest one was his least favorite.

"Are you First Platoon, Able Company?"

"Yes, sir!" came a more enthusiastic response.

"I believe First Platoon has a weak link! I'm about damn sure Able Company is not supposed to have a weak link!"

They were one of four platoons in Able Company, which was one of four in the Marine Third Special Operations Battalion formed in 2009. Out of a total of 672 men in Special Forces at Camp Lejeune, James Johnson's performance was dead last.

"First Platoon, Able Company is not supposed to have a weak link, but it does. Who is First Platoon's weak link?"

"Lieutenant Infidel!"

There it was.

"Who?"

"Lieutenant Infidel!" the men yelled in unison.

"Who?"

"Lieutenant Infidel!"

Sergeant Black always liked to get in an extra one for effect. J.J. felt a sting in his eye and wiped out some sweat. Yet it was nothing compared to the pain resulting from the downward spiral of his military career.

"What do you suggest we do about Lieutenant Infidel, the weak link?" the sergeant demanded as he made his way over to J.J. "I believe Lieutenant Infidel would like his platoon to stay on base this weekend and help him figure out why he finishes last in every run, and why he can't seem to recall what he is taught!"

Sergeant Black stood in front of J.J., took a purposeful glance at his forearm and walked away. The tattoo was the word "Infidel" inked in dark green with a gothic-style font, and since the standard PT uniform was T-shirt and shorts, it was blatantly visible.

"Hit the showers and report to the mess hall. Be sure to eat up, you'll need all the energy you can get. While the rest of your company is enjoying their weekend off base, you'll be practicing combat exercises in full gear! Fall out!"

Sergeant Black marched off.

The men walked into the barracks, heads held low, giving J.J. nothing but nasty looks. He decided to linger outside and give them a chance to cool off. He was starting to regret the tattoo, or at least for not putting it on a part of his body covered by clothing. It seemed like a good idea at the time, all his buddies were getting them. The enemy in Afghanistan called the Americans "infidel," so the marines began to mimic them. Then tattoos started showing up. Or maybe his remorse was the result of the life decision he had made a few weeks back.

"Johnson!" Sergeant Black had reappeared. "Colonel Grant wants to see you, let's go."

J.J. followed close behind as they traversed the manicured grounds of the base.

"Keep up Johnson, I don't want you falling too far behind."

Good one.

They soon reached a red brick administration building and turned up the walkway toward the front entrance. The American flag flew at half-mast due to an entire SEAL team killed in a CH-47 Chinook crash in Afghanistan, a country politicians in both parties had promised to exit long ago. After taking the elevator to the top floor, Sergeant Black left him at a receptionist desk.

"Have a seat, Colonel Grant will be with you shortly," the older woman said coldly.

J.J. sat on a bench by a large window overlooking the base. Camp Lejeune created in him a mixture of pride and heartache. He abhorred the path America had gone down. A former beacon of hope and freedom around the world, the country was despised globally more than at any other time in history. Once leading by example, the US lashed out at countries that posed no imminent threat. With every new conflict, the mission was increasingly vague and the troops less motivated to fight.

A soldier's job used to be to kill the enemy, but now they were police and security guards. In some countries they fought Al Qaeda, and in others they supported them. The conflicts in Iraq, Iran, and Libya were about oil, in Syria it was about a gas pipeline, in Yemen, Somalia, and Sudan it was about geographic control of the energy chessboard in the Middle East and North Africa. In Afghanistan, where James had been, they guarded the poppy fields.

Everything seemed upside down and inside out.

Soldiers were often afraid to fight since they were being imprisoned by the same government sending them overseas with those orders. One accusation of an "illegal killing" was all it took. It was better to avoid your job than to get prosecuted doing it. And despite promises to the contrary, whistleblowers were being convicted, and assassinated, at historic levels.

Many were sent to their seventh or eighth tour of duty by self-serving politicians and armchair generals who were more concerned with their life after retirement than in working for the best interests of the troops serving under them.

Mental breakdowns were common.

Their answer to stress was medical—drug the lab rats. Prozac, prescribed liberally by military psychologists, had been pushed on him more times than he could remember. He always refused. There was a reason a greater number of men were committing suicide than were dying in battle. Every person J.J. knew who killed himself had been on one of these drugs.

Every single one.

"You can go in now." The receptionist pointed to a nearby office.

Colonel Thom Grant was the name stenciled on the glass door. J.J. walked in and stood at mild attention in front of the man sitting behind the desk.

"Have a seat lieutenant," the Colonel said without looking up.

This office had an amazing panoramic view of the grounds. Camp Lejeune was named in 1942 in honor of the 13th Commandant of the Marine Corps, John A. Lejeune. The 246 square mile base had fourteen miles of beach along the Atlantic Ocean, eleven of which were capable of amphibious assault training.

"I'm Colonel Grant. I wanted to meet you and find out what's going on? I must admit, I'm vexed. You started out winning all the runs. Every PT exercise you finished first or close to it. You hadn't had many classes, but it appears you would have been an 'A' student, and three weeks later you're failing everything? Please explain."

J.J. wanted to say something, he hated being thought of as a loser. He was close now and needed to continue playing the part, demoralizing as it was.

"I don't know, sir."

"That's not an answer. Why has your performance become so poor?" Col Grant pressed.

"It's harder than I thought, I'm trying to keep up but I'm burned out. I just got back from Afghanistan after two years and I'm—"

"When a recruit goes downhill this fast, you know what I see? I see someone purposely washing out. Are you washing out?"

An involuntary rush of blood to his face affirmed to J.J. that the guy had just nailed it. He tried, but found it hard to speak. "I volunteered for this, sir. Why would I purposely wash out?"

"You tell me. Physically you're fine, unless there's something I'm not aware of?"

"No, sir."

"Do you not want to be here? I can throw you in the brig. That's what we do to marines attempting to wash out. We have a delightful facility on base, we'll lock you up and see if your performance changes?"

Purposely trying to get thrown out of the military was an offense that could land him in jail, so he had tried his best to do it gradually.

"Special Forces isn't easy. Not everyone is strong or committed enough to make it here. It's one of the most exclusive clubs in the armed forces."

He felt the sting again, aware the Colonel was using reverse psychology to shame him. Nonetheless, his temper started to boil deep down inside.

"I'll ask you one more time. Are you trying to wash out?"

J.J. imagined what his new career would be like and it didn't get more exclusive than a black-ops group. This helped him control his emotions. "I guess I'm just not cut out for this, sir."

The Colonel studied him. "I'm afraid if this continues something bad will happen to you. You're the least popular man on base. If you're washing out and I keep you here you could get hurt. If you're not doing this on purpose and I keep you here you could get hurt."

By "hurt," J.J. was sure the Colonel meant "hazed." He was actually surprised his platoon had not yet hazed him for his dismal performance.

"I don't want to take a chance, this can only get worse. I'm discharging you."

A wave of relief overcame him; it was finally over. The Colonel opened a drawer in his desk and pulled out some papers.

"Due to your exemplary service overseas, I'm going to give you an honorable discharge effective immediately. You will not participate in any more activities with your platoon, do you understand?"

"Yes, sir."

"It will take about a day to process this paperwork, so you are to go back to your barracks and stay there. I'll inform Sergeant Black. I doubt your squad's going to be upset you're leaving."

"Thank you, sir," J.J. said, not meaning it.

Colonel Grant stood up first, but instead of saluting they shook hands.

This guy wasn't so bad, J.J. thought as he left the building.

With an overwhelming wave of guilt, he sat down on a concrete bench and dropped his head. To stop his mind from racing was useless. Flashbacks haunted him with visuals of the strange meeting three weeks ago that brought him to this point.

The mess hall was empty and quiet. James Johnson sat by himself, nervously playing with his keychain. Sergeant Black had come to him in the barracks minutes earlier to deliver a message that someone wanted to meet him. The location was unusual, but he wasn't worried.

After just a week into Special Forces training, he was trouncing everyone in runs, obstacle course races, and he had received a perfect score on their first written test. He was already at the top of the class and it filled him with pride.

Interrupting his thoughts, a man dressed in civilian clothes entered.

J.J. stood and saluted.

"At ease, soldier," he said before sitting down, a folder in his grasp. "Lieutenant James Johnson?"

"Yes, sir."

"You're recently back from Afghanistan?"

"I stepped on a plane over there and got off here."

"So how's it going in *the graveyard of empires*? Long war, isn't it?"

"Sir, no one's sure what we're doing besides guarding the opium fields."

Blurting out a comment like this a year ago would have made J.J. kick himself. The truth was he couldn't wait to get out of Afghanistan. Brothers or not, when he was recruited to Special Forces he jumped on the first plane and said good riddance to the Mid-East without looking back. Year after year, draw-downs in both Iraq and Afghanistan were promised yet tens of thousands of combat troops had been left behind and renamed "security forces" to fool the public.

Whenever an election cycle approached, the president and Pentagon would pull out a few thousand to fulfill campaign promises, only to quietly replace them with men and women from other parts of the world. It was all a big shell game.

J.J. had come to believe the wars were not meant to be won, just sustained. With the massive manpower, military hardware, and corporate contractors, he guessed it must be money. War really was the health of the state. Meanwhile, the United States continued to expand the empire, bombing and invading sovereign countries that did not pose an imminent threat.

They didn't even call them wars anymore.

Contingency Operation,

Surgical Offensive . . .

The American public was being lied to and J.J. was fed up.

"I know it's tough." The man in civilian clothes opened the folder and scanned through it. "No mission, no goal, no clearly defined enemy, and no end game."

He looked early to mid-fifties, with a solid build under the red tartan shirt, and appeared strong as an ox. Khaki slacks draped over worn sneakers and a red baseball cap with USS Iowa BB-61 in gold stitching fit snugly on his head.

Clean cut and well spoken, J.J. suspected the guy was ex-military.

"James Johnson," he read from the file, "enlisted in the marines four years ago, only immediate family is a sister who lives in central Virginia, and never been in any legal trouble. Stationed in the KOP then transferred to Kabul for the remainder of your tour. You moved up to lieutenant faster than average, escaped Afghanistan without a scratch, and even saved your squad from a sniper after being pinned down in a firefight for thirteen hours. And demolitions experience, that can come in useful. You seem to excel at everything you do. No college though, why not?"

The question caught him off-guard. "College costs money, sir."

"Everything costs money, son. That's okay, it doesn't mean you're not smart or motivated."

"I'm sorry sir, I didn't get your name."

"My highest rank was Major," he said without looking up. "It's not easy these days. Not easy at all."

"Sir?"

"Good leaders are few and far between, young men with enough intelligence, strength, and loyalty to follow orders. To serve their country. I see why Special Forces wanted you. You do understand, if you're called into action you're headed overseas again?"

The Major closed the file.

"Yes, sir. That had occurred to me."

J.J. was excited to be in Special Forces, but he did not want to go back to Afghanistan, Iraq, or any other third world toilet the United States was currently involved in.

"I'm going to get right to the point. I work on black-ops projects, operations that are off-the-books, so to speak. I'm always on the lookout for men who have what it takes to be on my team."

"Off-the-books, sir?"

"There are plenty of threats here at home, son. Threats our guys in CIA, FBI, and Homeland Security can't handle. I wanted to see if you're someone who can do what we do, be part of the team. It's real *007* type stuff, completely under the radar."

Intrigued, he asked, "Who do you work for?"

"Let's just say my virtual office is attached to the Department of Defense."

"The Pentagon?"

"We don't have a home base. My team and I aren't tied down to anyone or anything, we operate independent of the military and law enforcement. You could run into another member and never know it. We're so top secret the secretary of defense is unaware we exist."

"What kind of work are we talking about?"

"We deal primarily with domestic intelligence gathering and internal threat evaluation with an emphasis on direct counter-action operations."

"What does that mean?"

"I can't tell you any more, unless you agree to join up. If you do come on board you'll have to sign a confidentiality agreement never to talk about what we do. I can promise you this, though, you won't have to go overseas again. It's not easy work, but it's here in America. Each of my guys has a pivotal role and you'll be in charge of yourself. Now and then you'll even assemble your own team for a mission. There's a lot of responsibility, it's an elite group. The pay stinks, but when you 'retire' you'll never have to worry about money again. I'll give you a few days to think it over."

The Major stood up to leave.

"I'll do it."

"Are you sure, son?"

"I don't want to go back to that hellhole." He took another moment before giving his final answer, then said, "I'm in."

"Decisive. I like that, it's a good trait."

The Major placed a contract on the table between them. He explained each paragraph and, hesitating a bit, J.J. signed the document.

"So, I'll go pack up my gear. Where are we going?"

"It's not that easy. There's something you must do. I need you to wash out of the program."

"Wash out?"

"Acting is part of this job. You're going to have to lie and create characters when necessary, and you'll have to be believable. Your first test is to become a disgruntled soldier and wash out of the training program."

"How do I do that?"

"Start failing. If it takes a week or a month, I don't care. You have to convince everyone you're bitter and you can't hack it. Finish your PT races last, fail the written tests, but do it gradually so it's not too obvious. Tell your comrades you hate the military and the government, and you regret signing up for Special Forces. Express to people, whether you know them or not, that you're angry at your country and the overseas wars. Say the only way America can survive is to get rid of the government. Can you do that?"

"Yes, sir."

Hating the wars will be easy, he thought to himself. *It's the rest I'll have to work on.*

"Good man. After your discharge I'll contact you. Then you'll disappear."

"Disappear?"

"This will give you credibility with groups you'll infiltrate and allow you to operate under the radar for me."

"Yes, sir."

"I'll be keeping track of your progress. When the time comes I'll get in touch and we'll begin." The Major stood up and said, "Sometimes failure is success, son. I'm counting on you. Don't let me, or your country down."

The *slam* of the door echoed throughout the room. James Johnson sat thinking about what had just happened, for longer than a few minutes.

CHAPTER 18

Tristan's vision remained cloudy and the sunlight shining into his face gave him a headache. He sat on the floor and tried to rub the throat pain away, wondering which one of them would speak first.

"Who are you?" came the low grumble from across the room.

He was now able to get a hazy visual of the man, crouching down, clasping his gun. "PFC Tristan Wood, First Platoon Falcon Company, US Marine Corps."

"Where were you stationed?"

"Firebase Vimoto, Korengal Valley." He attempted to focus. "You?"

"The KOP."

KOP was short for Korengal Outpost in Afghanistan, the US military base up the Korengal River, northeast of Firebase Vimoto. The KOP was the most dangerous base in the Valley at the time. It certainly suffered the greatest number of casualties.

"What are you doing here?" the man asked.

"Well, after I got shot they gave me a Purple Heart and I came back to the states."

"You know what I mean, smartass. Are you here to kill me?"

"Kill you? I'm FBI," Tristan said, shifting his position to avoid the blinding sun.

"FBI?"

"I'm looking for James Johnson, and I'm pretty sure that's you."

"What makes you think that?"

"I'm lead agent on the Train Bomber case."

"I got no idea what you're talking about."

"The assassination attempt of the president, in Union Station? You know exactly what I'm talking about."

"You got the wrong guy, friend."

"I saw the 'Infidel' tattoo on the Amtrak surveillance video."

James scratched his face with the gun and sized up the intruder.

"Show me your ID."

Tristan held it up.

"Toss it over."

With a flick of the wrist the badge landed at James' feet.

It struck Tristan that his impulse to say "damn the valley" had saved his life. It was an inside joke among the troops in the Korengal Valley, something they said to each other daily. It was also a phrase only marines from that part of the world would understand.

"Listen, my partner is out back, do me a favor and let him in. We need to talk."

The sunspots were clearing up and his vision was improving.

"What if I don't want to?"

"We can get the entire Washington, DC, FBI field office after you and do things the hard way. It's up to you, James."

After a moment of consideration he stood up and walked over to Tristan who winced, expecting a potential blow to the head.

"No one calls me James except my momma and she's dead. It's J.J."

He gave back the FBI badge.

"Can I have my gun? It's government issued, I'm responsible for it."

He engaged the safety and handed over the Glock, then opened one of the sliding glass doors. Tristan sighed in relief as a blast of warm air entered the room.

J.J. walked across the jaundiced pavement stones of the patio and unlocked the gate for Sebastian, who apprehensively followed him back inside.

Tristan struggled to his feet.

"What happened to you?" Sebastian asked.

"I was a little sloppy coming in through the window," he lied.

Small things like this showed good faith. It was imperative he gain the trust of a potential informant.

"Is this him?"

"This is James Johnson. His friends call him J.J." Tristan said with mild sarcasm before introducing his partner. "Meet FBI Special Agent Sebastian Graves."

J.J. held out a hand to shake, but Sebastian grabbed his arm, turning it over to look at the tattoo.

"So what were you doing on the Amtrak train, James?"

He buttoned up, not wanting to talk.

"Surveillance video doesn't lie. You followed the Train Bomber to Union Station and stuck around until he lit the fuses. Why did you do that?" Tristan asked.

"My job was to follow the guy and make sure he didn't get cold feet."

"But as close as you were, you would have been killed instantly," Sebastian pointed out.

"Except they were dummy fuses, right?" Tristan added.

"The bomb was never supposed to go off. He didn't know. That's why I was keeping an eye on him."

"For what reason?"

"I don't get those details. The Major tells me what to do and I do it."

"The Major? Who is that, your boss?"

"Before I tell you any more, I want to make sure you're not gonna throw me to the wolves. These people answer to no one. They will take me out, in a heartbeat."

"You should have thought about that before you started down this career path!" Sebastian said.

Tristan was now able to examine the man who had almost killed him. Somewhere in his late twenties, J.J. had pale skin and close-cropped blond hair with blue eyes, his biceps indicating he spent serious time in the gym. No wonder it had been impossible to break free of the choke-hold. Besides the tattoo on his forearm, the only other distinguishing feature was his crooked nose, which looked like it had been broken several times.

"Take me in."

"What?"

"I'll confess to everything but I want to be put into witness protection."

"We don't care about you," Sebastian berated. "You're worthless, you're nothing. We want your boss."

"The Major?"

"You bet."

"This is going to get me killed. If he finds out I'm talking to you, I'm dead. Do you realize that? I want witness protection!"

Sebastian slammed him up against the wall and FlexCuff'd him. The move surprised Tristan as much as J.J., who yelped in pain.

"What are you doing?"

"You're going to cooperate."

He snapped a picture with his cell phone.

"Come on, what the hell?" J.J. protested.

"You are going to play ball or I will plaster your name and photo all over the internet so this boss of yours can read all about how you got busted by the Feds. Then you can mutually settle your differences. Unless you want to start talking?"

So this is the temper I've heard about.

Attempting to brush off what had just happened, Tristan got back on point. "Who is the Major, J.J.?"

"Only because you're a marine. I'm only telling you because you're a marine," he spoke to Tristan. "I'm in over my head, this is all getting out of control, this is not what I signed-up for."

"You can trust us," he promised.

"I don't exactly know who he is. He recruited me out of Special Forces. He's the head of a black-ops group. He asked me to serve my country. I thought I'd be working domestic terrorism cases but once I joined, it became about entrapping people and setting up fake incidents."

"Fake incidents? You mean false flags," Sebastian corrected him.

"Yeah, false flags. He told me the real threat in this country is the militia movement, those who believe in small government, who want to get rid of the IRS and the Federal Reserve, Christians, even people carrying around pocket Constitutions. The Department of Homeland Security has been working for years to shift the fear of terrorists from Middle Eastern Muslims to white Christian males. They are trading in 'Islamic terrorist' for 'domestic terrorist,' singling out patriot groups like the Tea Party. At first I thought the Major was worried about anti-government attacks, but I realized it's because these folks are the ones who will resist."

"Resist what?" Tristan asked.

"Believe me, that's kept me up nights. I do know this, there's an organized campaign to discredit and blame them. They've been gradually changing public perception of members of the Tea Party and militia groups, through the media, to racists and terrorists. Right now they are making videos, infomercials, with all the terrorists as white males, moving the ads from the internet to television. There's a word he used . . . incrementalism. That's it."

"And you signed-up for this?" Sebastian sounded judgmental.

"I thought I was working to stop domestic terrorism, real threats! By the time I realized what was really going on, it was too late. I couldn't get out." J.J. leaned back against the wall, deflated. "I swore to never talk. I'm dead."

Tristan walked over and released the FlexCuffs.

"We'll look after you, but we are going to need you to do another job for this Major. We'll protect you."

"Oh, okay. You'll protect me?" J.J. quipped.

"Am I missing something?" Tristan asked.

"The Major is military. He's connected with the Pentagon. Everything he does is covert. If he gets suspicious I'm a rat, it's all over."

"That's why you thought I was here to kill you?"

"I've had bad vibes lately. You know the gut feeling you get when something terrible is coming?"

Tristan shot a glance at Sebastian before answering, "Yeah, I think we do."

"How did you find me?"

"We met your sister."

J.J. hesitated. "How is she?"

"Worried about you."

"Jill is my only family."

"What's your next job?" Sebastian got back to brass tacks.

"Don't know, I haven't heard from the Major since the Train Bomber gig. I was worried he'd get rid of me."

"How do you two communicate?"

"He gave me a phone number. I leave a message and he calls me back when he wants to. I've left a bunch of messages, but nothing."

"Okay, so try again," Sebastian said. "You keep bugging him until he calls, even if it's to tell you he doesn't need you. Then contact us."

"Contact you how? There are no secure phone lines or emails anymore."

"Do you have GPS on your phone?" Tristan asked.

J.J. held up his cell, "Yeah, I do."

"I'm going to give you my number, but only text me. We'll communicate using GPS coordinates. When someone texts a location, we get there within the hour."

"You'll work with us as an informant then, yes?" Sebastian wanted a verbal agreement.

"Yeah, okay."

Tristan confirmed the programing of his cell number into the phone.

"We'll head out the back door. Let us know when your boss contacts you." Sebastian pulled open the slider, letting in a rush of warm humid air.

"You guys better be careful," J.J. said as the agents headed out the sliders onto the patio. "From what the Major tells me, there are tons of spies in FBI."

Sebastian passed a bottle of water to Tristan who massaged his throat. He already had a black eye and hoped no visible marks would materialize. Allyson would kill him.

"What did you mean by false flag?"

"You remember the term false flag from your FBI field manual?"

"I think so. You attack your own side and blame it on your enemies to gain support for your cause, support you may not have," Tristan answered.

"A bomb that's not supposed to explode, yet appear as a presidential assassination attempt? It's a classic false flag."

"With what goal?"

"There are always multiple reasons for a false flag operation. The Train Bomber, I would guess, is being used to boost the abysmal presidential poll numbers and to add support to the National Defense Authorization Act. More importantly, I believe this one is to get the Patriot Act renewed again. It's due to be voted on at the end of the week and right now a majority of Americans believe it's unconstitutional. Watch the polls, if I'm right they'll swing to the other side and even the most draconian parts of the Patriot Act will pass. I think this time, however, it might be for something bigger."

"Like what?"

"Not sure. It could be specifically to ramp-up the police state. Look for a big push in the media to get body scanners into train stations, bus terminals, and smaller airports. Those scanners are worth hundreds of millions of dollars; follow the money."

"So if you follow the money, where does it lead?" Tristan asked.

"It always leads back to defense spending, in this case, the Chertoff Group."

"As in Michael Chertoff, the old Secretary of Homeland Security?"

"To get the airport body scanners we have now, the *Underwear Bomber* was used on Christmas Day 2009. It was my last case, in Detroit FBI, before I retired. Michael Chertoff was Secretary of Homeland Security from 2005 until President George W. Bush left office in January 2009. At the time, Rapiscan Systems was one of two manufacturers of the body scanners sold to TSA, and one of his security firm's clients."

"I remember that! There was some coverage in the news but didn't last long; it was a clear conflict of interest," Tristan said.

"They couldn't get the airports to buy and install them. The machines were incredibly expensive with no public support. Then an interesting coincidence happened. Just before Chertoff left DHS to work full time for his security group we had the *Underwear Bomber* incident on flight 253, and all of a sudden the politicians were calling for them regardless of the cancer risks from radiation and the constitutional violations. After the bombing attempt, Chertoff went on a national media tour promoting the use of the scanners without disclosing he was getting paid by Rapiscan. He got a couple softball questions about it but reporters basically ignored the subject and gave him a pass."

"I refuse to go through the scanners, never have. Treating Americans like criminals, guilty until proven innocent, it's a shakedown without probable cause."

"It violates the fourth amendment." Sebastian took out a pocket Constitution and read; "The right of the people to be secure in their persons, houses, papers, and effects, against unreasonable searches and seizures, shall not be violated, and no warrants shall issue, but upon *probable cause*, supported by oath or affirmation, and particularly describing the place to be searched, and the persons or things to be seized."

"The Founding Fathers are rolling over in their graves right now, aren't they?"

"Even Stalin and the Nazi's didn't have the gall to pat down their own citizens in such public situations. At least they had the 'courtesy' of dragging them into private cellars or gulags to violate their civil rights," he said.

"With the *Underwear Bomber*, why wouldn't they blow up the plane and scare us even more?"

"Because then whoever is in charge gets blamed for American deaths, they have to admit failure, and public support decreases. It's always about the next election and the subsequent power. You can't use the 9/11 excuse, that you were caught off-guard, when it's the same type of event you're supposed to be trying to prevent. The next one will have to be an entirely new type of attack. That way the government can claim it's something they never would have imagined."

"The *Underwear Bomber* sure did create fear."

"And remember when Chertoff's replacement, Janet Napolitano, actually came out and bragged that their procedures to protect the American people were a success?"

"I do; what a joke. The only reason the plane didn't blow up was because the bomb didn't explode, not because any security measures worked."

"The dirty little secret the media won't touch is, the bomber was allowed to get on the plane. It's quite a story, I'll give you the details another time. What's sad is Americans resisted the body scanners at first, and for much longer than the establishment expected. For the most part, now people are used to them. There are still isolated incidents of folks resisting, but they only get attention when the videos are uploaded to YouTube. The media no longer investigates or questions it. The reason for the airport scanners is not to protect us from terrorists, it's to condition us to obey the government."

Tristan rubbed his bad leg and shifted in his seat as Sebastian continued.

"This state of war we are in only serves as an excuse for domestic tyranny, and the 'war on terror' is literally never going to stop. By keeping the population in a constant state of fear, the globalists can erode liberties in the name of security. They've finally found the everlasting war. It's not like fighting a Germany or Japan. Now it's an enemy we can't name, can't see, and are dependent on the government to protect us from. There have been hundreds of admitted government sponsored terror attacks throughout history."

"Like what?" Tristan asked.

"There's the Reichstag Fire used by Hitler to take complete control of the government, and Himmler's other false flag; the Gleiwitz Incident. Nazis, dressed as Polish soldiers, took over the German radio station in Gleiwitz to create the appearance of Polish aggression to justify the country's invasion. Operation Ajax was the coup in Iran instigated by Kermit Roosevelt in the 1950s to overthrow the people-friendly Mossadegh for the oil-friendly Shah. More recently there's the Gulf of Tonkin Incident."

"The Gulf of Tonkin was a false flag?"

"The official story of the Gulf of Tonkin Incident was that on August 2 and 4, 1964, the North Vietnamese attacked US ships in the Gulf of Tonkin leading to President Lyndon B. Johnson's dramatic buildup of American troops in the region. The second incident, on August 4, specifically led to the approval of the Gulf of Tonkin Resolution, which resulted in the Vietnam police action and the death of over 58,000 American men. In 2005, an internal National Security Agency historical study was declassified. It concluded that the US Maddox had engaged the North Vietnamese navy on August 2, but since it did not create the desired public anti-North Vietnamese response, they staged an event on August 4. Data was skewed, facts ignored, and men were threatened into silence."

"But we're taught in school that this was an historic event, a slap in the face of America that prompted us to retaliate?" Tristan said.

"Textbooks still contain the official story, though it's admittedly wrong. There's even a CNN report on YouTube where Robert McNamara, LBJ's secretary of defense, admits he doesn't know what transpired that day. Traveling to North Vietnam, he asked General Nguyen Giap, the Vietnam Commander at the time, if there was indeed an attack on August 4? The reply was 'nothing happened'." Sebastian took a breath, and a gulp of water. "And of course, there's the biggest and baddest of them all; *Operation Northwoods*."

"I've never heard of that."

"You're not alone, most folks haven't. There is no other bit of proof that factions of our government sponsor, support, and carry out domestic terror attacks than Operation Northwoods," Sebastian was in the zone. "Again it's all admitted and out in the open thanks to the Freedom of Information Act. The documents can be viewed online. It came to light five months before 9/11 and has been branded, 'the most corrupt plan ever created by the US government.' In 1962, a year before the assassination of President John F. Kennedy and two years before the Gulf of Tonkin Incident, Attorney General Robert Kennedy ordered a stop to all anti-Castro covert efforts. So General Lyman Lemnitzer, chairman of the Joint Chiefs of Staff, decided the only option was to trick the American public into a justified overt war with Cuba. He brought a plan to Secretary of Defense McNamara called *Operation Northwoods*, which was presented to JFK."

"So what's the gist of it?" Tristan shifted in the seat.

"Operation Northwoods gave a detailed description of a false flag event to create the appearance that a Cuban aircraft attacked and shot down a chartered US civilian airliner en route to Jamaica, Guatemala, Panama, or Venezuela. The destination would be chosen so the aircraft would cross over Cuba. The passengers would be students, or another group with a common interest to support the story of why it was a chartered flight. A second aircraft, labeled 'drone' in the report because it would be controlled remotely, would be painted and numbered as an exact duplicate then substituted with the passengers boarding under prepared aliases. The chartered aircraft would land at an auxiliary field at Eglin AFB where the passengers would be evacuated."

"Eglin Air Force Base, in the Florida panhandle?"

"That's the one. When it passed over Cuba the drone would transmit a MAYDAY international distress frequency claiming the plane was under attack, to be picked up by pilots who could later testify to it. The transmission would be interrupted by the destruction of the drone, allowing ICAO radio stations in the Western Hemisphere to listen to what was happening in real-time. That way the US wouldn't have to 'sell' the story, the media would do it for them. Included in the elaborate plan, a submarine or small surface craft would disburse F-101 parts in the ocean to be found by dispatched search ships and aircraft, to reinforce the scenario."

"My Lord, it sounds like 9/11," Tristan said.

"There are quotes from numerous people, ex-intelligence, who stated as they watched the events unfold on September 11, 2001, that Operation Northwoods had finally been executed."

"The Joint Chiefs of Staff came up with this?"

"They brought it to JFK, who rejected it. Not long after that, and while working to get the US out of Vietnam, he was assassinated and the plan remained a conspiracy theory for thirty-five years. It can be downloaded as a PDF from the National Security Archive website for anyone to read."

"Hidden in plain sight."

"When something is mocked as a conspiracy theory because it's too elaborate, ask them if they know about Operation Northwoods. This is all public information, admitted by our own government, and easily researched. Yet a very small segment of our population is aware of it."

Tristan started the car's engine. "Let's get out of here." He located a pain pill and swallowed it.

"Is there something I should know?"

"War injuries," Tristan said as he put the car into *drive*.

As they left the housing development, Sebastian held a concerned gaze on him just a bit too long.

CHAPTER 19

D octor Allyson Wood tried to think happy thoughts to expel the butterflies from her stomach as she waited for Nurse Julie to finish assisting another M.D. Submitting the paperwork to the hospital's lab was causing her hands to shake nervously.

Before deferring to a gynecologist, Allyson had decided a reasonable first step would be blood work for her and a fertility test for Tristan. If the results were normal they could continue the natural way and avoid invasive testing. Besides, medical record privacy no longer existed even for healthcare workers, and hospitals gossiped like any other workplace.

She tried to divert Julie's attention from her fretfulness by pretending she had forgotten a signature. But the act was not Oscar-worthy and the veteran nurse saw through it.

"It'll be all right, dear," Julie said, squeezing Allyson's hands in an attempt to comfort her.

Allyson teared up and smiled, *thank you.*

She made her way back towards the Walter Reed Emergency Room and stopped in the cafeteria for a cup of hot tea.

Decaf, she thought, still trying to relax.

Allyson believed the individual was in control of most outcomes in life. Or at least, she told herself that. If there was a problem with either of them, it would be best to know and correct it. Though opiates did reduce male fertility, guilt tormented her for allowing Tristan to believe it could just as easily be his fault when she was unable to get rid of the intense feeling it was her, that she was being punished—

"Doctor Wood, please report to Doctor Michaels' office. Doctor Wood, please report to Doctor Michaels' office," came an announcement over the intercom.

Minutes later she was leaning against the familiar bookshelf stacked top to bottom with journals and magazines. The residents waited for their mentor to address them. He sat at his desk, a medical book open in front of him.

"I want us to be prepared when the ambulances arrive," Doctor Michaels said without looking up.

They exchanged confused looks.

"Sir?" Allyson spoke up.

Doctor Michaels had a habit of assuming those around him already knew what topic he was discussing, a quirk that annoyed the residents at times.

"Eight men, an army fireteam, simultaneously come down with headaches, disorientation, fatigue, dizziness, vomiting, and muscular pain. What might we have going on, any ideas?"

"Some kind of flu virus?" a female resident asked.

"Not likely with an acute manifestation in this many people at once."

"Where were they when they became ill?" Doctor Woo inquired.

"Well, we don't know that yet, so let's work with what we do know; the symptoms."

"Food poisoning?" someone suggested.

"The muscle pain makes me suspicious."

"Sounds like brucellosis to me," Allyson said, drawing laughs from the others.

"Gulf War Syndrome? That doesn't exist, it's a conspiracy theory," Woo ridiculed.

This made her feel sick to her stomach. She didn't understand why, but it did.

"What makes you think it doesn't exist?" Doctor Michaels snapped back. "Over one hundred thousand vets came home from the first Gulf War with an illness no one could diagnose."

Doctor Woo didn't seem to expect the challenge. "Well, my teachers in med school said it was never proven, many had a form of shell-shock and others imagined it."

"So all those men and women were afflicted with the same debilitating malady, and imagined it? That sounds like a conspiracy theory to me." Some of the residents chuckled. "Actually, Gulf War Syndrome is so common the Pentagon has been forced to admit it's a legitimate illness. After an investigation it was found the British and American troops became sick after receiving a series of untested vaccines. The French didn't receive the vaccines and did not become sick. And what do we know about vaccines?"

"They depress the immune system," Allyson answered when no one else would.

"Absolutely. When your immune system is compromised you become susceptible to any number of environmental agents. Saddam's stockpile of brucellosis mutated and became airborne, he had depleted uranium in antitank shells, and petrochemical fumes were released into the air from oil well fires. Expose someone with a bad immune system to all this and you get what we now call *Gulf War Syndrome*. Add in the stress of battle, and you've got a health disaster."

"But these guys coming in, they weren't in the Middle East?" another resident pointed out.

"Are you familiar with acinetobacter baumannii, the superbug the troops called Iraqibacter? Eventually it spread into the civilian population and the CDC labeled it Chronic Fatigue Syndrome. Back in 2010, CDC admitted there were over one million cases of it in the United States and over ten million with symptoms fitting the description. You've told me your father identified similar ailments in Vietnam, right?"

Allyson nodded yes.

He continued, "We first used Agent Orange and other chemicals on the enemy in Vietnam. It got into the air, food, and water affecting our own troops, and after it resurfaced in the 1990s Colonel Grant went public about it. Imagine watching those poor men tormented with a undiagnosed illness."

"Your father is Thom Grant?" Woo perked up. "*The* Colonel Grant?"

"Who's that?" another resident asked.

"You've never heard of Colonel Grant, the war hero? His squad was sent to blow up an enemy bridge over the Cua Viet River."

"What happened?"

"Everyone in the squad was killed during that mission. Private Grant . . . he was a private then, right? And young?" Woo confirmed.

"Eighteen years old," Allyson said.

"They were ordered to take out a bridge over the Cua Viet River, heavily guarded by the North Vietnamese along a supply route. When they got to their destination, they were ambushed. Everyone in his unit was wiped out, including the commanding officer. So Private Grant single handedly hauled the explosives himself, planted them and blew up the bridge, all while under enemy fire. But here's where it gets good; the North Vietnamese who fired on him, and witnessed what he did, put down their arms and let him go out of respect for his bravery. Oliver North actually did an episode on *War Stories* about him."

"Wow, your dad is a hero?" another resident asked.

"Like father like daughter."

Before anyone could ask what their boss meant, his office phone rang.

"The ambulances have arrived, doctor," a nurse announced over the speaker-phone, the noise of activity in the background.

"Thank you," he said before hanging up. "Everyone wears a mask and gloves." He put Allyson in charge of handing them out.

The group left the office as the first man, dressed in a strange type of uniform, was wheeled in on a gurney. The soldiers wore full-dress black, even the boots and hats. A patch with dark blue and red stitching contained a coat of arms with several animals including a lion and horse.

In the center of the design were the letters; *DHS.*

Within minutes all eight patients reposed on beds, two to a room. Doctors swarmed like bees, getting information from the EMS team and setting up IV racks and monitors.

Allyson checked one young army PFC, looking pale and weak. "How are you doing?" she spoke through her mask.

"Been better."

"Can you tell me what happened, private?" She inserted the IV needle and began to bandage the area.

"We were training and I got dizzy. At first I figured it was dehydration, but everybody else got sick too."

"All eight in your squad?"

"Everyone, except Corporal Lowery. He kept pushing us but people weren't feeling good so we took a break. Then it got worse. I heard something behind me, and when I looked back, one of the guys was facedown. We gathered around to see what was wrong and another passed out. That's when the corporal called-in for help."

"Where were you?"

"I can't say, ma'am." He vigorously scratched his left upper arm.

"What do you mean you can't say? You don't know or you won't tell me?"

The private occupying the second bed was now out cold.

"I'm not allowed to say, it's a classified training exercise," he wiped sweat from his forehead.

"If you don't tell me everything, the chances we can help you decline significantly. An entire squad comes down with the same illness at the same time? Sounds like an infectious agent to me. Probably life threatening."

"Infectious what?"

"A contagious disease, and most likely a nasty one. It's a long drawn-out painful way to suffer, bleeding from different parts of your body, one of the worst ways to die, actually." She felt bad scaring him but had no choice—a transmittable pathogen put her life in danger as well.

Scratching his left side again, he spoke almost in a whisper. "We were at the state fairgrounds, at Meadow Farm, down near Richmond."

"Richmond? Why did they bring you all the way up here? What were you doing?"

"Running drills on how to police a town after a gas attack, to keep people indoors during martial law, confiscate guns . . ." he closed his eyes as the blood left his face.

"What are these uniforms you're wearing? You're army, why the Homeland Security patches?" she posed it as a casual question.

Delirious, he replied weakly, "I follow orders, ma'am."

"Corporal Lowery, is that you squad leader's name?"

"Yes, ma'am."

"Did he do anything to you?" Eliciting no response, Allyson shook him but he did not wake.

The monitor showed stable vitals. She moved to the opposite side of the bed and lifted the sleeve where he had scratched several times. A silver dollar-sized circular rash on his upper arm surrounded a miniscule red dot of dried blood.

"Pin prick," she mumbled to herself.

Inspecting the second soldier, she discovered a similar mark in the same location on his arm. Allyson walked out, moving between rooms until she found Doctor Michaels, talking with the one man who did not display symptoms.

"Can I speak with you for a moment? Privately." She pulled her boss aside. "I want you to see something."

Allyson led him to the sick man in the other bed and rolled up the sleeve—another needle puncture. Dr. Michaels acquiesced with a nod. Anger overtook her. She approached the corporal and lifted his shirt but there was no mark. He slapped her hand away.

"What did you inject these men with, corporal?" Allyson demanded.

"What?"

"You heard me, soldier."

"I don't know what you're talking about, little lady."

"All these men, except for you, have a fresh needle mark on their upper left arm. They all apparently came down with the symptoms at the same time, what did you inject them with?"

"Listen sweetheart, I don't—"

"Don't call me lady, or sweetheart. I'm an Army Medical Corps officer. You're their squad leader, if just one dies because you didn't tell us what you injected them with, I will personally hold you accountable. Corporal Lowery is it?"

This made him nervous, yet still not eager to talk. He glanced at his wristwatch.

"This might be highly contagious, what do you think?" Doctor Michaels directed the question to Allyson, who picked up on the artifice.

"It could mutate. With these symptoms we may have a new Ebola-type microbe on our hands. If he starts bleeding from the ears, nose, and eyes, we'll have a better idea what it is."

Corporal Lowery began to squirm.

"This man is seriously ill," Doctor Michaels referred to the patient in the next bed. "If we confine these two in the room together, without ventilation, we will determine in a matter of minutes if it's pestilent."

"Good idea, faster than getting lab work done." They began to walk out.

"Jeez, okay. Look I didn't give them the shots."

"Then who did?" Allyson asked.

"I don't know exactly, we were running a biological attack scenario. I was told someone would come by, which they did, to give them test shots as part of the exercise."

"Test shots?"

"An experimental antidote for a simulated nerve gas attack."

"Why did you bring them here? Fort Belvoir or even Virginia Beach were closer. Think of the time you would have saved!?"

"I was just following orders. Damn, I already said too much, damn." He checked his wristwatch again.

A commotion erupted in the building.

"Finally," Corporal Lowery sighed in relief.

"Finally what?"

Allyson stepped out of the examination room to the thunderous sound of heavy boots. Multiple figures in yellow Level A/Type 1 hazmat suits stormed the hallway.

"CDC! This section of the hospital is quarantined!"

The impermeable uniforms included helmets equipped with built-in breathing apparatus to protect the person inside from infectious bacteria, viruses, and other contaminants. The CDC shifted into isolation mode, blocking off rooms and preventing staff from leaving the area.

"We are with the Centers for Disease Control and Prevention. This wing of Walter Reed hospital is now under the authority of the Department of Homeland Security," said the man in charge. "Everyone here, staff and patients, are quarantined until further notice. We appreciate your cooperation."

What distressed Allyson, however, was that these health professionals, in their yellow hazmat suits, had something else in common.

They carried automatic weapons.

CHAPTER 20

Sebastian Graves never imagined he would be attending his own son's funeral. He had decided to bury Jason in a secluded Virginia cemetery with wide open space and plenty of trees. It was a peaceful setting, though the heat was making it rather uncomfortable for the men, all of whom wore suits. An uplifting sermon from a Catholic priest seemed to comfort the twenty or so guests.

The turnout was dismal for a young man who had served his country in law enforcement, and the son of a decorated FBI agent. But Sebastian knew the reason—the spy accusation. Many would not show up simply because of the potential association with Jason. Paranoia was common in the Bureau, sometimes imagined and other times legitimate.

Reminiscing on the past evoked pains of guilt in his chest.

FBI policy, during most of his career, was to transfer special agents to a different field office in a new city every couple of years. Since agents served at the pleasure of the director they had no choice. Some families learned to adjust and others broke up.

Because of this lifestyle Jason was never able to establish roots, tough on an only child. While a freshman in high school, his mother left them, cutting off all communication. It sent Jason over the edge and he blamed his father. Sebastian did the best he could and worked hard to keep his son out of trouble during those teenage years. Somehow, Jason managed to graduate near the top of his class and go to college. But he never lost his wild side.

Robert Wood stood nearby with his wife. Sebastian had met them today for the first time.

Nice of them to come, he thought.

SAC Tufts, by himself and disjoined from the group, stared at the ground. The service came to an end and folks walked back to their cars, some stopping to express their sympathies. Robert and Sarah said goodbye and were the last to leave.

Finally, just Sebastian and Tristan remained.

"It was a nice service."

"I'm sorry Allyson couldn't be here."

"She is too. We're not sure how long the quarantine will go on."

"Is she okay?"

"No one, with the exception of the troops they brought in, has come down with any symptoms. She hinted that there was something big she knew, but couldn't talk about it over the phone."

"Was she able to tell you anything?"

"Only that the infected men were training at the Virginia state fairgrounds, down near Richmond, an area called Meadow Farm. I figured I'd drive down and check it out."

"Okay, let's go," Sebastian said without hesitation, loosening his tie.

"Are you sure you're up to it?"

"I don't want to sit around today. It's better to keep busy."

Little traffic impeded their drive south on I-95 toward Richmond. Sebastian used Tristan's smart phone to do some research on the internet during the trip. After a few minutes surfing the web he found the information he wanted.

"Yep, I thought so."

"What?"

"The State Fair of Virginia at Meadow Farm is a FEMA camp. Seems the company that operates the fair bought the 347 acre parcel in the summer of 2003 for $5.3 million. It's the birthplace of Secretariat. They even built a museum for the memory of the champion race horse."

"How can a state fair also be a FEMA camp?"

"They use the grounds for the fair a couple weeks out of the year, the rest of the time the government rents it out. It's not uncommon."

Sebastian switched the phone back to GPS mode and they exited I-95, heading down a deserted dirt road. A high metal fence appeared in the distance.

"I don't see any Ferris wheels or roller coasters?"

"Don't park right in front, let's drive around and find an alternative way in."

Tristan turned down a desolate pathway, overgrown with tall grass, but easily managed by his Jeep Wrangler. The chain-link barricade seemed to go on forever.

"There's another entrance up ahead. Stop here, let's walk," Sebastian said.

They left their suit jackets behind and followed the fence, looking for a better view inside.

"Why would FEMA rent out land used as a state fair?"

"The Federal Emergency Management Agency is in charge of the detention centers under the jurisdiction of the Department of Homeland Security. The overall plan of FEMA is to evacuate whole cities and use the camps as temporary housing, whether for natural disasters, or nuclear, biological, and chemical attacks under the pretext of planning for a war on terrorism."

Through the bushes and small trees Tristan could make out structures, but getting a clear view was difficult. They continued on.

"So what makes this a FEMA camp?"

"Well, most camps are currently situated on military bases, reported as closed, or designated *inactive* and maintained by skeleton crews. Others are on rented private property and operated directly by FEMA. Many have been around since WWII and were used to hold Axis prisoners during the war."

"You mean like the one hundred and ten thousand Japanese Americans FDR imprisoned in 'War Relocation Camps'?" Tristan recalled a bit of history no longer taught in public schools.

"Correct." Sebastian stepped over a small ditch. "According to their own website, the modern-day camps can be fully-functional within seventy-two hours and only appear deserted. They come complete with barracks, dining facilities, latrines, and showers. If the military has been training here, I'll bet the operation is under FEMA jurisdiction. Thanks to the Patriot Act and the NDAA, the president can declare a national emergency by executive order for any reason and take over the country without deferring to Congress, and force millions into FEMA camps. American citizens can now be indefinitely detained like those in Guantanamo Bay."

"Who needs the Constitution anymore, right?" Tristan struggled moving his bad leg through the high grass.

"FEMA has camps set up across the nation, and many appear to be for logical reasons. You would assume a FEMA camp in New Orleans was there in case of a hurricane, right? But the globalists hide their insidious agenda behind what appears to be admirable works. The road to tyranny is always paved with good intentions."

"This one looks pretty inactive to me."

"Yet the army was training here and a squad came down with some sort of contagion?"

"Allyson couldn't say it over the phone, but I could hear it in her voice. She has radar for this type of thing. Something stinks."

"If these camps are indeed for public safety, why doesn't FEMA or Homeland Security list the locations on their website? Remember the days when school basements had the yellow and black radiation signs, identifying them as a nuclear fallout shelters?"

Tristan laughed. "Actually I don't."

"Yeah, I guess that was before your time. When I was a kid, everyone knew where the nearest bomb shelter was. Many families had them in their basements or backyards, it was normal. Now you're considered a conspiracy theorist and a right wing extremist if you have one. The CDC provides radiation emergency information in case of a nuclear power plant accident or dirty bomb, but no list of shelters. They just advise staying at home."

Tristan stopped and pointed at something inside the camp. "What are those?"

Multiple black walls rose over thirty feet high. Upon closer inspection, they appeared to be stacks of some kind of containers.

"I don't believe it," Sebastian said in horror. "Back in 2008, people started uploading videos on YouTube showing stockpiles of plastic sealable coffins, in different camps across the country. After months of denials, FEMA finally admitted they were *coffin liners.*"

"What's a coffin liner?" Tristan asked.

"It's a plastic, water-proof container designed to hold a casket."

"For what?"

"To prevent deterioration from the elements in the ground. The reason most folks don't know about them is because they aren't there during the funeral, on purpose. After the guests leave, the casket is placed in a coffin liner and buried."

The topic was difficult for Sebastian to describe, considering.

"You can even keyword 'coffin liner' and visit websites that sell them. One camp near the town of Madison, GA, was reported to have at least half a million of them. Atlanta, a few miles west, is home of the Centers for Disease Control."

"Why would FEMA have them in the first place? And why store them in camps?"

"Good question, and one FEMA will not answer. I don't know how the government justifies being in the funeral business. The liners can fit one coffin, or two to three people without them. But that's not all. There are also videos of huge cement crypts under construction built right into hillsides with hundreds of two feet by two feet cubby holes, just big enough to fit a human body. In the last few months, a flood of these videos has been showing up online, once again, as if FEMA is preparing for something."

The foliage became too thick for Tristan who grabbed on to the chain-link fence for balance. Now just yards from the back entrance, they gained a better view of the interior. A huge white-aluminum warehouse towered over a playground, and rows of picnic tables were positioned under several metal awnings. Other similar buildings peppered the camp, all with large padlocks on the doors. The grounds were meticulously landscaped.

Then Tristan noticed something. "Look at the top of the fence?"

"I wondered if you'd spot that."

"Why would the barbed wire be pointed inside? Do they want to keep people in?"

"You tell me—" the metallic clicking of automatic weapons interrupting Sebastian's reply.

"Halt!" the voice came loud and clear. "Put your hands in the air and turn around."

Tristan and Sebastian obeyed as four men pointed AK-47s at them. Their appearance was military but dressed in all black, even the boots and hats.

"We're FBI, no need to point those at us."

"What are you doing sneaking around here?" the man who seemed to be in charge asked.

Thinking fast, Sebastian said, "We're investigating a missing child report. The family of the little girl suggested the fairgrounds as a possible area to search."

"Then I guess you'll show us your badges, right?"

"Of course."

One of the soldiers approached to examine their IDs.

"Have ya'll seen anything unusual out here?" Tristan asked, being deliberately vague.

"This area is off-limits."

"Sorry, we didn't see any signs."

The man in charge seemed to think for a minute before speaking again. "We'll escort you to your Jeep and make sure you get on your way out of here."

Both agents exchanged glances, picking up on "Jeep."

"Not a problem, we were just leaving anyway."

On the march back to their vehicle Tristan felt his phone, still on the vibrate setting since the funeral. He started the engine and they drove off. The men did not lower their guns until they were far down the road.

Checking his cell, the text message read;

38°53'21.48"N ~ 77°3'0.40"W

"Guess who?"

"It's about time."

Sebastian turned on the radio and searched for music as they headed off to meet their new informant.

CHAPTER 21

Robert Wood sat in a plush suite of a luxury hotel in Chantilly, Virginia, busy with all the things a senator's aide did. The fortification of trees visible from the window, shielded any view of the protestors outside the property wall. This was the location for the infamous Bilderberg Group meeting, an annual secret gathering of the richest and most powerful people on the planet.

Although the hotel was just a few minutes' drive from his home, Robert would be spending the weekend here. Per the rules, attendees and their aides were required to stay the entire three days on the resort grounds for fear of information being leaked to outsiders. Senator Matthews had attended Bilderberg every year for decades and bragged that his name had yet to be mentioned in any media report, what few there were anyway.

"Go ahead and confirm the meeting Thursday with the Speaker. Then clear my schedule on Friday, I'll need some time off."

"Yes, Senator."

"I used to be able to work seven days a week. I'm too old for that anymore."

"You've still got more energy than I do," Robert laughed as he looked at his Fossil wristwatch. "You are due downstairs in ten minutes."

The senator struggled out of the chair, slowly and with difficulty. Over the past month, small things had become more of a challenge. The senator's regular medical check-ups did not show any unusual health problems, at least for a man his age.

Robert wondered if it had to do with his wife's death, recalling what happened with his own parents. His mother was diagnosed with breast cancer and after unsuccessful chemotherapy and radiation, within six months she passed.

The brothers observed the steady decline of their father shortly thereafter. He had no overt medical problems, yet started coming down with mysterious illnesses the family doctor was unable to diagnose. Then one day he collapsed and never recovered.

"How do I look?"

"Dapper as usual, Senator."

Robert helped straighten his tie.

"This should only take a couple of hours, it's the meet and greet. Not too many new folks this year."

The Bilderberg Group met for the first time in 1954 at the luxurious Hotel Bilderberg in the small Dutch town of Oosterbeek. The freshman assemblage spent the weekend debating global affairs with Prince Bernhard of the Netherlands presiding. When it was over they decided to convene every year in a different location.

This was the fourth time this century the meeting had been held in Chantilly, Virginia, in addition to 2002, 2008, and 2012. Wherever they went, the Bilderbergers took over the entire hotel even kicking out guests if necessary.

"Don't forget this." Robert handed him the electronic keycard.

"When I get back we'll go to dinner. You think the food in Moscow was good?" the senator said before the door clicked shut behind him.

Robert checked to make sure he still had his required neck-badge, then took the laptop back to his own room and placed it on the table. After the computer booted, he opened a browser with the Drudge Report coming up as the homepage. The headline gave him quite a shock;

Doomsday Clock - 4 Minutes to Midnight.

The Doomsday Clock was created in 1947 and set to seven minutes to midnight representing the state of the nuclear world at the time. It dropped to three minutes in 1949 as the Russians successfully detonated their first thermonuclear bomb, officially kicking off the nuclear arms race and the Cold War. Its lowest position ever was in 1953 when it fell to two minutes to midnight as a result of the Soviet Union and United States both detonating atomic bombs within nine months of each other.

The link took him to an article explaining the reason it moved closer was due to the continuing conflicts in the Middle East, as well as the new *contingency operations* in northern Africa. Interestingly, it did not take into account Robert and the senator having been held hostage in Moscow, the ambassador to Russia refusing to come back to the States, or the admission that the START treaties were futile.

A bookmark brought him to Daniel Estulin's Bilderberg website, his main source of research. He found the high-powered attendees over the years to be fascinating: Bill Clinton, Henry Kissinger, Tim Geithner, Gerald Ford, Zbigniew Brzezinski, Tony Blair, Gordon Brown, Margaret Thatcher, various Rockefellers and Rothschilds, Alan Greenspan, Condi Rice, John Kerry, Richard Perle, Donald Rumsfeld, George Stephanopoulos, more names than he could remember.

The long list included heads of government, businessmen, politicians, bankers, journalists, and presidents of organizations such as the World Bank, Federal Reserve, International Monetary Fund, Trilateral Commission, Council on Foreign Relations, not to mention the biggest corporations on the planet.

This year the group consisted of about 140 participants, their total worth exceeding the combined wealth of all United States citizens. The press was banned and no statements had ever been released on the topics discussed. Not surprisingly the meetings were able to stay secret, for the most part, since many were in control of the media. Checking the list, Robert discovered the senator was correct; his name was nowhere to be found.

A docket included a series of bullet points outlining the confidential subjects the members would discuss over the next three days. There was, deliberately, nothing to identify it as being associated with any particular person or group. If leaked, as had happened in the past, it could not be directly linked to the Bilderbergers. The agenda was particularly Russian-heavy this year, Senator Matthews would no doubt be a popular guest due to his recent escapades at the Spaso House in Moscow.

❖ **Dismantling of Russian Acquiescence to Western Influence** – President Putin continues to divert humanitarian aid to nuclear, chemical, and biological weapons programs. Exemption from OPEC allows competition with the United States and its allies for control of vital energy reserves in Central Asia.

❖ **Russian funding and support of Third World Nuclear Programs** – As the world's top supplier of conventional weapons and nuclear supplies, Third World counties continue to pursue nuclear weapons programs to immunize against US military strikes/invasion.

❖ **Middle East and US Conflict** – Discussion of permanent military bases in Iraq, Afghanistan drug warlord crisis, and contingency operations in Syria, Libya, Egypt, Tunisia, Yemen, continued support of Muslim Brotherhood, Arab Spring, and Mid-East Union.

❖ **Collapse of the European Union and Expansion of NATO** – Discuss future of North American, Asian, Pacific, and African Unions. Expansion of the world army through NATO, and Russian reaction.

❖ **Breaking Down Boundaries** – Empowering international bodies to destroy their national identity from within and implement universal values set forth by the United Nations. Further empowerment of UN with jurisdiction over US law.

❖ **Current US and World Economies** – The continuing world economic crisis and the US role as it relates to Zero-Growth policy, social crisis, and ecological imbalance. UN Agenda 21 and sustainable development continue to be pushed as environmental-ism, the need to dilute private property is a priority.

❖ **Russian War Games** – Moscow schedules series of war games to unify former Soviet States, promote patriotism, with Putin supervisor; exercise vs. real world. The plan remains on-track, the timetable set . .
.

Robert was unable to continue down the list, it was giving him a headache. He read through Daniel Estulin's website, searching for any updates. He closed his eyes and tried to frame the big picture into some kind of context.

The structure of the world chessboard amazed him, the way a small group of elites manipulated entire nations with their money and power. In fact, it was mind boggling.

He never imagined he would be in Chantilly, the senator had sprung this on him yesterday. It was normal, for even returning members, to remain in the dark until the last minute. As time went on, increasingly drastic measures were required to keep the location and agenda secret.

The Bilderbergers paid groups to put out disinformation, and this year the misdirection was to fool people into thinking it would be held in Toronto. But with spies everywhere and the power of the internet it was nearly impossible to conceal the real location. The true die-hards, specifically Jim Tucker, Daniel Estulin, and Alex Jones, had been researching and exposing the group their entire careers and could not be deceived so easily.

The meeting was being held in the United States, once again, for a very important reason. Politicians were subject to the Logan Act, intended to prohibit unauthorized US citizens from negotiating with foreign governments. The American members of the Bilderberg Group had evaded exposure of their participation in these secret meetings for over half a century.

But thanks to the free exchange of information on the internet, they were finally being called-out for this traitorous practice. Convening on American soil in the presence of foreign leaders was also a violation of the Logan Act, but it made it less likely any of the attendees would be held accountable.

Senator Matthews had become quite garrulous on the drive to Chantilly, the intonation of his voice shifting into a low demonic pitch that caused Robert's body to shudder. In his excitement, he had revealed a number of things about the power of Bilderberg. It was within this group that the plan to bomb Iran's nuclear facilities had been debated and plotted. Ousting leaders in Egypt, Syria, Libya, and other countries was always on the agenda.

They also chose presidential and vice-presidential candidates for both parties, funded by the same banking interests, and often cabinet members as well.

Still blindsided by their discussion of the new Yars-M ICBM and emboldened by his boss's unusual candor, Robert asked how a nuclear scenario would go down if the Russians were to launch first. The description utterly shocked him.

According to the senator, the strategy would not be to wipe out the US populace. The Kremlin's plan would target thirty-or-so major cities and reduce the US population by up to 40 percent. Most Americans would be spared to rebuild their country as slave-labor, after being defeated, and forced to adjust to Communism. Anthrax and other bio-terror attacks would suppress the pockets of armed resistance.

What most worried the Kremlin was the Second Amendment in the US Constitution. Uncooperative citizens would be put into camps, already built under FEMA, and those who did not comply with Moscow's demands would be deemed "unsalvageable." This meant they could not be re-educated—and would be executed.

In addition, this tactic would conquer Western Europe without firing so much as a shot, the decades of planting and bribing Western European leaders finally paying off.

The old man seemed to glow with power as he spoke and it made Robert feel sick. Before turning off the computer, he searched the term that President Putin had been using so often in recent speeches.

Ola Gigante.

A Russian language website translated it to;

Tidal Wave.

He folded a copy of the Bilderberg Group agenda and hid it under his shirt, locking the door to the room behind him. In lieu of riding the elevator, he descended the emergency stairwell to the main level and exited through the back of the hotel.

Robert took off the neck-badge as he strolled down a path toward the protestors, now numbering in the hundreds. The group shouted at every vehicle that approached the entrance, snapping photos and trying to videotape the passengers inside. Blending into the crowd, he pretended to be a curious passerby.

One person in particular caught his attention.

"David Rockefeller admitted in his own memoirs that he wants to destroy the United States! He's a traitor!" yelled a man through a bullhorn. "The answer to 1984 is 1776!"

Robert recognized him as Alex Jones.

Daniel Estulin, whose website he had just been perusing, gave an on-camera interview to citizen journalist Luke Rudkowski. But the person he was looking for sat in a portable chair on the sidewalk. Jim Tucker, a reporter who had made exposing the Bilderberg Group his life's work, smoked a cigarette while he observed the action around him.

Tucker was famous for locating sources to leak him the group's program and was able to get it every year. Robert imagined that even he would be surprised to have a complete stranger hand him the current agenda on day-one of the conference.

He felt no betrayal toward his boss since names were not revealed. From what he knew of the veteran reporter, he would be getting a copy of this from someone anyway.

Attending covert gatherings with heads of foreign governments to discuss world policies on American soil was both unlawful and unethical. The way the senator had bragged about the power of Bilderberg, he would sleep better knowing he had helped the few American patriots actually aware of the group.

He casually walked over to the husky man taking a long drag off his cigarette, and handed him the agenda.

"Keep up the good work," Robert said to Jim Tucker before hurrying off.

CHAPTER 22

Tourists roamed the grounds of the National Mall as children fed crackers to ducks in the Reflecting Pool, situated between the Washington Monument and the Lincoln Memorial. The surface of the undisturbed water mirrored an occasional fluffy cloud drifting by while a soft breeze rustled through the trees. To the east, the white-stone obelisk rose from the ground like a giant phallic symbol of freedom.

The two men scanned unfamiliar faces in an attempt to identify their informant. Both were now dressed in suits, jackets on and ties straight, on-the-clock and representing the Bureau. Sebastian looked like an entirely different person. For the first time since they met, Tristan saw him as a true FBI agent.

He checked his smart phone again.

"This is the location, give or take a degree." The GPS position was rounded up slightly from the text J.J. had sent;

38°53'21.48" N ~ 77°3'0.40" W

"He's probably just running late."

"Maybe," Sebastian said. "I don't trust this guy."

"He'll be here."

Tristan fondly recalled the last time he had been on the National Mall, a frosty day not too long ago in which the Washington area was battered by its first winter snowstorm. He had brought his girlfriend, Allyson Grant, to ice skate on the frozen Reflecting Pool. A thick layer of snow, plus the absence of traffic noise, beget an eerie post-apocalyptic feel.

They were quite a pair. Allyson, a southern girl, had never been on skates in her life and Tristan had not yet recovered from his leg injuries. However, they enjoyed each other's company and ended up kissing for the first time.

"Something occurred to me, Sebastian. When I hear people talk about conspiracies they always say 'they' are doing this or 'they' are doing that. Who are 'they'?"

"If you're asking what the head of the snake is, it's the world's most elite banking families—not the one percent but the one-tenth of one percent. Using the wealth and power of the banks, these international bankers control public policy via secret and semi-secret round-table groups including the Council on Foreign Relations, Trilateral Commission, and the Bilderberg Group. They fund politicians who will back legislation favorable to the banks, lest they be ousted in the next election. They also support governmental organizations, from intelligence agencies such as the NSA and CIA, to others within the federal government like the Department of Education, Department of Defense and Pentagon, as well as consortiums including the World Bank and IMF. The agenda works its way down through a maze of bureaucracy until it reaches us at the local level."

"Sounds like a kind of trickle down tyranny?"

"That's a great way to look at it, think of it as a pyramid. Anytime you question something, follow the money up and you'll always arrive at the international bankers in the capstone. There are approximately 6000 people on this planet who control over 95 percent of the world's land and wealth, but the top of the pyramid consists of 13 dynasty banking families who own the Federal Reserve, Bank of England, and the central banks in every first-world country around the world."

Sebastian rattled-off several names, some of which Tristan recognized and others he did not.

"They are the International Bankers, the Insiders, who create the currency and loan it back to us with interest in exchange for our sovereignty. These elites are monopoly men who seek to dominate society from behind the barrel of a gun, while working to disarm the rest of us. They are intentionally destroying the producers, bankrolling power through the government like a vacuum cleaner, sucking up the wealth from the middle class and transferring the money to offshore banks, leaving a wasteland of cultural and economic rubble as they go . . ."

"How did a handful of families get so much power?"

". . . By controlling the currency of entire countries through their central banks. Since the founding of this country, there had been a concerted effort to install a central bank in America. Wars were manufactured to force sitting presidents to borrow interest-bearing money from privately owned banks to pay for the conflicts, but Americans resisted. In the nineteenth century, the twenty-year charters of both the First and Second Banks of the United States expired and the people consistently voted for anti-central bank presidents. Finally, the banker-elites realized their wars weren't working and needed to change their tactics."

"To what?" Tristan asked.

"Their new plan was to create economic panics through boom-bust cycles. No one was better at this than J.P. Morgan, the richest and most powerful banker in the United States. To generate a panic, Morgan's banks called-in one third of their loans all at once while deflating the amount of currency in circulation. For fear of losing their money, depositors scrambled to withdraw their funds which created runs on the banks. This led to massive unemployment and misery. Morgan was then able to buy-up the assets of the failed loans at fire-sale prices and take over smaller independent banks as they went out of business. Simultaneously, they put out propaganda through the newspapers they owned claiming that a central bank was the only way to prevent future panics and provide economic stability. So when things were in place, J.P. Morgan manufactured the Panic of 1907. Then in 1910 a group representing some of the wealthiest families in the country met at J.P. Morgan's Jekyll Island Club in Georgia, under fake names, and put together what would become the Federal Reserve Act, establishing a permanent privately-owned central bank in America. Represented there were the Rothschilds, J.P. Morgan, and the Rockefellers. They used their insider in the Senate, Nelson Aldrich, to strong-arm the bill through Congress on December 23 during the rush to leave for Christmas vacation in 1913. Later, their other banker insider, President Woodrow Wilson, signed the bill into law. Now, with a central bank to loan money to the US government, they needed a reason to increase the national debt. After all, more debt means more interest, which means more profit. And what is the best way to create massive debt fast?"

"War?"

"Wars, conflicts, and the enormous military industrial complex to support them. Every war the US has been involved in, since and including WWI, has been manufactured to create debt as profit for the international bankers. But the central bank was just the first of a three-part plan for the Insiders. Next was a progressive, or graduated, income tax—the second plank of the Communist Manifesto—but not to help the needy by redistributing wealth. It was created by the Insiders to destroy their competition and insure the debt payments. J.D. Rockefeller himself said that 'competition is a sin'."

"And the third?"

"The third part of their plan was to shield themselves from paying those taxes. They did this through tax-free foundations which were already set up by the time the income tax was passed. The Rockefeller Foundation, the Carnegie Endowment, the Rhodes Trust, and others were used to hide their income and wealth. And since a progressive income tax had been previously found unconstitutional by the Supreme Court in 1894, they forced the passage of the 16th Amendment to make sure that would not happen again."

"Why a central bank?"

"Because the way to control a country is by issuing its currency through a central bank. Amschel Mayer Rothschild admitted as much when he stated, 'give me control of a nation's money and I care not who makes its laws.' The Founding Fathers were aware of the tyranny of a central bank—the fifth plank of the Communist Manifesto, by the way—and it was Thomas Jefferson who said that a central bank was more dangerous to our liberties than standing armies. In 1913 the bankers were successful, from years of plotting, and we got the Federal Reserve."

"How does a central bank control a country?"

"When you take out a loan for a car, a bank loans you money with interest attached. But how do they ensure you'll make your payments?"

"Collateral."

"Exactly. You pledge the car as collateral. Stop making payments, they keep the money you've already paid and repossess the car. So if you're loaning money to a government, how do you make sure you get paid?"

Tristan shook his head.

"You threaten to fund their enemy. Those leaders will then do anything to make the payments and stay in power, even at the expense of the sovereignty of the people. And if there's no enemy you create one. It's a strategy called 'balance of power' politics. This is what we did with the USSR."

"What do you mean?" Tristan asked.

"The USSR was literally made in the USA. The Rockefellers and other globalists funded the Bolsheviks, then transferred technology, money, and food aid during the Cold War to make sure Communism succeeded in Russia. It's the Hegelian Dialectic, used to foment a perceived clash among different ideological sides, in this case East versus West, and Communism versus Capitalism. By keeping the conflict between two sides like a football game, they keep us angry and fighting amongst ourselves, distracted from the true agenda. And to ensure we don't get another Andrew Jackson or Abraham Lincoln, the globalists make sure they always own both contenders in any two-horse race. Every Republican and Democrat presidential candidate is pre-chosen before the election and funded by the international bankers through Goldman Sachs, Citigroup, UBS, and J.P. Morgan interests. That way they don't lose. The ideal situation is to put, for example, a George Bush up against his cousin John

Kerry, both Skull & Bonesmen, and globalists who will do the bidding of the elites. It's about creating illusion of choice . . ."

"I had forgotten those two really were cousins!"

". . . So after they had the central bank, progressive income tax, and tax-free foundations, the next step was to establish their New World Order and rule over a global economy. This was the reason for WWI, not just to make money, but to create the League of Nations which was the framework for world government. It convened in 1919 in Paris but many countries considered this a threat to their sovereignty and refused to join. Frustrated with Congress blocking it, British intelligence with the help of the Rockefellers, set up the Council on Foreign Relations in 1921 in New York City. The CFR's stated mission was to abolish all nation states in favor of an omnipotent world government ruled by a tiny elite."

"But the League of Nations failed."

"It did, but temporarily. In the lead up to WWII, the bankers again were able to fund both sides of the war to make billions in personal profits. The same people who started the wars claimed only global governance could bring about world peace and save humanity from annihilation, and they succeeded at setting up the United Nations. The building was constructed in Manhattan with land donated by John D. Rockefeller. Since then, the World Council has been working on the incremental creation of continental super-states as a stepping stone to world government. But they are overextended. They've created too much world debt and it will soon be out of their control."

"Economic collapse?"

"Which is why I believe they'll have to make a move for world government before it all comes crashing down. When our stock market crashes, unemployment will skyrocket, the housing and credit markets will dry up again, food stamps, welfare, and government checks will stop, and there will be riots in the streets. It could backfire on them. The only thing preventing the collapse of the economy is our Federal Reserve printing trillions of dollars in scams like Operation Twist and the endless Quantitative

Easing. But it's a band-aid on a bullet wound and can't go on forever. All this money-printing is artificially propping up the stock and housing markets but they can't continue the charade. They may think they're gods but they aren't. Our economy is a fixed racket for the Insiders, teetering on the edge of ruin, propped-up in a Keynesian bubble."

"Wasn't the philosophy behind Keynesian economics 'In the long run we are all dead'?"

"That's the basis of his whole economic theory. Spend recklessly today because you'll be gone tomorrow, and throw future generations to the wolves. John Maynard Keynes was a Marxist whose theories are the basis of every economics class in American high schools and colleges. It's taught not as theory, but as fact. This is why most of the so-called economists on CNBC, Bloomberg, and Fox Business promote Keynesianism—they don't know any better. And even if they did, they're incapable of thinking outside the box. When they hear opposing theories, they slip into cognitive dissonance and shut down. This is why they didn't see the dot-com bubble in the late '90s, or the subsequent housing bubble, and they don't see the government-spending and bond bubble we've been in for years. However, when this one pops, our republic is finished. And it's all planned."

Both agents turned to walk toward the Lincoln Memorial.

"When do you think they'll collapse the system?"

"Unfortunately, I believe it'll be soon. Very soon."

Tristan looked around—no J.J. He checked his watch.

"How about we separate? You check out the central hall and I'll walk through the lower chambers," Tristan suggested.

"Sounds good to me."

Sebastian walked straight up and into the memorial while Tristan took a left, entering the door below the stairs. Moving between the three rooms, he longed to spend time looking at the photos of Lincoln. This was his favorite historical landmark.

He thought about Allyson and hoped to one day bring their children here. That is, if they were able to have children. And more importantly, if this was all still standing years from now. He stopped to read a quote etched into the wall; "A house divided against itself cannot stand."

"Where you been?" J.J. asked, keeping his head down and glancing around nervously.

"We were outside. Agent Graves is upstairs."

They rode the elevator to the main level where the nineteen foot statue designed by Daniel Chester French towered above them. The effigy faced east toward the Washington Monument across the Reflecting Pool. This allowed Lincoln to begin each day watching the sun rise over the new Atlantis.

"Why did you have us meet you here?" Sebastian asked, clearly irritated.

"It's a public place," J.J. put his sunglasses on.

"Exactly. We can't talk, too many people."

"Well, maybe I don't trust you yet."

"You don't say?" he snapped back.

Tristan did not think it was a good idea to have the first meeting with their new informant at the Lincoln Memorial, yet he was not lost on the irony. The nation was never more divided than at any time since the Civil War.

"I know where we can go, follow me."

The monument was designed with a relatively narrow walkway surrounding the entire structure. They arrived at the backside, looking west at the Arlington Memorial Bridge. They found themselves alone. Tristan remembered coming here in high school with friends, it was a terrific place to bring a girl and make out.

Sebastian pinned J.J. against the wall and patted him down.

"What are you doing?"

"Shut up," he said, angrily.

The snitch was clean. What concerned Tristan was his partner's unpredictable temper which seemed to come out of nowhere.

"Happy?" J.J. pushed him away.

"Okay, so what's going on?" Tristan got back to the business at hand.

"The Major called me late last night, woke me up. I drove over an hour south to a motel off I-95."

"Named what?" Sebastian asked.

"Some flea-bag motel."

"What was it named?" he repeated.

". . . Bridge something. The Bridge Cross Inn, that's it."

"What room number?"

"Twenty-seven. Satisfied?"

Good man, Tristan thought to himself. Sebastian was testing him with detailed questions. Quick answers were less likely to be lies. J.J. was a marine, yet it was still necessary to treat him like any other snitch.

"So what's the plan?" Tristan asked.

"They're plotting a series of bombings, Oklahoma City style."

"Bombings of what?"

"He didn't say. I know who he wants to blame it on."

"I think we all do," Sebastian said.

"Who was there?"

"The Major, me, and two other guys. They were Russian."

"You sure?"

"Oh yeah, positive. It's still in the planning phase and the Major is putting the team together. He wants me to find a warehouse or something similar; big enough where we can meet, run drills, and build the bombs. It has to be in northern Virginia so it's easy to drive into lower DC."

"Bombings in lower DC? The White House, Capitol building, it could be any number of targets," Tristan said. "We'll get one for you. A place like that isn't cheap, how are you supposed to pay for it?"

"Same way he's been doing it all along, he has a bank account with money that isn't traceable. But he says he's having trouble lately, audits or something at the Pentagon, funds will be tight and we may have to be creative."

"What does that mean?"

"We're going to lift a lot of the materials from construction sites. He says there are all kinds of places to find the chemicals, and what we can't steal, we'll buy or barter. He said that's what made Oklahoma City so easy, it's normal stuff you can get anywhere."

Tristan understood. Since the bombing of the Alfred P. Murrah Federal Building, FBI had kept track of fertilizer and other sales at retail stores across the country. Anyone buying in large amounts, or small quantities on a regular basis, got a red flag in the database and a visit from special agents. Of course, most were landscapers and private citizens. It would be better to steal what they needed, and the only way to be sure it was untraceable.

J.J. continued, "I'm in charge of building the bombs, all except for the primer. He's going to get me the C4."

"And the blast caps?" Tristan asked.

"Fuses, again."

Sebastian looked to Tristan who said, "We can't use the same ones you made for the Train Bomber, those were too obviously bogus. I'll put together some better fakes. I don't know why he won't use electronic blasting caps?"

"Don't look at me," J.J. threw up his hands, "that's all I know. He wants a warehouse lined-up by the time he calls again."

"When's that?"

"No idea. He's anxious though, and it's not like this guy to be anxious. He trusts me after the Train Bomber job and I don't think he suspects anything."

A ship horn blared, in the nearby Potomac River.

Sebastian said, "Keep texting GPS coordinates, don't use any names, and we'll contact you when we get a warehouse."

"Good job, man," Tristan complimented. "Next time find an isolated location, okay? Public places are not secure."

"Yeah, no problem," J.J. gave Sebastian a nasty look as he walked off.

"No more monuments!"

But the informant was gone.

"So what now?" Tristan asked.

"I think it's time we persuade Homeland Security to let us talk to your Train Bomber suspect."

CHAPTER 23

Tristan and Sebastian sat in the office of their new SAC in the J. Edgar Hoover FBI building. The only thing different since Murphy left was the nameplate.

Andrew Tufts was an interesting character. He had transferred in from the Memphis office for a promotion, but Tristan had the impression he was given a desk job because he wasn't much of a field agent. No family photos kept him company and he wore no wedding ring. Quiet and soft spoken, he was even a bit creepy.

As they waited for Tufts to finish reviewing their report, it was impossible to discern whether he was genuinely interested, or just a slow reader.

"We're going to need to talk to the Train Bomber suspect, can you try and get us in to see him?" Tristan blurted out.

Tufts held up a hand in a *shush* gesture. Apparently, his newfound power agreed with him. SAC Murphy was profoundly missed.

"By the way, I received a disturbing call this morning. I was told FBI unofficially paid a visit to the residence of the Russian ambassador?"

"That was my doing," Sebastian confessed.

"That wasn't by the book."

"Tells you a lot about the book."

"They're diplomats, what were you thinking?" Tufts fired back, not appreciating the sarcasm.

"I thought I'd talk to this Lara Fedorov about the man who shot my son."

"And?"

"They claimed they didn't know her."

"Did you expect a different outcome?" Silence was the answer. "Internal Affairs is investigating Jason's case, not you. If the director found out, he may not have let you back in FBI—taking into account past circumstances, Agent Graves."

Tristan contemplated the meaning of the jab, but now was not the time to ask.

Tufts continued, "Don't do something like that again, you represent the Bureau now."

"Yes, sir," he said, sounding uncharacteristically subordinate.

The pain level in Tristan's leg, and his mood, had diminished as a result of the meds he had taken an hour earlier. He had attempted to detox the night before but the withdrawals were too intense. In addition, a nagging in the back of his mind pressured him to take the medication—not to dull the pain but to stop the withdrawals. The voice, if it could be called that, urged him to down a pill now and worry about the consequences another time. Unfortunately, Tristan was listening.

Shifting in the chair, his keys fell onto the floor with a *klank*. He leaned over to pick them up and in a subtle act of defiance, placed them on the edge of the desk. He exchanged a knowing glance with Sebastian who didn't quite know what to make of the move.

This earth-shattering bit of evidence, the *Tidal Wave 23* video, was now within arm's reach of their new SAC and he had no idea. Tristan could not decide if he felt guiltier about the stunt or for sitting on an important piece of evidence. He did, however, recognize the medication was beginning to cloud his judgment.

"Back to your case. I don't know who this Major is but once you get an image of him see if there's a match in the Data Warehouse." Tufts resurrected the conversation unfinished by Murphy; "I'm glad you finally acquired an informant, Agent Wood."

"Yes, sir."

"Any idea what their targets are?"

"Not yet."

"And where will these guys be meeting and planning this out?" Tufts dropped the folder on his desk and sat back in his chair.

"The Major wants our informant to find them a place to meet and build the bombs, a medium-sized warehouse."

"Pick one from the list, we have plenty of safe houses."

"No FBI safe houses, we need a fresh location," Tristan said.

"Why?"

"The guy goes by; *the Major*. Whether he's got a military background or it's just an alias, we can't take a chance, he may have connections in law enforcement."

"I assume you have a plan?" Tufts asked.

Sebastian jumped in. "We'll scout commercial buildings publicly advertised for rent, there's no shortage in this economy. We'll disclose we're FBI and pay the owners what they want on the condition they stay away. The last thing we need is a landlord coming around, checking up. And we'll give them a cover story in case anyone asks."

"It needs to look totally legit," Tristan added.

"Surveillance?" asked the SAC.

"We video-rig the whole place and put it on twenty-four hour watch."

"And wire the informant."

"I don't think that's a good idea, sir, one pat down and it's all over. We can get enough evidence on tape."

"This is standard procedure, Agent Wood."

"We don't need a wire."

"Says who?" Tufts asked.

"He's ex-military and disgruntled, he wants to help us." Tristan realized he was hanging out on a long limb for this guy, marine or not.

"Okay for now, but we keep all options on the table. What type of bomb are we looking at?"

"Fertilizer, similar to Oklahoma City. It's the easiest and most untraceable way to build a powerful conventional device. We don't know exactly what kind yet, there's any number of fertilizer compounds they could produce."

"How far along will you allow them to go?"

"This is where Sebastian enters in," Tristan said.

"We let them collect the chemicals but the blasting caps will be fake. When the day comes to build them, we get it all documented and arrest them in the act of building the bombs. Since we'll have access to the site we can switch out materials, if necessary. We need enough evidence for a clean conviction. If we bust them too soon and they're only talking about it on tape, we'll be lucky to get them on conspiracy. We can't allow a lawyer get them off on a technicality."

"Be careful, I don't want a repeat of the WTC bombing," Tufts stressed the point.

Although a common strategy in FBI stings, one event in particular stained the Bureau's reputation. In 1993, Middle Eastern terrorists successfully detonated a bomb in the underground parking garage of the World Trade Center, killing six.

This topic was no longer discussed either internally or externally in FBI.

The leader of the terror cell, an Egyptian bomb-maker named Emad Salem, was also a paid informant. The others in the group had been allowed to enter the country thanks to the CIA and national security overrides. Though aware of every phase of the operation, no arrest was made even with multiple opportunities.

The case was still considered a conspiracy theory and ignored by the media despite the publication of secret recordings by Salem, including the conversations with his FBI controllers that told the real story. He had wisely held on to the tapes as an insurance policy.

Salem had been a good informant and provided useful information, yet he was fired. One month before the bombing, they staked out the cell's meeting place on a farm near Harrisburg, PA, but made no arrest. Instead, the special agents were recalled to New York City and prevented from following the terrorists home.

With Salem out of the picture, the case was dumped on the FBI's Newark office. As a result, the plan to substitute harmless powder for explosives was not carried out, clearing the way for the attack a few weeks later with a real bomb. Salem was paid $1.5 million by the FBI, or rather the American taxpayers, to keep his mouth shut and the story was buried.

The future 9/11 Commission Report would say nothing about it, among the many other things it ignored. Most special agents were mindful, for fear of losing one's job, this was a subject no longer discussed.

"We'll need a surveillance van, and some Gs."

"The Bureau is facing massive budget cuts, as you're aware," Tufts said, "don't expect much."

"I'd like to have the location on twenty-four hour watch, if possible? Bedding down the subjects will make sure we don't miss anything," Tristan asked.

"I'll tell you right now, don't get your hopes up. But let me see what I can scratch together."

To help take some of the work-load off the field agents, a group of lower paid surveillance people called Gs were employed. They posed as joggers, bikers, skateboarders, and other average bystanders. Although it seemed unbelievable that FBI would fuss about providing man-power for its investigations, this was normal. The budget was always stretched thin and Gs, paid by the hour, added up to a big expense. In addition, with so many cases there were a limited number of them to go around.

"I'm concerned about this informant. Keep him on a short leash, agents. We can bust him at any time in connection with the Train Bomber. I'm keeping SAC Pascal informed of your progress, he's particularly interested in this one."

"Sir, we need to talk to the suspect. I'd like to see how he reacts to a photo of our informant and ask him some questions, it might help move the case along faster."

"Well, that won't happen, Agent Wood," Tufts said matter-of-factly.

"Why not?" Tristan asked.

"He's dead."

"What!?"

"He hung himself. They found him this morning in his cell."

"They didn't have him in a suicide vest?" Sebastian's face turned beet-red, his hands clutching the arms of the chair, ready to rip them off.

"Apparently not," Tufts acknowledged, oblivious to the anger brewing in front of him.

Tristan visualized his partner vaulting over the desk.

"Let me know if you need anything."

That was Tufts way of saying; *get out of my office.*

CHAPTER 24

Seth Pascal did not like spring in Washington, DC, nor did he like summer, for that matter. Fall and winter were his months, particularly when it was raining and dreary. He was not a fan of sunshine in general. It depressed him seeing people enjoy the weather, couples holding hands, and happy families spending time together. He did not know what made him this way but he felt jubilant only when others were miserable.

As the sun radiated without interference from clouds, he realized this was not going to be one of those days. However, knowing what would happen in the stock market, even the beautiful weather could not bring him down.

He drove the Lincoln Town Car west on Route 66 in northern Virginia, as rush hour traffic crawled along like a giant steel millipede toward the nation's capital. Pascal was glad to be moving in the opposite direction. It gave him a sick pleasure seeing the *sheeple*, as he thought of Americans, sitting in traffic on their way to jobs they hated.

Seth Pascal did not need to work. He came from money, and a lot of it. Where the average person put their earnings almost exclusively into stock-based investments hoping to retire on the appreciation, the Insiders understood the importance of tangible goods such as gold, silver, survival supplies, and fortified homes with military-grade bunkers. He had dumped any market dependent assets he owned years ago, in anticipation of what would happen in the DOW.

And it began today.

Normally he played music on a drive, but was compelled to listen to talk radio. It was quite a rush to hear the know-it-all neocon hosts speak about the daily headlines while being so completely oblivious to what was coming, ignorant of the Hegelian dialectic forming their narrative, and terrified of anything labeled a conspiracy theory. What they did not want to believe they simply did not discuss.

The one thing they were right about, however, was investing in precious metals. He felt no guilt when politicians tried to talk Americans out of buying gold, accusing them of being survivalist nuts and right wing extremists, when they themselves were invested in gold for the very same reasons. The elites knew gold was the only real currency, and Pascal knew they loved telling the American public just the opposite. The last thing they wanted was for the lowly commoners to be prepared.

Preparation meant less dependence on government and to the globalists this was even more dangerous than free speech. But they were not worried. Give an American the choice between an iPad and three months of storable food insurance, and they'd take the iPad every time.

This was precisely what the elites wanted.

Minutes after turning south on Route 81 he spotted the Shenandoah county fairgrounds, a well-known FEMA camp to insiders, then took the exit that would bring him to the town of Woodstock, Virginia.

Woodstock was a journey back in time, an entirely different world such a short distance from the city. These were folks who, like those in so many small towns, wanted to live life, fall in love, have kids, and be left alone by the power hungry politicians. These were the kind of people the globalists despised.

Pascal pulled the Town Car in between the bright white lines of his favorite parking space under a huge oak tree, right across from a small mom and pop grocer. He placed a portable FBI badge on the car's dashboard exempting him from having to drop a quarter into the meter. Dodging a couple of slow moving cars, he crossed the street and entered the store named; *Woodmart*.

After collecting his groceries he walked up to the register and set the hand-cart on the counter.

"Haven't seen you around, agent. Been doing a lot of travelling I gather?" said the lady he knew as *Mom*.

"Sure have. Bouncing between field offices, and now I'm back in DC—for a while, anyway." He handed her a credit card.

"How's your house coming along? Out to do some work on it?"

"I'm almost done with the upgrades, but there always seems to be something else to do."

"Isn't that the truth?"

She handed him a receipt to sign.

"See you later."

He carried his bags to the car and drove down a long unpaved road to his small rancher. Built in the 1970s, it had a basement and two acres of land. With his money he could have bought the biggest and grandest property in the area, but that wasn't the idea.

He needed to be low-key.

Upon his first assignment to the Washington, DC, field office he realized he should not assume he'd be granted access to an underground base when the big one went down. So if he had to fend for himself, Woodstock was perfect. It was far enough from major populated areas to be somewhat safe, and close enough to get to in haste.

He eased the car up the driveway and parked inside the garage, then keyed a five digit number into the alarm system causing the entire house to come alive with a series of electric hums. Storm shutters rose, revealing the windows and doors they were installed to protect and allowing light to flood the interior.

Pascal entered his kitchen. After putting the groceries in the refrigerator, he walked through the living room admiring the funky orange '70s carpet he never replaced. In fact, the main level remained unchanged from its original state, with the exception of the recently added storm shutters. But these were not for storms, or at least not the ones created by Mother Nature. If things went the way he expected, he wouldn't be spending his time on this level anyway.

The back door opened with a rusty creek and he walked through the yard to a storage shed. Inside were two large solar panels, which he lugged to the south side of the house. He detached a small air vent in the concrete foundation and pulled out a thick black extension cord, plugging in both panels and facing them toward the sun.

Checking his wristwatch, he realized the stock market was open.

The SAC returned to the kitchen and turned on a beat-up clock radio, weeding through static before tuning in a talk station. He started to cook breakfast. The radio wasn't the only old appliance. The stove was so ramshackle that just one burner worked.

Looking around the empty house, it was times like this that he pined for someone to talk to about all the things he knew. Seth Pascal had accepted years ago that he would likely end up alone, which he was.

Pushing those thoughts out of his mind as he had so many times in the past, he focused on the day ahead. He didn't know when it would happen, but it was going to happen. Two important pieces of legislation were being voted on in the House of Representatives in the days to come.

One was, of course, another renewal of the Patriot Act. This had always been easy to keep going. In recent years however, even ideologically opposed groups such as the ACLU and the Tea Party had agreed the law was not constitutional. The ACLU was bought and paid for but the Tea Party had become a real thorn in the side of the globalists.

It had looked for a while like the Patriot Act did not have enough support in the House of Representatives to pass. The quick fix was a false flag terror attack to remind Americans what they were scared of.

Mortalities were not necessary, a close call did the trick just fine. It could be a car bomb that almost exploded in Times

Square, or an underwear device on a commercial flight entering the United States from a foreign destination such as Amsterdam.

This time it was the assassination attempt of the President of the United States. Pollsters now showed a higher percentage of Americans believed the Patriot Act should be renewed again, and this reflected in the anticipated votes of their representatives in Congress.

Americans fell for it every time.

The second piece of legislation to be voted on was a bill to audit the Federal Reserve. This was more serious and required swift action.

Anytime Congress made a move to force the Fed to open their books and reveal the bailed-out banks, Goldman Sachs, J.P. Morgan, and the financial cartel wasted no time. The politicians, most of whom were bought by the banks, feigned support to placate the public. Usually, a bill such as this would be defeated outright unless the outcry was too loud, in which case it would be watered down with loopholes and exemptions until it no longer had any teeth.

The best way to stop this type of legislation dead in its tracks was with a different form of false flag; a temporary stock market crash.

First, the elites would send out their minions, such as the Fed Chairman, to threaten uncooperative members of Congress with an economic collapse should they dare challenge the bankers. If that didn't work, there would be an "incident." The stock market was the best way to send the message since the average American could witness the downslide in real-time, though the edict was intended for Congress.

When necessary, J.P. Morgan and Goldman Sachs would manipulate the high-frequency trading software controlling the DOW. After the market had dropped enough to cause a panic on CNBC, and throughout the halls of Congress, they would simply correct it; message delivered.

This type of false flag was useful with everything from audit bills and bank bailouts, to threats of regulatory legislation. Pascal had extolled these false flags numerous times in the recent past, and they had yet to fail even once.

On September 29, 2008, the House of Representatives rejected the $700 billion taxpayer funded TARP bailout plan for the banks by a vote of 228 to 205. The threats of imminent financial Armageddon from former Goldman Sachs CEO and Treasury Secretary Henry Paulson, Federal Reserve Chairman Ben Bernanke, and the Bush administration had failed. Then the DOW plunged 778 points amounting to the biggest single-day point loss ever, up to that time, eclipsing even the collapse that followed 9/11.

With threats of martial law, Congress was persuaded to pass the banker-bailout bill later in the week, before anyone had read it. Though the average person saw this as a chance occurrence, this economic model had been set up long ago with the creation of the Federal Reserve in 1913. The plan was to privatize profits and socialize losses, ensuring the banks would prevail regardless of the current economic situation.

On May 6, 2010, the bankers decided they would not wait for the House to vote before sending a message. This pre-emptive strike was a 1000 point market drop in ten minutes, a precision-guided high frequency trading attack by insiders at Goldman Sachs to show Congress who was boss. The first bill would have added undesirable regulations to the Federal Reserve and their fractional banking cartel, thus reducing their power. The second would have required the Federal Reserve to open their books for the first time in history.

Obviously, this would not be allowed to happen.

Executing a false flag on the stock market was brilliant considering it affected almost everyone in the country in some way. Although a majority of people did not much like the banks, the politicians always got the blame.

The first cover story blamed the May 6 crash on the actions of one trader who "hit the wrong button." This excuse, later labeled the *Fat Finger Foul-up*, was so ridiculous no one bought it.

Subsequent reasons followed over the weeks until the story dropped out of the news.

Pascal, through his sources, knew precisely what happened.

Goldman Sachs, JP Morgan, and the rest of the gang pulled the "buys" from their computer trading programs and voila; a manufactured temporary stock market crash. Thousands of day-traders sitting around watching CNBC instinctively jumped on the downward momentum bandwagon and unwittingly hijacked the crime for Wall Street. The financial terrorists were able to point to the day-traders and blame the market for the crash.

The sign of those responsible was recognizable by only a select few insiders. The New World Order elites loved sending each other coded messages in events like false flags, and Pascal had become very good at spotting them. The letter *F*, being the sixth of the alphabet, formed a sinister message giving even him the shudders.

"Fat Finger Foul-up" was code for "666."

This was put out by the Illuminati to the media; it was right up their alley.

After finishing his meal, he headed for the living room. Pascal removed a couple of hardbacks from the bookcase, an obvious newer addition to the home. Turning a handle, the bookcase sprung open like a gate. He entered an alcove and pulled up the carpet revealing a trap door.

This was the primary reason he bought the house. It was one of the few in the area with an original basement, now hidden by the faux bookcase. He had flown in two carpenters from California, put them up at the local motel and paid them a lot of money to do the work. The logic being, they would be too far away to get any ideas.

Pascal eased down a few steps and flipped on a light switch, set back in a recess within the wall. This space had room to stash the assault weapon he had yet to acquire.

The goal of the New World Order was to disarm the American people so they would be dependent on the government to protect them. The elites owned weapons and travelled with armed body guards, understanding guns were the best form of self-protection while creating propaganda for the general public stating the opposite.

The Second Amendment was the reason they worked so hard staging school shootings and spent so much money funding the politicians in favor of banning them.

Pascal made a mental note; *buy assault rifle.*

At the basement level, he stood scanning his bomb shelter. The dearth of windows made it rather drab, but several wall posters and colorful furniture transformed it from a Soviet gulag. He walked to a table and turned on a short wave radio, tuning it until he found a news station.

A reporter sounded concerned.

". . . the DOW, which opened on the upside this morning, is currently down over 200 points. Not a huge amount for anyone familiar with the volatility that has plagued the stock market in years past, but the drop is rather gradual, without many ups."

A rush of adrenalin warmed him as he waited for the security monitors to power-up and display a view of the home's perimeter. Another device showed the solar panels generating electricity and charging the battery backup system. In the far corner of the room were boxes containing enough long term storage food to last a year or more. Survival supplies were packed into every free space in the makeshift apartment.

The house was set up with a rain collection and filtration system capable of turning thousands of gallons into safe drinking water. His short wave radio needed no batteries, a few turns of a hand-crank gave it juice. There was an Xbox wired to a flat panel TV along with a stack of DVDs, plus a couple hundred books and magazines jammed in a cheap cabinet bought at a local yard sale.

He was well prepared with food, water, first aid, and even entertainment. The only thing lacking was companionship. Pascal sunk into his old pea-green recliner and listened enthusiastically.

-300 . . . -400 . . . -700 . . . -900 . . .

He almost jumped up and cheered as the DOW passed -1000. The reporter sounded on the verge of a heart attack. He loved when the average person suffered.

After an hour the market was still hovering around 1200 down. But unlike the other false flags, this one would not correct.

This time it was different.

It was the beginning of the planned economic collapse. What was coming would make 2008 look like good times. Pascal rested his head back in the chair and closed his eyes.

Yep, he thought to himself, *the American people fell for it every time.*

CHAPTER 25

Chrome walk-lights illuminated the path leading up to the turn-of-the-century row house. Allyson held hands with Tristan while Sarah clung to Robert's arm, as they took time to admire the immaculate multi-million dollar homes on one of the most posh streets in this part of the District. The Capitol Hill neighborhood had seen its ups and downs, but recently it had again become the trendy place to live.

As the working class faded away and Middle America sunk into a deepening depression, politicians and their cronies flocked back into this neighborhood like birds of a feather. Two classes of people were diverging as the income gap widened. In neighborhoods such as Capitol Hill, the lower class was quietly being forced into other parts of the city using eminent domain via the United Nation's Agenda 21. Builders renovated entire blocks with the help of insider deals, reselling them for top dollar.

Twilight gave the street the look of a Hollywood set.

Robert rang the doorbell, barely audible through the well-built walls of the house. The low humidity was a pleasant change for this time of year and Washingtonians knew to enjoy it while it lasted.

The air was still and Tristan could smell Allyson's perfume. Her long brown hair was pulled back in a loose braid and the low heals she wore elevated her to his height. He loved her natural beauty. She always dressed right; sexy and tasteful but subtle. She was not self-absorbed as most girls were these days and was what guys called "low maintenance." Allyson was the perfect girl for him.

If she could just relax about having children—

A lock unlatched and a middle-aged woman in a black and white maid uniform opened the door. After a tired greeting, she escorted them to the living room where Senator Matthews sat puffing on a cigar.

"Welcome, welcome!" The senator labored to stand up and tried to wave away the smoke.

Shaking his boss's hand, Robert reintroduced his wife as a formality, followed by Tristan and Allyson.

He apologized for the bad habit then turned on the charm. "It has been an eternity since I've had such breathtaking young ladies in my presence. May I have Martha get everyone a drink?"

Martha, the woman who had answered the door, listened intently then left.

"Thank you for having us over, Senator," Tristan said.

"It's my pleasure."

"Your home is amazing," Allyson observed.

It was obvious this room was where the former super-couple had done their entertaining. Antiques filled the space like a museum. Expensive art hung on the walls, and the impression was the furniture had been collected over the years from various parts of the world. But under closer scrutiny, the décor appeared threadbare. Once unique and elegant, it was now just aged.

"Please, sit." Senator Matthews snuffed out his cigar in the ashtray.

"Robert really enjoys working for you," Sarah said.

"Your husband isn't aiming very high, is he?"

The joke got a laugh all around.

"And this is the lovely wife of the FBI agent, the war hero, whom I read about? You must be sick and tired of hearing people say that, you can tell me the truth now, my dear."

"Yes, I suppose so," Allyson admitted.

"Well, some get fifteen minutes of fame and others a bit longer. Don't worry, in time it will fade."

A different servant entered with a tray of drinks, a younger girl who acted antsy. The smell of home cooking caused Tristan's stomach to growl.

"Before Mileva passed on she made me promise to hire someone to cook and clean and take care of her house. At first I was against it, but I confess it makes life easier. I lack the energy for routine tasks these days."

"How long ago did your wife pass?" Sarah asked delicately.

"Almost a year now."

An uncomfortable silence fell on the room.

"I wanted to thank you for getting Sebastian Graves back into FBI," Tristan said.

"One of the easier favors I've been asked."

"Robert told me later that you attempted to block Dufour's nomination for Bureau director. I didn't mean to put you on the spot, but it was a big deal."

"I must admit, it wasn't without some pleasure that I paid your boss a call. I like to think I still have pull in this town. They won't put an old man out to pasture so easily."

"What did you say to persuade him, if you don't mind my asking?"

"I'm a politician. I politicked." This drew more laughs.

"Can I ask you a question?" Sarah spoke up.

"Of course, my dear."

"What happens to politicians? Why do they end up corrupt after they get to Washington, DC, I mean?"

"Honey," Robert was taken aback. "That's not polite."

"It's quite all right," the senator said. "Some enter politics for the power and money, others for honorable reasons. Unfortunately, becoming a public servant even with the best of intentions rarely lasts. New politicians get a sit-down when they arrive in Washington, DC, by the people who funded their campaigns. They are told to throw their ideals out the window and conform to the status quo. Remember when the Tea Party had their grand victory in the 2010 midterm elections? Well, a year later most were in line, breaking their promise not to increase the debt ceiling and allowing government spending to continue. Washington is bought and paid for by lobbyists and special interests through the banks. No one can change that."

"And why did you enter politics?" She did not let him off the hook.

Tristan nominated Sarah as his new hero for having the guts to ask such simple, direct, and perfectly legitimate queries. Allyson squeezed his hand as though reading his thoughts. Neither liked politicians, but they still tried to give them the benefit of the doubt.

"I sold out long ago. I like to think I did some good along the way, though."

Robert was desperate to change the subject and said, "Senator Matthews has been in public service now for almost forty years."

The dinner announcement came, and to Tristan's amusement, got his younger brother off the hook. The group was led into the dining room where five place settings of fine china and silver were set on a grand table.

The food far exceeded any expectations and included filet mignon, lobster tail, sweet and mashed potatoes, and a medley of greens. A large basket contained hot bread and garlic butter. There were various sides such as cranberries and several types of pickles and olives, some stuffed with peppers. Bottles of Champaign, as well as red and white wines from Burgundy were within reach. They began to dig in with no inhibitions. It was the food of royalty.

The limited conversation consisted mostly of small talk and Tristan became bored. He wanted to talk about *Tidal Wave* 23 in the worst way, but knew it would come back to haunt him if he did.

"I'm sure you love talking politics after work, but I can't help myself. It's not every day I have dinner with a United States senator."

"You can ask me anything."

"We've got a real problem, the way we've expanded our wars from the Middle East into North Africa, and created more fiat debt than we can ever pay back? There's China, which we hear about often, and then Russia, a topic the media seems to want to avoid."

"You are more right than you know, son. China, Russia, and other countries are building up militarily while we go into historic amounts of debt to spy and police our own people, buy votes with welfare giveaways, and bail out banks and corporations. The troop and military movements around the globe are unlike anything I have seen in my lifetime." The senator talked in between bites of his steak. "China recently put three new aircraft carriers to sea— two conventional, the third nuclear. They bought the unfinished Soviet carrier Varyag from Ukraine in 2001, stating it would be converted to a floating casino, but we knew otherwise. Satellite imagery confirmed the renovation was for a military function. China is not our friend, neither is Russia."

"But Russia is the real problem, is it not, Senator? Ask the average person about Russia and what will they say?"

"They are moving toward Capitalism. They're our friends now," Sarah said.

"That's a fiction we're led to believe, right?" Tristan kept trying to lead the senator into the conversation. "President Putin appears to be creating a new Soviet Union?"

"Weren't the START treaties successful at reducing arms on both sides?" Allyson asked.

"The Russians have never, not once, lived up to their end of any START treaty requirements. Those in the Kremlin are masters of deception. They show our satellites and inspectors what they want us to see, while hiding their active weapons programs. Now Russia is flexing its muscles again."

"And yet we still send them billions in financial aid every year?" Tristan asked. "I never hear the media mention this?"

"This is why the Russians continue the charade, to keep our tax-dollars flowing. Since the collapse of the Soviet Union they have built tremendous nuclear, biological, and chemical weapons systems and all with the aid of US technology transfers and financial assistance. They are deploying on average, three brand new or updated ICBMs per month. Our last remaining nuclear weapon is the Minuteman III, and we don't upgrade our rocket systems, or build new ones."

"Is this because of PDD-60?"

The senator seemed caught off-guard.

Sarah kept him on the hook with the question, "What is PDD-60?"

"It's a Presidential Decision Directive, the 60th one under Bill Clinton and was meant to be a show of good faith to the Russian Federation."

"A Decision Directive?" Allyson asked.

"They are a lot like executive orders, issued by the president with the advice and consent of the National Security Council. They started back under Harry Truman and each president has called it something slightly different. Under Kennedy it was a National Security Action Memorandum, under Reagan, a National Security Study Directive, and Clinton called it a Presidential Decision Directive, or PDD for short. He issued about seventy-five of them during his eight years in office."

"Doesn't PDD-60 deal with military conduct, in cooperation with Russia?"

Robert was becoming uncomfortable again, but Tristan could not help himself.

"It stresses a similar response to a nuclear attack, rather than an all or nothing scenario. They fire one-hundred rockets at us, we fire one-hundred back. They keep half of their bombers grounded, we keep half of our subs in port," the senator responded.

"When you put it that way, it actually sounds reasonable," Sarah said. "If someone in Russia got control of one nuke and launched it at us, we wouldn't want to launch all of ours, right?"

"It's a deterrent, my dear. It is saying you pull out a knife and take a swipe, we pull out a gun and empty the barrel. The strategy is intended to say, you keep your nukes under control, or else. The nuclear deterrent is being ready to launch at any time."

"So what is the downside to this PDD-60?" Allyson took a sip of wine.

The senator continued, "In 1981 the Reagan administration created guidelines by which the United States must be prepared to win a protracted nuclear war. The policy was called, *Launch-on-Warning*. Before PDD-60, if Russia launched her missiles we could immediately fire back. This directive, however, set a new guideline; to retaliate in a 'similar response'."

"What does that mean?" Sarah asked.

"It means the United States would be required to absorb a first strike nuclear attack and evaluate the damage before retaliating. The real danger of PDD-60 is it removes the deterrent our nuclear arsenal is supposed to create in the first place."

"But a first strike by Russia would take down all command and control, including our bombers that would be sitting on their runways. We don't keep our bombers on constant alert, whereas Russia does, isn't that so?" Tristan asked.

"Regrettably, you are correct." The senator surrendered to a coughing fit before continuing. "Russia would also take out most of our land-based missiles, as well as satellite and submarine communications. When I was on the House Armed Services Committee during the Clinton years we were forced to reduce our B-52 Bomber fleet from 220 to 56, our B-1 Bombers from 90 to 60, our Strategic Defense Interceptor Aircraft from 36 to 0, and our army divisions were reduced from 18 active down to 10. And although it happened under Clinton, it was a bipartisan gutting of our defenses."

"How could President Clinton sign PDD-60, with such a radical change in US policy and no debate in Congress? How did he get away with it?" Allyson poured herself a fresh glass of wine.

"On the q.t. The media was obsessed with the extra-curricular activities going on in the Clinton Oval Office at the time, a scandal purposely leaked for multiple reasons, by the way. PDD-60 was so top secret only the president, vice president, and the Joint Chiefs of Staff had access. Nowadays, it's declassified and online for anyone to investigate for themselves."

"Did NSPD-14 under Bush change the policy?"

"Is that another executive order?" Allyson asked.

Tristan looked to the senator to explain.

"The directives under George W. Bush were called National Security Presidential Directives. NSPD-14 was a 2002 update of PDD-60. There has been no directive, by any president, on the subject since."

"But it didn't modify the policy or the ideology, did it?"

The senator's silence gave away the answer.

A chill ran down Tristan's spine. He had just received confirmation that what Sebastian told him was true.

"Now let me ask you all a question," another bout of coughing overtook him. "If there were a disaster today, how long would you last? How many days' worth of food do you have? Is there a shelter to comfortably spend weeks, months, with no electricity or running water? Supplies and first aid?"

This seemed to draw the response the senator expected. Both servants entered and began to clear away plates.

"We will hold off on desert for now Martha, thank you." Senator Matthews spoke again to the group. "Ever since the rise of the Bolsheviks in 1917 all of Russia's resources have been centered on building a world empire under Communism, with funding from western capitalists of course. They've never denied their goals or even concealed them, but we tend to ignore them. The Kremlin wants a Soviet Union again and they want to bring Communism to the rest of the world. As we drink beer and watch football, they are planning and preparing. You would be wise to heed my warning."

"Come on, this sounds crazy," Robert spoke up. "This is America."

"I want to show you all something," the senator said, struggling to get out of his chair.

In the kitchen, he entered four numbers into a keypad unlocking the heavy door in front of them. They descended a short flight of stairs to the basement, which turned out to be a rather luxurious bomb shelter complete with thick carpet and a leather sectional couch. The only personal effect in the room was a framed portrait standing upright on the coffee table—a sepia-toned photograph of the couple in their younger years, beaming with happiness.

"Is this Mileva?" Allyson asked. "She's beautiful."

"Thank you."

Tristan nodded in agreement.

Sarah approached an open closet, stacked bottom to top with plastic crates.

"Those hold enough long term storable food to feed two adults for over a year. Of course, my wife is gone. And see over there? That tank is a water storage system. After rain is collected, it goes through reverse osmosis and is stored here."

Sarah removed a pouch from one of the crates. "How do you cook this?"

"It's dehydrated, you mix it with boiling water. An electric hot plate does the job, with a solar oven as a backup. Solar panels on the roof charge a battery system daily. Everything is here: books, first aid supplies, toothpaste, mouthwash, you name it, I've got it. We buy health, car, home-owner, and life insurance, why not survival insurance?" He picked up the framed picture and smiled. "Value your family, gentlemen, keep them safe and keep them close."

"That's easier said than done lately," Sarah jabbed.

"I'm sorry," the senator pleaded. "I realize Robert has been spending more time with me than his family, but I'm going to take him away from you again. I have one last job for him before I retire."

"Where are you sending him now?" she asked, deflated.

"To an exotic location. Extremely cold, but very beautiful."

CHAPTER 26

Tristan and Sebastian were happy with the warehouse, nestled in a development surrounded by the trees and rolling hills of northern Virginia. They sat in their newly assigned surveillance van in a parking lot hidden among countless similar trucks. This commercial area, thanks to a Keynesian economy America continued to suffer in, was a ghost town. Tristan tried to imagine the time when plumbers, electricians, mechanics, and other tradesmen worked an honest day and took home a paycheck along with their pride.

Those days were gone.

And now that the DOW was crashing and the bond market imploding, it seemed the next depression was right around the corner.

"How's it recording?" Sebastian asked.

"Not too bad, we're looking good," said a thirty-something man with a Brooklyn accent.

Anthony Moretti, the only *G* assigned to them by SAC Tufts, hunched over the computer that controlled the surveillance equipment. He wore a Yankees jersey, Bermuda shorts, Nike sneakers, and his black bangs hung over his eyes, an allegorical shield from the crazy world he was forced to observe.

If they got one G, this was the guy they wanted. His decade of service was unheard of for this type of job. Everyone at the DC Bureau had worked with him at one time or another, even out-of-towners including Sebastian, on cases he had travelled to

Washington for. Tony was practically an FBI agent, he just lacked the badge.

"There's enough hard drive space to tape nonstop for weeks without a break, and it's motion activated. Anything the size of a cat, or bigger, moving around inside will get recorded." Tony stood up to stretch his legs.

The exterior view showed a brown 1970s Chevy station wagon with fake wood side-paneling, parked outside the front entrance. Each of the three interior angles captured J.J. sitting at a table shuffling a deck of cards. Tony's camera placement encompassed almost every square inch of the warehouse.

"Picture looks a little grainy, is that because of the light level?" Tristan asked.

"Yep. Gotta go with what we got, and there ain't much. Audio is good though, hear the cards shuffling?"

Tony was right. The sound was so crisp that every card was discernible as it brushed up against the next one. Lack of brightness aside, the cameras provided a nearly complete view of what was a rusty aluminum shell on an old cement slab, cracked and caked in a thin layer of dirt. The sliding double doors were large enough for two medium sized trucks to back into, with room to spare. The inside was empty except for multiple shelves full of automobile parts left behind by whatever previous mechanics business had gone bust.

"Can you try the zoom?" Sebastian asked.

Tony manipulated the outdoor camera followed by each of the three indoors. However, when he got to the last one it did not seem to work.

"Houston we have a problem," Tony said, attempting to focus a frozen zoom on one of the inside cameras. "Well, at least it's stuck on a wide view. We can fix it later when no one's around."

Sebastian grumbled. "It worked when I set it up, I'm sure of it. Damn."

"I'll get in there and find out what's wrong," Tony responded.

Sebastian took out a booklet from his pocket. "I've got something for you."

"The Leipzig Connection?" Tristan studied the cover.

"If you're going to have kids, and even considering sending them to public schools, you need to read this. It goes through the history of the school system and how it was sabotaged at the turn of the twentieth century to deliberately dumb down the American population, to delay learning to read as long as possible, and to socialize children like Pavlov's dog instead of educating them. There's a reason the elites brag about the public schools while sending their own kids to private ones."

"Thanks, this is right up Allyson's alley."

"It's packed with mind-blowing information. You'll scratch your head and wonder why you've never heard any of this before."

Tony interrupted, "Hey guys, check this out."

A maroon Ford sedan drove up and parked next to the Chevy. Two men stepped out and looked around. Both appeared to be late thirties and wore golf shirts with slacks. They lit cigarettes and walked inside.

"Who else are we waiting for?"

"There's supposed to be one more guy, plus the Major."

On the monitors, they saw the men approach J.J. and shake his hand, introducing themselves as Ivan and Petrev. Both had heavy Russian accents that were difficult to understand.

They sat down to start up a card game.

"Check the backup system and make sure it's recording," Sebastian said to Tony.

"You got it, boss."

Sebastian pulled Tristan aside. "I almost forgot to ask how Allyson is."

"She's fine, never came down with so much as a symptom. But it seems there was a reason."

"What's that?"

"She found needle punctures on the sick men. The squad leader denied it at first, then admitted someone showed up and gave them injections."

"What type of injections?"

"Some kind of nerve gas antidote they claimed were test vaccines. One of the soldiers told her they were running martial law exercises in case of a biological attack. She said the corporal in charge was acting odd and kept checking the time. Then CDC showed up and shut the ER down; with automatic weapons. They all had bad reactions, and two died."

"Two died? I haven't seen that reported?"

"So far it hasn't. Allyson has been trying to get a statement from the CDC, but they refuse to talk to her. She even got hung up on yesterday."

"I would suggest she let it go."

"Why?"

"If what happened is not supposed to go public, it will be kept out of the news one way or another."

"Well, that's going to be a little difficult. She has an interview set up."

"With who?"

"None of the networks returned her calls, it's one of the local stations. She's hoping it might snowball into more press. That's how our USAA story went national."

"Tristan, I wouldn't let her do that."

"You don't know her. Even if I tried to talk her out of it I'd be wasting—"

"Hey, hey, we got another one approaching," Tony cut in.

An old purple Pinto hatchback drove up and parked next to the other two.

"Jeez, these guys drive crappy cars," Tony observed.

"Cheap and paid for in cash, I'm sure. Untraceable."

The man had a thin build and light brown hair, mid-twenties, and by the looks of his clothes probably didn't have much money, or style. He entered the building and shook hands with the three men now playing cards, introducing himself as Liam. He appeared to be American and had no accent. From inside the surveillance van, the video monitors and microphones seemed to be working well.

"Where is this Major?" Sebastian wondered.

"Good question."

The new guy inspected the entire space, then sat down at the table. Through the speakers his voice was clear. "Ready to get started?"

Inside the warehouse, J.J. shuffled the deck, trying to act casual. He asked Liam, "Is the Major running late? We should probably wait for him."

"He won't be here today. You didn't know that?" He said arrogantly.

"I guess not," J.J. admitted.

"I got instructions for everyone. Ivan and Petrev, you research the guards at the Ukraine and Russian embassies and decide who to bribe. Choose two guys from each embassy. Whoever it is, they gotta have family in Russia. The Major says you know why."

"Yes, yes, we have done this before," the man named Petrev said, impatiently.

"We're bombing the Russian and Ukraine embassies?" J.J. asked.

Ignoring him, Liam continued, "You will also drive the bomb trucks. Got it?"

"We understand, yes," Ivan snarled.

"And James? Keep paying rent on the warehouse, the Major says make sure to pay on the first of the month, he doesn't want any problems. You and me are gonna collect bomb materials and buy the getaway cars. You report to the Major after each meeting, the usual way, whatever that is."

"Did he say what kind of bomb to build?" J.J. asked.

"Fertilizer."

"I know that, but what kind? There's any number of combinations."

"No idea, man."

"And where are we going to get the money for the materials and the cars? It won't be cheap, I spent everything I had on rent for this place."

"Most of the bomb materials we can steal."

"We still need money."

"And that's why the Major has a project for us," Liam said. "He's got buyers. We're gonna sell them guns."

"Guns?"

"AK-47s actually. The Major will set it up and let us know, when the time comes."

"Anything else?"

"That's all I got for now."

The two Russians lit up new cigarettes and walked out without speaking.

Before leaving, Liam said to J.J., "Nice to meet you," though he did not mean it.

From inside the surveillance van, the engines blasted through the microphones as the cars drove off. J.J. sat alone, staring into one of the cameras above him like a deer in headlights.

"Tony, download us still images of each suspect, try to get the best view of their faces."

"You got it."

Sebastian muttered to Tristan, "So that's it? The embassy bombings are the false flag; the catalyst to war with Russia? The embassies get bombed, the United States is blamed, or a rogue group within the US, and we go to war."

"Let's not jump to conclusions. But if you think that's the plan we better report it." He took out the flash drive with *Tidal Wave 23*.

"Not yet."

A knock came at the back door of the van.

"Remember Tristan, don't let the informant control the case."

J.J. climbed in and asked, "Did you get all that?"

"You did good. Do you know anything about these guys?"

"It's the same Russians from the motel, but this Liam, I never met him before. I'd guess he's another military recruit, like me. Probably not his real name though."

"No kidding," Sebastian gibed. "Where was your boss? Why wasn't he at the meeting?"

"I have no idea, you heard the conversation. We all thought he was going to be here."

"I'll tell you what I think," getting in his face, "I think this Major is made up."

"Yeah, right," J.J. said laughing.

"For all we know, you're him. You're the one calling these guys giving them instructions and planning the whole operation."

"Are you serious?"

"You are an informant, you got that?"

Tristan moved in to separate them but was surprised at Sebastian's strength. His partner's temper was beginning to unnerve him.

Then his cell phone rang.

"Hold on! This isn't solving anything!" he yelled before taking the call. "Agent Wood here."

"The only reason you're not in jail right now is because I say so, remember that!" He began to shove J.J. again.

"Quiet!" This time they obeyed. "SAC Tufts?" Tristan's eyes became wide as he listened. "What? Don't do anything, we're coming in now!" He hung up.

"What's wrong?"

"They're closing down the case!"

CHAPTER 27

Tristan and Sebastian walked through halls lined with glass offices, buzzing with activity as special agents and staff scurried to their destinations. Tristan watched faces pass by and wondered who the honest employees were and who might be up to no good. The J. Edgar Hoover FBI building held decade's worth of stories within its walls, from the humorous and lighthearted to tales of espionage and corruption.

They approached the secretary who seemed to expect them.

"Go on in agents," she said with a twinge of nervousness in her voice.

Tufts remained seated at his desk and gave them no time to speak. "SAC Pascal is closing down the Train Bomber case and handing the informant over to Homeland Security, to answer the question you were about to ask."

"He can't do that!" Sebastian began to pace. "We're finally making progress!"

"Things have changed. The bombing suspect killed himself and DHS has all the evidence from the assassination attempt."

"But we have the informant!" Tristan added

"Pascal is reassigning you. We're stretched thin on domestic terrorism cases. Besides, FBI wants to devote our resources to Justice Department guidelines. That's not public information, by the way."

"You mean the MIAC report. The bad guys are militia groups? Gun owners, constitutionalists, patriot groups?"

Tristan stepped in front of Sebastian to block him from moving around the desk where he could get to Tufts. The SAC appeared to grasp the potential threat, but ignored it.

"Are you done venting Agent Graves?"

"Where is Pascal? I want to talk to him."

"He's not in, and he's not reachable today. I'll relay any objections to him."

"The case is ours, you have to keep it open."

"You're bordering on insolence."

"What I mean is, they're trafficking guns now," Sebastian said.

"Excuse me?" SAC Tufts looked at Tristan who shook his head in agreement.

"The group is selling AK-47s to fund their operation. They're coming from across state lines."

"Is this true, Wood?"

"Absolutely. We also found out what the targets are."

"And?"

"They're planning to bomb the Russian and Ukraine embassies."

"Do you have a report for me? I need it in writing."

"We'll get it to you, today."

Tufts was unprepared for this new series of events. A gun sale meant FBI was obligated to follow through, and the SAC knew it.

"If you don't keep the case open, you could have another *Fast and Furious* on your hands," Sebastian reminded him.

This possibility created a paralyzing fear among the suits at FBI. Though the part about the guns crossing state lines was unconfirmed, it was most likely true.

The comment had the intended effect.

Not all the weapons had been recovered from the F&F debacle, another illegal act the government got away with. But firearms continued to surface, creating ongoing headaches for law enforcement; especially in the press. Since then, the mere mention of gun sales related to any investigation automatically moved it into a high priority status.

"This case needs to stay in FBI, sir," Tristan reinforced what his partner was saying.

"Well, I'll have to talk to Pascal about it."

"Okay, we'll assume the case is still open until you confirm it with your SAC," Sebastian said with a hint of *gotcha*.

They walked out of the office as Tufts tried to save face. "Get your report to me, ASAP!"

Tristan breathed a sigh of relief, and not just for the case. For the first time he was genuinely worried Sebastian was going to become violent.

They continued down the hallway until a revelation struck.

"That's where I've heard, 'the New World Order.' The MIAC Report!" Tristan exclaimed.

"You read it?"

"Not since it came out in 2009, it's been awhile, that's why I couldn't recall the term. I remember reading it on the internet and being blown away."

"Multiple websites still have it in printable PDF form. What's amazing is most of it has already come true or is currently happening, even though it was called a conspiracy theory." Sebastian said.

The Missouri Information Analysis Center, known as MIAC, issued a report they considered unclassified but law enforcement sensitive, meaning not for public consumption. It was handed out secretly to local and state police agencies, later reaching the media through leaks.

MIAC was one of about sixty taxpayer funded fusion centers across the country sponsored by the Department of Homeland Security. Many of the principles the MIAC report denounced, were ideals for which the Founding Fathers had pledged their lives, fortunes, and sacred honor.

"I remember it criticized Tom Clancy novels, Soldier of Fortune Magazine, and Rambo movies for portraying white males as morally upright and tough," Tristan recalled.

"It also described supporters of presidential candidates Ron Paul, Bob Barr, and Chuck Baldwin as militia-influenced terrorists, instructing the Missouri police to be on the lookout for vehicles displaying bumper stickers and other paraphernalia associated with the Constitutional, Campaign for Liberty, and Libertarian parties."

"And didn't MIAC blame the Y2K scare on militias?"

"It did," Sebastian said. "A majority of the US population, as revealed in polls, believed Y2K could happen but it was the media that sensationalized it. Hollywood even made a documentary in 1999 complete with actors and so-called experts who claimed a catastrophe would indeed occur. The militia members were simply the ones preparing for it with storable food and supplies."

"So if you believe in it, that's okay. But if you believe in it and prepare for it, you're a crazy right wing extremist?"

"It's nothing new. The same thing is going on now. The MIAC report is still used as a guideline in law enforcement and claims the real terrorists aren't Muslim extremists but Americans angry at the Federal Reserve and banker bailouts, those for fiscal responsibility and wanting to go back to the gold standard, to name a few issues. The MIAC report even calls anyone anticipating the collapse of the US government due to economic reasons, a conspiracy theorist."

They entered the computer room and sat down at the station as far from the others agents as possible.

"I'm dying to find out who these Russians are." Sebastian opened the intranet browser. "I never did get a username and password."

"I've got it." Tristan typed in his information.

The FBI computer database since 2003 was called the Investigative Data Warehouse, a continually evolving platform for the counterterrorism division. The system could now examine over a billion documents in over 200 different search engine servers and bring up results in seconds, a process referred to as "connecting the dots." They ran the data-mining software using the limited information on the two Russians, and received a quick response.

"Nothing on the names, probably fake anyway," Tristan said. "Let's try biometrics."

Inserting the CD Tony burned, they logged into the Facial Recognition Program and uploaded the images of both Russians.

"Keep your fingers crossed."

Before implementing the current database, the FBI information gathering process was embarrassingly primitive. Even following 9/11, the computers had no CD-ROM, mouse, or browsers, and were so old charities would not take them as donations. The Automated Case Support System did not connect to the internet and agents were forced to use forty-two separate programs for the same investigation. Because the processors could not handle graphics, it was necessary to have local police departments email photos to their home computers. Louis J. Freeh, the Bureau's director at the time, refused to upgrade the system but continued to spend millions every year on non-essentials.

"What the . . ." Sebastian was dumfounded.

The computer gave them no returns on possible matches.

"Did we do it right? Try one at a time," Tristan suggested.

They entered each face individually receiving the same results, then searched for the new guy, Liam, but again came up empty.

"So none of these guys have ever broken a law? One day they woke up and decided to be terrorists?"

Both special agents were at a loss.

"While we're here, I want to try something. Can you get access to the internet?"

"Sure."

Tristan closed out the *intranet* and entered his username and password into a different location. This brought up the Bureau's World Wide Web. It defaulted to a homepage showing current FBI news headlines as well as semi-public resources, exclusively for special agents.

The main headline read; "Patriot Act renewed!"

The next one down was; "Body Scanners Now Law!"

"Damned if you weren't right," Tristan admitted.

Sebastian typed "SAC Seth Pascal" into the search window and waited for results to generate.

"What are you doing?"

"The internal system won't give us any information about him. I want to see if his name pops up on the web."

Several articles came up, but one was particularly interesting.

"Holy—"

"What?"

The link led to a mainstream news article from 2010 titled; "FBI Spokesman for Underwear Bomber Case; Reports of Amsterdam 'Handler' and Additional Bombs on Plane Unfounded."

"The *Underwear Bomber* attempted to blow up the plane Christmas day 2009, but I retired on the last day of the year. The investigation was completely botched. During those six days I worked it as much as I could, then left it behind." Sebastian quickly scanned the article. "This suggests he was out pushing the official story."

"What can you do now? The *Underwear Bomber* is convicted and in jail."

"I'm going to make some calls. I've still got friends in the Detroit office, they may have some intel on this guy."

"Like what?"

"Not sure. But I know I've heard the name; Seth Pascal."

CHAPTER 28

The rotors from the Huey blew hurricane force winds down at Robert Wood who stepped onto the massive Nimitz-class aircraft carrier. The freezing gusts of sea spray whipping across the flight deck chilled him to the bone and caused an involuntary shutter. Seagulls floated in midair scavenging for their next meal. A navy ensign ran up and yelled something inaudible, he guessed it was an offer to help carry the luggage. With the choice of handing over his personal carry-on bag or the metal briefcase, he gave up the carry-on.

They hurried away from the helicopter.

"Welcome to the USS Vinson," the young man said.

Robert was now able to see the F/A-18 Hornet fighter jets up close. They had been quite a sight as the helo made its approach from the air. He was escorted to two officers who stood waiting.

"Mr. Wood? I'm Commander Hockman and this is Lieutenant Brett. Please follow us."

The ensign handed back the luggage and jogged off. Robert attempted to keep up as they made their way toward Primary Flight Control, also known as *the tower*.

"How was your trip?"

"Well, I flew into the Kenai Peninsula Airport in a prop plane, so I lost part of my hearing, and this was my first ride in a helicopter."

"Probably not as comfortable as the luxury private jets the politicians like to fly around in?" the commander derided.

"I'm glad I didn't lose my lunch."

"Did you have the barf-bag ready?"

"Never crossed my mind, sir."

"Good man."

The truth was he had battled some nausea, he just wouldn't admit it to these salty dogs. As they entered the tower, Robert noticed the seal above the door; azure and gold against a white background. An eagle poised to strike, its wings spread and talons extended. The beak was clamped down on a banner with the Latin phrase "Vis Per Mare" meaning "Strength through the Sea." The eagle was not only emblematic of the United States of America, but of Carl Vinson's call-sign as a pilot; *Gold Eagle*. This time Robert had done his research and hoped it would pay off somehow.

Entering the control tower was like moving into another dimension. An authoritative figure turned from a digital satellite map he was studying.

"I'm Captain Spears. And you must be our civilian guest from the states."

"Robert Wood, sir, nice to meet you." He held out his hand, which was reluctantly shaken.

"Welcome to the Vinson." He turned back to the nautical atlas.

Primary Flight Control was intense, resembling something out of a sci-fi movie. Despite the numerous men sitting at state-of-the-art computer stations it was quiet enough to hear a pin drop. There were no windows though most everyone appeared to face the bow. The nebulous blue glow emitted by the massive projection screen created a temple-like atmosphere. The Vinson, a 1970s carrier, had gone through a three year complex overhaul with high-tech upgrades impressive even by the standards of a civilian.

"Ever been on a ship?" Captain Spears was facing Robert again.

"Nothing bigger than a ferry I'm afraid."

"So why are you on mine?"

"Well, Senator Matthews sent me to deliver something to you."

He set the briefcase down and used a key to unlock the latches, then handed a large sealed envelope to the captain.

"By hand?"

"It's eyes-only. I was told to give it directly to you." On the trip over he had decided to use "sir" as a show of respect, even though he was not military. So far it did not seem to impress anyone. "I'll be out of your hair as soon as possible, captain."

"We're in the middle of war games, I'm not sure when we'll get you back out. You're lucky you got here in the first place."

"I understand."

Captain Spears looked at his second in command, "I'll be in my office, commander, you're in charge."

"Yes, sir!" Hockman saluted.

"Lieutenant, show Mr. Wood to his cabin and make sure he has a map so he can get around on his own."

"Sir!"

"Thank you," he said as the captain left.

Robert closed the briefcase, grabbed his carry-on, and followed Lieutenant Brett to an elevator.

"I wouldn't do too much exploring. There are five miles of passageways, even with the map you'll probably still get lost. We don't call it The Carl Prison for nothing." He pressed the down button causing the hydraulics to kick-in. "The aft galley is below us, it's open around the clock so help yourself to chow when you get hungry."

The doors opened and they stepped inside. The lift plunged into a rapid descent.

"I don't think the captain likes me very much."

"Anytime politicians start sending couriers with classified documents, he gets edgy."

They exited the elevator and soon arrived at a cabin door, which the lieutenant unlocked. "These are the guest bunks. It's not exactly the Hilton, but should be comfortable enough. And you have your own shower."

"It'll be fine, I'm sure."

The small room had a single bed and a workstation built into the wall. It smelled clean and the sheets looked fresh. All in all, it was better than he expected. The lieutenant handed him a key and a leaflet.

"Here's a map of the ship, but again—"

"I know, don't go exploring."

"My direct line is . . ." He wrote down his number, then gave Robert a small packet. "Here, take these."

"What are they?"

"Motion sickness pills."

"The boat is barely rocking."

"If you don't have experience *on the blue*, there's no telling how you'll react. It can sneak up on you, we don't know if you have sea legs. These will cause drowsiness, but there's plenty of coffee onboard."

"Okay, thanks."

"By the way, your cell phone won't work out on the Bering Sea and we're on communications lockdown during the war games, so you can't call the mainland. I have to get back. If you need anything, let me know."

Lieutenant Brett left, closing the door behind him. Robert took out his phone and turned the power off, setting it on the table next to the motion sickness pills.

The thought of taking medication that would make him drowsy wasn't enticing. He had never liked pills, not even aspirin. He unpacked his carry-on bag and took a shower. A slight rocking caused him to slide on the wet tile floor. Robert dressed and relaxed on the bed.

A knock on the cabin door came just as he began to doze off.

"Mr. Wood," Commander Hockman stood in the doorway.

"Yes?"

"Is your brother Tristan Wood? The marine?"

"That he is."

"Captain Spears would like you to join us for dinner."

"Sure, when?"

"Now."

"Okay."

Robert grabbed his wallet and locked the room behind him. As they made their way through the ship it dawned on him how massive the USS Vinson was. It was a city on the sea. They entered a loft with a large dining table and four place settings of fine china. The sunset provided a view of the Bering Sea that was spectacular.

Just then, the captain walked in followed by Lieutenant Brett.

"Gentlemen," Captain Anthony Spears said in a formal tone. "How good of you to join me for dinner tonight."

After they sat down, a cook began to serve them: steak, potatoes, and veggies.

"This is a fine ship you have, captain." The civilian attempted to break the ice.

"Yes it is," he agreed. "It's the third in the Nimitz-class of super carriers named after—"

"Named after Georgia Congressman Carl Vinson and commissioned in 1987," Robert interrupted. "Carl Vinson was a member of the House of Representatives for fifty years and Chairman of the House Naval Affairs and Armed Services Committee for twenty-nine of those. He had been the sponsor for the Vinson Acts, responsible for the massive ship building effort in World War II. In the early 1980s it specialized in chasing Soviet Charlie-class submarines, and was the first modern US aircraft carrier to operate in the Bering Sea."

The three men looked stunned. Robert took a big bite of his steak.

"Want more?" he asked, now emboldened. "The keel was laid back in 1975 and put to sea five years later. Congressman Vinson became the first person in the history of the United States navy to witness a ship's launching in his honor. It's over 1000 feet long, powered by two Westinghouse nuclear reactors, and can hold up to 130 fixed wing fighter jets and numerous helicopters, although it appears you currently have, I'd guess, about ninety F/A-18 Hornets on board?"

"Close enough," the lieutenant confirmed.

Robert smiled, knowing his research had been worth it.

"Impressive," the captain said. "You're the only civilian we've seen in months. What's the intel from the states?"

"Well, Washington remains broken and politicians are still corrupt," Robert managed to get a laugh. "You're probably aware the stock market is tanking, people are getting worried about the economy again." The reaction was collective agreement. "I saw other ships as we were flying in. How many are participating in the war games?"

"We've got Carrier Strike Group One here now, including the carrier Air Wing Seventeen, the destroyer Squadron 1, and the guided missile cruiser Bunker Hill."

"Forgive me sir, but it seems our relationship with Russia is deteriorating, yet there's nothing in the news back home."

"The media is clueless."

"What scenario do you practice in the war games?" Robert asked.

"The strategy designed by the Pentagon," Commander Hockman interjected.

"Which is what?"

Lieutenant Brett spoke up. "That's classified."

"I'm not asking for specifics. I'm just wondering, since Russia begins theirs with a pre-emptive nuclear strike, do you practice winning a war with them? Playing offense? Or do you plan for a response after we've been attacked?"

"We train for multiple scenarios," the captain said, dodging the question. "With the ongoing cuts in the defense budget, thanks to beltway politicians, we're lucky we have a leg to stand on."

Robert decided to give it a rest. The defensive tension at the table was giving him a queasy feeling in his stomach. He looked out the windows with his eyes squinted as the sunset turned the entire room a deep rich red.

"Sir, can I ask how you know Tristan is my brother?"

"Your Senator Matthews included a note along with the information you delivered to me."

"A note?"

The cook cleared away the empty plates and poured coffee.

"Apparently he wanted to make sure we treated you well." The captain blew on his drink to cool it off. "I read the USAA article. A fine couple, your brother and his wife. How are they doing?"

"Tristan's honorably discharged from the marines, he's an FBI agent, and Allyson is in her residency at Walter Reed Medical Center. She treats a lot of the soldiers coming in from the wars we rarely hear about anymore."

Robert's queasy abruptly changed to nausea.

"I've been to the new Walter Reed, it's impressive. We're going to need it, for all the new injured troops we'll have."

"New, sir?"

"You okay?" Lieutenant Brett asked. "You're looking a little green."

"I don't feel so good."

"Did you take the motion sickness pills I gave you?"

"Well . . ." The answer was obvious.

"I told you it would sneak up on you."

"I think I need to use your bathroom, please."

"Follow me." Commander Hockman led him out of the room.

Robert entered the lavatory and closed the door behind him. Another wave of nausea overcame him and he gave back his dinner. After recovering, he walked out to Lieutenant Brett who stood holding a hypodermic and a cotton swab.

"I hate needles."

"Would you rather feel this way for the next few days?"

He pulled up his sleeve and took the shot.

"What's in this?" Robert asked.

"A couple medications, one for nausea and the other is a bit of a sedative. It should start working almost immediately. You need to lie down for a while, then drink lots of water. First thing in the morning take those pills I gave you, and two more every twelve hours for the next three days, even after you're off the ship."

"Thanks."

"And stay hydrated, keep drinking water."

Robert returned to his room and fell into bed. It was a blessing the nausea was already gone, but he was groggy. He began to drift in and out of sleep with flashes of helicopters entering his dreams, dogfights with fighter jets, and off in the distance a bright flash followed by a mushroom cloud. Time blurred as he drifted in and out of consciousness.

Knock, knock.

"Yes? Hold on."

Realizing how much better he was, Robert opened the door to a man he did not recognize.

"Mr. Wood? I'm Lieutenant Hornell."

After a momentary torpor, he snapped out of it. "Oh, come in." He secured the latch and spoke softly. "What are you doing here, if someone comes to check on me—"

"Why are you on this ship?"

The question surprised him. "I came to deliver some intel to Captain Spears. Senator Matthews sent me."

"What is it?"

"I don't know, it's eyes-only. He wanted it delivered personally, so it must be sensitive."

"I have information for you. Russia is planning a series of war games, we were told today at our briefing. The ones we're running now are nothing in comparison. It's another simulated, and massive, nuclear first strike on the United States."

"How big?" Robert asked.

"Putin's snap check drills in 2013 had more than 160,000 troops, 5000 tanks, 70 ships, and over 320 tons of equipment including jet aircraft and helicopters, and rocket artillery. It was the largest Russian military exercise in history; until now. We are anticipating at least 300,000 troops and more than ten times the amount of hardware. It will be the biggest non-combat military operation of all time. This is the beginning of Putin's new Soviet Union."

"You said something about chemical and biological weapons when you called the senator?"

"Specifically, gas attacks. In this scenario, after America loses the war, areas of resistance, those who fight back with guns, will be gassed until they submit, or are wiped out."

"When are they planning these exercises?" Robert asked.

"July 4."

"Our Independence Day?"

"That's right."

"What's the United States doing about it?"

"Nothing, so far. You need to get off this ship, I've got a hunch this isn't training anymore."

"What do you mean?"

"I don't think it's going to be simulated this time. I believe this is going to be World War III."

CHAPTER 29

A rainbow pushed through the heavy mixture of mist and sunshine, one arch vanishing behind the United States Capitol. The FBI agents sat watching Ivan and Petrev who loitered in front of a mid-rise apartment building. They were not acting particularly subtle. Tristan aimed the electronic ear and turned on the recording device he had borrowed from FBI.

Then the Russians reacted to something.

A middle-aged man in shorts and a T-shirt strolled down the sidewalk singing along with music from an iPod. Oblivious, he nearly collided with them. Ivan asked for a light of his cigarette. The man searched his pockets, found a Zippo, and the three began having a conversation as they smoked.

"Great," Tristan said.

"What?"

"They're speaking Russian again. We'll have to find someone at the Bureau to translate."

Though the language was unintelligible, things became heated quickly. The confrontation came to a head when the man attempted to push by Ivan and Petrev who grabbed and led him to the far side of the building.

"What's happening?" Sebastian asked.

"They're out of range, I lost audio."

They held their breath. A minute later the guy scurried from around the corner, holding a hand over his mouth, and rushed into the lobby. Ivan and Petrev reappeared, obviously pleased with themselves. They finished their cigarettes and walked off. For the most part, this had pretty much gone the same way as hours earlier when they strong-armed another man across town. Their task was to persuade the embassy security guards—by any means necessary—to allow the trucks entry on the day of the bombings. The Russians were doing their job.

"Let's head back to the warehouse."

Tristan gathered up the surveillance equipment as the unmarked car pulled into the street and drove off.

"I finally watched *End Game*."

"Really?" Sebastian became excited. "What did you think?"

"Amazing! It was exhilarating, depressing, and exhausting, all at the same time. The pieces of the puzzle are finally coming together. I think I'm starting to understand the New World Order. The most insidious part of their program has to be eugenics and population control. And it's going on right in front of us. I didn't realize eugenics actually started in the US?"

"Most people don't. What's been essentially erased from the history books is that by the late nineteenth century the United States had joined fourteen other nations in passing eugenics legislation."

Tristan had done his own research after watching the documentary. The American Heritage Dictionary defined eugenics as "the study of hereditary improvement of the human race by controlled selective breeding." But it was a practice best described by its founder, Sir Francis Galton, an English psychologist who explained it as "the science of improving the stock to give more suitable races or strains of blood a better chance of prevailing speedily over the less suitable."

The objective was to determine who was dirtying the gene pool and fix it; through any means necessary. Eugenics-studies programs were promptly set up at Cornell, Stanford, Princeton, Harvard, and Columbia. Overseas, Winston Churchill became the director of the first International Congress of Eugenics in London that convened in 1912.

Sebastian continued, "By the late 1800s, thirty states had laws providing for the sterilization of mental patients and imbeciles and at least sixty thousand people were legally sterilized. California was the epicenter of the American eugenics movement with a group of race scientists who sterilized about ten thousand women, most considered bad girls, oversexed, sexually wayward, or passionate. California actually had sterilization mills in Sonoma, Napa, Norwalk, Mendocino, Agnews, Stockton, and Pacific County, funded by the Harriman railroad fortune, the Carnegie Institution, and guess who else?"

"The Rockefeller Foundation." Tristan didn't have to even think about it.

"Of course. The Rockefellers, Harrimans, and Carnegies contributed a combined $11 million to establish and fund the Eugenics Records Office in Cold Springs, NY, with Alexander Graham Bell as chairman."

The sedan passed through the Navy Yard.

"What bothers me is, when there's an agenda it gets turned into so-called science, in order to convince the masses it's legit," Tristan said.

"The scientific rationale for tyranny has always been attractive to the elites, giving them a reason to treat their fellow man as lower than animals. The history of eugenics includes a cast of evil and misguided characters. Robert Malthus advocated for his *Malthusian Catastrophe*, a mass food collapse to wipe out the poor. His ideas led to the *Theory of Evolution* created by Charles Darwin, a huge admirer of Malthus, with its chief tenet being, *survival of the fittest*. With the help of T.H. Huxley, called Darwin's Bulldog because of his strong support, the theories of evolution and eugenics were pushed into wide acceptance among key scientific circles first in England, then around the world. Sir Francis Galton saw an opportunity to advance Darwin's theory by applying it to social issues, creating Social Darwinism. It's the philosophy of useless eaters. Keep the slaves just healthy enough to produce what society needs to function and control their population via disease, war, sterilization through vaccines and chemicals like fluoride, and abortions."

As they crossed the George Mason Bridge into Virginia, Tristan said, "Allyson has told me how Planned Parenthood, which changed its name from the American Birth Control League, was an abortion mill disguised as a women's health clinic. I had no idea Margaret Sanger admittedly created the organization to get rid of minorities, specifically blacks."

"Margaret Sanger began a campaign to recruit black leaders to front sterilization programs directed against African-American communities, and it continues today. Jesse Jackson was anti-abortion before running for president in the 90s and openly expressed the view that abortion was just an excuse to wipe out the black race. When his campaign began, he fell in line with the globalists he needed funding from, and suddenly became pro-choice claiming white Republicans wanted to deny minority women this right—the Hegelian Dialectic in political action. These same eugenicists created the feminist movement for that very reason. How do you get a group of people to kill themselves? You convince them it's their right to abort their babies," Sebastian deplored.

"I also didn't realize Hitler got his idea for the *Final Solution* from American eugenicists."

"Hitler actually credited American eugenicists in *Mein Kampf*, and sent fan letters to Madison Grant, a eugenicist and conservationist, who wrote a book called *The Passing of the Great Race*. Hitler referred to it as his Bible while developing his plan of mass extermination of the Jews and other 'sub-races' based on Grant's writings. Interestingly, the most popular idea for euthanasia discussed in the United States in the early twentieth century was the employment of the gas chamber. By 1927 eugenics hit the mainstream and was aggressively pushed through schools, religious organizations, and state fairs. Churches actually had cash prizes to see who could best implement eugenics into their sermons, and church-goers were told Jesus was pro-eugenics. That same year, twenty-five states passed sterilization laws and the Supreme Court even ruled in favor of these policies. When Congress met in New York in 1932, it was the Hamburg America Shipping Line, controlled by Harriman associates George Walker and Prescott Bush, who brought prominent Germans to the meeting. One of those Germans, Doctor Ernst Rudin, was behind the Nazi Sterilization Act."

They weaved through northern Virginia traffic, the late afternoon sun overpowering the air conditioning inside the vehicle.

Sebastian was on a roll again, "When Hitler came to power in 1933 one of his first acts was to nationalize healthcare and pass eugenics laws based on those in the US. By 1936 Germany led the world in sterilization, euthanasia, and abortions. The Rockefellers sent scientists to Germany to help the Nazis fine-tune their extermination system. After WWII the Allies fought over who would bring home the Nazi scientists, with the United States getting the largest share under the program called *Operation Paperclip*. Although the elites were embarrassed by Hitler's brand of eugenics, it didn't stop them, it just manifested into different forms. Eugenics Quarterly changed its name to Social Biology, the American Birth Control League became Planned Parenthood, racial hygiene became population control, and Social Darwinism became environmentalism. Eugenics scientists chose to go underground and redirect their practices into other disciplines such as anthropology, biology, economics, geography, history, sociology, and even the law."

Tristan added, "And how many people know Thomas J. Watson, the founder of IBM, was a devout follower of Hitler and supplied the punch card computers and technicians to the Nazis in their death camps? The tattoos on the camp victim's arms were IBM human identification numbers, which fed into the computer system to keep an inventory. It's hard to imagine the first computers were designed for this purpose."

They turned off the highway and headed for the warehouse.

"Aldous Huxley," Sebastian said, "gave a speech at Berkley in the early 1960s in which he asserted that there would soon be a pharmacological method of making people love their servitude to produce a dictatorship without tears, producing a kind of painless concentration camp for entire societies. The citizens would in fact have their liberties taken away but rather enjoy it because they'd be distracted from any desire to rebel, by propaganda and brainwashing enhanced by pharmacological methods."

"Apparently it's already underway," Tristan lamented.

"The problem for the globalists is that it's not happening fast enough. The only way to quickly reduce the population is with one big event. Then the eugenicists can keep it under control so it doesn't get above whatever limit they set while weeding out the undesirables. Just like the Georgia Guidestones say."

"The what?" Tristan asked.

"The Georgia Guidestones, the globalist monument to the New World Order. You'll probably never see it up close and in person, check out the Wikipedia page. It resembles a scaled-down version of Stonehenge. No one knows for sure who built it, but it's under twenty-four hour surveillance by local law enforcement. Wild stuff."

They arrived at the van and parked.

"There's one more thing you need to understand, Tristan," Sebastian became deadly serious. "The New World Order plan is based on a very old ideology."

"What ideology?"

"The Order of the Illuminati." He continued, with trepidation. "They were publically founded May 1, 1776 in Germany by Adam Weishaupt. We know they exist because in 1785 a courier died en route to Paris while carrying documents including a tract written by Weishaupt outlining the secret society's long-range plan for 'The New World Order through world revolution.' They infiltrated the Freemasons, many of whom were Founding Fathers. By the turn of the nineteenth century the Illuminati was established at William and Mary, Yale, and other American institutions of higher learning including numerous organizations such as Skull & Bones. By that time they could not be stopped. These syndicates, these secret societies, are not a group of harmless frat boys as they claim. They are Luciferian."

"Satanists?"

"Not in the traditional meaning of the word. They believe Lucifer came to the Garden of Eden to save Adam and Eve from ignorance by eating the forbidden fruit. Gaining this knowledge freed Adam and Eve, and mankind, from being God's slaves. Lucifer actually means 'light bearer.' In their world God is the oppressor. Call them the Elites, Insiders, Globalists, whatever label you want, but their beliefs are those of the Illuminati. And their code is *do what thou wilt.*"

"What does that mean?"

"It means they can, and will, say anything to advance themselves within the cause. You may meet a member and not even know it. He or she could be an independent businessman, a corporate CEO, an entertainer, Hollywood producer, a media mogul, a politician . . . they will drip information to test you, it's a game to them, they'll even claim to be against the New World Order. You can research this yourself, there's no lack of books written on the subject. It's all around us. The signs of the Illuminati are everywhere, even built right into the streets of Washington, DC. They are powerful. Powerful beyond belief."

Before Tristan could ask more questions, Sebastian was out of the car.

The two special agents climbed inside the van and greeted their G, studying the monitors. Tristan placed the digital recorder on the table.

"What's going on, Tony?"

"Busy day, boss. Lots of activity."

Thanks to Sebastian, the Bureau did not have time to shut the case down after he revealed a gun deal was in the works. After consulting with the director, the history of the *Fast and Furious* scandal forced Pascal and FBI to back off.

"Did they buy a get-away car?"

"Two, actually. And these are even junkier than their regular cars. I don't get it."

The new automobiles included a 1980s LaBaron sedan and a black Trans Am, most likely from the '70s. The video monitors broadcast J.J. and Liam piling up sacks in the far corner of the warehouse.

"Is that fertilizer?"

"I counted twenty, or so, bags. They showed up an hour ago."

"How did this happen? Did you know about this?" Sebastian asked Tony.

"Nope, caught me completely by surprise."

Finishing their work, Liam announced an appointment he was late for and drove off in the Trans Am. J.J. waited until the car was out of site, then headed for the surveillance van.

"We're letting the informant control the case. We need to get this guy reigned in or something bad is going to happen."

Sebastian was right, they had to keep track of what was happening at all times. If not, they could lose valuable evidence, or worse. Tristan felt embarrassed. "I'll have a talk with him."

Not bothering to knock, J.J. opened the back door and climbed in.

"What do you think you're doing, snitch?"

"Huh?"

"You were out gathering bomb materials? You're supposed to tell us when you do that!"

"Why are you always riding me, G-man? The guy just showed up at my house. I was with him the whole time so I didn't have a chance to text you."

"Where did you get the fertilizer?" Tristan asked.

"Stole it. We went to different construction sites this morning. It was easier than I thought with so many unfinished building projects around."

"We can't protect you if we don't know where you are or what you're doing. You could get pinched, your cover blown, any number of things," Tristan explained.

"And the cars?" Sebastian asked.

"Liam bought them, with cash, a few days ago. He picked me up in the Trans Am, he seems to love that car. He drove me out to the LaBaron and we brought them back here. Those will be the get-aways we'll park by the embassies before the bombings, for the Russians to use."

"They don't look dependable."

"That's what I told Liam, but he had a mechanic friend check them out and they're okay."

"You *must* contact us if that happens again, all right?" Tristan attempted diplomacy. "Say you have to go to the bathroom or something, and text me."

"Yeah, fine."

"When is the gun deal going down?" Sebastian got back to the point.

"I'm not sure, but I get the feeling it will be soon."

"You get the feeling?" Fed up, Sebastian sat down and played the digital recording from their stake-out.

"What makes you think that?" Tristan asked.

"Liam made a couple of comments about it today, I suspect he's been talking to the Major but won't admit it." J.J. heard the recording. "What's that?"

"We followed the Russians this morning."

J.J. took a step closer to better hear the voices. "We need your help, comrade . . . you work at the Russian embassy . . . yes? You will be our new friend."

Sebastian looked up in disbelief. "What the hell?"

He continued, "When the time comes we will contact you . . . we need a favor. You will let us into the embassy . . . I can't do that . . . you have family in Russia, yes? We are KGB, if you help us we leave them alone . . ."

"You speak Russian?"

"Of course," J.J. said. "My father's Russian, it's the first language I learned."

CHAPTER 30

The plastic chair Doctor Allyson Wood sat on, outside the hospital's laboratory, could not be more uncomfortable. She kept her knee-length white lab coat on for warmth. Finally off-the-clock after a long day, fatigue began to set in. It would be nice to get home.

"A few more minutes, dear," said Nurse Julie from behind the counter. "Can I fetch you a drink of water? Coffee? Or if you don't want to hang around, I'll have you paged when the fax comes in?"

"No thank you Julie, I don't mind waiting."

Allyson felt sick to her stomach. She would soon have the results from the fertility test. One of them might have a problem, or both. There was also the possibility they were fine. Sometimes it just took longer, as Tristan constantly told her. She prayed it was the latter.

To take her mind off the wait she pulled out the booklet Sebastian had given them. The cover photo showed two despondent teenagers, and the full title was; *Basics in Education: 1, The Leipzig Connection* by Paolo Lionni. Having read it front to back once already, Allyson started over again to make sure she didn't miss anything. Counting the numerous photographs of various psychologists and universities it was still only about 90 pages long.

The information was shocking.

It explained so much, including how the public schools had become increasingly infested with drugs and crime since WWI. A clear linear series of facts documented why many seniors graduated unable to read, spell, or do simple math, and why no amount of money would ever solve the problem—even though funding always seemed to be the core of the argument.

The teaching method in schools today was rooted in psychology. At Georgetown University, Allyson had started out as a psych-major before switching to biology. But she did not recall learning the real history of the "science" and how it changed the educational system, as The Leipzig Connection revealed.

Before the mid-1800s, psychology simply meant the study of the soul. Then along came *Experimental Psychology*. She opened to the first page to read the man's name again; Wilhelm Maximilian Wundt.

Wundt was responsible for the fundamental revision in the study of psychology, the founding of experimental psychology, and was the catalyst for its spread through the western world. Wundt hypothesized that something was only worth studying if it could be measured, quantified, and scientifically demonstrated. And since this was not possible with the soul, which he didn't believe in anyway, he decided psychology should be physiological and not philosophical.

Wundt postulated that a human being was nothing more than a body with a brain and central nervous system, and a person's personality was a compilation of their experiences, consisting of actions and reactions. Wundt's philosophical basis for the principles of conditioning were later developed by Pavlov who researched physiology in Leipzig in 1884, five years after Wundt created his lab there.

To study in Leipzig, Germany, at the time was considered a prestigious honor. The Americans who studied under Wundt returned to the United States and founded psychology departments, securing positions of influence at major universities. In turn, they trained hundreds of psychologists who went off to train hundreds more. The eventual result was that American students would no longer be educated, but rather conditioned like Pavlov's dog.

A young couple fawned over a newborn wrapped in a blue blanket, capturing Allyson's attention. They strolled down the hall, oblivious to the world around them. Her body quivered with longing. She shook it off and continued reading.

John Dewey, the so-called father of education, published *Psychology* in 1887, the first American textbook welding experimental psychology to child education. The University of Chicago granted him $1000 to establish a lab where he could apply psychological principles and experimental techniques to the study of learning. Dewey believed, to prepare a child for a democratic society the school should be social, not individualistic. This was a sharp break from the traditional definition of "education."

The Wundtian redefinition of education meant feeding experimental data to a young brain and nervous system rather than the teaching of mental skills and critical thinking. This led to the role-change of the teacher who was no longer an instructor but a guide in the socialization of the child. The student was trained to adapt a specific behavior required of him to get along with his group. Successful, Dewey was able to implement and promote the interchangeability of psychology and education.

Edward Lee Thorndike was a first-generation Wundt graduate in the new discipline and performed experiments on chickens, testing their behavior and pioneering animal psychology. Thorndike, who concluded man could be studied in a lab like an animal, went to Columbia University and brought his two most intelligent chickens. His specialty was the "puzzle box" into which he put various animals including chickens, rats, and cats. The objective was to find their way out of the maze.

Thorndike was the first psychologist to study animal behavior in his experimental psychology lab and apply the same techniques to juveniles. The result of his work was the 1903 book *Educational Psychology*. He directly equated children with rats, monkeys, fish, cats, and chickens.

From his studies, Thorndike came up with laws that he applied to the training of teachers who went about integrating this new educational psychology into classrooms and schools. The idea was to give or withhold stimuli with the result producing or preventing certain responses—the origins of *conditioning*. Therefore, a teacher would reinforce a good behavior with a reward or eliminate a bad one, called negative reinforcement.

Within fifty years juvenile delinquency was rampant, illiterates poured out of schools, and teachers no longer learned how to teach. To keep the public ignorant of the truth, the Hegelian Dialectic—in this case the argument over lack of funding—was employed so fighting between both sides continued.

Allyson retained a vivid memory of understanding a sentence for the very first time, connecting the string of words into one thought. She sat with her mother who encouraged her to continue until she had finished the entire book. That cardinal experience had instilled a love of reading which Allyson hoped to one day share with her children. That is, if she were lucky enough to have them.

She continued with the Leipzig Connection.

It took hundreds of millions of dollars to turn education around in such a short time, and this money came from the Standard Oil Company owned and operated by J.D. Rockefeller. Rockefeller began his petrol business in 1863, and by 1880 he controlled 95 percent of US oil production. He dominated every aspect of the industry including the price of a barrel of oil. Rockefeller sabotaged his competitors, hired spies to infiltrate the businesses of his enemies, and squeezed out independent operators by carefully conceived secret contracts.

In 1910 when a glass of beer was a penny, a loaf of bread less than a nickel, a three-room apartment rented for five dollars a month, and a good pair of shoes cost a dollar, J.D. Rockefeller was worth $800 million, or tens of billions by today's inflationary numbers. Interestingly, for a man who helped institute an educational system that rejected natural born talents, Rockefeller himself considered his moneymaking abilities to be a gift from God and a talent, such as one's instincts for music, art, or literature. And because of his wealth he became one of the most hated men in America.

Although J.D. Rockefeller had written large checks to Baptist causes over the years, it did little for his reputation. His goal became one of improving his public image. The plan he came up with was to launder the Rockefeller money, to gain a monopoly on philanthropy and funnel cash into causes that would give him recognition. Because of the success of a grant to the University of Chicago, which helped his image among Baptists and educators, he decided education was a good way to go. The problem was the American public school system wasn't all that bad.

Thomas Jefferson had believed in order to maintain liberty, the population must be educated. Schools were established almost immediately after the colonization of new areas and the school system was deeply rooted in the beliefs and practices of the Puritan Fathers, the Quakers, and early American patriots and philosophers. Educational results in the 1700s and 1800s were far superior to the present, based on congressional records as proof. Students learned to read literature rather than comic books, and the math was much more advanced than today.

The south, however, had not recovered since the Civil War and was still under reconstruction. Few schools existed in rural areas, even for white children. To administer his plan, Rockefeller and his cronies formed the *General Education Board* and used one million dollars as an initial deposit while absorbing the other similar organizations in the south.

J.D. Rockefeller continued to be burdened with bad press and his health took a turn for the worse. His greatest desire at the time was to fund medicine and education to improve his name, while giving unlimited amounts of money to the Wundt psychologists for their ambitious designs of the American education system.

Allyson heard the familiar whirring of a fax machine and began to fidget. She breathed deep to clear her mind and calm her nerves. Returning to the book, she attempted to concentrate.

The Rockefellers funded *Columbia University's Teachers College* to implement their new psychology at a time when the numbers of school-age children were booming. Educational Psychology combined with Socialism became "Progressive Education." Then a $1.5 million grant from the Rockefellers to Johns Hopkins in 1913 went toward the development of chemical oriented medicine, or *Big Pharma*.

Since there was little profit in naturopathic medicine, Rockefeller money was steered to schools that disregarded naturopathy, homeopathy, and chiropractic, instead favoring surgery and chemical drugs. The combined funding of psychology and chemical medicine would culminate when in 1963 Ritalin was developed to treat children regarded as troubled or over-active.

Meanwhile, the General Education Board proceeded to attack traditional educational methods and became successful at eliminating the study of Greek and Latin. In addition, classical literature and formal English grammar would be dropped.

During WWI, Americans began to see this as an attempt by a minority of rich men to dominate everything taught in schools with an interest in shaping public opinion on matters just a few elites deemed important. The fight went to the US Senate, comparing this agenda to the government-controlled education of France and Germany. This was the last stand against the General Education Board and it failed.

In 1917, with the Wundt psychology and Rockefeller money combined, new textbooks were created and standard teaching practices revised. J.D. Rockefeller sent his sons to be taught under this Progressive Education but with disastrous results. Future Vice President Nelson Rockefeller himself did not learn to read or write correctly and frequently complained that reading was a tedious process.

One of the most damaging effects on the school system was the merging of history, geography, and civics into Social Studies—a vague class subject easily manipulated by political ideology. Testing would turn from open-ended questions requiring critically deduced answers, to a multiple choice format based on memorized regurgitation; Pavlovian learned-response training.

Followers of Progressive Education would make statements condemning Capitalism and property rights, with the plan to eliminate these concepts from the school curriculum altogether.

Progressive educators actually pushed for Marxism in the public schools and attacked Maria Montessori, founder of the Montessori School, for teaching reading, writing, and math at too young an age. Progressives would claim this impeded the child's creativity and therefore reading, especially, must be delayed.

Nurse Julie approached the counter and leaned over.

"Fax is coming through now, dear."

"Thanks, Julie."

Allyson had her parents to thank for her education. She was homeschooled until her mom surrendered to cancer, forcing her father to send her to public school starting junior year. Homeschoolers had always been considered odd, and increasingly they were being demonized by the government when in fact they performed far above the level of anyone in public and even most private schools. Allyson scored 1560 out of 1600 on her SATs, perfect on the verbal section but slipping up a bit on the math.

She quickly realized how depressing it was. Kids were entitled and rebellious, and a shocking number were on prescription drugs. Teens were obsessively preoccupied with their looks and entertainment, there was rampant drug use, and premarital sex. The only friend she made would end up as her first boyfriend, but she tried not to think about that.

Reading the Leipzig Connection reinforced her appreciation of homeschooling and brought back fond memories of the time spent with her mother.

"Here you go, Doctor Wood." Nurse Julie put the fax into an envelope. "I hope it's the news you want, dear," she smiled.

"Thanks Julie, have a good night."

"I always do," was the reply.

A short while later, Allyson sat in her car. Making a decision, she opened the envelope and read over the test results.

"Oh, my goodness."

Overcome by a rush of emotion, she began to cry.

After regaining her composure she wiped her eyes and pulled out of the parking lot, heading north on Old Georgetown Road. What she didn't notice was the car following her.

The mist and light rain made the visibility poor.

Allyson headed west on Democracy Boulevard, and sped up. So many thoughts raced through her mind she almost ran a red light in front of Montgomery Mall, triggering the anti-lock brakes on the slick pavement.

She took out her cell phone. About to make a call, the traffic light turned green and she tossed it onto the passenger seat. The vehicle behind her continued following at a safe distance.

She drove north on Seven Locks Road, the rain now pouring. Seven Locks was dark, hilly, and surrounded by dense clumps of trees. As the lanes converged into one, Allyson picked up the cell again and dialed Tristan's number.

In a flash, the sedan cruised alongside hers and a power window lowered.

She looked up from the phone just in time to see a large tree branch on the road ahead, and slammed on the brakes as gunfire erupted.

Allyson attempted to gain control of the vehicle.

Unable to maintain its traction the car began to spin, dropping into a ditch and kicking up mud. The momentum caused her to slide down into, then up and out of the gulley, flipping over.

A massive tree stopped the automobile with a deafening crash and it came to rest upside down.

The engine sputtered and died.

A wheel continued to spin, then slowed to a stop.

Seven Locks became quiet again, except for the clap of thunder.

CHAPTER 31

Tristan raced through the ER at Walter Reed National Military Medical Center. Various people waited to be seen by a doctor—active duty in uniform, seniors, parents with children—an emergency room was a depressing place. An orderly at the main desk confirmed Allyson had been brought in via ambulance. He hurried to the section of the hospital where his wife worked, and was now a patient.

"I'm Tristan Wood."

"I'm Nurse Julie, dear." She pulled him aside. "I've known Allyson a long time, she's a wonderful lady."

"How is she?"

"She's coming out of surgery any minute now."

"She needed surgery?"

"The paramedics recognized her and we called Doctor Michaels. He got here as fast as he could."

"What happened?"

"They found her car upside down on Seven Locks Road. I was just with her. She came to get her test results in the lab, then left to go home," Julie whimpered.

In large red digital numbers, the wall clock above the desk read; *11:11 p.m.*

A gurney burst through the double doors from the surgical wing. Allyson was unconscious. Tristan stood watching, his legs frozen in fear.

"Wait here," Julie said as she followed the gurney. "Let us get her settled in her room, okay?" She disappeared around the corner.

A doctor wearing scrubs stepped out. He handed a clipboard to a nurse who pointed at Tristan.

Walking over, he held out a hand. "I'm Doctor Michaels, you must be Agent Wood?"

He had a firm shake and looked him in the eyes as he spoke, something Tristan respected. Allyson crowed about her boss. As far as surgeons went, they didn't get any better.

"How is she?"

"Stable. There was internal damage, she has a bruised left kidney but both kidneys are functioning properly and the liver is fine. I did have to remove her appendix, gall bladder, and unfortunately her uterus."

"Oh no."

"The complication was the pregnancy. She was about a month along. I had to take out the entire uterus to stop the hemorrhaging."

"She was . . . she was pregnant?"

"I'm sorry, I assumed you knew." Doctor Michaels received a wave from the nurse. He placed a sympathetic hand on Tristan's shoulder. "You can see her now. The first twenty-four hours are crucial, but she should recover. She'll be in and out of consciousness for a while, it's best to let her get as much rest as possible." He walked away.

Tristan reluctantly entered Allyson's room, kissed her forehead and sat in a chair. She looked peaceful. He laid his head down on the bed next to her.

At times when he was alone, Tristan often reflected on the events that brought them together. The leg pain was a daily reminder. Although a teenager in 2001, he volunteered and signed-up for the United States Marine Corps because of 9/11 and the *war on terror*.

If not for Allyson, he would have died on the dirt trail that night. However, her assistance did not end there. After surgery, an infection set in and the doctors considered amputation. Obviously, Tristan refused.

Afraid a decision would be made while he was unconscious or incoherent, he took the smallest amount of medication tolerable in order to stay lucid. He remained vigilant, determined to keep his leg and fully recover from his injuries.

Allyson, whom he did not know, was his only ally in the lonely hospital halfway around the world. Acting as his advocate, she made sure they did not take his limb. Later, based on their experience, she admitted having a personal stake in Tristan's recovery.

And that was perfectly fine with him.

Firebase Vimoto in the Korengal Valley of Afghanistan was a dangerous place. When the troops weren't on patrol they were busy with chores such as fortifying the outpost or burning off waste from the latrine.

Much of their effort was spent gathering intel by listening to chatter with an interpreter over various radio frequencies. But most of their time was used defending the base. Attacks came regularly and sometimes more than once a day.

New troops, or "cherries," did not believe how bad it was until they actually arrived and witnessed it themselves. As for the old-timers like PFC Tristan Wood, they hated it here.

One half mile south of the Korengal Outpost, Firebase Vimoto was one of several smaller bases along the Korengal Valley in the Kunar Province. Kunar was one of the first places to rise up against the Soviet occupation in the 1980s giving it the label; *Cradle of Jihad*. During Tristan's tour, it was one of the most hard-fought and dangerous areas in Afghanistan.

The base had been renamed after the late PFC Timothy Vimoto of Fort Campbell in Kentucky, killed in the spring of 2007 when his unit was attacked by insurgents. The young man had followed the path of his father but his life was cut short at the age of nineteen in the very first firefight of his military career.

PFC Vimoto was loved by everyone. His marine brothers were so distraught when he was killed that renaming it was a no-brainer. The base was eventually shut down due to high casualty rates and low results.

In the *Valley of Death*, every day could be the last. Sniper bullets randomly flew by, and since they traveled faster than the speed of sound, the first one was not heard. Many American soldiers were killed this way—they never knew what hit them. And if it wasn't a sniper, the threat of a larger assault constantly loomed like a dark cloud.

The enemy would lob mortars, fire rockets, and shoot off Russian-made AK-47s. Waiting for daily attacks created an enormous amount of stress. Tough as the troops were they had the highest percentage of post-duty medication, highest rate of self-inflicted wounds, and the highest suicide rate.

Later, it would be discovered that more than fifty percent of those who had been in the KOP for a prolonged period of time were put on SSRIs such as Prozac or Paxil. Often they depended on drugs and alcohol to relax and sleep. The other half simply accepted it.

Most new soldiers were barely out of high school and had gone from living in their parent's house to fighting the first major war of the century. In the beginning, everything was novel with much to learn. Then, one day, reality would hit like a two ton heavy thing. They loathed it, yet no world existed outside the Korengal Valley.

And tonight, Tristan's life would change forever.

On that fateful evening, command had obtained intel there was going to be a surprise attack on Firebase Vimoto. This was not uncommon, but from the conversations they picked up it seemed to indicate the assault would be a suicide mission.

The Taliban were able to recruit young, angry, and desperate men willing to become martyrs while the cowards who enlisted them hid in caves far from harm. The goal of the suicide mission was simply to take out as many Americans as possible.

The squad was sent out late in the day to scout potential gatherings of the enemy and radio in the position for the mortar teams.

Tristan was assigned to First Platoon in *Company F* lead by Sergeant Morreno. Typically called Fox Company, they chose instead to call themselves Falcon Company because of the abundance of falcon species in Afghanistan. Where, in the States, it was common to see blackbirds and several types of ducks without thinking twice, it was the same with falcons in Afghanistan. They took on this company call-sign, in part because it was such a fierce predator, and also out of humility. They were proud to be Falcon Company.

It was not standard procedure to leave on a mission so close to dark. The decision was made to disrupt the operation rather than wait around for the inevitable. The plan was to follow one of the Korengal River tributaries south, then head west on a seldom used trail to Honcho Hill where they believed Taliban forces were gathering. The mission was not to engage but to report activity and positions of the enemy.

The squad consisted of eight soldiers including Platoon Sergeant Morreno. Four were designated *Fireteam Alpha* and four, *Fireteam Bravo*. They carried everything they needed and were supplied for several days, just in case.

Following an equipment check the platoon hoofed it out of base camp. The men stayed quiet as they marched, keeping all eyes open. The Taliban's best weapons were information and disinformation. They paid locals to listen in on the conversations of the Americans and observe their movements.

There were many similarities between the Korengal Valley and Vietnam, mainly because it was almost impossible to tell a civilian from an enemy unless they were holding a gun and firing. A sheep herder might guide his flock along a hilltop, followed minutes later by an attack on the base. Regarding disinformation, chatter filled the radio waves, often fabricated to throw them off. There was only a 50/50 chance of getting correct information from any given source.

After a half-hour of walking, the river road took a sharp turn to the left and the path narrowed. Tristan remembered this part of the trail, a narrow passage with no trees for cover; a great place to set an ambush. It would also be difficult for a Black Hawk to maneuver here if a rescue became necessary. By this time they had relaxed and a marine named O'Brien told jokes.

Then a *poof* of air preceded PFC Ajit collapsing.

What happened next was a barrage of machine gun fire and RPGs that exploded all around them. Everyone either hit the deck or ran for cover. The men hugged the ground, trying to evaluate their situation.

Platoon Sergeant Morreno bravely remained in the middle of the chaos and located a motionless PFC Ajit, using the radio to call in a mortar strike. Morreno then joined the rest of the squad, firing rounds at the ridge.

As Tristan moved to his sergeant's side, what he perceived as a lightning bolt, pierced his left thigh.

It spun him around 180 degrees and he fell to the ground.

Without warning, the shelling began. A deafening barrage of rockets caused the earth to quake beneath them. The projectiles came from a 155 Howitzer back at base, a huge smoke-colored gun that looked like it belonged on a battleship.

The explosions triggered an avalanche of rock and stone that tumbled down the ridge. The dust that was kicked up worked in the squad's favor by providing a cloud cover, but unfortunately did not last long.

The first round of shelling subsided, allowing for a brief evaluation of the scene. Ajit still lay motionless. Through the dust, another team member lay face-down on the path ahead of him. A few yards away his platoon sergeant was on his back, attempting to change the magazine in his M-4.

The ground erupted around them for a second time.

Tristan once again experienced *lighting* through his left leg, then everything went black.

In the reality of the hospital, Allyson squeezed his hand. A phantom glow from the medical equipment permeated the darkness in the room.

"Hi," she said weakly.

"Hey, how are you feeling?" Tristan asked, elated.

"Like I got in a car accident."

That made him laugh.

"Do you remember what happened?"

"It was raining and a car pulled up next to me on Seven Locks. I picked up the phone to call you with the good news and there were shots," she slurred, the pain medication making it difficult to concentrate.

"Shots? You mean gunfire?"

Allyson stroked the bandages on her abdomen. "What happened, did they operate on me?" Memories gradually returned.

"Who shot at you, did you see any faces? What did the car look like?"

She continued to inspect her bandages. "What did they do to me?"

The frequency of the heart monitor increased. "Doctor Michaels operated on you, you had some internal bleeding. He had to take out some organs."

"What? What did he take out?"

"Gall bladder, appendix . . ."

"And what? And what?"

"Your uterus."

"Oh no, no, no." Allyson began to cry.

"I'm sorry, I'm so sorry." He attempted to comfort her, but knew it would do no good.

"My baby, my baby! My baby is gone?"

All Tristan could do was hold her and let her grieve.

CHAPTER 32

Tristan tried to pay attention to the activity inside the warehouse, but found it hard to concentrate. The video monitors showed J.J. and Liam inspecting a pile of automatic weapons. They pulled back on the charging handles and slapped in magazines before placing each weapon into a large military-style canvas bag.

But his mind was in the hospital with the woman he loved.

Allyson had not asked him to stay, though he wished she had. They both knew this gun sale was a major part of his case yet he still felt guilty. At her bedside the words "I quit" had been on the tip of his tongue but they did not come out of his mouth. If the embassy bombings were the pretext to a nuclear war and they had a chance to stop it . . .

"Anytime you want to call and check in on her?" Sebastian said, bringing Tristan out of his reverie.

"Her father has been texting me with updates. And my sister-in-law is spending a lot of time there too." Part of him really did want to quit and take Allyson far away. But now that he was unplugged from the *propaganda matrix*, there was no going back. "Her doctor is optimistic. Despite some internal bleeding she seems to be doing much better."

"Did she see who shot at her?"

"No, it was raining and dark."

"Do you think it's because of the interview she planned on giving?"

"I don't know." Tristan recalled Sebastian's warning. "The timing sure is suspicious. And nothing about the CDC takeover of Walter Reed has made it into the news—"

"Here we go," Tony interrupted.

A red two-door Mustang drove up and parked in front of the warehouse next to J.J.'s Chevy. Two men got out and appeared to adjust concealed weapons. One of them removed a backpack and threw it over his shoulder. They knocked and a moment later Liam let them in.

"Recording?"

"You bet." Tony adjusted the focus on one of the cameras.

The sale transpired quickly with little talk between the men. The buyers opened the canvas bag and looked over the guns. Satisfied, the man with the backpack unzipped it and dumped stacks of bills onto the table. J.J. sorted through the money to estimate the amount.

"Whoa, who is this?" Tony pointed to the monitor with the outside view.

A police car crept down the road, emergency lights off.

"We can't let them get to the warehouse."

"Let's go."

Both leapt out of the van and took off in the Cherokee. Sebastian pulled in front of the squad car, forcing it to slam on the brakes. The cop jumped out and pointed his gun at them, shielded behind the door.

"Police!" he yelled.

The agents exited the Jeep, badges held high.

"We're FBI!"

Tristan moved around to the front, mirroring the submissive posture of his partner, only to have the officer switch his aim.

"Come on now, we're the Feds! We're on surveillance, you're putting our case in jeopardy."

The young cop walked over, his Glock aimed at Tristan, his eye on Sebastian. He took both IDs.

"I'm going to call this in." He went to his car and picked up the radio. In less than a minute, he returned. "This checks out."

"Can we ask what you're doing here?"

"We received an anonymous tip about suspicious activity in the area. They sent me to check it out."

Tristan found this odd since the complex was more or less a ghost town.

Sebastian said anxiously, "Can you get going? You're putting our case at risk."

The cop gave them an unpleasant look. "Have a nice day." He walked back to the squad car.

A noise caused them to turn around. The gun buyers stood by their Mustang watching. They put the canvas bag into the trunk and slammed it shut.

One of them drew a handgun and shot at Sebastian who dropped to the ground. A second bullet shattered the windshield of the cop car. The two men ducked into the coupe and drove off.

"Sebastian!"

Tristan sprinted to his partner, helping him to his feet.

"I'm okay. Got the wind knocked out of me."

A graze beneath a rip in his shirt began to turn blood-red.

"That's what they call, dodging a bullet," Tristan breathed a sigh of relief.

The police car kicked up dirt and stones as it sped off after the Mustang.

"Go after them!"

Sebastian jumped in the Cherokee and bolted. Tristan hurried into the warehouse, nearly trampling J.J., and stuck his gun in Liam's face.

"On the ground!"

Liam, in utter shock, did exactly as he was told. Tristan put a knee in the guy's back and FlexCuff'd him.

"Give me the keys to your car."

J.J. reached into his pocket and tossed them over.

"Come with me!"

Tristan ushered the two men outside to the beat-up Chevy.

Sebastian whipped the Cherokee into a dovetail, sliding from the dirt road onto pavement. As he flew down the highway he could see the cop about a quarter mile ahead, lights flashing as it gave chase. With serious ground to cover, Sebastian floored the pedal and the V8 under the hood responded. The route soon became a series of curves, forcing the Mustang and the police car to slow down. This gave the Jeep an opportunity to catch up.

The vehicles were now in a game of chicken. The road finally straightened and everyone hit the gas. The Mustang rammed the squad car multiple times before skidding off the asphalt. Regaining control, it miraculously found the highway again.

The police officer was doing a fine job keeping pace. Quickly approaching, however, was an intersection with a stale green traffic light. As the cars approached, it changed to yellow, followed by red. The 'Stang blew through the crossway and narrowly missed hitting another car. But the driver lost complete control this time and the coupe spun in circles across the gravel on the shoulder. After several 360s it slammed sideways into a wooden utility pole and came to a stop.

The cop braked, with Sebastian close behind.

Both lawmen jumped out of their vehicles, guns drawn, and approached the Mustang, now pinned against the telephone pole on the driver's side. The men remained motionless as smoke began filling the inside. The passenger door was so damaged from ramming the cruiser, it would not open.

"Roll down the window!" the cop tried to alert the men, dazed from the crash.

Without power, the electric windows did not move. Fire began shooting out the front grill.

"Break it!" Sebastian yelled.

The officer hurried to his car and opened the trunk, taking out a tire iron. As he ran back toward the Mustang, it ignited into a massive fireball. The deafening roar of the explosion created a flame-wall that scorched the utility pole.

Tristan arrived in the Chevy, with J.J. in the passenger seat and Liam FlexCuff'd in the back.

"Wait here, and watch him," he said to the informant.

Tristan joined the two men, but the intensity of the blaze prevented anyone from getting close to the burning car. The faint sound of first responders emerged in the distance.

"What happened?"

"We couldn't get them out in time."

Sebastian turned to allow his face relief from the searing heat. He realized, with a sense of dread, they would have to keep the details of this out of the news.

Two fire trucks and an ambulance came to a halt. The crew sprang to action, extinguishing the inferno, turning the car into a steaming pile of twisted metal.

Tristan's phone rang. "Hello? Okay, I'm on my way," he said before hanging up.

"What's wrong?"

"I need your Jeep," Tristan pleaded.

Sebastian handed over the keys to the Cherokee and a moment later he was gone.

Tristan dashed through the hallway of the hospital, unnoticed by anyone at the main desk. At his wife's room, the activity inside caused him to freeze in his tracks.

Allyson's father stood over the bed, stroking her hair. His brother and sister-in-law talked to a nurse who checked the nearby equipment, and there was a gentleman he did not recognize, dressed in black.

Sarah walked out with Robert and Colonel Grant close behind.

"What's wrong?" Tristan barely got the words out.

"She started crashing, the monitors were going crazy, I was so worried," she hugged him and began to cry. "They had to rush her into surgery." Robert put his arm around Sarah, leading her away.

"The doctors don't know what's wrong," Col Grant lamented. "The internal bleeding started again."

The man in black walked out—wearing a white collar. With a sympathetic nod, he ambled past them.

"Why is a priest here?"

"Father Byrne seems to think . . . she's dying of guilt. He gave her last rites."

"What?" Tristan felt his legs might give way. "I don't understand, she was stable and improving, we were talking and she seemed so much better?"

"Doctor Michaels says he can't keep opening her up, it just weakens her body and decreases the chances of recovery."

"What does that mean?"

"They can't operate. It's up to her now," Col Grant said. "We'll give you some time alone."

Tristan entered the room. The only sound was the exceptionally slow *beep* of the heart monitor. He sat down and held Allyson's hand.

"I'm not leaving you again. I don't care if the whole damned world goes to hell. You didn't leave me. I wouldn't even be here if it weren't for you." He hoped she could hear him. "Whatever burden you carry, whatever happened, it's in the past. You need to let go and move on."

He watched over her, hoping for a response. Allyson remained still and silent. He swallowed two pills. Not because of the pain in his leg, but rather due to the aching in his heart and the voice in his head.

Tristan Wood closed his eyes and begged God to spare his wife.

CHAPTER 33

When the call for the DUSTOFF rescue came in, Allyson Grant was relaxing on her cot. She had just finished dinner, a breakfast burrito, and was watching a movie on her laptop computer. Although the mercury had climbed above 60 degrees Fahrenheit today, it would soon drop into the 20s.

January was the coldest month of the year in the *Valley of Death*. She gladly remained tucked in with a standard-issue army blanket to keep warm. At the end of a long day soldiers liked to remove their heavy boots and let their feet breathe, but were always kept at the foot of the cot, laced and open, in case it was necessary to spring into action.

Word came in that a squad of marines was pinned down along a remote southern tributary of the Korengal River, and there were wounded. Allyson quickly fastened her boots, and grabbed the camouflaged jacket and medic's bag on the way out of the crude brick shelter. Heavy mortar fire had erupted minutes ago from a nearby base.

Was that the cover-fire for the squad they were going to rescue?

She ran up the path to the landing zone, or LZ for short, and struggled through the dust storm created by the rotors of the Black Hawk UH-60.

Allyson was an army medic and the Korengal Outpost had been her domicile for the last thirteen months. The base was little more than a dozen structures made of stone, wood, and sandbags built into the hillside modeling the nearby villages. Temporary or not, the troops defended their home with a passion.

The encampment was located in the Korengal Valley, a basin carved out by a tributary of the river and so isolated that its native inhabitants spoke their own language. Her job was not only to treat the wounded as they were brought in, but to ride along on MEDEVAC missions. MEDEVAC stood for *medical evacuation* and was conducted on a Black Hawk UH-60, or as they called it, their "hospital in the sky."

She was helped inside by her friend and team member, Jack Smith, nicknamed Smitty. As the Black Hawk began to lift off, she recalled the cold weather pack she had put together. It included a ski hat, scarf, gloves, extra blanket, and a second pair of socks among other supplies. Unfortunately, it sat where she left it; back in her brick hut.

Oh well, I don't need it, she decided as the helo ascended. *We'll be in and out in no time.*

Something on the LZ below wasn't right.

"What's up with the Kiowa?" Allyson yelled to Smitty over the roar of the twin turbines.

Two mechanics buzzed around the exposed engine of the Kiowa helicopter. Smitty gave her a hand signal indicating the chopper would not accompany them on the mission.

The Kiowa was a smaller version of the Black Hawk. Because of its compact size and high maneuverability it was the preferred air support for the bigger and slower medical bird. Plus, it was heavily armed. Due to military cutbacks, their base only had one, and it was grounded with mechanical problems.

In a matter of minutes they reached their destination. Craters pockmarked the ridge from the pounding of the shells. Mortar fire was the best way to eliminate foes from a safe distance. The quandary in Afghanistan was that the enemy was resilient and able to use the terrain to their advantage. Hitting them with tons of explosives did not, by any means, guarantee the battle was won.

And the number one rule in *the valley?*

Never assume it was.

The pilots slowed to a hover, then announced an all-clear over the radio. The steep ridge and the narrow path worried Allyson.

Not much room to maneuver a Black Hawk, she thought to herself.

The good news was, so far they were not being fired on. The enemy had no shortage of AK-47s, but in the hills their preferred weapon was the sniper rifle. As the medics prepared to descend, a gunner popped off occasional bursts as cover fire.

Smitty was locked into the harness and hoisted down first. An intense cross wind tossed him around but he made it without much difficulty.

Allyson clipped herself in and followed.

On the ground, the two medics began to evaluate the situation. The platoon sergeant, who identified himself as Morreno, continued firing rounds at the top of the ridge from his M-4 as blood pooled under his lower back. Allyson didn't know if he was shooting at something specific or if this was suppressing fire.

Although it appeared he may have life threatening wounds, Morreno insisted they attend to the rest of the team first; a true marine. She asked for a head count and was told there were eight in the squad. His labored breathing was not a good sign—this man would need medical attention ASAP.

Allyson jogged up the path to another marine lying face down. It was their radio operator and he was dead. She could see the exit wound in the back of his neck and decided he was killed instantly. After several minutes it was determined that six of the eight men were gone.

They agreed that Allyson would attend to the platoon sergeant while Smitty prepared the other wounded soldier to be hoisted up in the litter; slang for the basket.

A *poof* of air caressed one side of her face.

"Sniper!"

Allyson yelled to Smitty over the noise of the helicopter, but he was engaging the litter and did not hear her. As she called out a second time, Smitty's head snapped back and a thin red cloud expelled from his helmet. She knew before his body hit the ground that he was dead.

A flash of light drew her attention upward.

What happened next seemed to unfold in slow-motion; an RPG fired from behind a large boulder at the same elevation as the Black Hawk.

To her horror, the rocket hit its target dead-on. An explosion caused the 'copter to spin out of control. A moment later it dipped, lost altitude, and crashed into the tributary. The momentum of the rotors kicked up a wall of water and sand, spouting into the air before coming to a stop. The level of the river was not high enough to swallow the entire Black Hawk, which came to rest with half of the once mighty machine submerged.

Allyson grabbed Sergeant Morreno and attempted to pull him away from the enemy fire, but he was no longer breathing. Panic overtook her as she realized she was alone.

No, not alone.

She spotted the marine Smitty had been helping, now under an AK-47 barrage. He attempted to drag himself down the embankment. Allyson sprinted the distance between them as the gunfire shifted toward her, kicking up dirt and gravel around her feet. Upon reaching him, she grabbed his vest and they tumbled down the slope, almost ending up in the water.

More bullets struck the path above their heads, then stopped. After a moment of silence it seemed they were safe. With a quick inspection of the man next to her, she located the blood on his left leg and holes in the fatigues where the bullets had entered.

"What's your name soldier?"

Allyson reached into her med kit and took out a scissors, cutting a hole in the material around the wounds.

"PFC Tristan Wood," he mumbled.

"Well PFC Wood, you're hit in your left thigh. It appears two bullets got you. Are you injured anywhere else?"

"My calf," he said, gritting his teeth.

"Which one?"

"Same leg."

"I'm putting a blood-clotting bandage on your thigh wounds first and I'll need you to put pressure on it while I inspect your calf," Allyson ordered.

She applied the dressing and placed his hand on top knowing he would be unable to apply much force on his own leg. This was a technique medics used to keep the patient engaged by giving them a task.

She cut the fabric above his boot next and said, "You were shot once in your calf, but it missed the bone."

"Morreno, can you check on Morreno? He was hit, it looked bad."

"I'm afraid you're the only survivor, soldier."

"No!" He pounded a fist on the ground.

Allyson wrapped a bandage around his calf.

"Okay, I'm going to put a tourniquet on your thigh above the wounds. I won't tighten it now, it's a precaution in case we need to move you. I have to lift the leg to get it underneath, this will hurt."

She moved him slightly, to wrap it around.

"Agh!"

"I know you're in pain but I can't give you morphine yet. I need you to stay conscious until help arrives."

"You sure help is coming?"

A reasonable question, but Allyson decided not to speculate. She noticed they were losing daylight fast.

"Well, the good news is, I believe all three bullets exited pretty clean."

"Must be my lucky day."

She gave him a drink from her canteen and took one herself.

"Don't celebrate yet. You're still in the golden hour, but we have to get you to a trauma hospital. Here's the bad news. There is no way you can put pressure on this leg, which means you can't walk. We're going to have to sit tight."

"Anything else I should know?" he asked.

"Actually, yes. It'll be dark soon and the temperature will drop fast. If I give you morphine it will depress your blood pressure and circulation. The bleeding doesn't look too bad, but the cold may kill you."

"I understand." PFC Wood tried shifting his body to a more comfortable position.

"Redirect the pain. Squeeze my hand. I'll give you something to bite down on if you want. Stay with me."

Allyson reached back into her med-kit and took out a small blanket, draping it across his legs. She racked the slide of her 9mm and scanned the area for the first time since they rolled down the embankment.

Then her patient lost consciousness.

"Stay with me!" She shook him awake. The clock was ticking on this soldier's life. "How many radios in your squad?"

"One."

"I'm going to see if I can find it, I'll be right back."

PFC Wood drew his Glock from its holster. "I'll just wait for you here," he said, tongue-in-cheek.

He was still in the "golden hour," not an actual hour, but an indeterminate amount of time following an injury. If he survived the golden hour his chances were much better. The second hurdle was the ensuing six hour period. She couldn't be sure, but in this situation it was unlikely he would make it through that.

They needed a rescue team now.

Dusk was setting in and Allyson realized how quiet it had become. There had been no recent gunfire. The loudest sound was the water rushing around the Black Hawk, which lay in repose a short distance away. The former air ambulance had come to rest on its side and the rotors were gone.

Upon closer inspection of the scene, there was little chance anyone survived. If she ventured out into the river to investigate, she would be picked off by a sniper for sure.

Giving the marine his hand back, she crawled up the embankment toward a small boulder at the edge of the path. From a crouched position the limited view confirmed no movement, and she detected no survivors. Approximately twenty feet away was the large antennae of the AN/PRC-148 MBITR, still attached to the bulletproof vest of the dead marine.

She needed that radio.

Allyson took off her helmet and held it out. A bullet walloped the ground nearby—not a great shot, but good enough. The shooter must have a helmet-mounted night vision scope.

It never ceased to amaze her how well supplied the Taliban were. Ironically, most of the equipment came from Russia. The enemy they forced out in the late 1980s was now the one providing them with everything they needed to do the same to the Americans.

She pumped herself up and dashed to the radio, attempting to separate it from its former owner. The encroaching darkness made it difficult. Bullets threw up dirt and gravel and the adrenalin kicked in again.

After what seemed an eternity, she detached the MBITR and returned to her original position, diving down the side of the embankment like a baseball player sliding head first into home plate. She crawled back to the marine, unconscious once more.

"Hey!" Allyson said, trying to revive him.

PFC Wood woke up briefly then closed his eyes again. She began to call in a rescue, but something was wrong; it had no power. She had not seen the bullet hole that passed through the LCD screen.

Dead radio.

"No!"

She threw it into the river and examined her patient whose vitals had weakened. The beam from her flashlight revealed a problem—the blood-clotting bandage on his leg wasn't working. Chances were he had internal bleeding she was not able to see. If unattended, he would be dead in a matter of minutes.

She tightened the tourniquet causing PFC Wood to wake up in pain before drifting off again. Allyson located an IV bag of plasma, found a vein in his arm, and injected the needle. She readjusted the blanket around his legs to keep him as warm as possible, and considered what to do next.

"I'm sorry, I can't give you morphine, your pulse is too weak." She knew he couldn't hear her, but spoke anyway.

Then, above the sound of the river came voices. They were not English. Her heart started to race and the cold made her body shudder. The daylight was almost completely gone.

Over the embankment she could make out two figures moving down the hill. It was now or never. She would not allow them be taken prisoner only to be beheaded on camera after being tortured. If they were going to die, she would go down fighting, here, tonight.

Allyson waited until the footsteps on the path were close.

She stood up and emptied her 9mm.

One of the Taliban got a couple rounds off from his AK-47 but the shots were wide.

Both men fell to the ground.

She ducked and reloaded her handgun with the last clip.

More voices.

Refocusing on where the enemy had come from, her heart sank. Multiple figures descending from the ridge.

She was vastly outnumbered.

Now almost out of ammo, Allyson was about to make a last stand when the whirring of rotors emerged in the distance.

Within seconds, the Kiowa helicopter illuminated the entire area, firing everything it had above their heads.

Using her body to shield the marine from flying debris, she held his hand and hoped for a sign.

Elated, she felt him squeeze back ever so lightly.

CHAPTER 34

Tristan struggled to keep an eye on the car in front of him through the torrential rain. Few vehicles occupied the interstate in the early morning hour. The all-night drive was exhausting and he nodded off occasionally, despite the loud music playing on the rock station. A wave of water hit the windshield jolting him awake as an SUV passed on the left.

He regained a visual of the Cadillac ahead. The silhouette of Allyson in the passenger seat of her father's car caused his heart to skip a beat.

The two men had made a decision to get her out of the Washington, DC, area and had left just after midnight, in the cloak of darkness. Colonel Grant still lived in the home she grew up in, less than a mile from Camp Lejeune. With Tristan working such long hours on his case, they believed it would be best for her to recover in a familiar place and with constant care.

The unspoken reason, however, was the mystery surrounding her car "accident." It could have been related to the TV interview she was scheduled to do about the CDC quarantine, or maybe it was a coincidence. Either way, he now had a better idea of what may have happened at Walter Reed.

With nothing reported in the mainstream media, he went to Infowars.com and immediately found a news report by a reporter named Paul Joseph Watson documenting hospital take-overs all across the country. Though the end game was still speculative, it was being done by the CDC under the direction of Department of Homeland Security. The theory was that knowingly bad vaccines were given to unsuspecting guinea pigs—soldiers—who were then taken to major hospitals. This false flag was the excuse to requisition America's emergency health industry and transfer control to the federal government in anticipation of a major catastrophe.

But what catastrophe? Tristan asked himself.

They turned off the interstate and headed east toward the North Carolina coast. At first, Doctor Michaels had refused to discharge her arguing that she was still not recovering to his satisfaction. But after a discussion regarding the circumstances he agreed, on the condition she would be close to a hospital, which Camp Lejeune had.

The Wrangler followed the Cadillac into a housing development, and parked in the circular driveway of a three story home. Tristan helped Allyson out of the car and up a flight of stairs to her bedroom. He slipped off her shoes and put her into bed, then glanced around.

"Don't you say a word."

"I wasn't going to," he laughed.

The room resembled a college dorm. Clearly, her father could not let go.

The Colonel appeared in the doorway. "How about a grand slam breakfast? Chef Grant, reporting for duty."

"I'm starving," Allyson said.

His own stomach grumbled. "Me too."

"Give me a half-hour." He walked away humming.

"Lie down with me."

Tristan climbed into bed.

"I'm sorry. I always imagined you with a big round belly, having a house full of children. I didn't know how to say—to tell you that you'd never have babies. It's the hardest thing I've ever had to do."

"I had a dream, or a delusion, in the hospital. A mushroom cloud towered over a city I didn't recognize. There was a flash and I went flying through the air. Then something caught me. Everything was bathed in white light and all I could see were wings. Down below was complete destruction, red flames and rivers of fire, people suffering. I was so afraid. It was like Vergil was leading me though the valley of death. I turned to the light and a voice in my mind said my time here wasn't over, that I would see you again. The next thing I knew, I was lying in the hospital bed and you were holding my hand."

He kissed the bandage where the IV had been, the dark purple of bruised skin showing through the medical tape.

"I need to tell you something."

Tristan sensed what this was about. "You don't have to—"

"I want to, you deserve to know. I never told you why I graduated college a year late. After my mother died, I went to public school starting junior year. My first boyfriend . . . I got pregnant. Just a dumb mistake, but it happened. I told my father and he practically went insane. After a few days, we both had time to digest the situation and I decided to take a year off from school."

"You gave the baby up for adoption?"

"Well, the alternative never entered my mind, or my father's."

"So that's what you've been so guilty about all this time? What you've beaten yourself up over for so many years?"

"Actually no," Allyson continued. "We completed all the paperwork, I felt pretty good about putting her up for adoption."

"Her?"

"By that time, I knew from the prenatal tests that it was a girl. When I gave birth in the hospital, they immediately took her away from me."

"They don't want you getting attached, to second-guess your decision," Tristan surmised.

"I had an emptiness inside from that day on, and wondered why I did it. I could have been a mother. When I got to Georgetown I majored in psychology, thinking I'd counsel other women and help them before doing . . . whatever they would choose to do. I soon realized I was doing it for myself, to self-analyze, to understand why I couldn't shake the guilt. So I switched to biology and was accepted into the Army's Health

Professions Scholarship Program. I figured saving lives would be a penance and allow me to forgive myself."

"But it wasn't."

"No. I thought I had considered all the options, weighed the pros and cons, and made the right choice. But the one option I should have chosen didn't even occur to me. I have a daughter out there in the world that I willingly gave up, and I'll never know who she is—"

Allyson could no longer hold back the tears.

"When we were married I became worried I wouldn't be able to have children. As time went on, and it wasn't happening for us, I started thinking it was a punishment from God for what I had done. I was so afraid if you found out you'd leave me."

Tristan held her tight and let her weep.

"Don't worry. I'm not leaving you . . . ever."

"What do you mean?"

He reached over to the nightstand and handed her a box of tissues.

"I mean, I quit. I'll send in my letter of resignation to FBI. I shouldn't have left you in the hospital. You didn't leave me on that trail."

"You can't do that."

"Yes, I can."

"Tristan, you've done nothing but work on this case. This is bigger than you or me. Besides, Sebastian needs you."

"I'm not sure there even is a case anymore."

"Then you need to go back and save it."

"I can't abandon you again."

"I'll be okay."

"How do you know?"

"You mean besides my father's home cooking?"

"I'm serious."

She blew her nose and dried her face.

"I want to show you something," she said.

"Baby, you should stay in bed."

"Hush." She walked to the door. "Follow me."

Allyson led the way downstairs and past the kitchen where the smell of bacon and toast filled the air. Tristan followed his wife, who hobbled down the basement steps, arriving at a door made of thick metal. Inside, she turned on a light.

What Tristan saw astonishing him.

"My dad stocked up with over a years' worth of long term storage food, bottled water, and supplies. The door is bomb proof. The well windows are too, with removable steel panels."

"When did this happen?"

Tristan breathed in the crisp, cool air.

"He told me all about it on the drive down, I didn't know either. I've been giving him updates on your case, the *Tidal Wave 23* video, and he decided to be prepared. It was easy and not as expensive as he thought. A couple of contractors came in and did the work in a day and he's been stocking up on supplies ever since."

"Unbelievable."

"See? There's nothing to worry about. You have a responsibility, to Sebastian and the FBI, and to yourself." She smiled weakly and kissed him. "Now you have to do something for me."

"Anything."

"Get off the pain medication."

He held her in his arms and kissed her.

"Okay," he said, wishing he meant it.

Some hours later, Tristan drove the road approaching the I-95 exit that would take him back to Washington, DC. He pulled the car into the shoulder and stopped. Time to make a decision. It was now or never.

Allyson had finally allowed herself to vent and tell him the truth. With this massive burden lifted from her conscious she had devoured breakfast and fallen asleep almost immediately after. This gave him some peace of mind. However, Tristan's gut was talking to him again. The question was whether he'd listen.

Go for it.

Tires squealed as he stepped on the gas and headed south. Driving to central Georgia wasn't the best use of his time with such an important case pending, but his gut had not been wrong yet.

After an hour, the GPS guided him west toward Elbert County. He soon spotted the Georgia Guidestones; an ominous gray granite structure on a hilltop. Sebastian had explained it was *the* monument to globalism in the United States. Fate had brought him more than halfway here, his decision to complete the journey was the right one. Tristan parked the Jeep and realized he was alone.

Walking toward the *American Stonehenge*, as some thought of it, security cameras sitting high on poles kept watch over the perimeter. The massive stones really did parallel the original Stonehenge, located in Wiltshire England. Four slabs stood, surrounding a fifth in the center, with a capstone resting on top.

A stone ledger lay embedded in the ground a short distance away with technical data detailing the weight and measurements of the stones themselves. It also indicated a time capsule was buried here. Interestingly, there were no dates entered, either for when it was buried or when it was to be dug up.

Acutely aware of the cameras watching him, he located the ten guidelines engraved in eight different languages on the large upright stones. Each of the four faces had its own language including: English, Spanish, Swahili, Hindi, Hebrew, Arabic, Chinese, and Russian. The principles stated;

1) Maintain humanity under 500,000,000 in perpetual balance with nature.
2) Guide reproduction wisely - improving fitness and diversity.
3) Unite humanity with a living new language.
4) Rule passion - faith - tradition - and all things with tempered reason.
5) Protect people and nations with fair laws and just courts.

6) Let all nations rule internally resolving external disputes in a world court.

7) Avoid petty laws and useless officials.

8) Balance personal rights with social duties.

9) Prize truth - beauty - love - seeking harmony with the infinite.

10) Be not a cancer on the earth - Leave room for nature - Leave room for nature.

He hit speed dial on his cell. "It's me. I'm in Georgia."

"You're at the Guidestones? What do you think?" Sebastian asked.

"Incredible."

"Do you see how they try to make the guidelines appeal to emotions and sound vague, yet wrapped in world government with a twist of environmental eugenics?"

"Okay, so tell me more"

"There are two interesting astronomical features. Find the hole in the center column."

He moved around, searching.

"Got it," Tristan said.

"If it were night you'd be able to spot the North Star through it. Is there a ray of light shining on the same stone?"

"Yes."

"It's aligned with the sun's solstices and equinoxes. Each day at noon an inch-wide aperture in the capstone allows a sunbeam to pass through, indicating the day of the year."

His TAG wristwatch read; 11:45 a.m.

Sebastian asked, "Did you notice the cameras?"

"Yep."

"Well, Elbert County became the owner of the Georgia Guidestones site, which means taxpayers are on the hook for the video surveillance and whoever's hired to monitor it. Somebody named *R.C. Christian* deeded the five acres to the county immediately upon purchase of the land back in October of 1979."

"The ledger says R.C. Christian is a pseudonym but—"

"But pseudonym is spelled incorrectly, with an n instead of an m on the end," Sebastian interrupted.

"So who is that?"

"There are a few theories. The evidence, although circumstantial, seems to point to Robert Edward Turner."

"Ted Turner? The owner of CNN who gives interviews stating we need to get rid of 80 percent of the world's population and the only thing that can save us is the New World Order?"

"One in the same," Sebastian said. "And here is the real sinister part of what some characterize as, 'the Ten Commandments of the Antichrist.' From my research, the Guidestones were built by representatives of the Rosicrucians."

"It keeps getting better."

Tristan had read of the Rosicrucians, an international secret society from the seventeenth century devoted to the study of ancient philosophy and religion. The order was named after its founder, Christian Rosenkreutz, and meant the Rose of the Cross, or the Rosy Cross.

The ideology of the society was rooted in secrecy, and based on science mixed with magic. Rosicrucianism was also a precursor to the Illuminati. The Rosicrucian order, as well as other esoteric groups, used the term "illuminati" to refer to the higher grades of initiation.

"How is Allyson, by the way?"

"She's okay. Her father will take good care of her. I'm heading back now. I'm afraid to ask, but do we still have a case?"

"Call me later and I'll let you know."

"All right, I'll see you soon."

Tristan hustled into his Jeep and broke the speed limit on his drive toward Washington, DC.

His gut was starting to bother him again.

CHAPTER 35

12/25/2009

11:11 a.m.

As the Airbus A330 descended through thick patches of green and gray, the drab suburbs of Detroit appeared like a lighthouse beckoning to a ship lost in a stormy sea. Nothing but clouds, and a thin film of water droplets, rushed past the windows outside.

Almost no one paid attention to a young African man who removed a small bag from the overhead compartment and walked to the restroom. The plane, scheduled to land at 11:40 a.m., was running late due to a snow delay in Amsterdam. After an eight hour flight, passengers were waking up and preparing for a non-eventful landing.

11:35 a.m.

The man returned and settled back into seat 19A, mumbling something about having an upset stomach. He pulled a blanket up to his neck. Smoke began to seep from underneath, accompanied by a repulsive smell attracting the scrutiny of the person sitting next to him.

"What's wrong?"

The African man did not answer. The seatmate removed the blanket causing a large cloud of smoke to rise to the ceiling. More passengers caught on as he forcefully pulled the African man's hands from his pants. A small blaze erupted, lighting his own hands and lap on fire.

Then he noticed a syringe.

With adrenalin pumping, the seatmate grabbed the still smoking syringe and a series of *pops* filled the cabin. Another passenger from a few rows back reacted, jumping in to assist.

"Water! We need water!" he yelled.

Both men proceeded to put out the blaze, however, smothering the fire with the blanket only caused it to surge. The flames began to creep up the wall, burning another passenger who had rushed over to help.

Two flight attendants and several passengers extinguished the flames and secured the African man, now face down in the aisle. They stripped him down to search for weapons and dragged him to First Class.

"What's in your pocket?" the other stewardess asked.

"Explosive device," the African man said calmly.

To the few who realized this was a bombing attempt, the reality was that they were trapped in a flying aluminum prison from which there was no escape. With the hum of the landing gear opening, the plane lurched forward in a sharp descent.

They stripped the suspect's remaining clothes off to search for anything else dangerous and bound his hands behind his back with handcuffs, standard on all commercial planes since 9/11. As many passengers screamed in fear, those around the suspect found it odd that he was staring calmly into nothing, a hypnotic-like trance.

"Everything is under control!" the steward spoke into a handheld, broadcasting to the passengers. "Your federally trained flight attendants have the situation under control. We are now landing. The landing gear is down! Stay in your seats, we are getting ready to land."

The pilot said over the intercom; "Emergency landing."

11:40 a.m.

The male flight attendant called in to the cabin to inform them a man had lit something on fire and was presently secured. The door to the cockpit would not be unlocked or opened under any circumstances. Passengers braced themselves as the plane dove for Detroit Metropolitan Wayne County Airport.

Upon giving the pilots another update, the steward overheard one of them briefing the tower that someone had set off firecrackers, which he found odd. The pilot reported there were injuries, asking permission for an emergency landing. Before hanging up, he thought he heard air traffic control say that TSA and Fire & Rescue were on their way to meet them.

"There was an incident, and everything is under control. It is over. Fasten your seat belts. We are about to land," a copilot announced.

The engines whined with acceleration followed by another lurch forward. The plane continued its sharp descent as the flight crew strapped into their seats.

11:42 a.m.
FBI, Customs, TSA, and Airport Police all received word that a Delta flight from Amsterdam had an onboard fire and was making an emergency landing.

11:53 a.m.
Delta flight 253 from Amsterdam carrying 278 passengers and 11 crew touched down on runway 4R at Detroit Wayne International Airport with loud applause from the relieved travelers.

As it taxied, those with window seats observed multiple yellow emergency vehicles and a white SUV with flashing police lights heading their way.

Suddenly, Fire & Rescue turned around and headed back toward the terminal, strange considering there had been a fire on the plane minutes before.

11:55 a.m.
FBI Special Agent in Charge Sebastian Graves snapped the top button of his jacket as the van hydroplaned down John D. Dingell drive and passed the North Terminal. The windshield wipers

occasionally screeched across the glass to wipe away the drizzle as the five special agents shimmied inside the speeding truck.

It was a cold Christmas Day in 2009 and the engine had not had enough time to properly warm up the interior. The van took a soft right turn onto the service road behind McNamara Terminal, piercing a maze of orange pylons set up by airport security.

"We're approaching the terminal now. I'll give you a call back when we're inside," Sebastian said to someone on the other end of the cell phone.

12:00 p.m.
Flight 253 pulled up to Gate 24 Concourse A at McNamara Terminal, the sky-bridge reaching out to connect. Three TSA agents in yellow jackets immediately ran onto the plane and two returned with the bomber suspect, practically naked except for the blanket he was wrapped in.

He mumbled once again that there was a bomb on board while being escorted off. The airport was in the process of shutting down, with flights prohibited from taking off or landing. The African man was taken downstairs to US Customs and placed in an Immigration cell.

12:06 p.m.
The third TSA agent gathered information from the pilots in the cockpit as security worked to clear out a baggage area in Customs. Upon leaving the plane, the agent informed his superior of the hurt passengers, and the Fire & Rescue team was recalled to treat the injured.

12:10 p.m.
Paramedics arrived in their vehicles outside the International Arrivals section of the terminal, where three rows of unattended cars made it almost impossible to park. They cursed to themselves, realizing no one had thought to clear the area for them.

Forced to double-park, the first responders hurried upstairs to the gate. Adding to their frustration, the injured passengers were not allowed off the plane. After some arguing, the paramedics were able to get TSA to agree to let off the worst hurt man, who got applause as he exited. He was treated outside the door to the sky-bridge while the others received treatment on the plane.

12:20 p.m.
The van with Sebastian's FBI team came to a stop close to the terminal's back entrance, where the Fire & Rescue vehicles sat uncomfortably crammed in between cars. The five special agents jumped out, happy to get their muscles moving again. They climbed the stairs to Concourse A in McNamara Terminal and found Gate 24.

"Will you look at this?" an agent said to Sebastian as they arrived.

There were numerous uniforms from different agencies including Customs, TSA, as well as first responders and various segments of airport security. A man with sandy blond hair in a striped green shirt was being treated by paramedics, his hands wrapped in fresh bandages.

Outside the windows, the huge white plane with burgundy tail-wing sat wedged in between the other commercial jets. It was a Northwest Airlines airplane but a Delta livery. Two massive wing-engines dwarfed the security vehicles that cast their red and blue emergency lights on the belly.

"What is going on?" he asked himself out loud.

Approaching a group of TSA agents, Sebastian flashed his badge, as if the black jackets with large orange "FBI" didn't give them away. After three decades with the Bureau, he had become proficient at locating the highest rank at any crime scene; and today was no different.

"SAC Sebastian Graves. Why is this plane parked at the gate?"

The TSA agent took a look around, not sure what to say.

"You're TSA, right?"

"Yeah. I'm Agent Barros, I'm in charge."

"Not any more. This is now under FBI jurisdiction by authority of the Department of Homeland Security." Sebastian sensed the man was actually relieved. "What happened here?"

"A few minutes before arriving, the captain reported that someone lit off firecrackers on the plane, there may be injuries, and then requested an emergency landing. Turns out one of the passengers tried to set off a bomb in his underwear."

"His underwear?"

"Yeah, believe that? Actually sewn into his drawers. It didn't explode, but it caught on fire. Toward the end of the flight from Amsterdam the guy named," he had to look at a note pad to pronounce the name, "Umar Farouk Abdulmutallab gets up and goes to the bathroom. When he comes back he attempts to detonate the bomb. His seat was 19A, directly above the wing and its fuel tank."

"They came from Amsterdam? How long was the flight?" Sebastian asked.

The TSA agent looked somewhat perplexed by the question. "They were due to leave sheep . . . skeep . . . Amsterdam at 8:45 a.m. their time."

"Schiphol Airport, it's pronounced shkeep-hole."

"Yeah great, well it was delayed by snow and after the wings were de-iced it got off the ground at about 9:21 in the morning. It was scheduled to arrive in Detroit at 11:40 a.m. local time making it an eight hour flight, or so," reading off his note pad again. "What does that matter?"

"Why did the guy wait until the end of such a long flight to try and blow it up?" Sebastian wondered. "The passengers are awake, the crew is alert and preparing to land. Why not do it over the ocean when everyone is asleep?"

"Your guess is as good as mine, unless he wanted to detonate it over US airspace? You'd do a lot more damage blowing up a plane over a city than open water."

This made sense.

"We should be able to start interviewing the passengers once we get them off," Barros said.

"The passengers are still on the plane?"

"Yeah, it's on lockdown, we're waiting for a baggage area down in Customs so we can secure them."

"Secure them? There's a bomb attempt on a commercial airliner, the pilots park it at the terminal gate and you leave the passengers on?" He moved a few steps toward the window and looked down. Baggage handlers were unloading from the undercarriage. "Did it ever occur to you there could be another bomb onboard? Get those passengers off!"

The TSA agent took out his walkie-talkie.

"Where is the suspect?" Sebastian asked.

"In a cell, down in Customs." He spoke into the walkie, "Jackson, you got that Custom baggage area ready? Jackson, come in?" A voice answered back, letting him know it was. He looked at Special Agent Graves. "You're in charge. Do you want to round them up?"

12:25 p.m.

One half-hour after flight 253 made its emergency landing, Sebastian walked onto the aircraft to finally get the folks off, first updating the pilots. The burning smell was strong and had a strange odor. There was no doubt these were bomb chemicals. The passengers looked tired and agitated, and a couple of babies cried. The captain picked up the intercom on the wall above the food cart.

"We apologize for this happening, and we wish incidents like this would never occur. Apparently someone brought firecrackers on the plane. Please prepare to exit, we realize some of you need to make connecting flights and we apologize for the delay. If Detroit is your final destination, please stay seated and let those who are making connecting flights get off first."

Sebastian decided to ignore the firecracker comment figuring it was to keep the passengers calm. Disobeying the instructions, everyone got up at once and scrambled to collect their things from the overhead compartments, pushing and shoving to get off as fast as possible.

It was logical to have them exit without their bags, then have the *Bomb Squad* do its work, however, he had been given explicit instructions by his SAC at the Detroit field office that they should take their carry-on luggage with them. It made no sense but Sebastian was just happy to get them off the aircraft.

After the plane emptied, he returned to the terminal gate where the passengers were being herded like cattle down the escalator toward US Customs. TSA Agent Barros busily gave orders over his walkie-talkie.

12:35 p.m.
Everyone entered the Customs baggage area, now guarded by airport security. With nowhere to sit, some folks relaxed on the carrousel while others attempted to get comfortable on their luggage. A few minutes later Agent Barros arrived with an announcement.

"Listen up!" He demanded the attention of the large crowd. "You are being quarantined for a reason. There is no cell phone use and if you need to go to the bathroom you must have one of us with you."

Sebastian found this statement to be rather arrogant. Though yellow police tape was put up in an attempt to isolate the passengers, this area was anything but secure. The only thing actually containing them was their willful cooperation. Random airport patrons walked by, entering and exiting the baggage claim, talking on cell phones and otherwise oblivious to what was going on.

Then a group of plainclothes officers stormed in with an obvious sense of self-importance and authority. Oddly, the man who appeared to be the leader wore a sweater, athletic shorts, and sneakers. Only the neck-badges made it evident they were official.

"Who's in charge here?"

Sebastian simply raised his hand and stated, "FBI."

Barros identified himself as lead Customs agent.

"I'm directing this operation now."

"Says who?" Sebastian squinted to read the man's badge, but could not make out the name.

"The FBI Director, that's who."

Sebastian called his SAC in Detroit to confirm, then they brought the new guy up to speed on what had happened thus far.

"From now on," he said, "everything goes through me."

Agent Graves finished the briefing. "The passengers just got off the plane and the luggage has not been checked by Customs. There have been reports that the suspect mumbled something about a bomb being on the plane as they were bringing him off, but nobody has searched yet."

"We're taking care of it, thank you," the new SAC cut him off and walked away.

12:55 p.m.

An ambulance waited outside as three Customs agents escorted the paramedics who wheeled the *Underwear Bomber* suspect out of the terminal. Although the young man still looked dazed and confused, he was strapped tightly to the gurney under a thick wool blanket placed over what they had determined to be second degree burns to his inner thigh and genitalia.

Handcuffed to the metal bar, the suspect was secure.

One Customs agent jumped into the ambulance while the others confirmed the destination as the burn center of the University of Michigan Hospital in Ann Arbor. As the doors were about to close, a young female flashed her FBI badge and hopped in. Before anyone could protest, the emergency vehicle sped off, lights flashing but no siren.

In the Customs baggage area Sebastian mentally patted himself on the back. Inserting a special agent from his team would help him keep track of what they did with the bomber suspect. There was something terribly wrong with this entire operation. No sooner did he begin to feel optimistic then various baggage handlers began hauling in the luggage.

"What are you doing?"

"What do you mean?" Barros asked.

"You're bringing the luggage in here, with the passengers? You want Customs to search for a potential bomb in bags right next to the people we're supposed to be protecting?"

"I'm just doing what I'm told. You're not in charge here, he is." Pointing at their new friend, the plainclothes was meeting with his team in one of the small rooms along the back wall of the claim area.

1:20 p.m.
His stomach sick with worry, Sebastian ascended the escalator where Delta flight 253 remained parked at the gate. Two men in yellow jackets guarded the door to the sky-bridge. He overheard a passenger, with bandages on his hands, tell Customs agents he saw the bomber suspect with a carry-on bag, and believed it was still on the plane.

1:28 p.m.
Sebastian received a call from his special agent on the ambulance. She informed him they had arrived at the hospital, but the staff had found an unknown powder residue on the suspect requiring them to go through an extensive decontamination procedure before entering the ER.

The Customs agent asked some standard questions during the trip. The young man eventually revealed he had trained with Al Qaeda in Yemen. When he claimed the device was made by a bomb-maker in Saudi Arabia, the Customs agent read him his Miranda Rights, at which point he shut up before she could ask him anything.

Not knowing what authority she had, she did not protest, and promised to call back after their decontamination was complete.

1:37 p.m.
Customs announced that the inspection of the check-in luggage by their bomb-sniffing dogs turned up nothing. This made sense since they already knew the suspect did not check-in a bag.

Sebastian located the plainclothes man, now in charge. "I believe it would be a good idea to move the aircraft out onto the runway before the *Bomb Squad* inspects it, to get it away from people and other planes. We understand the suspect may have had a carry-on bag that could still be onboard."

"Are you asking me agent?"

"Yes, sir," he said begrudgingly.

"Okay, go ahead and do that."

1:45 p.m.

Sebastian felt guilty, forcing the pilots to return to a plane that might currently have a bomb, and move it to the tarmac where they should have ended up in the first place. As the two captains turned to walk down the sky-bridge, one purposely lagged behind.

"You're FBI right? I don't know what you've heard, but we were told there was going to be a terrorism drill near the end of the flight; a fake bomb, which would be firecrackers. We wouldn't have taxied to the gate if we thought there were real explosives."

Before he could digest this statement the pilot was gone. The sky-bridge retracted and the plane backed out.

Sebastian entered the closest bathroom and paced around before punching one of the stall doors. The emotional release veiled the pain that radiated up his arm.

After composing himself, he returned to the gate. The plane was now isolated on its own runway surrounded by cop cars, the airport fire truck, and an ambulance. But all eyes were on the bomb-disabling robot at the bottom of the stairs leading up to the aircraft.

2:15 p.m.

Back in the US Customs baggage claim area, FBI Agent Sebastian Graves stood close enough to hear the latest command coming from their new SAC. The plan was to bring in the bomb-sniffing dogs to search the carry-on bags the passengers had now held in their possession for almost two hours. Minutes later, a lab and a pair of German shepherds began to eagerly circle the people and sniff their luggage.

One German shepherd, named Jordi, made his way to an Indian man approximately thirty years of age wearing an orange suit, and sat down by his bag. Customs quickly surrounded the *Man in Orange* and led him to one of the nearby rooms. After initially leaving the carry-on, someone returned for it.

Including passengers, crew, security, and agents, there were upwards of 350 people in this part of Customs baggage claim. Neither Sebastian nor anyone on his team directly observed the interrogation of the *Man in Orange*.

The new SAC was busy giving instructions on what he felt was the best method of questioning. They began interviewing couples, families, and those traveling together in groups rather than each of the 279 passengers and 11 crew individually, which would have been a daunting task.

Finally, Sebastian thought, *something that made practical sense.*

2:20 p.m.
On the tarmac, the airport's bomb-detecting robot prepared to search the aircraft, but ran into a problem. After more than thirty minutes of prep time, the robot was unable to climb the airstairs because the treads kept slipping on the steps, slick from the rain.

They went to plan B.

2:47 p.m.
An explosives expert made his way slowly and carefully up the airstairs. Donning a bomb suit, he entered the plane. Each overhead compartment was checked and every seat inspected until a bag was found, one and a half-hours after they had been made aware it might exist, and three hours after the jetliner pulled into the gate.

The carry-on was removed and an X-ray revealed nothing of interest. Nor could they confirm it belonged to the terrorist suspect. Next, bomb-sniffing dogs were sent through but no explosive materials were found. Delta flight 253 was then moved to a maintenance hangar.

3:02 p.m.
Sebastian's phone rang; it was his ambulance *plant*, reporting an update. What he was told left him speechless. The decontamination process had ended without any conclusive results, thus everyone was released. Abdulmutallab, the bomber suspect, was brought into a University of Michigan Hospital conference room and sat in front of a judge who was there to arraign him.

He was smiling when they wheeled him in, wearing a light green patient's gown with blue socks, and bandaged hands. No one knew who authorized the hospital-courtroom scenario.

The justice confirmed he was pronouncing the name correctly and asked Abdulmutallab if he understood the charges against him, which he did. Although able to sign an affidavit, the young man still appeared to be under the influence of something.

The judge assigned a public defender, setting a detention hearing for January 8, 2010. After about twenty minutes Abdulmutallab was prepped and taken to Milan Federal prison.

Sebastian hit END on his cell, his head spinning.

3:15 p.m.
As the team questioned passengers, they failed to notice some of the plainclothes exit the room with the *Man in Orange*. His personal bag was still inside, its contents strewn across the table. Words were exchanged before placing him in handcuffs and taking him away.

Sebastian was engrossed in an interview with a young couple who had some very interesting information. They recounted sitting on the floor in Schiphol Airport in Amsterdam, approximately ten feet from the gate, playing cards while waiting to board the plane delayed by the weather.

As the one facing the boarding gate, he viewed a young African man with an older Indian man, around age fifty, in a tan suit. He concluded this *Sharp Dressed Man* was probably the adult chaperone for the teenaged African man who, despite the chilling temperatures of winter in Amsterdam, had neither luggage nor a coat.

The witness recollected the two being an odd couple. Minutes later, the *Sharp Dressed Man* asked if the ticket agents would allow the young African man to board without a passport. The answer was no, to which the *Sharp Dressed Man* replied, "He's from Sudan and we do this all the time." The ticket agents told him to speak with their manager, so they were directed down a hall still in the secure part of the airport.

That was the last he saw of the African man until he tried to explode the bomb. The couple had searched for the *Sharp Dressed Man* in the crowd, and suggested the possibility he never got on the plane at all.

Sebastian's team interviewed several passengers who provided fascinating information. A mother traveling with her daughter saw a man videotaping the suspect for almost the entire flight, but they could not agree on what he looked like or the clothes he wore.

Two separate passengers recalled seeing an Indian man in a gray suit taken away by Customs while in the baggage area. The *Man in Gray* was leaning against the wall when one of the bomb-sniffing dogs took an interest to him. He was immediately handcuffed without a struggle and led away.

From what Sebastian figured, this *Man in Gray* was different from the *Man in Orange*, and also the *Sharp Dressed Man* in a tan suit. He had almost finished his current interview, when the group of plainclothes came over and announced their new plan.

"You are all being moved to another area because this area is not safe. You all just saw what happened and are smart enough to read between the lines and figure out what is going on."

Sebastian guessed he was referring to the *Man in Orange* who had recently been arrested. They began to move the passengers into a nearby hallway. It became apparent that this case was so badly mismanaged, it would be best to just observe. He would later write down a detailed account of the day to make sure he remembered everything.

3:35 p.m.
Squeezed into the narrow corridor, Sebastian listened to the plainclothes in amazement.

"We have had a serious incident today, we thank you for your patience but we have to wait and sort this all through. We realize you have been delayed and want to get you home to your loved ones."

This brought angry responses from passengers demanding to see their lawyers. Some asked for food and water, which they were told they would receive soon.

The SAC continued, "But every single one of you will need to be interviewed today before you go home. How many people here don't speak English? Raise your hand."

This prompted some laughter, including Sebastian, who wondered how a person unable to speak English would understand the question. Another plainclothes began walking up and down the corridor with a new query.

"We have been told someone was videotaping the incident. If you were videotaping the incident can you please make yourself known?" A few passengers confirmed this, even suggesting four possible seat locations, but no one was identified.

"Have you arrested or detained anyone today?" Sebastian asked the SAC.

"No one."

He knew this was not true.

"Has anyone you interviewed mentioned a person who was videotaping during the flight?"

"No one," Sebastian lied back.

3:45 p.m.
As the team continued to question passengers, the search for the person videotaping unexpectedly stopped, despite several

witnesses who were able to narrow down the possible location to rows 31 and 32.

The SAC appeared again, to make yet another announcement. "We have those we believe are responsible for this in custody, we will now be doing interviews with each of you and then you are free to go."

Sebastian found it interesting he spoke in the plural. "I thought you told me you didn't arrest anyone?"

"We got the bomber."

"Only him?"

"Are you finished interviewing?" he said, shamefully ignoring the question.

"We're not even halfway through, is my guess."

"Well, let's go, I want to get out of here sometime today." The SAC defiantly walked away.

6:19 p.m.

Everyone was exhausted and all the passengers were questioned. Folks with Detroit as their destination were allowed to leave. Those who had missed their connecting flights received a complementary overnight hotel stay at the nearby Embassy Suites, plus a dinner voucher.

Sebastian was all too happy to wrap it up and head home. In just six days, over thirty years of a distinguished career with the Federal Bureau of Investigations would come to an end. SAC Sebastian Graves felt depressed that he was looking forward to his retirement.

CHAPTER 36

Tony, the FBI G, slept in the passenger seat of the surveillance van, snoring lightly. He had been pulling long hours and Sebastian wanted to give him every chance possible to rest. The Major's team had been busy, most of the bomb materials were now bought or stolen.

The Russian translations J.J. provided had confirmed Ivan and Petrev were doing what the Major wanted—bribing and threatening embassy guards—and Tristan had made several phony fuse caps that he would give to J.J. when the time came to build the bombs.

Unfortunately, they did not know when the bombings would happen. This troubled Tristan. So far J.J. had been unable to get the Major to reveal a date, and not for lack of trying.

A near disaster, the gun deal almost brought down their entire case. Once again Sebastian had saved the day. He had J.J. call the Major to report that Liam never showed. The informant turned out to be quite a good actor. He yelled, complained, and put him on the defensive by threatening to quit, regardless of the consequences to himself. It seemed to work.

The gun sale was successful and the money secure, so the boss assumed Liam got cold feet and disappeared. Since the Russians had been out working on the embassy guards and the car fire had remained nothing more than a news-blurb, the Major was none the wiser.

Sebastian called in a favor from an old friend in local law enforcement. ATF placed Liam in an isolation cell with a suicide vest and no communication with the outside.

At the moment though, Tristan was fascinated by the *Underwear Bomber* case. The story had been a long time coming.

"So let me get this straight, this guy bought his ticket in cash, did not check-in any luggage, and he came from Yemen, one of the hotbeds of terrorism in the world? Did everyone suddenly forget about 9/11?"

"It gets worse. The bomber's father was a wealthy Nigerian banker who had gone to the US Embassy in Abuja a month earlier. He warned that his son had been spending a lot of time in Yemen and was probably involved with terrorists. He was concerned about his radical religious beliefs and Abdulmutallab's name was even put in the TIDE database."

TIDE was the acronym for Terrorist Identities Datamart Environment, a computerized information bank managed by the Washington-based US National Counterterrorism Centre. It contained about 550,000 names that funneled into a second list called the Terrorist Screening Data Base, or TSDB, with over 400,000 names.

"And he was still able to get on the plane?" Tristan asked, amazed.

"Under normal circumstances, that would have been more than enough to revoke the guy's visa and place him on the no-fly list."

"How did he get past security?"

"He was allowed on."

"How do you know?"

"Because in January of 2010 in hearings before the House Homeland Security Committee, Patrick F. Kennedy, the Undersecretary for Management at the State Department testified that an agency, which he would not reveal publicly, had asked them not to revoke the bomber's visa."

"Come on."

"The Undersecretary has the power to abrogate passports, without consulting FBI or CIA. But if the person-of-interest is under watch, busting him could disrupt an ongoing investigation. So standard practice is to contact the various agencies and ask before making a move, potentially triggering a *national security override*. Kennedy said they had information Umar Farouk Abdulmutallab was a dangerous person and were ready to revoke his visa. Nevertheless, in his congressional testimony he stated, point-blank, that he was ordered not to."

"Patrick Kennedy actually said that, under oath, in public hearings?"

"This protocol is business as usual, it's nothing new. Various 9/11 hijackers operated for extended periods of time inside the United States, under the cover of national security overrides. How did these men enter and leave this country, obtain visas and driver's licenses, rent apartments and cars, acquire checking accounts and credit cards, register vehicles, attend flight schools, and repeatedly fly on US domestic airlines? How did they escape arrest for traffic violations, which some of them committed?"

"What are you saying?" Tristan asked.

"Remember when actor James Woods revealed he was on a commercial flight with several of the 9/11 hijackers on a dry run? A stewardess warned the pilots, who locked the cockpit door. A report was filed with the FAA but ignored, along with all the others stating commercial airliners would be commandeered and flown into US targets. The truth is, 9/11 was also allowed to happen. These men had been made untouchable to ordinary law enforcement with *national security overrides*, making them immune to arrest and keeping their names off no-fly lists."

"I don't understand. If a US intelligence agency stopped the undersecretary from arresting the *Underwear Bomber*, a man they knew was a terrorist, what was the reason?"

"It was a false flag," Sebastian said.

"So, he was a patsy?"

"I believe the guy was a terrorist, and perfectly willing to die as a martyr. He was trained in Yemen to detonate a real bomb which never supposed to go off. They also showed him what to do in case the blasting cap failed. Plan B was mixing the two liquids using a hypodermic needle; a concoction his handlers knew wouldn't explode. When the moment of truth came, he searched his bag in the overhead compartment and found no blasting cap, forcing him to go to Plan B. In the bathroom, he drew the liquid using the hypodermic then returned to his seat above one of the fuel tanks. So he wouldn't check his luggage before the flight, they had an airport employee in Amsterdam stow away the bag for him. That's why passengers reported seeing him without luggage. He was drugged to reduce anxiety, and the man videotaping him was there to make sure he didn't get cold feet. Sound familiar?"

"The Train Bomber suspect also appeared drugged up and J.J., his handler, was admittedly there to make sure he didn't get cold feet. The blasting caps were fake and the bomb was not meant to go off."

"Voila; a false flag."

"Why? For what reason?"

"Follow the money," Sebastian continued. "It led right to body scanners, a multi-billion dollar business, and an increase in the police state in line with the New World Order. Now the Train Bomber is being used to expand the scanners to other forms of public transportation, and to give the Executive Branch extraordinary power. They didn't want the underwear-bomb to go off any more than the bomb in Union Station, but they need them to try. If you stop them before they commit the act the story is gone in a few days. It's meant to scare the American people with a close call so they can claim they stopped a terror attack, then ask us to give up more of our rights or next time the bomb will go off. And those who dissent are labeled as heartless people who don't care if children die."

"You said there were reports of three different Indian men; one in an orange suit and another in a gray suit at the Detroit Airport, plus the *Sharp Dressed Man* in the tan suit in Amsterdam who helped the bomber get on the plane? Who were these men?"

"We still don't know, they never released the surveillance video from Schiphol airport. Regardless of multiple witnesses, since day-one they have refused to release any tape. Out of frustration, some of the passengers blogged their accounts on the internet and told their stories on alternative radio, like the Alex Jones show. They were ignored, even by our own FBI."

"If the official story is true, then why not release the tapes?"

"Local Detroit media asked that question, among others, but backed off when 'conspiracy theory' reared its ugly head. Amsterdam security eventually admitted the *Underwear Bomber* was not required to go through normal passport check-in procedures, but by then it was old news."

"I don't remember hearing about any of these details in the media?"

"There's always a pattern of spin around a false flag, which is how the story changes within days and sometimes hours. What they do is release the 'official' story and let the media run with it. Any obvious lies or discrepancies can be dealt with later. The social engineers understand the human mind, and what they know is, the first story is the one most people remember. The media will accept it as truth if it comes from an official government source like the Pentagon or the White House. Then the discussion organically moves into Democrat versus Republican, or left versus right."

"The Hegelian Dialectic."

"That's right, and any questions conflicting with the official story are dismissed as 'fog of war.' Fog of war is a free pass, it's like saying 'I don't recall' during a trial. Look at how the accounts of Pat Tillman and Jessica Lynch changed, both proven to be completely false after the official story was released. Most people to this day still only know the first version. Donald Rumsfeld said 'I don't recall' over seventy times in the Tillman hearings, then laughed and joked with the armchair generals who testified with him, as the Tillman family watched in disbelief. The bin Laden story is a classic example, a Santa Claus fable for adults. Do you know bin Laden was never wanted for 9/11?"

"What?"

"His Most Wanted poster never said anything about 9/11. It's still on the FBI website. You can go there and see what it says, or rather, what it doesn't."

"Which is?"

"He was wanted in connection with the 1998, bombings of the United States Embassies in Tanzania, Nairobi, and Kenya. When asked why 9/11 was not mentioned on his Most Wanted page, FBI admitted they had no hard evidence connecting him to the attacks."

Tristan asked, "Then what happened to bin Laden?"

"The killing of bin Laden is another example of an entire story proven bogus within twenty-four hours. It was well documented he required daily kidney dialysis, even before 9/11, and could not have received treatment hiding in caves and bunkers for all those years. Bin Laden actually died from kidney failure due to Marfan syndrome in late 2001 in an American military hospital in Dubai under the close supervision of CIA. However, he was a useful political tool, especially to keep the war on terror going. There's a long list of intelligence analysts who confirmed his death over the years including veteran CIA officer Robert Baer, Pakistani Prime Minister Benazir Bhutto, FBI head of counterterrorism Dale Watson, Senator Harry Reid, government insider Dr. Steve Pieczenik, and Fox News even reported in December 2001 that bin Laden had died a month prior and was buried within twenty-four hours in an unmarked grave in accordance with Wahabbist Sunni practices. The official narrative of the raid and supposed killing of bin Laden in 2011 unraveled within days of its announcement. There've been so many versions of the bin Laden story over the years it's impossible to keep track of them all."

Tristan dropped his head into his hands, in frustration. "How many versions of the *Underwear Bomber* case were there?"

"Five distinct versions. Of course, most folks only remember the first. Version one was the official story, Umar Farouk Abdulmutallab was the only person involved and the only one detained, that he cleverly slipped by airport security due to flaws in the system and his bomb just happened to fail. This story lasted five days, much longer than usual, but local media would not stop asking questions and frustrated passengers began posting their own accounts on the internet. So, on December 30, 2009, version two was released admitting a second man was indeed taken into custody and being held indefinitely on immigration charges. Version three came out later the same day and stated the man taken into custody had been from another flight, even though multiple passengers contradicted this claim. Version four came out December 31—"

"Your final day at FBI," Tristan pointed out.

"And the last of my involvement in the case. This fourth version came in the form of an email sent out to apologize to select reporters, not the passengers. Besides all the lies, tell me if anything in this letter stands out?" Sebastian handed Tristan the copy, but it was the signature that made him gasp.

All, Good Evening,

Thank you for your patience and accuracy in reporting the events of Dec. 25 at Detroit Metropolitan Airport.

Everything we have talked about has been accurate concerning these events. That being said I have just received a piece of information that I did not previously have and hope it will clear up this matter. As I have explained, there were no other passengers from flight 253 arrested or detained. The eyewitness accounts coincided with a separate issue concerning a passenger from a separate flight arriving at the airport. That passenger was escorted from the arriving plane to the CBP area. He was handcuffed at that time and could have been observed by the passengers from flight 253.

This still remains true; however, I now know that a passenger from flight 253 did have a canine alert to his carry-on bag in the baggage area of the CBP facility. He was placed in handcuffs and escorted to an interview room where he was interviewed and searched. There was nothing found during that search. Following the negative search results, he received an explanation why. He thanked the officers for doing their job and departed the facility along with the other passengers from flight 253.

I cannot provide any other information about the individual because again, he was not arrested or detained and we have to protect his privacy. This information is consistent with the eyewitness accounts. I accept full responsibility for this information not being made available to you. I did not access the correct report that contained this information. I take pride in providing my media contacts complete, accurate information and I did not accomplish that this time. Please accept my apologies for any difficulties this may create.

Respectfully,
SAC Seth Pascal
Foreign Counterintelligence Investigations, FBI
Detroit Field Office

"Pascal?" Tristan almost fell over.

"I didn't need to go too deep into the rabbit hole to find out why his name is familiar. Pascal was brought in for damage control. His job was to discredit any witnesses who contradicted the official story of the *Underwear Bomber* and debunk the 'handler' theory."

"It says he was in the Detroit field office. I thought you didn't know him?"

"He wasn't part of my office. I contacted someone who was with me that day. In fact, I sent her along in the ambulance with the bomber to keep track of what was happening while I was at the airport. After a few calls she found a reporter who held on to a copy and forwarded it to me."

Tristan studied the letter again. "You said there was a fifth version?"

"Well, after no one bought the first four, and the story would not go away, Pascal went directly to Detroit News and claimed his account was a composite of two events and blamed it on not being able to quarantine the area the passengers were held in. He wasn't even there, but the media didn't think to ask that."

"What did FBI's case file say?"

"It doesn't exist. At least, not anymore."

Tristan exhaled, trying to digest it all. "I always had a bad feeling about this guy. I'm glad we haven't given him the *Tidal Wave 23* video."

"I have something to confess. I uploaded it to YouTube."

"When?"

"While you were down south. I created an anonymous account."

"I thought we were going to keep it to ourselves?"

"I wanted it in the public domain. If anything happens to you or me, it hopefully won't be lost forever. At the moment, it's any other video out of millions on YouTube."

Tristan thought before saying, "Actually, I think you did the right thing."

Sebastian's cell phone rang, the caller ID read; FBI.

CHAPTER 37

Sebastian exited the elevator with purpose, weaving in and out of agents and staff walking the halls of the J. Edgar Hoover building. The veteran special agent was having a hard time containing his rage. In fact, he barely remembered the drive over after receiving the phone call from SAC Tufts.

First they tried to shut down the Train Bomber case and now they were going to close the investigation of his son's death, allowing the spy allegations to remain. It made Sebastian so angry he could barely contain himself. He wanted answers.

They arrived at the office, confronted by the wiry receptionist.

"He's not here Agent Graves."

"Where is he?"

She hesitated before saying, "He's in a meeting with SAC Pascal." Sebastian's eyes opened wide. As he turned to leave she pleaded, "Agent Graves!" The expression on her face was undeniable.

Be careful.

They hustled down another corridor, and barged in on the two SACs sitting across the desk from each other.

"What the hell are you doing Pascal?"

"Don't blame me, Internal Affairs decided to shut down the case."

"Reopen it, give it to me."

"You know I can't do that, it's against FBI policy to let agents investigate family members." Pascal stood to face Sebastian, feigning bravado.

"Did they find his girlfriend?"

"She is a guest of the Russian ambassador and has diplomatic immunity. The embassy will not cooperate."

"Did I.A. question anyone, or investigate at all?"

"The file is sealed. You've been an agent for a long time, you know how this works."

"I don't think they did anything. I think they washed their hands, to get it out of the news so the Bureau won't look bad."

"FBI is stretched thin, we do the best we can and move on." It was obvious Sebastian would not be satisfied so Pascal ended the conversation by saying, "Go cool off."

"You gonna turn this into another *Underwear Bomber* case? Release disinformation and harass witnesses? You're a stooge for the New World Order!"

A look of shocked culpability crossed Pascal's face. "Your son was a spy, Graves, you need to accept that!"

Sebastian lunged at Pascal tackling him to the ground. SAC Tufts watched in trepidation as Tristan barely managed to stop a raised fist from dropping. Insane with anger, Sebastian felt he was observing the confrontation from outside his body. With difficulty, he was pulled off by his partner.

"Get him out of here!" Pascal roared.

He charged once more, held back by Tristan.

"Sebastian, stop!"

Breaking free, he stormed into the hallway, pacing as others stopped to watch.

"Are you cool? Sebastian! Are you cool?"

"I'm fine."

"I need you to relax!" Tristan implored.

He leaned against the wall and attempted to calm down.

"I'm going to check on Pascal. You all right?"

After a deep breath he managed to vocalize a "yes."

Tristan reentered the office where the angry SAC continued to vent. Suspecting only the man's ego was injured, Sebastian broke into a slow jog down the hall.

He did not see anyone again as the elevator doors closed.

Adrenalin pumped through Sebastian's veins as he sat in front of the residence of the Russian ambassador to the United States. He held the photo of Lara Fedorov in his shaking hands. It was a stupid thing he had done. His mind raced and he felt depressed.

In three decades of service to the Bureau he had never assaulted a fellow officer, let alone a superior. There were plenty of altercations with suspects, overlooked or ignored by FBI, but never anyone above him in the chain of command—except for one incident in particular, over twenty years ago.

Sebastian had been out on the town with other off-duty FBI and ATF agents in a Georgetown bar. After several hours of drinking Jack Daniels shots, he had returned from the bathroom to find a stranger hitting on his girlfriend, Miriam. The *man in the flannel shirt*, as Sebastian remembered him, whispered in her ear while simultaneously making eye contact with him.

A real alpha male move.

Blinded with rage, Sebastian punched the guy in the face instantly dropping him to the floor.

By the time his friends could pull him away, he had kicked the younger man into unconsciousness. The family was lawyered-up one month later when he awoke from his coma. FBI was able to keep the incident out of court, and out of the press, with a massive cash settlement.

Sebastian came to realize they bought his silence by not firing him. Instead, the Bureau transferred him to another city where he underwent anger management therapy for two years, and managed to stay off the bottle for ten more.

Before the move, he proposed to Miriam who accepted. The same jealous rage she viewed as fervid devotion in their youth would drive her to leave him later. The deep-down anger he could not relinquish, combined with the guilt for what he had done, eventually brought him back to the drink.

There's still time to ditch, he thought to himself.

A secluded home waited for him far, far away, in the southern hemisphere. It would be easy to flee, to leave it all behind. But right now he needed to concentrate on the task at hand, to cool his head and think clearly. The ambassador's residence bustled with people coming and going, an unusual amount of activity compared with his previous stake-outs—

"I don't believe it."

After what had seemed like an eternity, a familiar looking woman hustled out the front door. She wore a lame disguise including a wide brim hat, silk scarf, and sunglasses much too big for her face. Through the binoculars, a blonde ponytail was visible.

Lara Fedorov moved quickly into a taxicab and headed west, with Sebastian close behind in the Jeep Cherokee.

It crept up M Street, NW, in dense Georgetown traffic before coming to a stop at Wisconsin Avenue. The Russian left the cab and ducked into the *Shops at Georgetown Park*, a former tobacco warehouse dating back to 1838 and converted into an underground shopping mall in the 1970s. Sebastian swung the Cherokee into the Park's subterranean garage.

He parked and hurried to the elevator, then stepped into the lower level with a wave of dread. Finally, he had found Jason's illusive Russian girlfriend only to lose her in a mall.

With three levels, hundreds of shops, and a floor-plan that included alcoves, fountains, planters, and various barriers, this would be like finding a needle in a haystack. Sebastian tried to act normal as he searched.

After completing a walk-around, he spotted her standing in front of a gourmet coffee kiosk. After she paid for her drink, he followed at a safe distance.

Sebastian was stupefied.

He had imagined confronting this girl many times but never thought about what he would do when it finally happened. If he approached her in the middle of the mall she could scream bloody murder. He continued to follow, and then caught a break when she entered the ladies room.

Deciding to seize the moment, he walked to the restroom door and listened.

Now or never.

He drew his Glock and skulked inside. A paper coffee cup sat on the edge of a porcelain sink, its image reflected hundreds of times in a wall mirror surrounded by thousands of tiny aqua-colored tiles.

A toilet flushed.

As the girl left the stall, Sebastian pinned her up against the wall cupping his hand over her mouth.

"I'm not going to hurt you, I just want to talk. Okay?"

Eyes wide open, she nodded yes. But as he removed his hand, she let out a yelp. He gagged her again.

"I said I'm not going to hurt you, I'm an FBI agent." He kept the gun barrel pressed into her neck. "Lara Fedorov?" He received no response. "Is your name Lara Fedorov?"

She nodded.

"Do I look familiar?"

She did not react.

"I should. I'm Jason Grave's father. Will you talk to me?"

She nodded yes.

Sebastian took his hand away again, but the gun remained in her throat. Every sound in the room was exaggerated as it bounced off ceramic and glass.

"Who shot my son? Who was that man?"

A slight woman, he had no trouble holding her against the wall. The dark roots and crow's feet at the corners of her eyes revealed her age close up.

"It does not matter," she finally said, with a heavy Russian accent.

Sebastian released the safety with a *click*. Then he put his finger on the trigger as intense anger consumed him.

"It matters to me!"

"He is agent. He works for our embassy. But you will never find him."

"How do you know that?"

"He has gone back to Russia."

"I want a name."

"I say it does not matter, because we have men like him all over Washington, DC. If it had not been him it would be another. This is how Russian embassy works."

"What is *Tidal Wave 23?* His FBI partner found the flash drive after you left him to die."

"I'm sorry." She began to weep. "I did not want that to happen."

"What is *Tidal Wave 23?*"

The restroom door opened, casually. An unsuspecting woman entered, took a moment to digest what was happening, and ran out.

"I'm not going to ask you again."

"You have watched it?" she asked.

"More times than I can count."

"It is Russian intelligence. I have not seen it but I do know it was important to our embassy."

"It must be if they shot my son over it."

"One time he came to pick me up. I showed him the embassy. We went into ambassador's office. He took it when I was not looking and asked for one hundred thousand dollars. They were very mad, they almost killed me."

"Is that why you met the man along the canal?"

"We were going to embassy in the morning," she continued in broken English, "but they did not wish to wait. They wanted me to bring him down to canal for meeting. Our agent asked for the return of the flash drive and they would forget that it happened. Jason got angry and demanded more money, and he shot him. Then the other FBI man yelled, he must have followed us, we did not have time to search for flash drive."

"They killed him because he wanted more money?"

"They killed him because he saw the video. They did not want to take a chance he would give it to FBI, or your government."

Sebastian lowered the gun and released her.

He sat on the floor and buried his face in his hands, utterly exhausted. All this time, he had hoped it wasn't true. Or perhaps Jason was framed.

"I am sorry," she said with a whimper.

Completely alone in the world, he had no wife, no son, and would not have a job much longer. He waited for the sound of the door indicating Lara Fedorov had left. Instead, she leaned against the sink, eyes closed.

"Why are you still in the United States?" Sebastian asked.

"I wait until Moscow calls me back. They say it will be soon."

"Will it be safe there?"

"I do not know. But it will be safer than here."

The restroom door opened and two security guards cautiously entered with guns drawn.

Sebastian didn't bother putting up his hands.

CHAPTER 38

Tristan sat on a bench inside the Jefferson Memorial, a place he liked to go when he needed to think. It was open twenty-four-seven and had incredible views of the District with Virginia on the opposite side of the Potomac River. To the north, the Lincoln Memorial and Washington Monument were now illuminated with artificial light as darkness crept over the city. The lone sound was the din of traffic from George Washington Memorial Parkway across the river.

Although his gut was telling him something bad was coming, Special Agent Tristan Wood of the Federal Bureau of Investigations felt completely helpless to stop it.

Not only was he seeing *11:11* on clocks, but now *9:11* as well.

Taking in the cityscape, he no longer saw the same metropolis, random and unplanned. There was a deeper esoteric meaning. He unfolded the street map from his Jeep's glove compartment and tried to focus his tired eyes on the area he was in.

The Governmental Center.

Tristan's cell phone, on the bench at his side, was a silent reminder of how alone he was since leaving Allyson in North Carolina. He chased down two pills with some water and admitted to himself that he most likely had a problem—an addiction to opiates.

Though exhausted, he could not relax. In lieu of sleep, he had been spending time researching the New World Order, specifically the Illuminati and Freemasons. The conversation with Sebastian had haunted him ever since.

And what he learned did not provide comfort.

The buildings and street layout in the District were designed by Freemasons, and with an open mind, the symbols were obvious. Grievously, they all pointed to something very bad. Tristan was not religious, in the organizational use of the term, but he knew evil. And it was here in Washington, DC.

John Russell Pope was the designer of the Jefferson Memorial, which stood on land liberated from the marshland of the Potomac River across from Foggy Bottom.

Pope also built the most esoteric structure in the city; the Masonic House of the Temple, designed for the Scottish Rite Freemasons. Located at 1733 16th Street NW, it was the only architectural pyramid in Washington, DC, and resembled the truncated pyramid on the back of the one dollar bill.

Constructed from 1911 to 1915, the design for the Temple was adapted from the tomb of King Mausolus at Halicarnassus, in ancient Turkey. What he found interesting was that Pope, to meet the architectural and interior demands of Masonic ritual, employed the help of Elliott Woods, a 32nd degree Mason who had also designed the United States Capitol building.

The Freemasons were the most famous of all the secret societies. It was generally accepted that they composed the layout for the District of Columbia. Masons were stoneworkers and builders, but the term *Freemason* was used to distinguish the upper class from the lower blue-collar Masons.

A Mason was "free" because he could travel across national borders and work on any great building project. By possessing a secret password, he was able to identify himself to others in the society, thus getting preferential treatment in obtaining employment.

The Founding Fathers, many of whom were Masons, were influenced by various forms of mysticism, occultism, and Illuminism, and used the tools of astrology, alchemy, as well as the Kabbalah in their designs. The Freemasons were famous for inserting esoteric symbols into their art, and had a name for this technique.

Hidden in plain sight.

Secret societies were an ancient tradition formed because the knowledge they guarded was so profound it could not be made available to the average person. Freemasonry had thirty-three levels, though few reached that far, and along the way members were directed in the service of a higher power referred to as the Divine Architect.

Those able to escape the order, and not killed, claimed their master was God in reverse, or Lucifer, and the symbols they included in their work were Luciferian in origin. The ultimate goal of America, according to the secret societies, was to assume the global leadership in the plan for the New World Order.

Tristan breathed in the river air, the steady green light on his cell phone continuing to taunt.

He reflected on the fascinating street design surrounding him. After the conversations with Sebastian, Tristan had acquired a strong desire to investigate. Besides, if he were to learn about the New World Order it was best to begin with the origins.

Freemasons had planned the layout of the city with patterns designed in the streets, rotaries, and cul-de-sacs, and quite obvious if one knew what to look for. Schoolchildren were taught that America was founded on Christian values by Christian men, yet aside from a few Biblical characters there were no crosses or other religious signs to be found. On the contrary, Egyptian and occult symbols were everywhere.

The most powerful and obvious occult symbol in the District of Columbia was the inverted pentagram connected to the White House. Masons claimed because one small section did not connect, amounting to a mere ten percent, that it did not exist. Rhode Island Avenue stopped at Connecticut Avenue. Had it continued southwest to Washington Circle, the pentagram would be complete. But the esoteric knowledge the Masons possessed was that the unfinished pentagram was considered more evil and powerful in the occult world than the intact symbol.

Tristan traced the outline with his finger.

The pentagram was actually three objects in one; the pentagram, the pentagon, and the Baphomet goat head. The top four points of the "White House pentagram" represented the four elements of the world including Earth, Air, Fire, and Water, and were located at Washington Circle, Dupont Circle, Logan Circle, and Mt. Vernon Square, with the fifth point being the White House. This fifth point represented the mind of Baphomet the goat, or the spirit of Lucifer. The same goat head could be found in multiple places on the one dollar bill.

The square, with its vertical lines, represented the ethereal force moving from heaven to hell and the horizontal lines represented the movement of time as well as the heavenly bodies across the sky from east to west. Mt. Vernon Square was placed on the east side of the pentagram. In occult doctrine, east was the direction from which a person received spiritual knowledge and guidance from the rising sun.

Scott Circle was located at the top of the pentagon, also the bottom of the inverted pentagram, and represented the flame of the candle, meaning spiritual illumination. A circle was considered the most important of all units in magic symbolism and intended to denote spirit forces, as in a halo above a person's head to give them a divine appearance.

The middle of the goat-head pentagram was where 16th Street ran north to the Masonic House of the Temple, the North American Headquarters for Freemasonry. Placing the Masonic Temple north of the White House was important in that it represented the place of governmental control, with the power of the president coming from the Temple.

On the south side of the building was R Street, the eighteenth letter of the alphabet, a common code for six, plus six, plus six; 666. It was also located thirteen city blocks north of the White House starting with the first block north of Lafayette Square.

The number *13* had a long history in occultism, representing rebellion against God's authority. In the Bible, Lucifer's intention was to overtake God's throne by force to establish his own reign "above the stars and in the uttermost north." North, the location of God's throne, was where occultists believed governmental authority dwelled. This meant the White House was spiritually controlled through the House of the Temple, with Lucifer as the Divine Architect.

Tristan involuntarily checked the bars on his cell, the signal strong, the phone in hibernation. He resisted the urge to call Allyson, fearing he would wake her. She needed rest.

Turning his attention back to the map, he focused on the most sacred symbols of Freemasonry—the Mason's Square, the Compass, and the straight-edge Rule—the tools used to build their monuments. All three were designed into the streets of lower DC.

The owl was yet another powerful image in the occult world, representing the spirit of Satan. The street design that beset the United States Capitol was a horned owl, the two irregularly shaped cul-de-sacs on the east side as the ears, and the circular drive around the building outlining the face.

The one dollar bill contained owls hidden in plain sight and the owl was also a symbol of various secret societies including the Bohemian Grove, an all-male annual retreat in northern California once infiltrated by Alex Jones and made into a documentary. Therefore, with the southern point of the Baphomet goat-head pointing to the White House and the owl image surrounding the US Capitol, both the Executive and Legislative branches of the government were under the symbolic control of Satan.

Tristan cast his gaze on the most obvious occult symbol in DC, lit with floodlights and circled by American flags, the world's tallest obelisk;

The Washington Monument.

The four-sided stone pillar, with pyramidal top, was designed to replicate the ancient Egyptian monolith believed to house the spirit of the sun god; Ra. The only other obelisk in America was the one transported in 1881 from Alexandria, Egypt, and placed in Central Park in New York City.

Freemason ideology was based in the Illuminati belief system going back centuries. It mattered not if the average American believed in any of this, what mattered was the global elites did. Although skeptical in the beginning, after scrutinizing the DC street map, these images were far too obvious to be mere coincidences. He had even searched the layout of other major cities and found no pentagrams, owls, or Freemason symbols built into the streets.

The cell phone rang, and he answered, "Agent Wood."

Tristan noticed his own voice sounded tired.

"It's Tony."

"What's going on?"

"Your man is here."

"You're kidding?"

"He's inside the warehouse right now."

"You recording?"

"Yeah, but it's darker for some reason, almost like there's a fog surrounding everything. The equipment seems fine, I'm trying to get something useful."

"Who else is there?"

"One of the Russians. I don't know for how much longer though."

"I'm on my way. If he leaves, call me immediately!"

Tristan hit END on his cell and ran down the steps of the Jefferson Memorial to his Jeep, the pain in his leg dulled from the meds. He sat in the driver's seat for a moment before deciding he was okay to drive.

Minutes later, with the George Mason Bridge and Arlington National Cemetery behind him, he contemplated whether or not to call Sebastian. The guy had been through a lot, however, this was too important. He deserved to know. After all this time, their "white whale" had finally appeared. Speed dialing the number, it went right to voicemail.

Figures, he thought, before leaving a message.

"Sebastian, it's me. He showed up, the Major showed up. I'm on my way to the warehouse, call me back or just head over."

Less than a half-hour later Tristan slipped into the van.

"Is he still here?"

No answer was required. Tony listened through headphones as he worked the video controls. Even in the low light, Ivan was recognizable.

"So that's him?"

"The Russian has been calling him Major, and he seems to fit the description."

His G was right. The Major was over six feet tall with a bit of a gut. He had the baseball cap J.J. claimed he always wore, making it even more difficult to see his face. They were sitting at the table.

"Where is Agent Graves?"

Tristan ignored the question and asked, "What's the Major doing here? What have they been talking about?"

"They seemed to be going through a checklist, taking inventory and discussing the bomb materials."

"Is that his?"

Parked in front was an old black Mercedes with tinted windows.

"Yep."

Regardless of the grainy image, it was obvious the car had seen better days. It even missed a hubcap. The drab citrine light revealed small dents and scratches that peppered the body, and dried mud covered much of the back end.

As the conversation between the two seemed to wind down, the Major shook Ivan's hand and left.

Tristan jumped out of the van.

"Where are you going?" Tony asked.

"To tail him. If Agent Graves shows up, tell him to call me."

Tristan started the engine and waited for the Mercedes to drive off, then followed at a safe distance. The lack of traffic at this hour allowed him to follow far behind. He called Sebastian again and got voicemail but did not leave another message. The Major exited GW Parkway and entered the loop that brought him to the west entrance of the Pentagon.

Unsure what to do, he pulled the Jeep Wrangler into the shoulder of the highway and watched with binoculars. A guard came out to inspect the driver, waving the car inside. The Major took a hard right and drove to the south side of the building. It was late and the Mercedes was the only moving vehicle on this section of the Pentagon parking lot.

Tristan slipped out of the Jeep and made his way down the hill, avoiding the overhead street lamps.

Planting himself behind a road barrier, this was as close as he could get without being seen. He crouched down and searched with the binoculars, momentarily losing sight of the black Benz until the flashing lights of the alarm system revealed were he had parked.

Instead of heading for the main entrance, the Major walked toward an inconspicuous stairwell that disappeared below grade. He no longer wore his cap, giving Tristan a good look at his face. An overhead lamp illuminated the area with a dim glow. At that moment, sheer terror sent a tremor through his body.

The Major turned once more before heading down the stairs. Then Tristan saw, or thought he saw, someone different. The facial aspect changed to crimson and the eyes stretched out, becoming jet-black. Two small horns appeared, protruding from the forehead and morphed into a demon. The binoculars fell from his trembling hands, and his legs weakened.

"Get a hold of yourself. You're tired and you're seeing things."

But the image burned in his mind's eye.

In fact, Tristan was sure he had just seen the face of Baphomet.

CHAPTER 39

Tristan walked through the halls on the seventh floor, a part of the FBI building he had never seen. This level consisted of administrative offices and small conference rooms. SAC Tufts had called early this morning asking him to come in for a meeting. He knew the reason but the location was puzzling.

Tristan reached the end of the corridor and found the room; *7272*. From behind the door came the faint sound of voices. He decided not to knock and slumped into a nearby chair. If Sebastian arrived soon they could talk about what happened before meeting with Tufts.

Exhausted, he had gone home after following the Major to the Pentagon. Lacking the energy to climb the stairs to his bedroom, he collapsed on the couch until morning. Tristan had fallen into a sedated sleep, again dreaming of nuclear war, and had missed an important call.

The message was devastating.

Sebastian was in jail after confronting Lara Fedorov, who confirmed the spy allegations and revealed the flash drive with *Tidal Wave 23* had come from the Russian embassy. This would be the end of the line for his new FBI partner. He had physically attacked Pascal, with witnesses. Sebastian's anger demons had finally prevailed.

The thought of continuing the Train Bomber case alone was terrifying. The voices inside the room became progressively louder until the door opened, revealing a grim face.

Sebastian walked out, with Pascal standing behind him.

"I'm going to get some sleep. I'll give you a call later."

He gave no indication of what happened, and was gone.

"Agent Wood, come in."

Following SAC Pascal inside, a rush of nervous adrenalin surged through his veins as he realized why he was here. Special Agent Tristan Wood, the wounded marine who fought for his country in Afghanistan, sat down in front of a polygraph.

"This is Agent Lopez with I.A."

The man nodded and went back to changing the paper in the machine. Late morning sun entered the conference room.

"What is this?"

"We've had a lot of leaks this year, and a spy or two. This shouldn't be a surprise."

"So Internal Affairs has time for this, but we're stretched too thin to investigate who shot and killed my partner?"

"Watch yourself, Agent Wood."

Tristan was strapped in, with an armband to measure blood pressure and a pincher on his finger to track heart rate.

"Okay, I'm going to ask a series of questions," Agent Lopez said. "You must respond to every question and please answer only with yes or no."

Taking a deep breath, he told himself there was nothing to worry about. He hadn't talked to anyone in the media, nor was he a spy. It couldn't be the medication—

"Is your name Tristan Wood?"

"Yes."

Agent Lopez began to mark spots on the paper as it moved.

"Do you reside at . . ." the man read Tristan's address off an agent bio.

"Yes."

"Are you currently a special agent with the Federal Bureau of Investigations?"

"Yes."

"Are you currently working on a case involving the attempted assassination of the President of the United States?"

"Yes."

"Have you talked to any members of the press about this case?"

"No."

"Are you married to Allyson Wood?"

"Yes."

"Do you have children?"

This question felt strange, considering . . .

"No."

"Have you talked to your wife about this case?"

Tristan paused, caught off-guard, "I don't . . . I don't understand what this has to do with anything?"

"Yes or no only, please," Agent Lopez reminded him.

"Yes," Tristan would have given Pascal the evil eye if the man had been facing him.

"Is your brother's name, Robert Wood?"

"Yes."

"Does he work for a Senator Matthews?"

"Yes."

"Have you discussed this investigation with your brother?"

"No." He had Robert ask the senator about *Tidal Wave 23* but that was as far as it went.

"Is Sebastian Graves your current FBI partner on the Train Bomber case?"

"Yes."

"Besides your partner, have you discussed the Train Bomber investigation with any other non-family members?"

Tristan ruminated before answering, "No."

This was true as well. He recalled the dinner at the senator's house and realized he did not speak specifically about the case.

"Was Jason Graves your former FBI partner?"

"Yes."

Indignation welled up inside him.

"Did you witness the shooting?"

"Yes."

"Do you know who shot him?"

"Are you kidding me?" he said involuntarily.

"Yes or no only, please."

"No."

"Were you involved with Agent Graves' spying activities?"

"That's it!" Tristan took the device off his finger followed by the arm band. "I'm done. You've asked enough questions."

Pascal looked at Agent Lopez. "Well?"

"No deception."

He waited for a double-check, which was confirmed with a nod.

"See? No deception, can I go now?"

"You talked to your wife about the case."

"And?"

"I was crystal clear, do you remember the meeting, when I warned not to discuss ongoing investigations with anyone? Not even family."

Pascal's ring finger was bare and Tristan wondered if he had ever been married.

"Agent Wood, you are to turn in your badge and sidearm immediately."

"You can't be serious? We are on one of the biggest cases in the history of the Bureau, and you're going to take Sebastian and me off this case? There is no case without us!"

"Not Sebastian, just you. He passed the polygraph. He didn't discuss the investigation with anyone."

"You're making a big mistake, we're close to . . ." he stopped himself, ashamed at the sound of desperation in his own voice. Fatigue was affecting him.

"I'm suspending you. Hand them over."

Tristan placed his Glock on the table and reluctantly tossed his FBI badge next to the gun. He had no choice. With nothing left to say, he walked out to the empty hallway. Standing alone, the silence was deafening. He speed dialed a number on his cell and headed for the elevator.

"Hey, it's me. Can we talk? Not on the phone. How about the usual place, in a half-hour? See you then."

Tristan walked through a diner, busy with their weekday lunch crowd, and spotted his brother at the counter in the back. The J. Edgar Hoover Building was a stone's throw from the Russell Senate Office Building and this was their favorite place to eat. Tristan often bragged they had the best malted vanilla milkshakes in town.

"You look straight from hell," Robert observed.

"Then I'm headed in the right direction." A waitress placed a menu in front of him. "Coffee, please. Large."

"No milkshake?"

"I need the caffeine."

"What's up?"

"I got suspended from FBI."

"When did that happen?"

"About ten seconds before I called you."

"Why?"

"They gave me a polygraph. I wasn't supposed to discuss the Train Bomber case with anyone, even Allyson. So they suspended me."

Robert took out his phone. "I'm calling Senator Matthews, I'll have you back in FBI by the end of lunch."

"No, no," Tristan grabbed the cell away. "Not yet. Let me get my head straight and think this out first."

"What about your case?"

"I can't . . . wait, yes I can. I'm suspended, I can talk to you about it now."

The waitress poured a cup of coffee. "Would you like to order?"

"Can you give us a few minutes?" Tristan said. After she walked out of earshot, he spoke again. "The Train Bomber was a false flag."

"A what?"

"The bomb in Union Station was never supposed to go off, it was a false flag meant to scare the American people into allowing more body scanners and pat downs and sway public opinion to renew the Patriot Act. Sebastian and I found the *handler*, a guy who followed the bomber to make sure he didn't get cold feet. We flipped him as an informant and we've had the terrorists under surveillance while they plan their new job."

"Which is what?"

He surveyed the diner, worried someone was listening. "They're going to bomb the Russian and Ukraine embassies. We think it will be blamed on a patriot group, or America as a country. Russia will use it to . . . to launch a pre-emptive nuclear war. Remember I texted you about *Tidal Wave 23?*"

"Of course."

"It was a video of a nuclear strike on the United States. Jason lifted it from the Russian ambassador's residence; it's Soviet intelligence. He was trying to extort money for its return. Apparently that's what he got shot over."

"When are they planning this false flag?"

"We haven't been able to find out. I know it all sounds crazy, I hear myself saying it and I can't believe it."

"I'm not so sure."

Tristan was surprised by his brother's response.

Robert continued, "When we were in Russia, the ambassador said there was a 'storm' coming and begged the senator not to return to the US. Putin has been repeating a phrase in speeches; 'Ola Gigante.' It means 'tidal wave.' He's been saying a tidal wave is coming. And we've been getting eyes-only intelligence reports on Russia. This year they completed two massive underground bases with high-tech command centers that our government has been keeping track of for years, but can't get inside. In the last few days, there's been a flurry of activity with trains going in and out around the clock. The CIA doesn't know why, or claims they don't. Then there's something the senator told me when we were in Russia that I haven't been able to stop thinking about."

"What?"

"He said the KGB, renamed the SVR, is still in power and has been using the billions in financial aid we send them every year to upgrade their nuclear, biological, and chemical weapons systems. They have an entirely new line of ICBM called the Yars-M. These rockets are so fast we can't shoot them down." Robert hesitated and glanced around. "They believe they can win a nuclear war."

"Sebastian told me the same thing."

"But why a nuclear war?"

"Have you heard of the New World Order?" Tristan asked.

"Sure, it's a conspiracy theory."

"Maybe not."

Tristan spent the next few minutes telling his brother what he had learned about the New World Order and their agenda.

"Okay, so bust them right now. Stop it today."

"We can't. If we don't catch them in the act this will just resurface at another time. The guy in charge, the Major, is connected with the Pentagon. We don't want to get the low-levels, we need to expose the New World Order and show the American people what it is."

"I don't know if this will mean anything to you, but before I went to the Bering Sea, a navy pilot called the senator. He was concerned that the military is being trained with the framework of a new version of the MIAC report, via the Pentagon. Their exercises aren't to fight Russia but to play defense following an attack and then control segments of the American population, while under martial law, after we lose the war."

"Control them how?"

"When I visited the USS Vinson, the pilot came to see me. He said gas attacks would be used to suppress or wipe out areas of resistance."

Tristan tried to comprehend it, "That's why hospitals all over the country are being seized by Department of Homeland Security. Allyson was attacked to keep this out of the news . . ."

After a moment, Robert said, "He said there are Russian war games planned for July 4, the biggest in history."

"The Fourth of July? Tomorrow is the first!"

"You think they might try and bomb the embassies on Independence Day, as something symbolic?"

"It's possible," Tristan said. "Let's watch for signs."

"What kind of signs?"

"The elites know it's happening, but they'll need time to get to their shelters or leave the country. You have access to FAA activity reports, right?"

"Ever since 9/11, we get daily briefings from DHS."

"Look for unusual air traffic, especially a large number of private jets requesting permission to fly out of the US. Keep an eye out for military movements, drills, or FEMA camp activity, things like that."

"What about you?"

"Now that I'm suspended, I'm not sure I can do anything. I may drive down to Lejeune to be with Allyson. I hope nothing happens, but if it does—"

"What's this?" Robert interrupted.

A news bulletin on the television behind the counter showed a wide angle shot of an aircraft carrier surrounded by rescue ships, with helicopters hovering on the horizon. The ticker on the bottom of the screen repeated the same message.

Pilot Missing in Bering Sea . . .

"Excuse me?" Robert called to the waitress at the register. "Excuse me!"

She turned around, annoyed.

"Can you turn up the volume?"

She found the remote and cranked up the sound. It appeared to be a frantic search and rescue operation.

The report was in progress, ". . . the ship's crew, although trying to stay optimistic, are not holding out much hope Lieutenant Hornell will be found alive. Even if he managed to eject from the plane before going down, it's doubtful he would have been able to put on his survival suit in time. In the frigid water of the Bering Sea, it can take a matter of minutes for the body to go into shock. When asked if this was related to the ongoing US war games, the response was 'no comment.' Reporting from the Bering Sea aboard the USS Vinson; Eyewitness News."

"Oh, no, I can't believe it," Robert said. "They killed him!"

CHAPTER 40

JULY, 1

Tristan Wood was a young boy again, running on a sandy beach of the Delaware shore with his younger brother, Robert. The youngsters laughed uncontrollably and held out their arms pretending to fly, lost in complete freedom from worry and stress. Faceless figures walked the water's edge under a colorless sky.

It all came to an abrupt end with a flood of intense heat on his back. Turning around, multiple mushroom clouds rose in the distance. He wanted to run but his legs would not move. Without warning, the brothers were hit by a wall of sand and debris launching them into the air. As Tristan tumbled out over the ocean, a ringing slowly woke him up. He opened his eyes and stared at the ceiling trying to regain his senses.

The cell phone rang again and he reached to answer it.

"We need to talk," J.J. yelled over traffic noise in the background.

"What's wrong? I can barely hear you!"

"I have to meet with you right now!"

"What are you doing? Stick with the plan! Text me the location and we'll be there."

"Okay, but I need to tell you that something has changed—" A truck horn blared, drowning out the rest of his sentence, followed by a dropped call.

Tristan threw the phone down in frustration, remembering his FBI suspension. He hobbled into the bathroom to clean the bad taste in his mouth.

The mirror reflected the face of someone he barely recognized, tired and haggard. Weight loss was now undeniable and his skin pale. At least his eye had finally healed and was no longer black and blue. He reread the back of the tube of toothpaste.

"Keep out of the reach of children under 6 years of age. If more than used for brushing is accidentally swallowed, get medical help or contact a Poison Control Center right away."

Hidden in plain sight.

The phone rang again, this time with the tone specific for a text message. The display read;

39°03'73"N ~ 76°91'0.59"W

Tristan speed dialed Sebastian.

"It's me. The informant called, he sounds frantic."

"Did he tell you why?"

"No. I'm going to text you the GPS location now."

"Come pick me up, we'll meet him."

"I'm suspended, I can't."

"Yes, you can."

"I don't want to get you in trouble too, you're the only hope on this case."

"I need you there, the informant doesn't trust me, or like me."

This was true, and Tristan was more than a little worried that if Sebastian and J.J. were alone for even a short amount of time, it could all blow up.

"Okay, I'm leaving now."

Within a half-hour they were speeding along MacArthur Boulevard with the Potomac River to the south.

News reporters on the radio were in near panic about the bond crisis, which had caused the DOW to drop almost thirty percent in the last week. Though the New York and other stock exchanges remained open, the growing consensus among economists was to halt trading and close the markets.

Across the water, CIA headquarters in Langley appeared from between the old growth trees, a landmark indicating the Capital Beltway was fast approaching.

Minutes later the car was winding through the makeshift dirt roads of a construction site, closing in on the GPS coordinates. They parked outside the shell of a mid-rise apartment building, next to the brown Chevy, and got out.

"Up here." The informant waved from one of the higher levels.

The special agents walked up cement stairs to the sixth floor where mixing buckets and other building materials littered the space. The absence of walls created a wind tunnel effect that pleasantly cooled the temperature several degrees.

"We got a big problem." J.J. paced like a caged animal. "They moved up the time table!"

"What are you talking about? When?" Sebastian asked.

"Tomorrow."

"Tomorrow?" The shock of the situation hit Tristan instantly. "Why so soon?"

"They didn't tell me."

"Have you talked to the Major?"

"He's calling me when it's time to meet, but it's going down tomorrow. It's too quick, this is too soon!"

"I knew something didn't feel right!" Sebastian blustered.

"Are you sure he's not trying to throw you off? He calls, says it was a false alarm, *I'll talk to you next week?*" Tristan asked.

"I don't think so."

"Why not? How can you be sure?"

"We're parking the get-away cars outside the embassies tonight. And the Major wants the Russians to give the signal to their contacts at the guardhouses. Once they do that, there's no going back."

"Okay, for now we need to keep the plan the same. Let's stay calm and level-headed, we don't want to make any mistakes."

"We're putting a wire on you," Sebastian insisted.

"You do and I'm as good as dead!"

"We need to get everything recorded, if we miss just one conversation it will be devastating for this case!"

"No, no, I'm out. I can't do this anymore."

"You're not out of anything," Sebastian grabbed J.J., backing him up near the edge of a forty foot drop. "We're wiring you or so help me I'll put a bullet between your eyes right now!" He drew his Glock, dangling J.J. over the potentially fatal fall. "What's it going to be?"

Tristan moved in fast to break it up.

"We all need to keep our heads and think straight. You!" he spoke directly to J.J. "Get out of here." He ushered the informant toward the exit. "Listen to me. We're not going to make you wear a wire. You call me as soon as you hear from the Major, no more GPS texts, just call. I want to know everything he tells you. Got it?"

"No wire?"

"No wire. We stick to the plan."

Somewhat allayed, J.J. rushed down the stairs. The sound of wheels kicking up dirt and stones echoed off the walls.

Sebastian was livid.

"Why tomorrow? It's July second, why the second?" Tristan wondered. "Russia is having massive war games on July 4, that day would make sense. A terror attack on American soil on our Independence Day is logical. Why July 2?"

"I think he knows more than he's telling us."

"We can't put a wire on him Sebastian, as nervous as he is, it will be a dead giveaway. If they wand him once, or pat him down, they'll either call the whole thing off, or kill him. Or both."

"We're losing our options, fast."

"I understand, but our job is to prevent a nuclear war and the way to do that is to bust them trying to blow up the embassies."

"Our priority is to expose the New World Order plot and the people behind it, or there will be another false flag to do the job this one didn't. I'm starting to wonder whose side you're on, Tristan."

"I'm trying to make sure this case goes according to plan."

"The way this is going, there is no case."

Sebastian, seething with anger, walked across the platform and down the stairs as a strong gust of wind pushed Tristan in the opposite direction. The investigation was now clearly weighing heavily on both of them.

He stood for a moment pondering the long drive home.

Sebastian Graves checked his wristwatch, the glow of the hands indicating it was roughly midnight. The dashboard lights combined with Pink Floyd's *Brain Damage* coming through the speakers created a phantasmal atmosphere inside the Jeep Cherokee.

From coast to coast, folks would be settling in for the evening, perhaps dreaming about the upcoming Independence Day celebrations with friends and family. They had no idea what was stirring in the nation's capital. A phrase from Macbeth came to mind;

Something wicked this way comes.

The world would quite possibly change overnight and the American people were completely in the dark. Speaking of dark, this part of the Dulles International Airport parking lot was almost pitch-black.

His cell phone buzzed.

The caller ID displayed Tony's number, no doubt wondering where he was. Sebastian took a carry-on bag from the back seat and headed for the terminal. After a long walk, automatic doors slid open and dry crisp air surrounded him making it easier to breathe. Locating his airline, he fell into line behind waiting passengers.

The knots in his stomach were not from nerves, but from guilt. He tried not to think about what he was going to do; skip out and leave for his new home halfway around the world. This case was over as far as he could tell. There was nothing left to do.

His predictions had come true. The economy was now in free-fall collapse, yet the Hegelian-influenced talking points continued to dominate the news. The media-heads and talk show hosts preached the "accidentalism" theory as fingers pointed back and forth between the two parties. In reality, both sides were under the control of the international banker elites.

This was all part of the plan.

If the American people were going to keep electing the same New World Order globalists over and over, keep falling for the same government lies and phony terror attacks, keep asking for handouts and freebees, and keep living in willful ignorance, then he would leave them to their fate. But justifying it this way did not make him feel any better.

"Next in line," asked a beautiful young woman, prompting Sebastian to advance to the ticket counter.

"I bought an e-ticket."

"Driver's license and passport please?"

After some typing, she printed a boarding pass and wished him a happy flight.

He walked across the terminal and stopped at the first security checkpoint where passengers lined up, removing their shoes and entering the body scanners.

A middle-aged woman talking with a male TSA agent caught his attention. She explained that she could not pass through the scanner due to an implanted pacemaker but he demanded proof. She searched her bag and handed over an official looking document.

The man escorted her off to the side where a female agent gave her a pat-down. The woman squirmed and fidgeted, obviously uncomfortable with the manner of touching. Then she began sobbing.

The agent stopped, rolled her eyes, and threatened to keep her from proceeding to the gate. Two male agents approached, standing over her in an intimidating posture, which only made it worse. The groping continued and she started to cry again.

Sebastian lost it. He stormed over and flashed his FBI badge.

"Stop that!" he tried controlling his rage. "Ma'am, come with me."

The agents reacted predictably, unsure what to do when their authority and power were challenged. They stood bewildered as Sebastian comforted the woman, escorting her around the security checkpoint to her shoes and luggage.

"Thank you officer, you are a saint." She spoke with watery eyes and hugged him.

A rush of emotion coursed through his veins. The TSA agents huddled together like a pack of threatened wild dogs, giving him dirty looks.

"Can I see you to your gate?"

"I'll be okay now, thank you."

She kissed him on the cheek. He watched until she had disappeared into the crowd. Walking back around, FBI Special Agent Sebastian Graves took his luggage and dialed a number on his cell phone.

"Tony? Sorry, I got held up. I'm on my way."

CHAPTER 41

Sebastian entered the warehouse carrying a tall step ladder. One camera had been plagued with problems since the beginning, and now a second was acting up. Tony needed someone to work on them while at the controls, which he could not do by himself. To be on the safe side the inside lights remained off. Sebastian's only means of guidance was a flashlight.

"Keep an eye on the outside, you see a car or anything at all, tell me ASAP," he spoke into the walkie-talkie.

"Will do," Tony replied.

"Let's make this quick. What camera do I work on first?"

"Start with the one with zoom problems—back, west corner."

"West? Where is west?"

"After you walked in the door, when you turned right you were facing west." Tony's voice boomed through the empty space.

Spotting the camera in the narrow beam of light, Sebastian climbed up to it.

"Okay, I'm here. What do you want me to do?"

"See the black plastic ring around the lens? I'm going to operate the zoom, tell me if it rotates?"

"Nope."

"Try moving it manually."

"Seems to be stuck."

"It might be jammed. Push the tabs in and lift the top off."

A loud crash outside startled him.

"What the hell?"

He held the flashlight in his mouth and used both hands to remove the cover, adjusting a loose section. He tightened it up and closed the lid.

"Try it now."

"It works! Okay, on to the next one. Head over to the opposite side of the warehouse."

Two rows of shelves reached almost to the ceiling and extended to the far wall. The hundreds of automobile parts cast eerie shadows from the murky light as Sebastian plodded between them—then the sound of another animal.

Or maybe not?

"Tony, I keep hearing things."

"I don't see anything, there's no one here."

"Well let's get on with it; this place gives me the creeps."

"Okay, look up on the second shelf from the top, against that back wall. It's buried in the clutter, somewhere in the middle."

Sebastian positioned the step ladder and climbed, searching for the camera—another noise.

Was it a clang or a bang?

He froze, listening intently, body weary and concentration nil.

"I need sleep."

Not even adrenalin improved his vigor anymore.

As he reached for the camera, the flashlight slipped from his hand and hit the floor with a metallic thump—the light extinguished. Cursing, he stepped down and rummaged blindly in the dark.

"Hey, what's going on? Did you find the camera?" Tony's voice roared over the walkie.

"Gotcha," he said to himself, finding the flashlight.

But after struggling to his feet, he realized it was dead. Sebastian slapped it against his leg, with no success.

Dirt and gravel crunched beneath shoes just ahead, directly in front of him, a few feet away. *Footsteps, I'm sure of it!*

"Hello?" he called out.

The last thing Sebastian Graves heard before his life ended was one deafening gunshot.

Tristan Wood stood on the front doorstep of a grand colonial home on a quiet street in Chevy Chase, Maryland, ringing the doorbell over and over again. Wind rustled the trees in the early morning tranquility. Even the birds slept soundly under the gray skies above. Multi-million dollar homes lined the block, affordable only by the well-connected.

With the recent DOW crash, the Federal Reserve could no longer manipulate the economic numbers to fool the average person into believing things were getting better, so they didn't bother.

All the stimulus, bailouts, and quantitative easing gimmicks had run their course. The Fed's bag of tricks was finally empty— the bubble was bursting. The few who actually showed up for congressional hearings, those who did not disappear into thin air, simply *pleaded the Fifth*.

Even the mainstream media was forced to report on the depression they now foresaw as imminent.

But it was too late.

The largest wealth transfer in the history of the country was complete. For the last century, the Insiders had hidden money in offshore accounts and tax-exempt foundations, designed to avoid paying taxes. The elites had stayed in business and out of prison under the justification of *too-big-to-fail* and *too-big-to-jail*.

"Don't move," said a voice.

Something pushed into the back of his head, followed by the sound of a revolver hammer.

"Director Dufour? It's Agent Wood."

"Agent Wood?" The FBI Director lowered his gun and asked, "Son, what are you doing at my home?"

"Please sir, I need to speak with you, it's urgent."

"You're bleeding."

"Not my blood, sir."

Director Dufour took a careful glance around. "Come in."

The massive brick colonial was decorated, wall to wall, with Oriental furniture. He locked the door behind them and inspected Tristan.

"I almost shot you."

Dressed in bathrobe and pajamas, he placed the handgun inside a drawer of an antique escritoire in the foyer.

Dapper, even at four in the morning, Tristan thought.

"Agent Graves is dead, sir."

"Come with me." He led the way to his home office. "What happened?"

"He was fixing equipment in the warehouse and someone shot him."

"Who?"

"I don't know. Our G called, I went to the safe house but by the time we got him to the hospital he was DOA."

"You don't have much luck with partners, Agent Wood. What is the status of your case?"

"They're planning on bombing the embassies sometime today. The Major will contact our informant with the details, he's the team leader—"

"I'm familiar with the cast of characters. Remember, I'm the one who got the call on Agent Grave's behalf. From what I understand your brother works for the good Senator?"

"Yes, sir."

"I've had quite an interest in this investigation, to say the least."

"Then you realize, SAC Pascal suspended me. We have no one left. I'm begging you, please let me finish it."

"Do you want to put a team together and bust them right now?"

"We need the Major. I don't know where to find him until he shows up at the warehouse to build the bombs." Tristan reflected for a moment. "Sebastian was concerned, that if we're not careful, a lawyer could get them off on a lesser charge. It has to be a slam-dunk."

"I'm well aware of what lawyers are capable of, Agent Wood."

Trying not to sound forlorn, he said, "Sir, no one but me can carry on."

"SAC Pascal suspended you for a reason."

"Because I talked to my wife about the progress of the case, nobody else. You're married, Director Dufour, you understand."

"I don't like how this whole thing is going."

Tristan believed his pitch was solid, yet the director exhibited little enthusiasm despite all his work and the potential world-shattering consequences. He had a strong hand, but it was finally time to play his trump card.

"Sir, it is impossible to fathom the scale of this case."

"What do you mean?"

He removed the flash drive from his keychain.

"Can you turn your computer on please?"

After the PC booted, the director plugged in the flash drive and played the video file.

— Приливная волна 23 —

Tristan waited for a reaction.

"What is this?"

"*Tidal Wave 23*. I found it on Agent Graves. Jason, not his father. He had it on him the night he was shot."

"The spy? Where did he get this?"

"He took it from the Russian ambassador's house, and was trying to extort money for its return."

"What is it?"

"Russian intelligence. We believe the embassy bombings are meant to be a catalyst . . ."

"A catalyst to what?"

Tristan hesitated before saying, "To a preemptive nuclear strike by Russia. This video shows the targets."

"Am I the first to view this?"

The question was bound to surface. "Yes."

"Why didn't you give this to your SAC?"

"I held onto it until I could figure out what it was."

"So you were withholding information on an active investigation?"

"Yes." He swallowed hard.

The director played *Tidal Wave 23* again, then sat back in his chair. "Can I have this?"

"Of course."

He decided not to mention he had made several copies, and that Sebastian uploaded it to YouTube. Be that as it may, the man was not naïve.

"All right, Agent Wood," he said reluctantly. "I'll reinstate you, temporarily. When it's done I want a full report and we'll reevaluate your current employment with FBI at that time. I'll have your SAC reissue your badge and gun."

"Sir, I need backup. There will be three men to arrest plus my informant, and two vans with the bombs. I also need the *Bomb Squad* on stand-by."

"Let SAC Pascal know what you require for the sting."

Tristan's heart sank. "But Tufts is lead agent."

"Andrew Tufts has been transferred out of the DC field office."

"What? When did that happen?"

"Last evening. I'm handing this over to Mr. Pascal, this is his area of expertise. Especially with the Russians."

"I'm not sure that's a good idea—"

"You want this case? Then be happy with what I give you."

"It's just . . . it hasn't been easy getting assistance from SAC Pascal. In fact, it's been like pulling teeth."

"You have any trouble you come to me, I'll be keeping a close eye on your progress."

Not placating him, Tristan decided to push it now that he had the FBI Director's full attention.

"There's one more thing, Director Dufour, it's my understanding that the Major works for the Pentagon."

"What makes you think that?"

"I followed him there."

"Have you been able to ID him, get a real name?"

"He's been extremely illusive. Sir, if it turns out this is somehow connected to the government, we need to expose it. No matter how high up. I don't want another *Fast and Furious* where evidence is suppressed, witnesses are threatened, and everyone else pleads the Fifth and gets away with it."

"Whoever these people are, whoever they are connected to, we'll get them. You have my word."

The director held out his hand to seal the deal with a handshake, but Tristan's gut was talking to him again.

CHAPTER 42

JULY, 2

The monitors in the surveillance van showed the activity in the warehouse, the hard drive recording. Tristan had just finished giving instructions to the four special agents, in two unmarked cars, assigned by Pascal to assist. It wasn't as much manpower as he would have liked, but at least he was back on the case. With Liam in isolation, there were now three suspects to arrest—the two Russians and the Major.

The Russian named Petrev was moving bags of fertilizer, opening them with a box cutter and emptying the contents into the barrels at the direction of J.J. Watching from a nearby chair sat the other Russian, Ivan. The Major was not yet here, but Tristan knew it wouldn't be long.

This was his show.

He was also providing the military-grade C4 as the primer for the bombs. The doors to the warehouse were wide open and both trucks were backed in, ramps leading up inside.

"It's getting ready to go down. Are all the cameras working?"

"So far so good. Number one is still grainy, but it's passable. That's the one Sebastian didn't get to." He gave Tony a sympathetic pat on the back. "I had the strangest dream last night."

"Let me guess, a nuclear war?"

"How didja know?"

"Just a hunch."

"It started out insanely quiet," Tony recollected. "There was a bright flash and a mushroom cloud. Then a shockwave hit me—"

"Wait," Tristan reacted to something the G said. "Did you check the video from the warehouse?"

"Of course I did, but it was too dark to see anything."

"There would have been a flash from the gun."

Realizing what this meant, Tony began working frantically on the computer. He found the sound of the shot that killed Sebastian. "This was the closest camera to him."

Tony played the seemingly barren video.

"Okay, isolate the first frame of the gunshot," Tristan said.

"On it."

Tony moved forward, still by still, until they located a faint circle of light. It showed the blurry outline of a figure.

"That's as good as it gets."

"Can you work on the image of the face?"

"Not with what's here. I gotta spend some time back at the Bureau on their computers. And we're kind of busy today."

"I know, but first chance you get, see what you can do."

"You got it."

Tristan unclipped the walkie-talkie from his belt.

"Team Alpha ready?"

"Ready."

He placed two FBI agents in an unmarked car three hundred yards away in the small parking lot of an abandoned gas station.

"Okay, wait for my signal. Team Bravo, ready?"

"Roger."

The second response came from the other pair of agents, parked inside a half-built carwash. Team Bravo was positioned on the opposite end to make sure both sides of the commercial complex were covered.

"Wait for my signal."

Further off-site was the *Bomb Squad*, sitting in a fire station a mile north on the route the trucks would travel to get into the city.

J.J. had the dummy fuse caps Tristan rigged to look real. Although the bombs could not be set off with them, the volatile chemicals combined with the C4 made the devices very dangerous.

"I think he's here," Tony said.

The black Mercedes drove down the road and parked. The Major and another man, holding a red backpack, got out of the car and walked into the warehouse.

"Whoa, who is that?" Tristan asked.

"No idea!"

Tony turned up the volume on the monitors so they could better hear the conversation inside.

The stranger received suspicious looks, but there was no explanation and there were no introductions. The Major tossed his car keys to Ivan who left in a hurry, followed by Petrev. The two Russians raced off in the Mercedes.

The Major inspected the barrels—now packed with fertilizer—and asked, "How we doing?"

"I need the C4."

He took a brick out of the red backpack and tossed it to J.J.

"Time to fire 'em up boys," the boss clapped his hands in anticipation.

They poured the liquid nitro into the first barrel and secured the lid. J.J. grabbed the dolly, and with the help of the new guy, they used all their strength to move bomb number one up the ramp and into the truck's cab, then installed the first C4 brick.

"You have the blast caps?" the Major asked.

J.J. pulled a clear plastic bag out of his pocket and held it up, reluctant to allow him a close look. Tristan had filled them with beeswax, giving the appearance of a real pyrotechnic ignition mixture. He also added a non-flammable chemical creating a similar odor to the initiator, a formula he had discovered in Afghanistan used by arms dealers attempting to sell fakes.

"You want me to arm them?"

"Not until we're ready to pull out of here," the Major answered.

After adding liquid nitro to the second barrel, he secured the top. The two men pushed it up and into the other truck, attaching the next C4 brick.

"Let me see the blast caps."

"Sure," J.J. jumped down and handed them to the Major.

Then they heard something outside.

"What is that?"

"You ready? Moment of truth," the Major said.

"Are those trucks?"

"A slight change in plans."

Two vehicles, exactly like the ones they already had, pulled up and sat idling outside.

"I decided we needed some decoys."

"Good thinking." J.J. tried acting casual.

Ivan and Petrev hurried into the warehouse.

"Let's get everything loaded into the trucks. I don't want to leave anything behind."

J.J. walked over to the unused bags of fertilizer and bent down to pick one up. The Major tossed the dummy fuse caps on the table then shot a glance at the new guy who pulled something out of his back pocket.

As J.J. turned for the door with the heavy bag on his shoulder, he was clutched from behind, his throat slit with a knife.

James Johnson, the FBI informant and ex-marine, dropped to the floor like a sack of potatoes.

Back in the surveillance van Tristan almost had a heart attack. "Oh, no!" he yelled involuntarily. "No, NO!"

They watched the monitors as the Major took a new set of blasting caps from the backpack, each with a black wireless transmitter where the fuse would be. He handed one to Ivan and the other to Petrev who affixed them, completing the bombs.

"What are those?" Tony asked.

"Electronic blast caps."

The Major picked up a container of nitro and spread it around the warehouse, drenching the leftover materials, the furniture, and even the dead informant.

As the Russians pulled the ramps off and rolled down the doors, the Major lit the flammable liquid with his zippo. Engines roared as the bomb trucks drove away.

The Major grabbed the backpack and ran outside, with his new accomplice, and into the decoy vehicles. The bags of fertilizer quickly caught fire hastened by exploding bottles of nitro.

In less than a minute the entire warehouse blazed.

"Team A, go! Team B, go!" He called into his walkie, but got no response. "Team Alpha, are you there? Team Bravo?"

"We're here," affirmed one of the agents.

"There are four trucks now. I'll get the one with the Major and you stop the trucks with the Russians!"

"We can't do that, Agent Wood."

"What are you talking about?"

Tony looked at Tristan, dumbfounded.

"We have orders to follow, but only to observe."

"I didn't give that order!"

"We were given new ones a few minutes ago."

"From who?"

"The top."

Tristan jumped out of the back of the surveillance van.

"Where are you going?" Tony asked.

"After them. Stay here with the equipment and call the fire department!"

The Jeep Wrangler kicked up rocks and dirt as it sped off. He dialed a new number.

"This is Agent Wood, I need to speak with Pascal!"

The secretary replied that the SAC was expecting the call, and put him through.

"Pascal here."

"What are you doing? It's time to make the bust!"

"I want to catch them in the act."

"That's not necessary, everything's recorded! We have all the evidence we need!"

"I want them to attempt to blow up the embassies, it's the only way to make sure. They can't detonate them anyway."

"They're not using our blast caps, the Major installed his own, and they're electronic. They killed my informant and set the warehouse on fire. The bombs are hot!"

"Agent Wood, follow them and wait for further instructions."

"Let me speak with the director!"

"Director Dufour has put me in charge of this operation, I'm your SAC. You follow and let them attempt the bombings." He hung up.

In utter disbelief, Tristan tore out of the commercial complex and spotted the two unmarked cars following the trucks further up the road. The Washington Monument and US Capitol were now visible on the horizon.

He called the number of his Bomb Squad contact—they weren't even picking up.

Tristan followed a football-field length behind Team Alpha and Team Bravo, the Potomac River drawing near. The trucks crossed the George Mason Bridge bouncing from lane to lane, overly reckless considering the cargo they carried.

"Team A, come in! Do you know which ones have the bombs?"

"No," was the monotone reply.

As they entered the district, all the trucks moved into the center lane, forming a line.

"What are they doing?" Tristan asked himself.

A fork in the highway approached. Two trucks swerved left, taking them north on Route 1 and the other pair veered right, continuing on I-395 heading east into the city. Either way would get them to the embassies, however, he had no idea which vans were which, or who drove them.

"Team Alpha, go left! Team Bravo, go right!" It did no good, both unmarked cars went left. "No!"

Tristan went right, all by himself. He tried speeding up, to look inside and determine who was driving, but the twists and turns in the highway, plus the mounting traffic, prevented him from gaining much ground.

They continued the distance on I-395, taking the exit onto First Street NW, with Tristan doing his best to keep up. As they reached the Capitol building, one of the trucks reduced speed and pulled into a no-parking zone, next to the huge steel beams separating road from sidewalk.

Two DC Metro cop cars were stationed on-guard outside. The box truck slowed, preparing to stop. It then spasmodically slammed into one of the police vehicles.

"What the—"

Tristan brought the Jeep to a screeching halt and jumped out, gun drawn. The Metro cops were caught completely by surprise. Moving around to the driver's side of the vehicle, the Major's new accomplice sat in a servile position, his hands resting on the steering wheel in a surrender posture.

"Diversion!" Tristan realized what it was. "Out! Get out of the truck! Keep your hands where I can see them!" The door opened and he grabbed the guy, throwing him to the ground as the cops arrived. "I'm FBI!" He showed them his badge. "Detain this man, he is a terrorist!"

This truck did not have a bomb.

Tristan returned to his Jeep and headed north searching frantically for the other. But the accident had caused the disorder it was meant to, and traffic slowed to almost a stop.

"Come on, move!" he yelled at cars in front of him, knowing full well it would do no good.

In desperation he hooked a sharp left through the intersection, running a red light and causing a minor accident. Tristan's head was spinning, trying to locate either one of the Russians driving a bomb truck, or the Major who would detonate them.

Unsure what to do, he continued in the direction of the embassies.

The Major pulled into a wide fire lane and sat with the engine running. He checked the volume on his walkie-talkie and placed it on the dashboard.

Next, he unzipped the backpack and removed a remote detonator. Flipping on the power button caused a series of red LEDs to light up and move back and forth before changing to a single solid green. This meant it was communicating with the bombs.

Ivan and Petrev would soon be parked at each embassy, allowed to enter the premises by their new contacts in the guardhouses.

Then there was a knock. A District Metro police officer motioned to roll down the window.

"Do you know you're in a fire lane?"

"I do, officer. My engine started sputtering and I thought it was going to shut down. I didn't want the truck to break down in traffic. It's bad enough this time of day." The Major flashed an easy smile.

"It sounds fine to me." The cop listened closely.

"When it idles, it seems okay. When it's in drive, it starts acting up."

The cop studied him before saying, "License and registration, please."

"Of course."

He took out his wallet and gave the driver's license to the officer.

"The truck is a rental, hold on, I have the lease agreement."

Inside the glove compartment he found the document, giving it to the cop who walked back to his car.

The Major reached under his shirt to disengage the safety on his handgun and positioned it between his legs. He placed the detonator on the floor, tucking it under the seat. In the side view mirror he could see the cop exit his car and head back. The only sound inside the truck was the slide, chambering a round.

"I'm sorry, sir."

"For what, officer?"

"I'm sorry to take up your time, my apologies." The cop handed the license and rental papers back. "Would you like me to call you a tow truck?"

"No, I'll let it sit for a while longer, if you don't mind."

"Stay as long as you want. Have a nice day."

Nothing like a national security override.

He engaged the safety on the gun as the cop returned to his cruiser and drove away.

The solid green LED on the detonator persisted.

Then Petrev's voice came over the walkie, loud and clear;

"Русский"

Ivan's voice followed.

"Русский"

It was a beautiful July day in Washington, DC. Birds chirped on tree branches surrounding the Russian and Ukraine embassies as wind rustled the leaves. Clouds drifted overhead and an unusual quiet enveloped a typically hectic city—until the explosions.

The simultaneous blasts blew out windows in the guardhouses, killing those inside, and shattered glass in the buildings across the street. Nearby structures shook with the force of an earthquake, and the roar of the fertilizer bombs could be heard well into Virginia and Maryland.

Anyone close enough would behold a white fireball quickly turning yellow and orange, hurling the respective box truck thirty feet into the air before falling back into the six foot crater created by the explosion.

The heat from the inferno lit trees, grass and bushes on fire while scorching everything in a fifty-foot radius. The shock wave set off car alarms as far as a half mile away.

Razor-sharp shrapnel consisting of glass and metal was propelled 360 degrees at thousands of feet per second, with the force of 150,000 pounds of pressure per inch.

As each fireball extinguished and the dust settled, black smoke rose up from what was left of the truck that expelled it. All that remained was a chassis, engine block, and four wheels flattened and melted.

Most of the damage was inflicted on the embassies a few yards away. A structural collapse at both locations preceded blast clouds that ascended into the sky, visible for miles around.

Only a trained ear, or a recording played in slow motion, would have revealed the almost simultaneous explosions, prior to the initial blast—explosions that came from inside the embassies, causing a demolition the bombs were incapable of doing on their own.

Like the Murrah Federal building in Oklahoma City in 1995.

And the Twin Towers in New York City in 2001.

CHAPTER 43

JULY, 3

Robert Wood sat across the desk from Senator Matthews in his Russell Senate Building office. Washington, DC, was in near panic. The media was reporting pockets of riots erupting around the country due to growing social unrest. At the same time the politicians pointed fingers of blame back and forth between the parties.

The American people were in a perpetual state of denial.

Governors of several states had issued curfews and outlawed the sale of alcohol, guns, and ammo. There were rumors the president would soon declare martial law and suspend habeas corpus as Lincoln had during the Civil War.

With Independence Day looming, the media had an excuse to put a smiley face on what they did not understand, happily announcing the fireworks shows to come. The president was scheduled to speak on the embassy bombings from the Oval Office tomorrow, July 4, at noon.

The computer on Robert's desk was open to the Drudge Report's current headline.

Doomsday Clock; 2 Minutes to Midnight.

The photo above it was a black and white from the 1950s, a group of men observing a mushroom cloud rising in the distance during a nuclear test in the desert.

The Doomsday Clock was now tied with the closest position it had ever been, not just from the bombings but also because President Putin and the Russian Federation were directly blaming the US and threatening revenge. Putin's passionate rhetoric was exciting the Russian people into a frenzy, and an unprecedented anti-American fervor was spreading through the country, particularly in Moscow.

The buildings set on fire, the stores that were looted, the citizens who were assaulted, all the anger was directed toward "the great Satan," a term revived by Putin and repeated often. However, the president of Russia was not calling for the embassy bombers to be brought to justice, but rather for justice to be brought upon the United States of America.

It was a message resonating worldwide.

"Russia is moving troops to the Georgian border. Satellite images are also picking up movements down toward the Kuril Islands," Robert read to the senator from the latest intelligence report. The senator's mind seemed to be elsewhere.

"Already?" he snapped out of it, momentarily. "I didn't think it would happen so fast."

The Kuril Islands, located between the Kamchatka Peninsula and northern Japan, stretched a distance of over 800 miles. Since WWII the two southern-most islands had been claimed by Japan as territories while Russia considered them to be under their administration, resulting in the *Kuril Islands Dispute*.

In February 2011 President Medvedev began deploying French made Mistral-class amphibious assault ships and installing anti-air missile systems, as he publicly declared the islands to be an inseparable part of the country and a strategic Russian region. The dispute with Japan had always been a sore spot for the Soviet Union and now they seemed prepared to take them back.

"There's lots of activity at Vladivostok. CIA reports the last Delta-class sub has left port. All active Russian subs, Delta III, Delta IV, and Typhoon-class are at sea. China is also mobilizing. They must be spooked over a potential conflict between Russia and the United States. China's aircraft carriers appear to be heading toward Taiwan and the Senkaku islands. And North Korea is moving troops along the southern border." Robert flipped through the pages of the report. "Sir, all this could not have been organized since the embassy bombings?"

"You are right, it could not."

This confirmed that many world leaders had prior inside knowledge. He continued scanning the security brief. "Russia just recalled their ambassadors and embassy staff."

"That is to be expected," the senator mumbled.

The current response to the bombings and to Putin's inflammatory statements baffled Robert. It seemed Americans did not know how to react. As with the Train Bomber, the media was announcing another Tim McVeigh, reporting a home-grown right wing terrorist who was the mastermind behind the embassy bombings. There was no evidence whatsoever to support this.

He did not understand how they could, in good conscious, make such a claim after getting it wrong so many times in the past. America was being blamed and the media was fanning the flames, regardless of the facts, or lack of them. No one had yet been arrested and the limited information was given to them by a spokesman in FBI.

Someone named SAC Seth Pascal.

Stocks had opened so low at the opening bell that the SEC had halted trading, announcing all US markets would be closed until after the holiday. Everyone on Wall Street was sent home and government offices were shut down.

But across the country there was a strange denial in the air; bars remained full, people obsessed over sports, and all the same distractions preoccupied the populace.

Robert's cell phone rang and he left the office to take the call.

"Hey, what's up?"

"We need to talk," Tristan said.

"Yeah we do. Where are you?"

"Look outside."

Stepping to the window, he looked down. Tristan waved.

"I'll be right down."

Robert met his brother who paced on the sidewalk in front of the building. Observing the pedestrians confirmed the strange vibe he had felt. Folks seemed to walk around like zombies.

"What's going on? What's the latest intelligence?" Tristan asked.

"It's bad. Russia seems to be preparing for war. China and North Korea are mobilizing, they're on high alert. Russia recalled their ambassadors and staff. And I checked with the FAA. Private jets all across the country are requesting permission to leave US airspace."

"That's the one I was waiting for. The rats are jumping ship."

"You need to go to the media," Robert suggested.

"I'm worried about creating a mass panic. Either that, or no one will believe me."

"What do you want to do?"

"If I could speak to the president directly, I could tell him what's really going on."

"How do you know he's not part of the New World Order?"

"I don't. But I don't know what else to do?"

"Right now, the president is in the White House bunker, he's untouchable."

"Isn't he giving a statement from the Oval Office tomorrow?"

"That's a set, in the bunker. One of the few well kept secrets inside the beltway."

"Is there anyone high up in government to talk to?"

"The Speaker of the House is in a closed meeting right now. The Capitol is on lockdown, but I can get us in."

"Let's give it a shot," Tristan said.

They walked back inside the Russell Senate Office Building and passed through security. The design of the rotunda was impressive. Robert had always found it odd that there was so much ancient Greek architecture in the city.

He led his older brother down a flight of stairs.

"All this time, I bet you never knew a tunnel spanned the distance from the FBI building to here, did you?" Robert asked.

"Believe me, there are a lot of things I've realized I didn't know."

He searched a set of keys and chose one, unlocking a door leading to a long hallway. The cement floors were polished and shiny, reflecting the fluorescent lights that dimly illuminated the corridor.

The brothers began to walk.

"This is amazing."

"There are thousands of miles of tunnels below DC, dating back to the Civil War and even earlier. And it's not just here, many cities have complex tunnel systems, in and outside the United States. The senator showed me one under the Spaso House, complete with a magnetic levitation train system."

"Really?"

"It was wild. Moscow not only has an extensive labyrinth of tunnels, but an underground base as well. It's fully functional, run from a state-of-the-art central command center, and stocked with supplies in case the heads of state and other elites need to get to safety. Apparently, there are numerous similar bases scattered all over the US including a deep one under the Pentagon."

They arrived at a T-section, a door before them, and complete darkness in both directions. By now, Tristan was limping.

He watched his brother swallow two pills then lean against the wall to rest. "You okay?" Robert asked—a question with multiple meanings.

Tristan brushed it off with a nod.

He decided to insist they talk, heart to heart, sibling to sibling, when this was over. The steady decline in Tristan's health had bothered him for some time and this was the worst his older brother had ever looked.

Unlocking the door, they climbed two flights of stairs and entered the Capitol building. Robert had traveled this route many times and took them to the area where closed conferences were in progress.

After some searching they came upon a door guarded by Capitol Security, a message board on a tripod announced the time blocked out for the meeting.

"It should be over, they're running late."

They did not have to wait long.

The doors opened and out came the Speaker of the House of Representatives, along with other congressional members.

"Mr. Speaker, can I have a word?" Robert called out.

Regardless of his persistence they were ignored. Then security decided the brothers had worn out their welcome.

"Fight the New World Order!" Tristan shouted.

The man who was third in line to the presidency stopped dead in his tracks. "Who said that?"

"I'm an FBI agent, Mr. Speaker. May I have a minute of your time, please?" Tristan pleaded.

An aide tried to pull him away, but the Speaker ignored her and walked over.

"If you haven't noticed we're in a bit of a crisis, agent . . ."

"Wood. Tristan Wood, sir." He showed his badge. "This is my brother Robert, he's Senator Matthew's aide."

"Please, make this quick."

"I was one of the FBI agents assigned to the embassy bombing case."

"Mr. Speaker, he was *the* agent," Robert insisted.

Pulling them to the side, the Speaker waved off security and his entourage, begging some privacy. "That phrase you yelled out. Is there anything I should know?"

"Sir, the bombings were a false flag," Tristan said. "It was planned and orchestrated by someone in the Pentagon."

"Who in the Pentagon?"

"We never found out his name. I had some . . . difficulties on the case."

The Speaker glanced at his pocket watch. "Get to the point, son."

"The embassy bombings were meant to provoke a nuclear war with Russia. They needed a catalyst to launch first."

Robert added, "Mr. Speaker, I just saw the latest intelligence report, as I'm sure you have. Russia is mobilizing. This was all planned, but it can be stopped. The president must know the truth."

"I assume you have proof of this?"

Tristan handed a new flash drive to the Speaker before saying, "This video shows the blueprint for the attack. It's called *Tidal Wave 23*. My partner took it from the Russian ambassador's residence."

"Took it?"

Handing over a business card, he said, "Sir, the director is fully aware what's going on, give him a call, he can confirm everything I'm saying."

"Okay, I'll take a look at this." The Speaker was pulled away by his staff. "Director Dufour better know what this is about."

The brothers stood, with Robert feeling a mutual hope between them for the first time in a long time.

Tristan inspected the artwork on the walls with morbid curiosity. Still seated, the senator carved a symbol on top of his desk with an antique letter opener, a grim look on his face.

The symbol was a pentagram.

"Senator, you remember my brother Tristan?"

He continued to move the letter opener through the grooves he had engraved.

"Does he realize what's going on?"

Robert nodded yes. He then said, "Senator, you must speak to the president. We have to inform him the embassy bombings were a false flag, and make sure the Russians don't launch."

The politician mumbled incoherently, speaking in tongues.

"Sir, we need to get the word out—"

"There is nothing you can do. It has been planned for a long time."

"The New World Order?"

"Even today, with all that has happened, the people watch sports and drink beer, living in willful ignorance that everything will be fine. They put faith in leaders who will cower in bomb shelters or leave the country, expecting the military to fight when it will stand down," the senator rambled in a voice that did not seem to be his own.

"Why won't the military protect us, sir?" Robert asked.

"The Pentagon split up our aircraft carriers and nuclear subs. The other half are in port. Our bombers and fighters are grounded, which is where they will remain. Tomorrow, the war games will distract any response or retaliation, the same way they did on 9/11."

"I was on the Vinson, they seem prepared to me?"

"They will stand down."

"Why?"

"Because, you conveyed the orders, Mr. Wood. We had couriers travel around the world to deliver eyes-only directives to ships, subs, bases, and their commanders. You delivered the stand down orders to the USS Vinson."

"PDD-60?"

"No. A new executive order built on its framework. The United States will lose the war with Russia and we will have a New World Order."

"Can it be stopped?" Tristan asked.

"We are the Illuminati, son. We cannot be stopped."

"Are you going to sit back and let this happen? Hide in your bomb shelter during Armageddon?" Robert choked up as he thought about his wife and children.

"No, I'm not."

The senator removed a handgun from under his desk.

He put it into his mouth and pulled the trigger.

CHAPTER 44

INDEPENDENCE DAY

"Good Afternoon,

Two days ago, our fellow citizens, our way of life, our very freedom came under attack in a pair of deliberate and deadly terrorist acts on the Russian and Ukraine embassies. The victims in the buildings had their lives suddenly ended by evil, despicable acts of terror. The images of the devastation have filled us with disbelief, terrible sadness, and a quiet, unyielding anger. These acts were intended to provoke tension and conflict with our friends, the Russians, as well as frighten our nation into chaos. But they have failed. America is strong. As our economy struggles to get its footing in the continuing financial downturn, our nation once again saw evil, the very worst of human nature. The embassy bombings have shocked the world, but be assured, we will bring those responsible to justice.

Immediately following the attacks, I implemented our government's emergency response plans. Our military is powerful, and it is prepared. To maintain order, I am suspending the sale of guns and ammunition across the country until further notice. We are also implementing curfews in major cities, through local and state law enforcement under authority of the Department of Homeland Security. In addition, I am granting FEMA the power to activate shelters in case of new crises. The functions of our government continue without interruption.

The search is underway for those who were behind these evil acts. I have spoken with FBI Director Dufour and what we know is; this is the result of homegrown terrorism by a radical right wing group of Americans much like Timothy McVeigh and the men who perpetrated the Oklahoma City bombing. FBI believes the man who orchestrated the attacks was a member of both the Tea Party and an anti-government militia, the same group that tried to detonate the bomb at Union Station during the ceremony I attended for the Next-Gen high-speed rail system. The suspect was killed as a result of explosives he detonated by accident, burning down the building where the operation was planned. Therefore, we may never know all the details. I called President Putin today to assure him we will do what is necessary to restore trust with the Russian Federation. I have directed the full resources of our intelligence and law enforcement communities to bring those responsible to justice. We will make no distinction between the terrorists who committed these acts and those who harbor them.

I appreciate so very much the members of Congress who have joined me in strongly condemning these attacks as we stand together to win the war against terrorism. America has stood down enemies before, and we will do so this time. We urge you to enjoy the baseball games, fireworks, and family gatherings. Your government will protect you. Happy Independence Day and God bless America."

Tristan watched the television in disbelief. He had hoped meeting the Speaker of the House yesterday, and giving him a copy of *Tidal Wave 23*, would have produced better results. It certainly did not reflect in the president's speech, which was filled with doublespeak and misinformation. And the words were strangely familiar.

The Speaker, due to make a statement of his own, would hopefully address the real issues. Everything Sebastian said about shifting the terrorist image from radical Islam to the media's stereotypical view of pro-Constitution patriot groups had come true.

The FBI Director knew exactly what happened, this could not be misconstrued so dramatically in a phone call to the president, if indeed there had been one.

Frustrated, he muted the TV and went into the kitchen for a cold bottle of water. An empty prescription bottle sat on the counter, its contents flushed. He dropped his head and took in a deep breath, smiling to himself.

It was finally over.

Tristan had made the decision to detox from the opiates and get off the meds once and for all, determined to find other ways to deal with the leg pain.

The senator's suicide was the wake-up call.

The thought of descending to that level, for any reason, was terrifying. After giving a statement to the police, he parted ways with Robert and rushed home.

He first broke the news to his wife about Sebastian, then gave her the details about the embassy bombings. Then he confessed the real reason he called.

Allyson did not anger or judge, but stayed on the phone while he went through the ordeal. The withdrawals started with simultaneous hot and cold sweats, his eyes stung, muscles ached, and nausea set it. Then the anxiety hit, a horrendous winding in his chest with body shakes.

He paced the house like a caged animal for hours until the abdominal cramps and vomiting began. Tristan could not recall how long he stared down into the toilet, slipping in and out of a delirious state. As bad as it got, he knew it was necessary. This was something he needed to go through, to remember, in case he experienced a moment of weakness in the future.

The worst of it ended as the sun came up. He said goodbye to Allyson and crashed on the sofa. After only a few hours' sleep his strength had returned, both in body and spirit.

I'm clean, he thought. *Damn straight!*

His resolve stemmed from Allyson. Fighting back from near-death and expelling her own demons, he would never have guessed she almost died that night in the hospital. Her miraculous improvement was obvious in her voice every day.

Tristan returned to the living room and turned up the volume as the Speaker approached the podium. He essentially reiterated the president's speech, also claiming to have talked to the FBI Director.

Stunned, his intellect wanted to make excuses. Maybe the Speaker did not watch the video, didn't believe it, or was told by the director that it was bogus? But his reaction to Tristan yelling, "Fight the New World Order," had bothered him ever since.

His gut was saying Sebastian was right—again. The president and those in the highest levels of the American government were part of the New World Order. He could think of no other explanation.

Tristan's phone beeped with a text which read;

Anyone you know?

The photo attachment was the image Tony had been working on, the dark single frame from the warehouse. He had forgotten all about it.

"Son of a . . ."

Though murky, the person was unmistakable.

It was Pascal.

What gave him a dreadful chill was the indescribably evil expression of the mouth, stuck in a grin. The jet black eyes, the redness of the face, it reminded him of his what he had seen at the Pentagon—the Major. This was unexpected, but it was proof.

SAC Pascal shot and killed Sebastian.

He speed dialed a number. The FBI Director's secretary picked up after two rings.

"This is Agent Wood."

"He's here."

"You're kidding?"

"Hold on, I'll put you through."

A pause, then the call dropped.

"He hung up on me?"

Minutes later, Tristan was racing downtown in his Wrangler.

A strange vibe lingered in the city. Traffic was at a minimum and few people were outside despite the pleasant weather. Every couple of blocks he passed youths roaming the streets like packs of wild dogs, some appeared to hold bats, or were they pipes? Smoke rose in the distance, from what he thought was a residential neighborhood. Tension was building; riots were not far off.

His cell phone interrupted his thoughts.

"Hello?"

"Can you believe it?" Robert asked.

"It's like we never even met the Speaker."

"Where are you?"

"I'm heading to FBI. I'm going to get the director to go public, panic or not, the truth has to come out. They may not believe me, but they'll have to listen to him."

"I'm not sure how much good it will do."

"What do you mean?"

"The military just went to DEFCOM 5."

"What?"

"They didn't want to announce it before the president's speech; it will be public in the next few minutes. They're not going to cancel the war games, the Pentagon is now calling them a 'defensive exercise.' There will be so much chaos no one will be able to tell the difference between exercise and real world."

"And that's the point."

"I was told that immediately after the speech the president got on the phone and began calling world leaders telling them they're on their own, that the United States will not be in a position to help defend any of our allies. We've already given up."

"Robert, you need to get Sarah and the kids and take shelter."

"We got a fresh intelligence report. Russia is arming her warheads. I can't believe I'm saying this, but it looks like they're preparing to push the button."

"The senator won't be using his bomb shelter, can you get into his house?"

His younger brother did not answer.

"Robert, can you get into his house?"

"I've got keys."

"You need to get there as fast as you can. I have to go, I'm pulling up to FBI now."

"This can't be happening."

"Happy Independence Day," Tristan said facetiously.

The cell lost reception upon entering the underground garage. He parked and rode the elevator up. Director Dufour had given his word they would go to the media if necessary, and Tristan was going to hold him to that promise, even if it was at gunpoint.

He flew down the hallway weaving in and out of other FBI agents, many behaving strangely disoriented.

Hunched in her chair, the secretary stared at her computer.

"I need to see the director."

"He's gone," she said, in a stupor.

"I spoke to you a half-hour ago, you told me he was here!"

"A helicopter picked him up on the roof. I think he's leaving the country . . ."

Perplexed by her demeanor, Tristan moved around to check out what she was reading. The Drudge Report headline was bold and red.

DEFCOM 5!

The photo above it was now a single mushroom cloud.

"What's going on?" she asked, genuinely confused.

"You need to go home, there's no reason to be here." He helped her out of the chair. "Do you have a basement?"

"Yes."

"Collect as much fresh water and food as you can. Keep track of the news, and stay inside."

"Okay. You should tell SAC Pascal too."

"Pascal?"

"He was walking down the hall with a backpack on. It looked like he was leaving."

The elevator descended with an energetic hum until the doors opened on the parking level. Tristan disengaged the safety on his Glock and racked the slide. He held it close and made his way into the garage, listening intently with sharpened senses and surging adrenalin.

A shot rang out.

He instinctively hit the deck, taking cover behind the nearest car.

"Pascal!"

"Agent Wood! Nice to see you again!"

The echo of both voice and gunshot made it difficult to pinpoint his location. A second shot came nowhere close.

He's trying to scare me, Tristan thought, *he doesn't know where I am either.*

"Were you coming to find me? Well, bring it on!"

Tristan almost answered, but decided to move. He meandered in between cars, seeking out Pascal's location. Then he thought of a way to get the guy talking.

"I'm going to expose the New World Order, Pascal. I'm going to stop the nuclear war!"

"That's what you think!"

Maneuvering aggressively now, Tristan adjusted his path as another shot rang out.

"This is bigger than you, or me. This is bigger than the director. Hell, it's bigger than the president! A lot of very powerful people have been planning this for a long time. It's time to trim the fat, get rid of the dead wood, thin the herd, reduce global population, and put the slaves in their place. We live in a prison planet, and I'm one of the guards!"

Tristan rounded a large SUV and came up behind Pascal, pressing the barrel into the back of his head.

"Give me your gun."

"Come on, Agent Wood, let's talk about—"

"Shut up! Hand it over or I'll paint the floor with your brains."

Pascal held up his Glock and Tristan grabbed it.

"I ought to shoot you, the same way you did Sebastian—in cold blood."

"You should be thanking me."

"Yeah? Why is that?"

"It could have been your wife. But she got lucky, I rarely miss."

"What did you say?"

"Going to the press to rat out the CDC? Trying to stop the New World Order? Who do you people think you are?"

Tristan's face flushed with anger as he thought of Allyson, and his baby.

His finger began to tense.

"Go ahead do it, Wood. Pull the trigger, put me out of my misery."

After what seemed like an eternity, he lowered the gun.

"You're not worth it, Pascal. You'll get yours."

Tristan ran to his Jeep as the man bellowed in rage, his voice creating a guttural demonic sound. He tossed the sidearm onto the back seat and drove out of the garage.

Across the street, a flash mob shattered the glass of an Apple store, stormed in and began stealing everything they could carry.

He hit a speed dial number on his phone.

"Allyson?"

"Tristan, what is going on?"

"It's all falling apart, we're at DEFCOM 5. Robert is taking Sarah and the kids to the senator's bomb shelter. You and your father need to get into yours."

"The media keeps saying this is overblown, they're not even cancelling the fireworks. Putin says the embassy bombings were a preemptive declaration of war, and he's warning America not to attack Russia," she said.

"He's setting the narrative as they fuel their rockets."

"Where are you going to go?"

"Actually, I'm headed for a shelter right now. I'll call you later. I love you."

"I love you too," Allyson whispered back.

Tristan hung up and pressed the pedal to the floor, causing the Jeep Wrangler to lurch forward.

CHAPTER 45

It all felt surreal to Seth Pascal. He had gone through this scenario in his mind for so many years and now it was finally happening. It made him sick and excited at once. The world would never be the same after today, the New World Order was here. He was bitter for not getting a pass into an underground base, but had prepared for that likelihood.

Little traffic bothered him on the familiar route to Woodstock, as most were celebrating Fourth of July with family and friends. Sports stadiums across the country were filled and the National Mall was packed with folks gathering for the huge pyrotechnics display.

The denial of any impending danger was utterly staggering.

Dusk approached and amateur fireworks lit up the horizon. Pascal looked at the empty seat next to him and had an acute awareness of how alone he was, and would remain. With no one to love, the isolation of the bomb shelter seemed much more daunting. Emotion built up inside and he realized he was weeping. It was not for the coming devastation or for the countless Americans who would die, but for himself.

Then he buried the feelings and let the anger back in.

Woodstock was safe from the nukes, of course, it was just a small town far from Washington, DC. However, every part of the country would be affected eventually, either directly or indirectly. The nuclear fallout was going to kill tens of millions. Those who did not die from the initial blasts or radiation poisoning would soon run out of food and fresh water, willing to do almost anything to survive. And it would all happen as he remained safe and secure in his shelter.

Pascal turned up the radio attempting to regain his composure. He needed to keep his head on straight and think clearly. Another news-break repeated what had been said for the last two hours. While Americans celebrated their Independence Day, politicians from both parties were working hard to resolve tensions between Russia and the United States.

As the fabric of society began to unravel, the message was to spend money, eat, drink, live for today, and don't worry. It was exactly what the elites wanted.

"Looting and vandalism are on the rise across the country, and we are getting reports of flash mobs and riots in major cities," came the pleasant female voice with a slight southern accent. "Authorities are advising people to enjoy their holiday weekend and report any suspicious activity to their local police. And now, back to the best music, commercial free—"

Pascal switched over to the CD player. A moment later his favorite classical song began. *Air on the G String* by Bach came through the speakers, creating a background soundtrack for his arrival in Woodstock.

The Woodmart grocer was up ahead and he decided to go in one last time and say goodbye, not that the couple would know what he meant by it. They'd probably guess he was moving on to another transfer in a new city. But as he approached the familiar landmark, it was obvious something was wrong.

Pascal stopped the car and took in the scene.

Inside the store, someone wearing a soiled white apron draped down to the knees was lying motionless on the ground. It was the man he knew as *Pop*. Then he saw *Mom*, attempting to crawl outside the front door as a shelf full of food crashed down behind her. At least four young men ran up and down aisles, smashing things with baseball bats, howling like wolves and yelling about the end of the world. Pascal reached under the seat for his gun before remembering Agent Wood had taken it.

What was the use trying to help them, he thought?

They would not survive the next few days anyway. Deep down he wanted to be a hero and save Mom and Pop. The urge was to go in and waste these thugs. But if the cops came, he could end up in the local jail and be stuck in a cell when the war started. It was too risky, any number of things were likely to go wrong.

He put the car in drive. Mom looked up at him, reaching out in a gesture for help.

Last chance to do something good?

But it was not to be.

His foot depressed the accelerator and he pulled out, into the street. The next thing Seth Pascal recalled was the loudest sound he had ever heard; the crunching of steel on steel. Without his seatbelt on, he would have been thrown out of the vehicle. A sharp pain shot through his right thigh and down his leg as it came up against the steering wheel, followed by what a boxer punched in the face must experience.

The pickup truck clipped him, lifting the passenger side of his car up in the air for a brief moment before gravity brought it back down. Seconds later it was over and everything was quiet.

He no longer had sight out of one eye. The rear view mirror reflected blood dripping down his face. Wiping it away, he was relieved to have binocular vision again. While assessing the situation, he became aware of voices building in volume and getting closer. One of the thugs walked over and crouched down next to him, holding a bat.

"It's the end of the world." The guy slammed the bat on the car inches from Pascal's head. "Chaos reigns!"

The thug opened the door and dragged him out by his shirt. He screamed and held his leg, almost blacking out from the pain.

"It's the end of the world!" he repeated.

With a diabolical grin, Pascal said, "Only for the peasants."

The thug became agitated and kicked the FBI agent, who cried out again. He searched the pockets retrieving his wallet and badge.

"You see this? None of this matters anymore!"

The money, credit cards, and driver's license fell onto the ground. He put the badge into his own pocket, laughed and walked back to his friends loitering in front of the store.

Pascal struggled to his feet and grunted in misery. He decided his leg must be broken. Blood once again ran down his face and he squinted to see inside the pickup, embedded in the side of his car. The driver was head-down on the steering wheel, either passed out or dead. He realized the truck had raced through the stop sign and side-swiped him in the intersection.

Both vehicles were totaled.

He found the garage door opener in the center console and staggered across the street. Stopping to glance over his shoulder, one of the young thugs gave him the evil eye. Pascal concentrated on the task at hand; getting home.

He limped his way down the road but it was slow going. Unable to apply weight, he practically had to drag his injured leg behind him. Blood continued to drip into his eye and he now had a ringing in his ears. He tried to take his mind off the pain by playing *Air on the G String* in his head. Delirium was setting in and it was hard to think straight. The sound of random fireworks exploded in the distance.

Exhausted, he reached his driveway and staggered toward the house, the daylight waning. Relief overcame him as the remote successfully raised the garage door.

In the living room, he entered the secret bookcase and descended the stairs to the bomb shelter, locating the first aid kit. Pascal took out a bottle and swallowed a handful of pain-killers. Preparing to splint his thigh, he remembered he had left the garage open.

After a short pep talk, he began to hobble back up. The pain in his leg was excruciating, able to move only one step at a time. At the top of the stairs he looked up to the very last thing he wanted to see.

The thugs from the Woodmart grocery store stood before him.

They held bats and pipes.

His hand was in the space where the assault weapon would have gone, had he bought one.

The final emotion Seth Pascal felt, as multiple weapons struck him, was regret.

CHAPTER 46

Tristan cruised east on George Washington Memorial Parkway and passed Arlington Cemetery before turning onto Route 27, the highway American Airlines flight 77 flew over before hitting the Pentagon on 9/11. Then, with nightfall approaching, he saw something incredible.

All three heavily-guarded security entrances were busy admitting vehicles, backed up in long lines. Slamming on the brakes, the Jeep skidded to a stop on the shoulder of the road. Through the binoculars it was apparent the driver of each vehicle had some kind of ID, scanned using a handheld device by the guards. They parked in the massive lot and trudged in the direction of the Pentagon carrying their luggage.

His idea of gaining entrance to the epicenter of the United States military industrial complex had just become much more difficult. Sure the Major was inside, he needed a plan.

Tristan drove his Jeep off the highway and got in line behind the others, inching their way toward the checkpoint on the west side of the complex. The security guards who first looked military now appeared to be dressed in all black, identical to the men who had confronted them at the Meadow Farm FEMA camp in Virginia.

He abandoned the Jeep on the side of the road and jumped the guard rail, disappearing among the cars and trucks in the parking lot.

At the north entrance, a hundred or so people waited to enter the Pentagon, with more filing in. Each person possessed a laminated badge, about twice the size of a credit card and attached to a chain. Some wore them around the neck while others held them tight in-hand. There were no photos or names, only a large barcode and string of numbers. Tristan realized without one, the probability of getting in was zero.

He glanced down.

A carry-on bag in front of him was being pulled by a woman nervously chatting with her husband. A badge hung from the handle of her luggage. Short of cutting the chain, it could not be pilfered. Then he got lucky.

The woman let go of the bag to search for something in her purse, her husband preoccupied by the checkpoint ahead. Carefully, he lifted it and headed for the front of the queue. Thinking quickly, he hung the security badge around his neck and took out his FBI ID.

Tristan presented both to the closest guard, while boldly pushing his way through. "FBI; I'm in a hurry."

The guard, taken by surprise, scanned the barcode. After a long delay the handheld device beeped several times. Satisfied, Tristan was allowed to proceed.

He had almost made it inside when two corpulent security thugs blocked his way.

"What are you doing there, buddy?"

"I'm FBI, I'm late. The Major expected me an hour ago, I got caught up in traffic," Tristan said, improvising.

He had no idea if they would know who the Major was.

"You're not supposed to be cutting line, for any reason. Let me see your identification."

The stolen badge was checked again with another handheld scanning device, followed by a visual of his Bureau ID.

"You're FBI?"

"Not for much longer," he said, trying to detract from their task.

The man snickered before saying, "Okay, go on in."

Special Agent Tristan Wood entered the Pentagon.

Additional guards herded those already inside toward a series of nearby elevators. A lift door opened, the crowd rushing and shoving, reminiscent of a sporting event or rock concert. The mounting anxiety level required security to intervene. This presented an opportunity.

Tristan tactfully backed up, hugging the wall, then entered a stairwell. Moments later he found the inner of five rings, the windows overlooking the deserted central courtyard. Trees, grass, and walkways were dimly lit by random floodlights under the Cimmerian sky.

Somewhere, there would be a main command center, as Robert had pointed out, most likely underground and near the middle of the complex.

He arrived at the 9/11 crash-site and the *September 11 Memorial Chapel*, and suddenly felt lost. The almost 600 acre complex was so massive there was little chance he'd reach his goal without help, especially with his bad leg. Tristan stepped onto the orange-carpet inside the chapel and sat down in a mahogany pew.

Behind the pulpit, in the back of the room, was a backlit multi-colored stained glass pentagon built into the wall. Knowing the meaning of this symbol made the hairs on the back of his neck stand up. He said a prayer for all those killed on 9/11 and in the globalist's "war on terror." Anxiety urged him to press on and continue his route, following the ring.

A klaxon sounded, calling out an alarm. Flashing red lights, mounted to the wall every fifty feet or so, came alive.

Two guards dressed in black rushed by, almost knocking him over. He followed, trying his best to keep up. They ducked into a nearby stairway arriving at a door labeled—*2B*—the lowest basement level. On the other side of the door was an elevator where the two men waited. Tristan approached, attempting to act casual. They spoke in hushed tones and ignored him.

The doors opened and all three men entered.

"Where to?" asked one of the guards.

"The command center."

"That's off limits, only authorized personnel—"

Before he could finish, Tristan's Glock was in his face.

"The command center. Please."

The man slowly opened a small hidden panel below the main one and pressed a button followed by a numeric code. The elevator descended, alleviating some stress from Tristan's leg. In seconds the doors opened and he cautiously glanced out.

"Which way?" With no answer forthcoming, he asked again while brandishing the gun.

"Go left, then another left, and it's at the end of the long hallway," the other instructed.

Tristan pushed the call button for level 5, the top floor, sending them back up. After the doors closed he broke into a sluggish jog. Left, then left, and at the end of the long adit he burst through the doorway.

Made it.

The command center was breathtaking. It reminded him of NASA mission control during the Apollo moon project. Rows of people sat at their computer workstations, arranged in a stadium seating design, with the focus on a massive wall of monitors. Almost every seat was filled and several men in suits seemed to oversee the operation.

The wall of screens showed different images including satellite, infrared, Doppler, and even live feeds of several US cities. Other transmissions consisted of ICBM silos and Russian mobile missile trucks preparing to launch.

One monitor in particular captured his attention.

Tidal Wave 23.

Battleship gray outlines of the Russian states, drab army green landscape, vertical cursor with a steady pulse, like a heartbeat.

Time code static and deathly still.

00:00:00

All was quiet, for now.

Little interest was paid to Tristan as he wandered around, taking it in.

"Agent Wood." The Major approached, saying hello like an old friend. "Your tenacity surprises even me."

"You know who I am?"

"We know more than you could ever imagine, son."

"What is this?"

"We're ready. It's almost time."

"*Tidal Wave 23*?"

"Operation *Tidal Wave 23*, officially."

"I don't understand."

"Of course you do, you figured it out."

Tidal Wave 21 – 9/11, Tidal Wave 22 – planned economic collapse, Tidal Wave 23 . . .

Tristan found it difficult to say out loud. "The New World Order."

The Major simply smiled.

"So it's all planned, just like Sebastian said?"

"Nothing happens by chance, we just make it appear that way."

A tone sounded and the *Tidal Wave 23* time code flashed several times on the monitors, like an automated reminder.

00:00:00

"I want to show you something," the Major said, putting his arm around Tristan and ushering him out of the command center through a different door. "There are over 140 DUMB bases in the United States under the authority of FEMA. This is the mother of them all."

"DUMB?"

"Deep Underground Military Bases, connected with MAGLEV trains. The Pentagon is the largest in North America. We have over six million square feet of floor space on seven levels, including the two basement levels. That's on the public record. What's classified is another ten times that below us. It's an entire city, Tristan, and this is not the only one."

The pair made their way through a maze of passages and hallways. Tristan wondered if the route was random or if he was actually being led somewhere.

The Major continued, "We always attach a black-ops project to a legitimate one. J.J. told you, that's what I do—black-ops. Sometimes it's hidden, sometimes it's hidden in plain sight. Do you recall when Donald Rumsfeld announced on September 10,

2001, that $2.3 trillion went missing from the Pentagon? Well, we did that on purpose. We knew the next day no one would remember it, or care, and anyone who questioned the timing was laughed at as a conspiracy theorist. The money was used to build one of the most secretive high-profile projects in the country; the DUMB base under the Denver Airport. It's almost as big as this one."

"How can something so massive be done in secret?"

"We had many whistle blowers, but it was easy to discredit or silence them. You've no doubt seen the news reports about the various US cities experiencing strange underground explosions? That's us. We've been building two new bases a year in different parts of the continental US and we've become quite good at it. Back when the DC Metrorail was built in the 1970s, they dug ten times the amount of tunnel actually needed. The system starts up north in Maryland and connects Camp David to the White House, over here at the Pentagon, and down into Virginia."

"So the president can get out of the White House bunker to a more secure location in case of a nuclear war?" Tristan assumed.

"The president is never in the White House bunker, that's for lower level people like the vice president and Speaker—expendables."

"What?"

"We tell the press that. Politicians too. It makes them feel important. Others believe he's at Camp David. But only a select few are privy to where he really is."

"Mount Weather."

The Major appeared impressed. "That's right."

"Well, it's the logical choice. Mount Weather Emergency Operations Center is the brains of FEMA, and was built to be the major relocation site for the highest level of civilian and military officials in case of a natural or man-made disaster. It's meant to assure a continuity of government in time of a national crisis, though you never hear about it."

"Hidden in plain sight."

"So the president is part of it?"

"The Bilderberg Group decides who runs for president, in both parties. The only way to win a two horse race is to make sure you own both horses. And we always do."

They arrived at a beautiful archaic door made of hand-carved wood, towering at least twelve feet high. The ornamental engravings and gold trim gave it an eastern religious quality. A central plaque was beset with a phrase Tristan recognized;

Novus ordo seclorum.

The Major placed his hand over the plaque and without having to exert any force, the portal opened. Both men walked into a large rotunda.

"We call this 'The Temple'."

What he saw made his knees weak. Before him was an exact duplicate of the Georgia Guidestones. Three church pews faced the monument, dark wooden benches with red velvet cushions in the shape of a crescent moon. The room was lit in a soft light and there was absolutely no echo of sound. The drone of a wind harp played a low frequency tone that seemed to be in his mind.

His sight was drawn to the zenith, above the Guidestones, to a multi-dimensional effigy consisting of luminous stars against a dark sky. Angels floated among the clouds, though it was not immediately apparent what they actually were. He walked across the marble floor, a massive etching of an owl. Looking up again, the figures he had thought to be angels were actually winged demons.

"What is this place?" Tristan asked.

"The soul of the Pentagon. The spiritual center," the Major said, sitting down on a bench.

"Is this the Illuminati?"

"No one becomes commander-in-chief, or even gets the opposing party's nomination, if they don't swear allegiance to the Illuminati and loyalty to the New World Order."

"What's going on, up top? Who are those people?"

"The genetic lottery winners. Some paid their way in or had a connection. Political favors aren't just for campaign donations. Others are physically and intellectually superior, worth saving to continue the gene pool. All across the country today, the elites have been moving into underground bases, or flying to their homes outside the US." He paused. "What did you come here for, Tristan?"

"To stop the nuclear war."

"You can't. This has been planned for centuries, in one form or another, by the richest most influential families on the planet. Right about now President Putin is making his last speech before the war. He's warning America not to attack, before Russia launches her nukes."

"The . . . the ultimate false flag," Tristan stuttered.

The Major checked his wristwatch and stood up. "We'd better head back."

They left the Temple and made their way down a long corridor, the fluorescent lights reflecting a ghostly hue on the drab yet highly polished floors. His leg was beginning to hurt again especially now that he was no longer on medication.

"I've got one more thing to show you."

At a dead end was an unimpressive freight elevator with scuffed cherry-red doors and no UP-DOWN call buttons.

The Major entered a code on a keypad, opening the doors.

He grabbed the FBI agent by the back of the neck and shoved, causing him to strike the far wall. "Agh!" He collapsed to the floor and clutched his bad leg, wincing in pain.

The Major punched another series of numbers into the keypad and saluted.

"I'll catch you later, Agent Wood," he said as the doors closed.

Tristan's body lifted off the ground as the elevator went into free-fall.

CHAPTER 47

Tristan Wood fully expected his life to end. But in a matter of seconds the elevator went from rapid descent to controlled deceleration, followed by a jarring stop. The doors opened and he struggled to his feet, limping out. Reaching the egress of a long hallway, something materialized he could never have imagined;

A massive underground city, just as the Major had claimed.

The people formerly on the ground level roamed the streets using handheld maps to guide their way. The buildings, most of which appeared to be multi-family residences, resembled three-level nineteenth century row houses. Each front door had a list of numbers with barcodes, identical to those on the badges. This subterranean metropolis was complete with sidewalks, faux cobblestone streets, and gas lamp replicas on every corner. In fact, the entire mise en scène reminded him of Georgetown.

Gazing up, he saw what must be an illusion; a deep blue "sky" with fluffy white clouds drifting across the expanse. It was impossible to get a sense of the ceiling height. Natural-looking daylight flooded the complex, without a "sun."

Tristan walked to a Chestnut Oak, a type of tree he loved to climb as a child, and pulled a leaf off to confirm it was real. The chirping sound of birds came from an imitation rock at the base of the trunk. The landscaping included genuine grass, shrubs, plants, and flowers. Obviously, the entire design was meant to replicate Earth's surface, minus the wildlife.

Anxious to talk to his wife, Tristan took out his cell—no bars.

Across the street he spotted a structure resembling a mall directory map. It stood as a monolith in the center of a four-way intersection. He joined a young couple who studied it, trying to get their bearings.

The layout segmented into three color codes.

Green areas included; *Cafeteria, Barracks, Library, Restrooms*, and a blue *H*, the universal symbol for *Hospital*.

Yellow sections; *Computer Center, MAGLEV/Tube*, and *C/C TV Studio*, which Tristan figured must stand for Closed Circuit Television Studio.

Red portions of the map were simply labeled; *Restricted*. The few with names were; *Generator, Power Plant, Water Storage, Sewage, Hydroponics, Air Purification, Desalination Plant*, and something called, *Nuclear Port*.

Tristan found what he wanted, *City Central Control*, and set off in that direction.

He weaved in and out of folks investigating their new home. The air smelled remarkably fresh and clean. Past the final row of dwellings in the residential sector, a massive wall of glass appeared out of nowhere.

A sign read; *Hydroponics*.

Wiping condensation from the casement affirmed that this was not the lowest level of the base by a long shot. The cylindrical structure of green leafy crops descended so far down it appeared to have no bottom.

Next, he came to a duplicate of the DC Metrorail, a MAGLEV train parked at a platform. Regardless of the lighted interior and open doors, it did not appear to be operative.

Quick to continue on, he arrived at a nondescript building with no windows and one door.

City Central Control.

Tristan entered a scaled-down version of the Pentagon's command center above with twenty-or-so flat panel displays against the wall. Soldiers in black sat at computer stations, diligent in their work, the energy palpable. An older gentleman wearing a suit bounced from station to station, asking questions and giving directions.

"This area is off-limits." A soldier in black had sidled up next to Tristan.

He flashed his badge. "I'm FBI."

"That means nothing down here." He became physical, saying, "You gotta leave or I'll have to—"

"Let him stay," said the suit with a nefarious grin. He motioned to the soldier to return to his station. "It's going to be quite a show."

Tristan nodded a *thank you* knowing this would be his only opportunity to witness what might happen on the surface.

A nuclear war is not imminent, he told himself.

But if World War III started today he prayed Robert, Sarah, and their kids made it to the senator's bomb shelter, and that Allyson and her father were safely locked in theirs.

The flat screens began to show activity. One alternated between numerous Russian ground silo locations, their bunker-lids open. Light from inside projected a kaleidoscope of colors diffused within the steam pouring out. A different monitor scrolled through live images of ICBM mobile-trucks, their missiles now pointed at the sky. Another showed Russian bombers flying in formation.

During the height of the Cold War, the Soviet Union had concentrated on mobile rocket launchers as the primary strike force. These could be continually moved, and thus more difficult to locate. The United States invested in silos, later recognizing this serious tactical flaw. Gradually, the American military converted the main concentration of nuclear power to its submarines, and to a lesser extent, high-altitude bombers.

"Get ready, here come the EMPs," a soldier announced, raising his hand.

All eyes turned to a satellite image of North America where multiple points of light traveled across the map toward Alaska from the direction of the Bering Sea. They flared up before disappearing.

"Targets?" called out the suit.

The soldier, sitting at his computer station, kept his hand up until he spoke.

"Warning Radar Network, Eielson AFB—Fairbanks,

Space-Radar Base—Shermya Island . . ."

He announced the destinations as they were hit.

After Alaska, several EMPs headed for the US mainland from submarines in the Pacific Ocean. A white comet-like tail made it easy to track their progress on the monitors. They quickly exploded over their destinations.

"Naval Station Everett—Washington state," he continued.

"Edwards Air Force Base—California,

NORAD, Peterson Air Force Base—Colorado . . ."

Three fired from subs in the Atlantic, the missiles shooting up and out of the geysers they created.

"US Army Signal Corps—Fort Gordon, Georgia,

Cheyenne Mountain Air Station—Colorado."

He hesitated before saying, "Pentagon—Virginia . . ."

The EMPs exploded within seconds of each other. Electronics in the room flickered and everything went black. Tristan felt claustrophobic until the ringing tone of a backup system preceded a dimmer level of light. He guessed the EMPs were used to knock out communications—a tactic directed toward the American people rather than the military or the government.

"Here we go!" another said excitedly.

Several monitors changed to *Tidal Wave 23*. The map remained still, the time code frozen on the bottom right side of the screen.

00:00:00

The slow steady blink of the cursor in the lower left corner awaited . . . the quiet before the storm . . . then *Tidal Wave 23* came alive.

Tristan watched in horror as TOPOL-M and Yars-class ICBMs exited their silos and fired from mobile launch pads. This first wave would target sites researched since the Cold War. Over the years as US bases moved or closed, the locations were updated in the Russian guidance mainframe. While Americans lived their lives, the men in control of the military industrial complex played virtual war games on massive computers plotting the destruction of their enemies.

The maritime ICBM was an SLBM, or submarine-launched ballistic missile. A wide view of open sea displayed multiple plumes of water from Russian submarines fulfilling their purpose. One after another, hundreds of nuclear rockets propelled by reddish-orange flame, burned in the primary stage as they lifted into the sky. It sickened him that only Russian nukes were dispatched.

America would not fight back.

So this is it, Tristan thought, *the end of world as we know it.*

A second wave fired, closely following the first.

The nation's capital had fallen into darkness with dusk engulfing the west coast. Live feeds of major cities showed enthusiastic crowds cheering the colorful fireworks. The one that caught Tristan's eye was a view of the National Mall and the Reflecting Pool where he had taken Allyson ice skating, and where they kissed for the first time. Fourth of July was the one day of the year when the collective conscious of America fixated on the heavens.

It was the perfect day to start a war.

The time code calculated the speed of the journey over the North Pole, reminding him of Robert's intel.

Missiles . . . so fast we can't shoot them down; Even if that were the plan.

The first wave of ICBMs cleared the Canada-US border. Points of light filled the *Tidal Wave 23* map. Within seconds they would be in a sub-orbital spaceflight entering the third and final stage of propulsion.

To some in the northern states it looked like a meteor shower, others guessed it was simply part of the show. A cluster stood out, distinguishing itself from the background. The lights arced downward, this last phase manifesting as stars to the average person.

The flicker indicated reentry from their elliptical flight paths, en route to strike. A shower of warheads from the MIRV stage cascaded at three miles per second. For most Americans it had been a long day of holiday festivities including food, drink, and family. Many of those on the National Mall became aware of something unusual.

But it was too late.

The initial explosions created a momentary flash on all the flat panels causing Tristan to flinch. A massive fireball appeared, followed by a second, third, fourth, and a fifth. As the warheads exploded, the searing heat incinerated everything below.

The first to strike were in the Midwest. Tristan knew these locations had one thing in common. They retained the only three ICBM complexes left in the United States; home of the Minuteman III.

The *Tidal Wave 23* cursor jumped into action listing the targets, the formerly Russian names now in English.

Francis E. Warren AFB—Cheyenne, WY,

Minot AFB—Minot, ND,

Malmstrom AFB—Cascade County, MT . . .

Every military base was hammered from north to south, and east to west. Shock waves propelled out from each blast site at more than the speed of sound.

Dover AFB—DE,

Camp Pendleton—CA . . .

Buildings were flattened, cars and trucks hurled around like toys. Trees were uprooted and turned into flying kinetic-energy weapons.

Chemical Warfare Center—Dugway Proving Ground, UT,

Marine Corps Air Station—Yuma, AZ . . .

Anyone unlucky enough to be looking in the direction of a blast was instantly blinded.

Pearl Harbor—HI,

Eglin AFB—Valparaiso, FL,

Then . . .

Camp Lejeune Marine Corps—Onslow County, NC.

Tristan's legs began to tremble as the monitors shifted focus to the capital of the United States of America.

Lives of the thousands gathered on the National Mall were immediately snuffed-out. The Metrorail system, which had experienced random power outages from the EMPs, was now completely down. The tunnels would be useful only for sheltering survivors lucky enough to get inside.

USS Ohio-class submarines carrying Trident SLBMs were targeted as well as their respective command and control centers.

Tristan knew, because of the PDD-60 policy and subsequent Presidential Directives, the US only deployed one-third of its Navy at any given time. The rest of the fleet remained confined to port. As a result, the initial blow would soon take out most of the submersible force;

Michigan, SSGN-727,

Henry M. Jackson, SSBN-730 . . .

Big-deck amphibious warfare ships were struck, the Wasp, Peleliu, Boxer, the Iwo Jima, the warheads hitting the water instead of hovering in the air as they did over land.

Deployed aircraft carriers each received a TOPOL missile;

USS Dwight D. Eisenhower, CVN-69,

USS George H.W. Bush, CVN-77,

USS Enterprise, CVN-65 . . .

After just a few short minutes, the entire military industrial complex of the United States of America was obliterated.

The second wave of nuclear rockets had been timed to strike as quickly as possible after the first. These appeared to be bound for civilian, governmental, and transportation centers, power plants, hydroelectric dams, and hospitals so the wounded and dying could not be treated.

What else would justify the Statue of Liberty getting its own warhead? Tristan thought.

Rumbles of ground-thunder beneath his feet quelled any doubt this was actually happening. A hushed and humble silence replaced the previous excitement in the room.

Light from the fireballs illuminated the radioactive clouds rising high into the troposphere. The Washington Monument was no longer standing and the people on the Mall had been vaporized. The United States Capitol and other historic governmental buildings lay in ruin. One monitor showed a row of mushroom clouds stretching for miles. Washington, DC, or ground zero as almost everyone in the free world thought of it, was leveled.

Across the country, civilian airports, hospitals, monuments, anything with strategic and historic significance was annihilated.

Sports stadiums were not spared. A woman in a Navy uniform sang God Bless America—during the seventh inning stretch—to a sold-out ballpark in San Francisco. A brilliant flash ended the transmission halfway through the song.

Willful ignorance to the end.

The men in the room gradually broke out of their collective trance as the second wave waned, then returned to their work stations.

Tristan wondered if this compared to what J. Robert Oppenheimer and the Manhattan Project scientists experienced in New Mexico during the Trinity test of The Gadget in 1945; *Now, I am become Death, the destroyer of worlds.*

Several of the monitors morphed into a live shot of a podium weighed down with microphones. Various people scurried about, connecting cables and testing equipment. Tristan did not recognize the podium-seal, a red shield with an all-seeing eye gazing down on a yellow hammer and sickle, surrounded by a black winged-dragon and a lion. The all-seeing eye was the same from the US one-dollar bill.

A moment later, President Vladimir Putin stepped up. A young military officer repeated his statement in a heavy Russian accent;

> "Today, on their Independence Day, the United States of America launched a pre-emptive strike against Russia and its territories, which have once

again joined in unity to defeat our long-time enemies. In self-defense, we activated our anti-ballistic missile system destroying most of America's nuclear rockets. We then unleashed a tidal wave of Russian firepower, displaying the strength of the new Soviet Union. We have crippled the Great Satan. No longer will the western imperialists invade countries or control the world's economy, desolating entire nations for their own personal gain. We ask our brothers and sisters in the Middle East to rise up and destroy all US embassies and military bases. We also demand that Western Europe immediately surrender and submit to Russian forces. The New World Order is now a world soviet system. Thank you, and God bless the Russian Soviet Socialist Republic."

President Putin left the podium after what was the first speech of the New World Order.

Tristan overheard two men talking.

"Run a system check on the MAGLEV, the Major is going to Mount Weather," said the man in the suit.

"I'm checking for seismic damage now," the other replied.

A flat panel showed an elevator door open on their level. The Major walked out, surrounded by multiple security soldiers in black, the group moving swiftly.

"Looks good, everything is a go."

"Hey, FBI agent, what did you think of the show?" the suit asked.

But Tristan was gone.

He made his way back toward the MAGLEV station using buildings and other structures as cover. With the platform in sight, he remained hidden and waited.

The Major and his security entourage walked up and entered the train. The doors shut with a whoosh, and it took off into the tunnel at incredible speed.

Tristan ran to the edge and peered down the passage only to see the lights fade, disappearing in the darkness.

The air flow reversed directions, pushing out the opposite side of the shaft. He leaned back as another MAGLEV train shot by, almost taking his head off. It came to an abrupt stop, the doors opening.

Tristan stepped into the lead car and located the operator controls in a small cabin at the front. A bluish-green glow from the computer cast a ghostly aura inside the cramped space. The touch-screen appeared to be semi-automated and not difficult to figure out. After several tries Tristan brought up a list of stations and selected one.

Mount Weather Emergency Operations Center.

A digital timer began the count-down, announced by a pleasant female voice.

30, 29, 28, 27, 26, 25, 24, 23 . . .

Tristan sat on the spongy orange bench and waited.

A series of beeps followed one long tone, then the doors closed. The MAGLEV shot into the tube. A mild G-force pressed him back into the seat, subterranean lights the only reference for the rapid speed of the train.

He drew his Glock and popped out the clip to verify it was full, then racked the slide to chamber a round.

The Major and the president were minutes away.

FBI Special Agent Tristan Wood checked his watch, which read;

9:11 p.m.

ACKNOWLEDGEMENTS

Alex Jones is my *Morpheus*, and I have him to thank first and foremost, along with his amazing Infowarrior team at prisonplanet.com, infowars.com, and prisonplanet.tv, including but not limited to: Paul and Steve Watson, Aaron Dykes, Paul Craig Roberts, Kurt Nimmo, David Knight, Jakari Jackson, David Ortiz, Dan Bidondi, Mike Adams, Rob Dew, GiGi Erneta, LeeAnn McAdoo, plus anyone not mentioned, thank you to the entire Infowars team!

I urge you to become a www.prisonplanet.tv subscriber, supporting the truth-media is a worthy cause. Joining allows you to watch both the radio show and nightly news, plus all the documentaries and special reports; well worth it for just pennies a day.

The topics covered, and most easily researched, are: the Hegelian Dialectic, Cognitive Dissonance, Public Water Fluoridation, the Russian Threat, False Flags and Stand-Down, SSRI's including Ritalin and Prozac, Gulf War Syndrome, DUMB Bases and MAGLEV Trains, the Police State, the Federal Reserve and Fractional Reserve Banking System, and International Bankers, Tidal Wave 21, the Underwear Bomber, the Propaganda Matrix, Eugenics, Vaccines, Slow Kill Population Control, Georgia Guidestones, 11:11, 9/11, the "War on Terror," Gulf of Tonkin, Operation Northwoods, FEMA Camps, Bilderberg Group and Secret Societies, Public Schools and Education System, Oklahoma City, PDD-60, War Games and the Military Industrial Complex, Freemasons, and the Illuminati.

I also want to thank the patriots in the truth movement who have worked tirelessly and contributed so much: Popeye on www.FederalJack.com and his show Down the Rabbit Hole, a guy who interviewed me on the radio when no one else would. Also, Gerald Celente, Jason Bermas, Luke Rudkowski and WeAreChange.org, Dr. Webster Tarpley, the late-great Bob Chapman, Max Kaiser, Lord Christopher Monckton, David Icke, Jim Marrs, the entire 9/11 Truth movement, Dr. Paul Craig Roberts, Dr. Steve R. Pieczenik, Clyde Lewis and his Ground Zero radio show, Joel Skouson and his father Cleon, and the Coast to Coast crew including George Noory, John B. Wells, George Knapp, and Ian Punnett.

This novel would not have been possible without the amazing influence of my favorite authors, with links on www.TidalWave23.com: Jim Marrs, Dr. Webster Tarpley, Peter Schiff and his father Irwin, Ron Paul, J.R. Nyquist, Bill Cooper, Mark Dice, John Perkins, Governor Jesse Ventura, Mark Dice, Daniel Estulin, Dr. Robert Hieronimus, Paul Naudon, Dr. Richard Sauder, Rose Koire, Dr. Stanley Monteith, Gary Allen, Fletcher Prouty, Ralph Epperson, and Charlotte Iserbyt, to name a few.

God bless the United States of America and fight the New World Order!

www.ingramcontent.com/pod-product-compliance
Lightning Source LLC
Chambersburg PA
CBHW032131190626
46814CB00005BA/1647